THE DEMON ALWAYS WINS

TOUCHED BY A DEMON BOOK 1

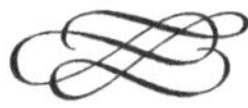

JEANNE OATES ESTRIDGE

The Demon Always Wins

Cover art: Paper and Sage, www.paperandsage.com

Editor: Karen Dale Harris, www.karendaleharris.com

ISBN: 978-1-949451-00-9

First edition

September, 2018

Also available in paperback:

ISBN: 978-1-949451-01-6

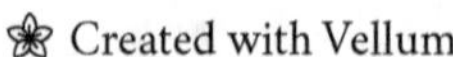

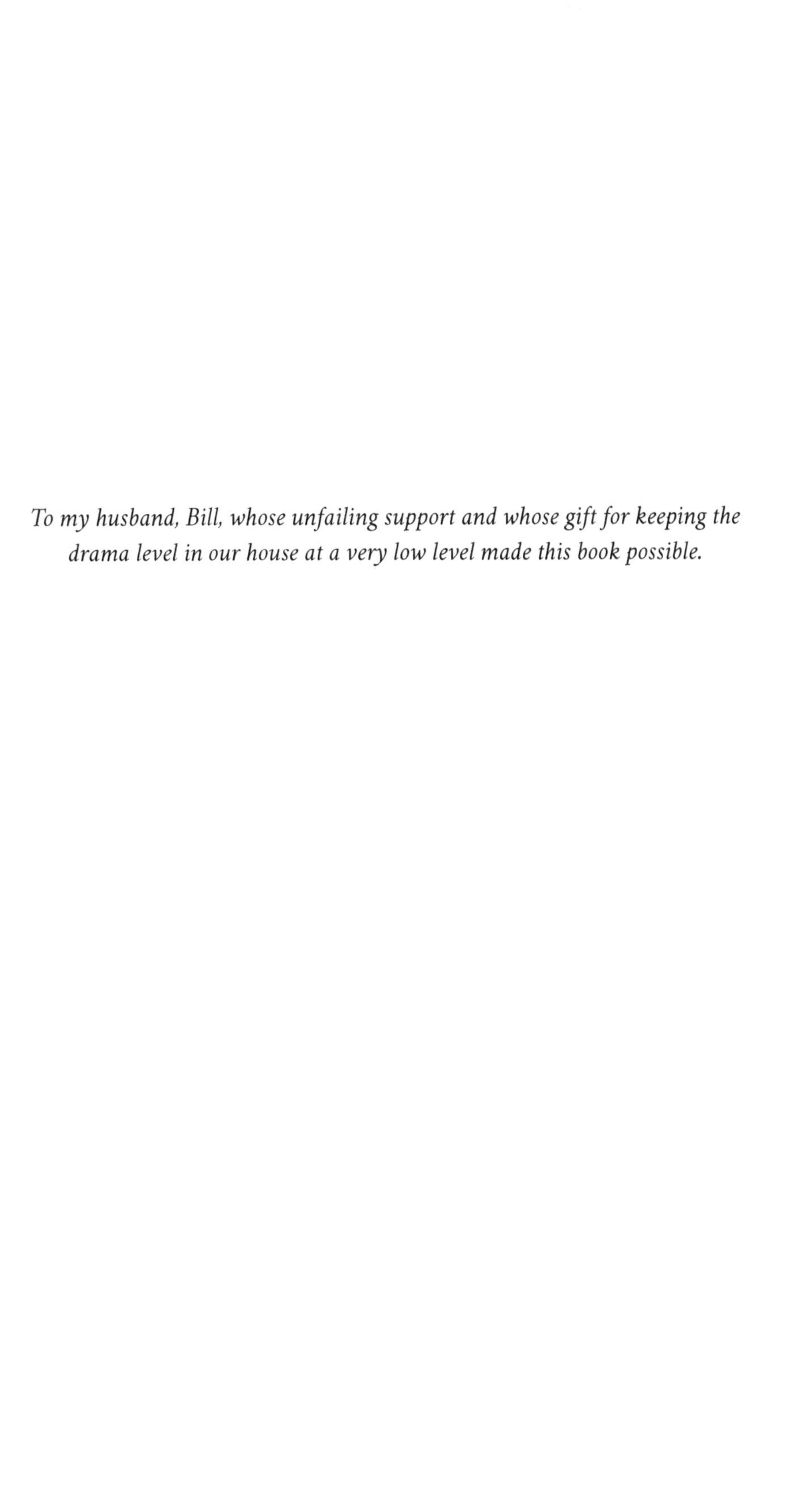

To my husband, Bill, whose unfailing support and whose gift for keeping the drama level in our house at a very low level made this book possible.

CHAPTER 1

It was poker night in the Ninth Ring of Hell and the demon Belial was in trouble.

After ten thousand years of exposure to brimstone and heat, his skin had grown too leathery to sweat easily, but now he wiped his palms on his thighs. It was one thing to win a hand of poker. It was another to snatch victory away from the Lord of the Underworld in front of his peers. And Satan expected to win. The syncopated tap of his fore-talon on the table was a tell Belial had seen too many times to mistake.

Cuban cigars perfumed the air, obscuring the usual stench of sulfur. Overhead, Mick Jagger crooned his sympathy. Belial weighed his options. He could fold, throwing away the best hand he was likely to see all evening, or he could stay in and earn top billing on the boss's shit list. Satan was notorious for being a sore loser. If Belial called, it would show the other players he was his own man, not a sniveling coward afraid to win a hand of cards for fear of offending his short-fused boss.

"Are you in or out?" Loki's palm slammed the table, making his beer stein jump. Amber lager slopped onto the green baize.

Belial added some chips to the pile in the center of the table. "I'm in."

"All right, ladies, let's see what you've got." On his right, Zeus laid out his cards, a paltry two pair.

"*Jeg vinner!*" Loki slapped down three of a kind.

"Not so fast, reindeer-fucker." Satan fanned out three sixes and a pair of queens.

Loki's pale face reddened as Satan stretched out his skinny arms and dragged the pot toward him. Belial held up one finger. One card at a time, he laid down his hand—four jacks and an ace.

Satan dropped his hands, abandoning the pot.

Belial turned to the Enemy, the final player at the table. "What have you got?"

With a faint smile, his former employer pushed his cards, face down, toward the center. Cigar clamped between his teeth, Belial raked in his winnings.

Loki's gaze traveled from Satan to Belial and then back again. Beneath the Norse god's helmet, with its ridiculous twisting horns, his eyes gleamed. He nodded toward Belial.

"This is the guy you're promoting to chief executive demon?" he asked Satan.

Satan hissed like a steam locomotive. The surrounding air seemed to grow three degrees hotter. "I haven't decided."

Belial sucked in a breath. Surely the boss wouldn't withhold his coveted promotion over a hand of poker? No one was that bad a sport. He studied Satan's face. Smoke issued from his horns and his pupils had gone square as a goat's. Maybe he *was* that bad a sport.

Lilith, the highest-ranking she-demon in Hell, sidled up beside Belial on her signature stilettos. She leaned over to empty his ashtray and murmured in his ear, "You are so screwed."

He turned his head so the boss wouldn't hear. "I was screwed either way."

"Guess that's the price of playing with the big boys." She turned to sashay away, but before she could make her escape, Zeus slipped his hand beneath her skirt. Any demon that dared touch Lilith uninvited would draw back a stump, but the boss had given strict orders about the treatment of tonight's guests. Lilith froze, her crimson lips drawn back in a parody of a smile, her fingers twitching as the Greek's hairy hand crept up her thigh. Lilith was a pain in the ass, but this was bullshit.

"Heads up." Belial picked up his lighter and hurled it at the Greek's head. Reflexively, Zeus grabbed for it. By the time he set the lighter on the table and reached for Lilith again, she was already halfway across the room. The Greek's lower lip jutted out in an epic pout.

Belial risked a glance across the table. Satan had seen this by-play and wasn't happy. The smoke issuing from his horns was black as oil.

Something crept over Belial's limbs, taking control. He tried to move his jaw, but it was locked shut. He went to push back his chair, but his legs were frozen. Even his fingers refused to respond to his command. It was as though a spider web of steel filaments encased every muscle, every tendon, every joint in his body.

Satan smiled and the smoke thinned a little. "Something wrong, demon?"

It was thrall, Satan's ability to take over a demon and operate him like a puppet. Younger, weak-minded demons stayed enthralled until Satan released them, but veterans were another story.

Belial pushed against the thrall and felt it push back. He prodded at every corner, but there were no weak spots. Even his lungs refused to inflate. Satan couldn't kill him this way—as a fallen angel, he was immortal, or nearly so—but Satan could subject him to the humiliation of keeling over in front of everyone. Every eye at the table, every eye in the room, watched as he silently struggled. It took every bit of his strength, but with a loud grunt, he finally broke free. Satan smirked at him. Common sense said let it go, but pride was stronger.

"You're getting better at that." Belial managed to say the words without gasping, though his lungs ached for oxygen. "You should keep practicing."

Loki howled with laughter and beat his fists on the table. Zeus guffawed so hard ouzo snorted from his nose. Even the Enemy smiled, but Satan's horns smoked like a tire fire.

"Whose deal is it, anyway?" Satan snarled. For a moment, Belial thought the entire table might go up in flames.

"Mine." He gathered the cards and shuffled them.

Across the table, the boss's lips pinched tight and his eyes were mere slits. It was the face he wore when he was dreaming up punishments. If Belial didn't figure out a way to cool him down, and quick, the promotion he'd worked toward since Satan first lured him into joining his organization ten thousand years ago would be up in flames.

It wasn't Belial's interference with Lilith, or even his win in their little wrestling match, that had pissed Satan off. He'd worked with the Lord of the Underworld for too long to think that. Making Satan lose face in front of the Enemy—that was the problem. Satan didn't give a damn about these other yahoos, but he hated looking foolish in front of their old boss.

Fortunately, the old devil was easily distracted. All Belial had to do was come up with a diversion powerful enough to redirect Satan's attention. He shuffled the cards, his mind racing even faster than his fingers. What would best beguile Satan? That was easy. An opportunity to score points over the Enemy.

That was it.

Setting up the boss to win over the Enemy—that was how he'd get his balls out of this vise. The two already loathed one another. All Belial had to do was create an opportunity for them to go at it, diverting Satan's attention away from him to other, more profitable, matters.

"You know, the boss is right to keep a tight rein down here." He tried to sound casual as he divvied out the cards. The Enemy paused in the act of lighting his cigar to cast him a glance of amusement. Loki rolled his eyes.

Belial held up his hand. "I don't always like it, but a galley travels fastest when its crew rows as one."

"It's too late to start licking ass now, demon." Satan's voice was rich with the promise of torments to come.

Belial pretended he hadn't heard. Slouching back in his chair, he surveyed the Enemy through half-closed eyes. "One of your humans, operating on her own, wouldn't stand a chance against the boss."

The Enemy stared down his large, aquiline nose. "We tried that once. I won."

He was talking about Job, of course. It wasn't exactly Satan's finest moment—that human doormat stayed faithful through everything the boss threw at him. Satan hissed through his teeth, the very sound a threat. It was a fine line Belial was treading. This next bit was critical if he was to get any traction.

He took a deep breath. "I was talking about the time before that."

The Enemy didn't pretend to misunderstand. "You're speaking of Eve?"

Belial shrugged and straightened his cards. "I could argue that the boss is actually ahead by one, since he managed to compromise Adam in that round, too."

"That's true." Satan's horns sparked. "Those kids fell into my hands like a pair of ripe pomegranates."

The clench in Belial's gut relaxed a little. He picked up a remote and pressed a button. At the far end of the room, blood-red panels slid apart, revealing a billboard-sized screen. He pushed another button and the screen glowed silvery-gray with a tiny black dot in the middle. The dot grew larger, until it became a blue-and-green ball.

"Seven billion people on that planet." The floating ball drew closer, until mountains as well as oceans appeared on its slowly revolving surface. "Three and a half billion, just counting the women. Surely, out of three and a half billion women..." He focused on the Enemy and drew the phrase out to let the enormity of the number sink in. "There must be one you can trust with all that free will you've given her."

Satan went very still. It had been four thousand years since the Enemy had last agreed to pit one of his puny humans against the powers of Hell. The day-to-day work of enticing souls away from the light and into the darkness was ongoing, of course. And there had been that attempt to lure the Boy over to their side, but everyone knew that effort was doomed to failure from the start. The last time Heaven and Hell had gone head to head over a purely human soul was Job.

The boss was practically drooling at the idea, but the Enemy's brows drew together like storm clouds. Beneath the cavernous ceiling of the Ninth Ring, thunder rumbled and lightning crackled. Swallowing, Belial wondered if he'd pushed it too far. Satan might punish him for centuries, but the Enemy had eternity at his disposal. Then the Enemy smiled.

"Well played," he said, shaking his finger at Belial. "Well played. As it happens, I do have a woman I trust."

Ignoring the remote, the Enemy pointed at the screen. The image zoomed in on North America, narrowing in on the Florida-Georgia border. The landscape grew more detailed, until the streets of a small town dotted with sand pines and moss-laden oaks filled the screen. A sign whizzed by—"Welcome to Alexandria, Florida." Still the zoom continued, until it focused on a flat-roofed cinder-block building. The building was cream-colored, with flamingo-pink awnings over the windows. Over the handicapped-accessible door hung a sign that read, "Matthew A. Strong Memorial Clinic."

The view melted through the walls, coming to rest on a woman in her mid-thirties, seated at a desk stacked with medical charts. Involuntarily, Belial leaned forward, inexplicably drawn to the image on the screen. Across the table, Satan shot him a sharp look. Belial hunched his shoulders and narrowed his eyes to show he was merely sizing up his adversary.

And what an adversary. She lit up the screen like a torch flaring in the darkness. Her face, with its wide-spaced gray eyes, had the luminous beauty of a pre-Raphaelite Madonna. Her hair hung down her back in a honey-colored braid so long he doubted she had ever cut it. A stethoscope around her neck drew his eyes to burn scars at the base of her throat. They were strangely alluring, with their hint of fire and death. Her hands, with their long, tapered fingers, should have been beautiful, but more scar tissue disfigured the backs. The third finger of her left hand bore a plain gold band.

"A doctor?" asked Zeus.

"A nurse," the Enemy corrected. Then he added, softly, "She is my daughter, with whom I am well pleased."

For an instant, Belial felt something akin to pity for the woman on the screen. If history was anything to go by, he was better off in Satan's doghouse than she was as the Enemy's favorite.

"Her name is Dara Strong," the Enemy said.

The boss eyed the image on the screen, licking his lips with both forks of his tongue. The Enemy watched him, his lip curling with distaste.

"Let's agree on terms," Belial said, before the Enemy could change his mind. "A win for us consists of getting her to curse you, aloud and in public."

"Agreed."

"Time frame?"

"Seven days."

If the woman were that easy, the Enemy would never have chosen her.

"Seven times that," Belial countered. To his surprise, the Enemy inclined his head in agreement.

Seven weeks would be more than sufficient. Belial held out his hand to seal the wager, but the Enemy shook his head. "First, let's discuss the rules."

"Rules?" Belial couldn't remember the Enemy setting any boundaries on past wagers.

"You may not kill her."

"Of course not." Why would he even bring that up? Killing her would be counterproductive.

"Also, you may not kill anyone close to her before their time."

That was tougher. Without the ability to take away those closest to her, it would be impossible to push the woman to her limit.

Satan hissed. "What are you trying to do, demon—set me up to lose?"

"That's not how we've played this game in the past." Belial directed his words to the Enemy. He was pleased with how cool he sounded, not at all like a demon facing a century in a larvae pit.

"It's not necessary." The Enemy pointed his finger at the screen and the focus relocated to a hinged picture frame on Dara's desk. The frame held two photographs. On the left was a faded picture of a little girl in a frilly dress and patent-leather shoes, flanked by smiling parents. Although the child couldn't have been more than three or four, she was already recognizable as the woman at the desk. The other photo showed an unscarred, twenty-something Dara in white lace, radiant beside her young groom.

"She's already lost them." Sadness weighed in the Enemy's voice. He was far too attached to those billions of disposable souls.

"The usual stakes?" Satan's tone was brisk.

The Enemy nodded. One human soul.

The taut muscles in Belial's belly relaxed. His distraction had worked. On screen, the woman typed something into a computer, her brows drawn together in concentration. The scars on her throat rippled each time she swallowed.

"Since this was Belial's idea," Satan said, "he will be my principal, as the Strong woman is yours. Win this, Belial, and you'll have that chief executive demon job you've been after."

It was all Belial could do not to give a fist pump. Finally, the other C-level demons—Abaddon, Mammon and Asmodeus—would have to acknowledge his superiority.

"What's your strategy?" asked Loki. "Will you tempt her like Eve? Or try her like Job?"

Belial nodded toward the photographs of the woman's dead loved ones. "It appears that she's already been tried. I think it's time for her to experience pleasure." He infused the word with a garden of earthly delights.

The Enemy's lip curled again, and his gaze seemed to drill straight through Belial. Belial's shoulder blades throbbed like his wings were being torn away, though they'd been gone for a hundred centuries.

He shrugged off the discomfort. It would be amusing to go

Aboveworld again. He'd confined himself below for far too long. Earth was a demon's playground.

"Remember," the Enemy said, "this contest is about free will. If you usurp her will in any way, make any choices for her, I will consider it a forfeit and I will claim one soul that would otherwise have been yours. You have seven weeks to get Dara Strong to curse my name. Agreed?"

Satan rubbed his hands together, his triangular smile gleeful. "This will demonstrate, once and for all, that giving humans free will was a mistake."

"What if he loses?" asked Loki.

"He won't lose," said Satan.

"In ten thousand years, I've never bedded a woman and failed to corrupt her." Belial smirked at the thought of his unbroken string of successes.

Loki ignored him. "He's screwed up before."

Belial's smile froze. Hundreds of years had passed since that incident. Would his single failure never be forgotten?

"I didn't bed that one." He hadn't gotten even that far.

Satan continued to smile, but his eyes glittered. "If he loses, he'll restart his career as our newest greeter at the entrance to Hell."

Belial pictured himself dressed in red polyester pants and matching vest, sporting a name badge. His mouth went as dry as the Negev. That was worse than the maggot pit.

He had to win this wager.

CHAPTER 2

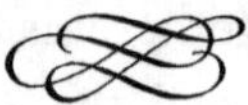

Dara Strong slid her credit card through the reader and waited for the gas pump to authorize her purchase. In the darkness beyond the concrete apron, crickets called sleepily from the grass.

The air was heavy with moisture and mid-September pollen. Her hay fever had gotten so bad earlier she'd taken an antihistamine, leaving her a little fuzzy-headed. On the plus side, she could smell ocean in the warm, damp air tonight.

She tilted her head left and then right, trying to stretch out her trapezius muscles. Her late husband, Matt, used to say he could bounce a quarter off her shoulders when she was stressed. Tonight that coin would have shot halfway across the gas station.

The evening clinic had been unusually busy for a Monday night. It was after nine when Dr. Bell walked out the door. He wasn't happy, and she couldn't blame him. Such a long evening of volunteer work after a full day of work was a lot to ask. She hoped his frustration wouldn't translate into a lost volunteer.

The gas pump dinged, almost drowned out by the thunder of an approaching motorcycle. The little window above the credit card slot read, "Declined." Drat. She must be maxed out.

She leaned in through the passenger window and stuffed the useless card back into her wallet. She dug to the bottom of her purse, scrounging for cash to fill her tank, at least enough to put in fuel to last till payday. A few minutes' fishing netted her only a handful of ones. She grimaced. She'd have to fall back on the high-interest card she tried never to use. The motorcycle glided up to the pump behind her.

It was a Ducati, all black except for the gleaming chrome. The rider, too, was dressed in black—black t-shirt, black jeans, black boots with chains around the heels, black helmet. Even though it was night, he wore his tinted visor down. She didn't usually feel threatened by bikers—most people who owned machines as expensive as this one were lawyers or accountants—but something about the shadowy figure sent a shiver down her spine.

His t-shirt outlined every muscle in his torso. He kicked the stand down and leaned the bike on it, slinging his leg over the saddle in a move that was almost balletic in its grace. His body was so flawless it didn't seem quite human. Without raising his visor, he tugged a leather wallet from his back pocket—no mean feat, given how snug his jeans were—and slid his credit card through the reader. It was accepted. No surprise there.

He unscrewed the gas cap and pushed the button for high-octane fuel. Black fingerless gloves covered his hands, but his forearms were muscular and scattered with dark hair. He lifted the nozzle from its holder and thrust it into the gas tank. Low in her belly, something clenched.

She stared at his hands. The tautness in her belly intensified and a languor swept over her limbs. What would it be like to share a night of love with a handsome stranger, a night without responsibility or regret?

She gave herself a shake. She didn't know what that would be like, but she knew what it wasn't like: her. She didn't even date, much less share nights of passion with anonymous strangers.

It was impossible to see through his visor to tell what he was thinking, or even what he was looking at, but she knew his gaze was trained on her. Beneath his helmet, his throat was like a bronze column. He might have been an alien, come to Earth as a scout for an aggressive race.

The featureless visor remained fixed on her, and, although he didn't move, she felt him willing her closer. *Come to me,* he seemed to say. *Let me show you pleasure beyond your wildest fantasies.*

She shook her head, trying to clear it. He might be gorgeous, all mystery and metal and leather and danger, but she was a thirty-five-year-old nurse in pink scrubs and rubber Crocs, hardly a figure ripe for seduction. What she needed to do was pay for her gas and go home—alone.

With that resolve, she took a step, but for some reason, her feet didn't carry her toward the pump. Instead, she moved toward him. He stilled, like a hawk sighting a mouse far below. She quivered. His broad, muscular chest seemed to beckon her closer. She took another step.

What are you doing? Her rational mind was horrified. *This is not who you are. This is not how you live your life.* With an effort of will, she angled her foot toward the pump and set it down, but she couldn't pull her eyes away from the figure in black.

He held out a black-gloved hand and flexed his fingers. *Come to me.* This time, the command was unmistakable. She took another step toward him. The smell of gasoline and ocean faded away, replaced by the fragrance of petrichor—the smell of rain as it strikes hot cement—fresh and sweet, but with a faint undertone of sulfur. In the back of her mind, an alarm clanged. That smell meant something, something perilous, but she couldn't recall just what. His scent wound around her like the tendrils of a vine, drawing her to him. She took another step.

Another ding sounded. Without turning his head, he removed the nozzle and slotted it back into the pump with a smooth thrust that made her mouth go dry. The image of those black-gloved hands on her body returned. She wanted to stroke the wall of muscle that made up his chest, to lick his throat and taste his flesh. Like a robot, she took another step.

What was behind that visor? Was his face as flawless as his body? That was why she was moving toward him. Not to avail herself of the pleasure he offered, but to discover the man behind the mask. As though in answer to her unspoken question, he pushed back his visor with one black-gloved hand.

He had swooping, dark brows above eyes so dark they looked black, and a jaw Michelangelo might have chiseled. His full lower lip promised sensuality, but the upper one was thinner, hinting of cruelty. His nose brought back the image of a hawk once more. He didn't smile, just watched her with hooded eyes, silently commanding her to close the distance between them.

From some deep well of self-preservation, she managed to drag her eyes away and walk back to her own pump on shaky legs. It took two tries, but she swiped her card through the slot. It was accepted. She turned to jam the nozzle into her tank, but her hands were shaking so badly the spigot banged into the Toyota's rust-speckled fender instead.

She hadn't heard him move, but his hand closed over hers, guiding the nozzle into the opening. The scent of petrichor and vanilla enveloped her, so delicious that saliva flooded her mouth. What would he do if she ran her tongue up his throat? He had removed his helmet, and his profile reminded her of heads she'd seen on coins from ancient Rome. His short hair was as black as his eyebrows. He was so beautiful it was almost otherworldly.

He still wore his gloves, so his palm didn't touch her hand, but as he guided the nozzle into the tank, his fingers brushed hers. The instant their skin made contact, intoxicating images filled her mind, images of things she had never done with Matt. Her eyes flew to his. His shark-like smile said he knew exactly what was going through her head. Her blood raced.

"Get your hands off me." She attempted to speak firmly, but the words came out as a strangled whisper. She tried to drag her hand from beneath his, but her pitiful effort gained her nothing.

"Is that really what you want?" His voice was as melodious as the strum of a guitar, and his words caressed her like a silken scarf drawn across her naked body. The movement of his lips drew her eyes and her vision tunneled in, until all she could see, all that seemed to exist in the world, was his mouth. His scent wrapped itself around her, and the very air seemed to buzz, like a thousand bees drawn into one nectar-filled flower. Heat unfurled low in her belly. Inside her scrub pants, the crotch of her cotton panties grew damp.

His gloved hand slipped behind her head and twined itself in her braid, holding her head immobile as his lips descended toward hers like a hawk dropping from the sky. She thought he would kiss her—she wanted him to kiss her—but his mouth moved past her lips without touching them.

"Because I'm not sure it is." His breath was warm and moist on her ear. Gooseflesh dimpled the entire left side of her body. Inside her bra, her breasts felt heavy, the nipples painfully sensitive to the rasp of the fabric.

"Let me show you your true nature." His hand wound deeper into her braid, dragging her head back till she had no choice but to look into his face again. His irises were as black as his pupils. Tiny demons seemed to dance there.

She tried to summon an image of Matt's face, but all she could see were black gloves stroking her bare flesh. She'd never wanted anything as badly as she wanted to have this man's mouth on hers, to feel their bodies slide together, skin on skin. The crazy urge to lick his throat returned.

As if he knew what she was thinking, he angled his jaw away, offering her access, as though she were a vampire and he an uncorrupted innocent, although she knew the opposite to be true. Unable to resist, she stroked her tongue up the column of his throat. His flesh tasted as delicious as it smelled, but beard stubble scraped her tongue like a thousand peppery needles. It was a warning. Any pleasure found with this man would yield full measure of accompanying pain.

She tried to heed that warning, to drag herself away, knowing she would not be successful, that his pull was just too powerful, when a nasal voice called, "Hey, Dara—are you okay?"

She jerked. The voice was like a bucket of ice water. On the other side of the gas pump, a patrol car had pulled up, the driver's-side window rolled down. She yanked herself free of the stranger's grip. The images in her head melted away like they'd never been.

"Yes, thanks, I'm fine," she called, trying to catch her breath. She felt as though she'd just sprinted the length of a football field. Donnie Benson, an old classmate from Alexandria High, got out of the patrol car. He stared curiously from her to the mysterious stranger and back.

"This gentleman was helping me pump gas." The words tumbled out in a breathless rush.

For the first time, the stranger's beautiful lips lifted in a smile. "Is that what I was doing?"

Hands on his chubby hips, Donnie glared at the stranger, who sauntered back to his bike and climbed on board. He gave her one last look, holding her gaze captive.

"Until we meet again." He revved the engine and roared off into the darkness.

Donnie stared after him, frowning. Then he turned to inspect Dara. "You sure you're okay? Do you want me to chase him down and get some ID?"

She swallowed. She had been that close to zooming off into the darkness with a total stranger. Even now, the scent of petrichor clung to her like a threat. *Until we meet again,* he'd said. It would be good to know who he was, what his purpose was in coming here. In a town the size of Alexandria, though, gossip could hurt her reputation and, by extension, the clinic.

"I'm good." A stray breeze picked up a few strands of her hair and set them fluttering. Her cheeks burned as she realized that her braid had come undone. Swiftly, she re-braided it, banishing the memory of the stranger's fingers winding through her hair. Donnie still looked doubtful.

"I'm fine, really." The last thing she wanted was to start rumors.

"If you say so," he said, and turned to gas up his squad car. She finished filling her tank and got into the Toyota.

The scent of vanilla and petrichor got in with her.

CHAPTER 3

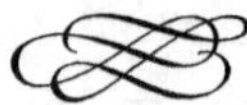

Dara paused outside the door of her grandmother's room at the Mercy Care Assisted Living Center and checked her watch. It was after eleven, late for a visit, but she hadn't made it by before work this morning. She was willing to bet Nana was still up, hoping she'd drop by. She reached for the doorknob and the faint scent of petrichor rose from her scrubs. After that bizarre encounter at the gas station, she might find comfort in a visit herself.

As expected, Nana was curled up in a corduroy recliner, facing the television. On screen, a televangelist exhorted his audience to send money, but Nana didn't hear him. She was fast asleep, her chin resting on her chest. Her face was a future version of Dara's own—widely spaced eyes, cheekbones middling high, stubborn chin. Her life hadn't been easy. She'd buried her only child, Dara's father, as well as her husband. All she and Dara had left were each other.

Dara leaned over to press a kiss on top of her gray head. Nana shifted in her sleep, and the tattered scrapbook on her lap fell to the floor with a bang. Her gray eyes sprang open. She clutched at the ruby-encrusted cross that had hung around her neck for as long as Dara could remember.

"Lord save us," she said.

Dara bent to pick up the book. It was so worn that she worried the spine had split from the impact, though maybe that wouldn't be such a bad thing. A quick inspection revealed it was intact. She set it on the end table beside Nana's chair. "Sorry, Nana, it's just me."

Nana sneezed into a handkerchief retrieved from the cuff of her robe. All hint of drowsiness had fled from her face, replaced by wide-eyed vigilance. She sniffed the air like a bloodhound. "What's that smell?"

Argh. Dara should have seen this coming and skipped tonight's visit. The last thing she wanted was to tell Nana about the handsome stranger at the gas station. She knew exactly where that conversation would lead.

"I showered this morning." She made a show of sniffing at her armpits, trying to pass it off as a joke. "I guess that was a long time ago."

She crossed the room and perched on edge of the bed, putting herself out of range. Nana took another long sniff. Only when her thin shoulders relaxed did Dara's do the same.

"How are you feeling?" she asked, trying to catch a glimpse of Nana's ankles to check for water retention.

"Better than I have a right to." Nana tucked the pink-and-yellow afghan tighter around her legs, hiding her ankles. That was the most Dara ever got out of her on the subject of her health.

"How did your presentation go today?" Nana might be ninety-four, but she was still as sharp as ever. "Will the county commission give you your money?"

"They said they'll be able to renew our contract at the current level, maybe even give us an increase." With relief, Dara turned her attention away from the handsome stranger to her real life. "That still leaves us a little short for our drug costs. By the next board meeting, my trustees will want to hear I've got that covered."

"If you were still at Deliverance, you could ask Pastor Bodine to take up a love offering."

The pastor who took over the pulpit at Deliverance Mission Church when Granddad retired would probably have let Dara request a donation for the clinic in honor of Nana and Granddad's lifetime of service, but she couldn't very well ask for money from a church she hadn't attended in five years.

"It wasn't the same after Granddad retired," she said, but they both knew that wasn't the real reason. The last service she went to was Matt's funeral. She waited for a homily on her non-attendance, but Nana moved on to a new topic, one even less welcome than a lecture on skipping church.

"That nice Dr. Stevens was in yesterday."

"What did he say about your edema?"

"He asked about you. I think he's sweet on you."

"Jeremy is a volunteer at the clinic, Nana."

"That shows what a nice man he is. And he's a good doctor."

"He is. Did the good doctor say anything about changing your diuretic?"

"With a little encouragement, I believe he'd ask you out to dinner."

Dara stifled a groan. "I don't want him to ask me out to dinner. Dating volunteers is a bad idea." She had no interest in men, except as clinic volunteers. At least, that was what she'd thought before tonight.

Nana snorted. "Where else are you going to meet anyone, working ninety hours a week? Trying to keep a clinic going that barely manages to survive in spite of everything you do? A woman your age needs a man."

The image of the handsome stranger at the gas pump took front and center in Dara's brain. He smiled down at her, enticing her to...

She touched the seed pearl necklace Matt had given her as a wedding gift, and Matt's freckled face replaced the olive-skinned stranger's.

"I had a man," she said.

Nana's voice softened. "And he was a good one, honey, but he's not coming back."

She knew that. She'd had five years since the car accident that took her husband and unborn child to come to terms with that fact. Familiar anger roiled in her chest. Why had God taken them?

"Matt wouldn't expect you to spend the rest of your life alone," Nana said.

Make that every person but one. "I'm not alone. I have you," Dara said.

"I won't always be here. You need a family."

"My team at the clinic is my family."

With a grunt that made her opinion clear, Nana picked up the scrapbook and opened it.

Dara swallowed a sigh. They'd been through that book so many times she could describe the contents from memory. Black-and-white newspaper clippings and full-color magazine articles filled its pages. Lonnie Perdue had been famous, back in the day. Nana leafed past a photograph of him preaching, and another where he was leading his congregation in praise. She paused at a picture of him kneeling and ministering to a woman as she writhed on the floor.

Dara's grandparents believed in demons as a real and present danger to human beings. They thought demons came to Earth on missions to corrupt and destroy, and that much of the evil on Earth was because humans were in a constant state of siege. Granddad had claimed skill, both at freeing people possessed by demons and at driving off demons that came in their own forms.

"That man could cast out demons like no one I've ever seen." Nana snuck a look at Dara out of the corner of her eye. "You could have been as good, if you'd stuck with it."

Dara remembered kneeling on the floor between rows of pews when she was about twelve. She breathed in, drawing putrid green smoke from between the lips of an unconscious man. Then she blew out the smoke, sending it spiraling through the open pane of a stained-glass window. The man awoke, freed of the interloper that had tormented him.

"Lonnie said he never saw another young 'un with as much promise as a healer as you had," said Nana.

"I'm still a healer," Dara said. "I heal bodies."

Nana pursed her lips disapprovingly. "You can't take your body into the next world."

"And you can't get along without it while you're in this one."

"It's not too late to get back to it."

Another memory. Dara was sixteen. Her best friend Sarah lay in that very same aisle. Dara tried pulling Sarah's breath into her lungs, but nothing came forth. Her friend didn't wake.

Dara locked eyes with Nana's. "I'm a nurse now. I use science to heal."

Nana was first to look away. She pointed at a clipping in the book with one age-thickened fingernail. The photo showed a clearly skeptical Mike Wallace interviewing Granddad. "This is when he was on *60 Minutes.*"

As Nana launched into the oft-told tale, Dara let her mind drift. *Until we meet again,* the stranger had said. Heat rose in her body, and the warmth evoked the smell of petrichor and vanilla again. She could feel his fingers weaving themselves into her hair and see his lips descending toward hers. Fear and desire mingled in equal parts.

She squeezed her thighs together, shocked by the strength of her yearning. She'd all but forgotten what desire felt like. What had gotten into her? She touched her pearls, but the talisman effect didn't work this time.

"Did I ever tell you about this she-demon?" Nana's question was a welcome interruption, even if the subject wasn't. She had reached the last page of the scrapbook, a hand-drawn portrait of a young woman. At first glance, it appeared to be an inexpert rendering of a beautiful female. It was doubtful anyone could have identified the woman from the picture, except for one thing. Her eyes had rectangular pupils.

A hundred times. Dara bit back the harsh response, restricting herself to a nod.

Nana traced her crooked forefinger over the drawing. "When they get mad, their eyes go goat, you know."

Nana had shown Matt the scrapbook once. When she came to that picture, he admired it politely, but on the way home, he said, "You don't really believe any of that stuff, do you?" Then he went on to lecture Dara on how evolution meant human pupils couldn't be rectangular. She hadn't responded. There was nothing to be gained from debating the subject.

Matt had never stopped trying to convince her that her grandparents were crazy, and Nana never stopped trying to bring her back into the fold. These days, Dara viewed herself as a demon agnostic. Maybe if she'd ever seen a demon's pupils turn rectangular she'd feel differently.

"So I hear." She crossed the room to plant a goodbye kiss on Nana's head. Nana pulled her close for a hug. In spite of their disagreements, the bond between them remained strong.

Before Dara could straighten, Nana sneezed again. Her eyes went wide, and she clutched Dara's arm. "That's demon I smell."

Dara stifled a groan. This was exactly what she was trying to avoid. She patted Nana's hand. "It's not demon scent. It's aftershave." Particularly delicious aftershave.

The old woman's gaze sharpened. "When were you rubbed up against a man to where he'd leave his scent all over you?"

Heat flooded Dara's face at the memory of the stranger's muscled chest pressed against her breasts, his melodic voice in her ear. If she told Nana how he'd roared up out of the darkness to beguile her, Nana would insist he was a demon, sent from Hell to corrupt her. Which, in turn, would send Nana's blood pressure soaring.

Dara hated lying to her grandmother, but she couldn't have her upset. What would calm her down? Dara needed to account for the smell in a believable way.

"He's a doctor," she said, "a friend of Matt's from college."

Nana's gaze raked her up and down. "He took you out to dinner in your scrubs?"

Maybe if Dara lied more, she'd be better at it. "It was casual. We're just friends."

"That's a lot of smell for just friends."

Before Nana could take another sniff, Dara retreated to the doorway. "He gave me a hug."

Behind Nana's bifocals, her eyes were so narrowed Dara could barely see their pale blue. "What made you decide to go out with him?"

"I was trying to convince him to volunteer."

Nana threw up her hands. "That clinic is all you ever think about."

"Mostly." Dara turned the door handle. "And right now, it needs money. Let me know if you come up with any ideas."

"Don't ask me," Nana said. "Ask God."

Unfortunately, Dara couldn't do that. She and God weren't on speaking terms.

CHAPTER 4

The cavern that housed Demon Security, a.k.a. DemSec, the bureau responsible for outfitting demons for Aboveworld assignments, had changed beyond recognition since the last time Belial was there. Formerly a dank cave with piles of moldy paperwork and groaning clerks chained to army-surplus desks, it was now a well-lit grotto filled with modular workstations. Only the groaning clerks remained the same.

The transformation was due to Abaddon, the Demon of Sloth, known to his fellow demons as Bad. Short, dark and hairy, he had tiny horns protruding through the brim of his fedora and an arrow-tipped tail. He was a Hade, a member of the indigenous tribe that peopled Hell long before Satan arrived with his band of fallen angels.

It would be a mistake to underestimate him. Bad was, without question, the smartest demon in the Underworld. Few Hades ever left the mines and metal shops of their kind, but Bad was different. Six months ago, Satan had promoted him to chief technology demon. With that advance, he became one of four demons competing for the chief executive demon slot. Satan may have publicly promised Belial the CED job, but his promises weren't worth much. If Bad made it look like his technology was responsible for the win, he could still edge Belial out.

"What have you got for me?" Belial wouldn't have been here at all if not for a direct order from the boss.

Bad pushed the heavy frames of his glasses up on his nose and peered at the screen of a hand-held device. "We're putting together a dossier on the target. Also, based on the mission description you sent me, we're building an identity for a physician."

Just the kind of tech wizardry that had Satan fawning over the geeky demon. "I don't need that stuff."

"With the advances in human medicine, you won't be able to pass as a physician undetected without it." Bad's eyes ran over Belial, assessing. He punched something into the device. "We'll adjust your pheromones to improve your enticement quotient and splice in some homo sapiens DNA to make you appear more human."

Belial lifted his chin. "No need for that. I'm fine the way I am."

"No, you're not. You've been down here so long your skin is like leather and your hands are curling into claws." One of the most annoying things about the nerdy demon was his way of making rude statements in a matter-of-fact way.

Belial thrust out his chest. "The success of my initial foray with the target suggests you're wrong." His first meeting with the target had actually been a bit of a letdown. He'd expected more resistance from the Enemy's chosen one.

Bad poked a button on his device and a tiny hologram of a man and a woman standing beside a gas pump appeared. He pointed at the male figure. "The halogen lights at the gas station cast an orange glow that disguised your skin tone. And those gloves obscured your hands."

In the hologram, a black-and-white squad car pulled up on the other side of the pumps and a chunky police officer got out. A few moments later, Belial roared off into the darkness. The look of relief on Dara's face was impossible to miss. The demon in the hologram didn't look nearly as close to success as Belial had felt at the time.

He clenched his fists. "Where did you get that footage?"

"The security camera at the gas station. DemSec captures the feeds from all Aboveworld cameras and audio recording devices."

Belial frowned. "You mean there's nowhere up there I can go where the boss can't watch?"

Bad scratched his nose and thought about that. "Unless you hang out with total Luddites, probably not."

In the old days, there was a fair amount of room to freestyle. The boss sent undercover demons to spy, but it was easy to spot them. Now it sounded like there was no getting away from oversight. On the upside, the cameras would beam back Belial's successes, keeping his image front and center. It would give the tadpoles a chance to see how the big frog did things, *and* make clear why he was the best choice for CED. If he needed privacy, he'd just have to locate some technology-free zones.

"We got you a house in"—Bad consulted the little screen again —"Alexandria, Florida, out at the beach. And Travel leased a Porsche 911 for you to drive."

Travel, like Accounting, reported to Mammon, chief financial demon and the most miserly fiend to ever walk the lava floors of Hell.

"A Porsche?" Belial's lip curled. "I'll need a Lamborghini Aventador." Half the fun of taking on Aboveworld missions was playing with the toys.

"Won't happen," said Bad. "We pushed the budget to the limit getting you the Porsche."

"Budget? What do you mean, 'budget'?"

Bad squinted at him. "When was your last mission?"

"Nineteen-eighty-one." When Bad didn't react, Belial added, "The assassination of Pope John Paul II."

Bad frowned. "John Paul II wasn't assassinated."

"Exactly."

Bad clicked his tongue and, for the first time, grinned. "Gotcha." Then he shrugged. "These days, the boss wants to see a return on investment."

"This is the most important mission since Job. How am I supposed to seduce the target with a...*Porsche*?"

Bad shrugged. "You'll have to take that up with travel."

He'd better believe Belial would, too. "If I were to agree to let you adjust my appearance, when could you make that happen?"

Bad checked his device. "Thursday."

Thursday was four days away. The mission only had a seven-week timeline. "I can't wait that long."

Bad shrugged. "We have a full schedule down here."

He was clearly trying to impede Belial's progress. Belial had come into Hell at the bottom of the food chain. In Heaven, he'd been a Virtue, one of the lowest orders of angels. It had taken centuries to get to where he was today, on the cusp of the highest job any demon had ever held. He hadn't reached this point by letting other demons sabotage him.

"This is the most critical mission we've undertaken in centuries," he said. "Move me to the front of the queue."

"No can do." Bad pulled up a text from Satan. It said not to give any demon preferential treatment.

"This mission wasn't even on the table when he wrote that."

"He would have to tell me to make an exception."

Belial pulled out his phone, prepared to dial 666, but stopped himself. He wouldn't earn the second-in-command position by whining to the boss. He looked at the other demon. Every demon, like every human, had a weak spot. In some, it was a desire. In others, a fear. Either way, once you figured out what that weakness was, you could manipulate it to get what you wanted. He glanced around the room, taking in the sleek workstations.

"Are you getting enough budget to do what you need to do?"

"Are you kidding?" Bad said. "This is the top-producing department in Hell. We pay back double for every cent we spend. The boss gives us whatever we want."

Belial's score sheet tallied damned souls in the hundreds of thousands. He doubted Bad could claim direct credit for more than a handful, but his creations—TNT, the cotton gin and laser-guided weapons, along with a host of others—destroyed lives by the millions.

If money didn't lure him, what would? A half-serpent she-demon slithered up with a clipboard. "That new shipment of memory came in." She handed Bad the clipboard. "Should we start installing it?"

He initialed the document. "That would be great, Lamia." His eyes followed her coils until she was completely out of sight.

"Would you like to fornicate with her?" Belial asked.

Bad tried to cover his interest with a shrug, but Belial didn't buy it.

"I could arrange it," he said.

Bad stared down the hallway where Lamia had disappeared. "Nah, I've got this."

If Bad wasn't susceptible to bribery, they'd have to go with fear.

"Once I complete this mission successfully—and I will—this department will report directly to me."

"No chance. The boss loves this department. He says it's where the most happening stuff in Hell is happening."

"Be that as it may, once I take over as CED, he plans to move into a more strategic role." Belial hadn't earned the title "Lord of Lies" by being squeamish about a little falsehood. "There are entire corners of the galaxy we haven't explored. He wants to focus on new opportunities."

From Bad's expression, this was news to him—and believable news.

"It would be a shame," Belial said, "when that happens, if I felt like this department needed new leadership. I'm going to talk to Travel. I'll be back in thirty minutes. Be ready for the load when I return."

Bad stared at him, open-mouthed. "There's no way I can..."

Belial pointed at him with the phone. "Half an hour."

CHAPTER 5

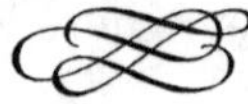

Dara gritted her teeth and pressed down on the accelerator of her twelve-year-old Corolla. Her windshield wipers slapped at the heavy rain without much success. The Toyota's engine whined a complaint, but the speedometer crept up to fifty-five.

At the top of the next exit ramp, the light turned a soggy green. Her public health lecture at the nursing school up in Jacksonville had run longer than expected, but if she could make that light, and every other stoplight between here and the clinic, she could still start triage on time.

She eased the car into the exit lane. When the turn signal on the blue Honda in the next lane began to blink, she sighed and slowed to make room. A black Lamborghini cut in, missing her front bumper by inches.

She stomped on the brake pedal, her antilock brakes thumping like she had a demented mechanic trapped under the hood. She glared at the Lamborghini. Inside, the driver had his head cocked to the side. He was talking on his cell phone.

Of course. She snorted. Cell phones were an invention of the devil.

Just as that thought crossed her mind, his eyes met hers in his rearview mirror. They were so dark they reminded her of the guy at the gas station the night before. She pushed the thought away. No more fixating on the handsome stranger.

Ahead, the light turned yellow. She wouldn't make it, which meant the waiting room at the clinic would be full of sick, wet, cranky people who'd been kept waiting.

When the Lamborghini reached the top of the ramp, it sped up, careening under the traffic signal, now red. Its tires threw a spray of dirty water on her windshield, temporarily blinding her. She stomped on the brakes again, scowling at the Lamborghini's receding taillights through the murk.

After a long minute, the light changed again. She turned left into the residential area that surrounded the clinic. Outside, the rain tapered to a drizzle. Live oak trees lined the streets and grayish-green Spanish moss dripped water onto Cape Jasmine hedges. As they did every September, the firespike bushes sported tubular scarlet flowers.

It was exactly five o'clock when she pulled into the lot behind the white cinder-block clinic. There were three reserved slots near the back door for the volunteer docs. A Volvo that was even older than her Corolla occupied one of them. Dr. Wilson was already here. She hoped that was because he got bored and decided to come in early, not because he had forgotten, once again, when clinic hours started. One time, he'd arrived at two o'clock and they'd had to entertain him for three hours.

She drove deeper into the lot, to her own slot, only to find it was also occupied. By a black Lamborghini. She stared at it in disbelief. Alexandria was too small to have an abundance of Lamborghinis. What business could Mr. Welcome-to-My-Universe have with the clinic?

She nosed the Corolla across the street to the overflow lot and the sky opened up again. Stacking her purse on top of her head, she dashed toward the clinic.

"Dara. Thank God you're here." Kelsey Saunders waited for her inside the back door. Kelsey had planned to be a ballerina until a torn meniscus destroyed her dream. As a favor to Kelsey's mother, a longtime volunteer, Dara was teaching Kelsey to write grant applications, a skill she could take back to the dance world.

In her late twenties, she still moved with the perfect posture and fluid grace of a dancer. She took a second look at Dara and blinked. "You're wet."

Wet was an understatement. Dara's suede pumps squished with every step and her polyester suit clung like wet bandages. A bolt of thunder shook the building.

"A little bit." She fought back a sneeze and realized she'd forgotten her antihistamine that morning. "Could you please grab my scrubs and bring them to me? I don't want to track water through the building." She'd change clothes in the staff bathroom and be ready to go.

But Kelsey shook her head. She was so excited that she was vibrating.

"There's someone in your office." She rose on the balls of her feet, hands at her waist, like she might suddenly whirl in a pirouette. "A doctor. He wants to volunteer."

So Lamborghini guy was a doctor. That made sense.

"Turn him over to Javier." Javier Guerrero was their volunteer coordinator. Except for a tiny staff of full-timers, the clinic ran on volunteers. With the back of her hand, Dara wiped a rivulet of water from her forehead.

Kelsey stayed where she was. "He asked to talk to you."

Of course he did. Anyone who drove a car like that would expect to deal with the director, not a lowly coordinator. She checked her watch. Five after five. There were nurses and medical students awaiting orders. If she didn't start triage soon, not only would the patients be kept waiting but so would the docs when they arrived at six.

She plucked the soaked fabric of her pants away from her thigh. A pair of dry cotton scrubs hung on the back of her office door. Should she take the time to see him? There were never enough volunteers, especially doctors, but based on his car, he was probably an orthopedist or cardiologist, possibly a plastic surgeon. Such specialists were of limited value at a clinic designed to deliver front-line care to the poor.

Kelsey wet her lips with the tip of her tongue. "He has these shoulders." Her hands sketched a pair of broad shoulders. "And his jaw..." She let out her breath in a sigh. "It reminds me of a Michelangelo sculpture I saw in Florence when I went there in high school." Her eyes had a faraway look, envisioning this godlike creature. "Wouldn't it be wonderful if he volunteered here?"

A glimmer of how Dara felt when she first met Matt came back to her—that rush of oxytocin as you realize you've met The One. She looked at Kelsey's enraptured face. Oh, what the heck. The clinic's patients were used to long waits and slow service. She could spend a few minutes stroking Dr. Lamborghini's ego, then ask him to come back another time. A few more minutes wouldn't kill anyone. She hoped.

"Okay, okay," she said, laughing. "I get the picture. Ask Gabby to collect the patient information cards, please. Tell her I'll be there as soon as I can. And send Javier to my office."

"Thank you." Kelsey danced away.

Belial stared out the rusted casement window to the rain-drenched asphalt of the clinic's parking lot. Florida. He could almost feel mold growing on his skin. Hell might be hot, but at least it was a dry heat.

"I hope you didn't screw this up by jumping the gun at the gas station." Satan's voice on his cell phone was like the whine of a mosquito in his ear.

Bad had apparently wasted no time sharing the hologram with the boss, along with his completely false interpretation. The look of relief on Dara's face had been a trick of the light.

"She's met the man of her fantasies," Belial said, "and now he's here to help with her life's work. Things are going exactly according to plan."

"If you'd waited till Bad had your identity ready, you might have consummated on day one."

And let Bad claim credit for the win? "Not a good idea. Her desire needs time to build."

Satan ignored that. "Have you read her dossier?"

Belial had scoured the document DemSec provided, such as it was —a single page listing some dates—her birth, her parents' deaths, her high school and college graduations, her wedding and subsequent widowhood. She'd founded the clinic just six months after the accident with the money from the insurance settlement. "I didn't find much that was useful."

"Pay close attention to stuff about her grandparents."

Belial frowned. The only mention of her grandparents was to say they'd adopted her following her parents' deaths while on a foreign mission. Before he could follow up, Satan was on to another topic. "It looks like she needs money."

The worn carpet, water-stained ceiling tiles and decrepit laptop computer all attested to a pervasive cash shortage, but how did Satan…? Belial's eyes fell on the webcam built into the laptop. Cameras had become ubiquitous since his last Aboveworld mission. Once he was on staff here, he'd have to locate some device-free areas so he'd have room to maneuver.

Behind him, the door opened. He caught a glimpse of her reflection in the window. The image in the glass was faint, but she seemed different than she had at the gas station—crisper, more in command. She cleared her throat and he held up one finger to let her know he'd be off the phone in a moment.

To his surprise, her full lips flattened into a straight line. She was annoyed. At the gas station she was passive, like Job before her, but here she was irritated by a tiny inconvenience. Maybe there was more to her than he'd realized.

"The problem with that approach is," he told Satan, watching her face in the glass, "it doesn't make a deep enough connection for what we're trying to accomplish."

"So we start out shallow and worm our way in. I don't want you—"

Dara checked her watch and looked at the door. If he didn't get off the phone soon, she'd walk out and leave him standing there.

"Let me call you back," he said.

Satan grunted, and Belial punched the disconnect button. Mustering his most dazzling smile, he turned to face his foe.

For just an instant, her eyes widened. Ah. She recognized him as the stranger from the gas station. Then her eyelids swept down to cover her reaction. She offered her hand. "To what do I owe the pleasure, Dr.…?"

"Lyle, Ben Lyle."

She pulled her hand away as soon as courtesy allowed. She was treating him as though they'd never met. Well played. His interest notched up another point.

"I'd like to volunteer," he said. "I have dual credentials in family practice and endocrinology, if that would be of any use to you."

Her eyebrows lifted at that information. Grudgingly, he awarded points to DemSec. Clearly, they had engineered this identity to be exactly what the clinic needed.

"How did you hear about us?" she asked.

"I just returned from a volunteer stint in Angola." He recited the cover story provided by DemSec. If she followed up, a paper trail would corroborate his statements. "I plan to set up my own practice here in Alexandria. In the meantime, I thought I might volunteer here."

She stared at him, pursing her lips. For a long moment, he thought she might actually refuse. Was Bad right? Had he started things off on the wrong note there at the gas station?

"Do you have time to fill out an application?" she asked.

He breathed a sigh of relief as she turned to rummage in a low file drawer, displaying a derriere like two perfect globes. He licked his lips.

Then he realized what she'd said.

"Application?" He pulled his gaze from her delicious backside. Demons didn't fill out applications. Demons swayed people to their will with their overpowering beauty, luscious scents and hypnotic voices.

"Application." Her tone was brusque as she straightened and handed him a printed form. "We'll have to verify your credentials and make sure your malpractice insurance is up to date."

Credentials? Malpractice insurance? What was wrong with this woman?

She'd found him irresistible the other night, as did all human women. Even Joan of Arc, monomaniac that she was, had displayed an initial attraction to him—at least until the voices from the other side drowned him out. He'd think there was something wrong with the identity Bad had issued him, but the little dancer who escorted him to Dara's office had reacted normally. He'd practically had to peel her loose.

He stepped closer to ensure Dara was breathing in his scent. She inhaled and her eyes widened in alarm. She lifted her foot to step back, but before she could retreat, her shoulders relaxed. She set her foot back down. Much better. Another breath and she would be ready to yield to his sculptor's touch. She gave him a drowsy smile and breathed in again. Excellent.

Without warning, she sneezed, bringing up the crook of her elbow barely in time to cover the explosion. He took half a step back. She sneezed a second time. He offered her his handkerchief, but she waved it away, blotting her nose with a ragged tissue pulled from her pocket. She shook her head, like a dog coming out of water.

"I don't know what aftershave you're wearing." She grabbed another tissue from a box on the file cabinet and blew her nose. "But I think I'm allergic to it."

He drew himself upright. That was preposterous. Humans didn't develop allergies to demon scent.

She shook her head again—more a shudder than a shake—and tossed the sodden tissue into the wastepaper basket. A knock sounded on the doorframe and she turned. A dark-haired man in his early thirties stood in the doorway.

"Javier." Her relief couldn't have been more evident. "Could you answer any questions Dr. Lyle might have? I need to start triage."

"I'd like to come with you," Belial said, "to observe the clinic in action and get a sense of how things work." He creased the blank paper in his hands as a subtle reminder that he hadn't committed yet.

For a second, he thought she would refuse. Then she said, "Of course." Her accompanying smile was so brief it was almost nonexistent.

Application in hand, he followed her out the door, his eyes on her backside again. This was going to be more of a challenge than he'd thought, but that was all right.

If it were easy, any demon could do it.

CHAPTER 6

Dara made her way to the front of the clinic, wet shoes squeaking with every step. Her pantsuit was damp and itchy and she would be wearing it for another four hours, thanks to the man at her side. If, in fact, he was a man.

Argh. She'd spent the last seventeen years convincing herself demons weren't real, that the things she'd seen as a youngster were smoke and mirrors and Granddad's hype. She'd never forgiven him for Sarah. He'd spent months trying to draw the demon out of Dara's friend. By the time Sarah's parents took her to a doctor, her brain tumor had metastasized. She'd died a week before graduation.

Much of what Nana and Granddad considered demon possession, modern science called mental illness or cancer. And what they called demon infestation was just people making selfish choices.

Four years of dating a non-believer, followed by five years of marriage to him, had further eroded her belief in the supernatural. Over time, the church's activities and beliefs had faded into a distant memory, refreshed only by strolls down Scrapbook Lane with Nana.

When Dr. Lyle—if he was Dr. Lyle—shook her hand, warmth had traveled up her arm and across her throat, settling in her lips and making them tingle as though she'd been kissed. She'd all but snatched her hand away. And his scent. Sweet goodness, if sin came in a bottle, it would smell just like that.

Thank heaven for her allergies. But why had it made her sneeze tonight, but not at the gas station? Then she remembered. Antihistamines. She'd taken them yesterday, but not tonight.

So where did that leave her on the man versus demon question? His pheromones might trigger her desires in a way no other man ever had, but that didn't make him a supernatural being bent on evil.

She racked her brain, trying to recall methods to identify a demon. If you rubbed their skin with a mix of herbs Nana called demonweed, their flesh would erupt in blisters. You could obtain the same result with holy water. Granddad said Catholics were wrong about everything from the rosary to celibate clergy, but they knew how to fight demons. Unfortunately, Dara had neither demonweed nor holy water on hand.

What she did have was work to be done.

Beside the high, u-shaped counter known as The Pit, Dr. Wilson had already traded his suit jacket for a lab coat. Dara heaved a sigh of relief when she saw fourth-year medical student Andrew Walz standing next to him. Andrew's red hair stood straight up, making him look like an exclamation point. His family belonged to Deliverance church. When she was a teenager, she'd taught his Sunday school class. She stopped to introduce Dr. Lyle.

"Thinking about joining us, are you?" Beneath shaggy gray eyebrows, Dr. Wilson regarded Dr. Lyle with approval.

"I am." Dr. Lyle's eyes appraised the old doctor as they shook hands. Dara tensed. Dr. Wilson had passed the point where he should still be seeing patients, but he kept up his license just so he could volunteer at the clinic. She didn't have the heart to turn him away. Andrew would let her know if any of his work needed to be reviewed by another doctor, and Dr. Wilson could tutor Andrew in the soft skills needed to be a good physician. It was a solution where everyone won.

Beyond the huge reception window, the waiting area was standing room only. It would take a miracle to see them all.

"Big crowd," Dr. Lyle said.

Dara shrugged. "Average."

Agreeing with Dr. Lyle on any topic felt like she was letting him win. If he was a demon, she didn't want to do that. After that stunt at the gas station, even if he wasn't a demon, she didn't want to cede him any territory.

She scooped blue patient information cards from a plastic basket labeled "Triage" and skimmed through them. At the bottom of the stack was a card with the name "Viola Finch" in purple ink. On the line provided for patients to list their symptoms, the card read, "Stomach." Aware of the man at her side watching her every move, Dara stifled a groan. Viola had seen every doctor at the clinic and none had been able to alleviate her heartburn. That was, at least in part, because she refused to follow treatment plans.

Dara pulled out cards for half a dozen must-sees and handed them to the lead nurse. Then she opened the door to the lobby. Viola hovered right outside. An orange beret with a purple pompom covered her wiry gray hair. As soon as she saw Dara, her jaw jutted forward.

"I come here to see a doctor." Viola thumped her orthopedic cane on the tile floor.

Dara nodded sympathetically. "Let's see if we can make that happen. Tell me about your symptoms."

"You're just a nurse." Viola glared at her. "I want to see a doctor."

"As you can see, we're pretty crowded tonight." Dara kept her smile pinned firmly in place. She hated the lack of resources that made her turn away patients or delay care. "So we may not be able to see everyone. Why don't you describe—"

"I been here since four o'clock." Viola's pompom trembled with outrage. "Them people"—she pointed to a group along the wall—"just got here."

"That's a long wait." The clinic saw patients based on who was sickest, not who got there first, but Viola already knew that, so there was no point in repeating it. "I'm sorry that happened to you."

"Sorry don't feed the bulldog." Viola's eyes blazed. "My stomach's bothering me at night something terrible."

"And you've done the things Dr. Lawrence suggested?" Most of the treatments for nighttime heartburn involved lifestyle changes.

Viola thumped her cane again. "They didn't do me a bit of good." A crafty look came over her face. "Tonight my breathing's bad, too. And my chest hurts something terrible." She wheezed and stuck out her chest.

"You're having chest pain?" Dara slipped the tips of her stethoscope into her ears. "Do you mind if I listen?"

She pressed the diaphragm against Viola's ribcage. Her heartbeat was as steady as the drip of the faucet in the staff bathroom.

"I can take a look at her if you like."

The voice in Dara's ear was as pleasing as a bow across cello strings. Gooseflesh rippled down her neck and shoulder at the feel of his warm breath on her skin.

Dara's jaw tightened as Dr. Lyle bathed Viola in the full wattage of his smile. Viola preened beneath his gaze. Modern medicine had become an assembly line, encouraging doctors to give each patient a fraction of their attention, but Dr. Lyle seemed one hundred percent focused on Viola. Would a demon do that? And if so, why?

"If you'll show me which room to use?" he said.

"I appreciate the offer, but we need to verify your credentials before you can see patients here." Even in her own ears, she sounded prissy. That annoyed her even more.

"Are you gonna just let me suffer?" Viola's voice grew louder, and her pompom quivered like sea oats in a high wind.

Other patients in the lobby looked up from their magazines and cell phones. Viola wanted human attention more than she needed medical care. Dara's eyes fell on Dr. Wilson standing next to the counter, chatting with Andrew.

"Dr. Wilson." She raised her voice to draw his attention. "Could you please take a look at this patient? You can use room two."

One of the student nurses escorted Viola into the room. Andrew guided Dr. Wilson after her. Dr. Lyle's gaze followed his tottering progress.

"How old *is* he?"

Color warmed her cheeks. "Seventy-nine."

Dr. Lyle blinked. "Seventy-nine?"

She crossed her arms. "He takes continuing education classes. And tonight he'll be a godsend. I've got six patients with flu symptoms. He can see all of them." She hated the defensive note in her voice.

"It must be very difficult to recruit enough volunteers in a town the size of Alexandria." He sounded sympathetic.

It felt so good to have someone finally understand the uphill battle she fought to keep this clinic running. The tension in her shoulders relaxed.

Beside them, Javier cleared his throat. "Maybe now would be a good time to show you the rest of the clinic, Dr. Lyle? And then I can help you with the paperwork."

Dr. Lyle turned toward him and said something so softly that Dara couldn't hear. Javier's eyelids fluttered.

"But I can't do that now," he said. "I have something in my office I need to attend to." He turned and headed toward his office.

What just happened?

"You could pair me up with Dr. Wilson tonight," Dr. Lyle said. He was back to the sympathetic, understanding tone he'd used with her before. "And then have Javier put me on the schedule for the rest of the week."

She started to nod but pulled herself up short. "After we verify your credentials and malpractice insurance."

"Of course." He gave in so gracefully she wondered if she'd imagined his effort to sway her. "Are you sure Dr. Wilson is still competent?"

"I would never allow him to see patients otherwise."

"Of course not," Dr. Lyle said. "It's a difficult balance. How do you make full use of your resources while still ensuring patient safety?"

His tone was so honeyed, his face so sympathetic, that she shared her backup plan.

"I always pair a fourth-year med student with him," she said. "He thinks he's mentoring them, but they've been instructed to report anything that looks questionable."

Behind her, someone cleared their throat. A very elderly someone. She closed her eyes. *No, no, no, no, no.* She turned around.

Dr. Wilson's face was pink all the way to the top of his bald crown. "That woman's heart is as sound as a bell." He jerked his head toward the examining room. "If you don't believe me, you can check with my *mentor.*"

Her face went hot with shame. "Dr. Wilson, I am so sorry. Please believe me…"

Without answering, he took off his lab jacket, hung it on a peg and retrieved his suit coat. She followed him, apologizing over and over, but he didn't respond. At the back door, he settled his gray felt hat on his head and walked out.

Tears burned her eyes. She'd known he'd have to leave someday, but she'd never anticipated it would be under circumstances like these. Dr. Wilson had been her family physician since she was a child. He'd seen her through poison ivy when she was a middle schooler and mono when she was in college. It was he who had confirmed the joyous news that she was finally pregnant.

He was the first physician in town to volunteer at the clinic, and his standing in the community had done much to bring other doctors and nurses to her door. And he'd been Nana's physician until the day he closed his practice. Nana would be horrified to hear how Dara had insulted a man who'd shown her nothing but kindness.

"I would be happy to help out tonight," Dr. Lyle said, looking noble.

Had he deliberately engineered that situation to push Dr. Wilson out the door? If he were a demon, the answer was yes. Demons made mischief just for the sake of mischief. She tried to think of a reason that a human doctor might push out another doctor to secure a volunteer position but came up dry.

"Thanks for your offer." She forced more courtesy into her tone than she was feeling. "But no. In fact, we're currently overwhelmed with volunteers, so I don't think you need to bother filling out an application."

Dr. Lyle might or might not be a demon, but he was no fool. His olive complexion darkened and his jaw clenched. So he was angry, was he? Well, that was fine. She was even angrier. Then she noticed his eyes. They were different, somehow. She peered past his ridiculously long eyelashes to the center of his dark brown irises, where his pupils had sharpened into rectangles.

Like a goat's.

Involuntarily, she stepped back. Looking down at her shaking hands, she told herself, *Biology. Evolution. Humans cannot have goat eyes.* She looked again into Dr. Lyle's angelically beautiful face, now dark with anger. His pupils remained telltale rectangles.

The man was a demon.

She dug deep, and Nana's lecturing voice arose from her childhood. *If you spill anything with grains, a demon must stop and count them.* There was the bowl of dry rice on the front desk that housed pens, but she didn't want him to know that she'd recognized him as a demon. Her hand crept to her throat, to her necklace. She hated the idea of destroying Matt's gift, but she hated the danger to the clinic even more. Each pearl was tiny, no bigger than a grain of rice. Would they be small enough to work?

There was one way to find out. She gave a sharp, unobtrusive tug. The frail thread gave way and pearls flew everywhere. She focused on Dr. Lyle.

His eyes scanned the worn carpet, seeking out the grain-like pearls, his lips moving soundlessly as he counted. It was so rapid that if she hadn't been looking for it, she might not have noticed.

When he was able to tear his eyes away from the mess on the floor, she took his application from his hands. She bent over and flipped a switch. The cross-cut shredder used to shred confidential patient documents awoke with a growl. She fed the edge of the form into the shredder, reveling as it chopped Dr. Demon's application into confetti. Her anger felt more than justified. It felt righteous.

"Thanks for your offer," she said, "but we can do without your kind of help."

Dr. Lyle's eyes swept over her, and it was as though a flame danced across her flesh. If his goat-square pupils and compulsive counting weren't enough to convince her of his subterranean origins, that scorching gaze would have given him away. She stood her ground, silently commanding him to shake the dust of her clinic from his Italian loafers.

He smiled, but it was a travesty of the comforting expression he'd worn before. He raised his hand in salute. "Until we meet again."

CHAPTER 7

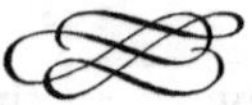

In ten thousand years, no mission had ever begun as badly as this one. On rare occasions, targets had avoided Belial. Once or twice, a subject had even taken a dislike to him. But never had anyone simply dismissed him.

His cell phone rang.

"What the fuck just happened in there?" Satan roared.

"Nothing." Belial forced himself to sound upbeat. "Trust me, she'll be begging me to come back in a day or two."

"Who are you trying to shit? She threw you out."

"A temporary setback."

"She made you."

"She did not make me." Only rank amateurs got made right out of the gate.

"Then what were the pearls about?"

"She's clumsy." But even as Belial said the words, he knew they weren't true. Although she'd pretended it was an accident, Dara had spilled those beads deliberately.

"We should have foreseen this." Satan's tone made it clear that when he said "we," he meant "you."

"She is Lonnie and Esther Perdue's granddaughter."

"Why is that significant?"

"Didn't you read her dossier?"

"Of course I read her dossier. The only thing it said about her grandparents was they adopted her following her parents' death."

There was a rustle of paper as Satan opened a folder. "There was a hyperlink. You must have missed it."

"I didn't miss anything."

"A lot of older demons struggle adapting to technology."

Said the demon that made his secretary copy everything onto parchment. Belial was willing to bet the observation about older demons had come from directly from Bad.

"There were no hyperlinks in the copy I received." Was that an oversight, or intentional?

Satan grunted. "The point is, Lonnie Perdue was once the foremost demon-fighter of the twentieth century."

"What happened?"

"Lucifer took him down."

Lucifer's specialty was pride. Like grandfather, like granddaughter? Belial tucked that away for future reference. "I'll go back and review the dossier again."

"It's too late for that. I'm replacing you. It'll take a couple of days, but I'll send in Asmodeus."

Asmodeus was the Demon of Lust as well as chief marketing demon, another contender for the CED slot. He was also bosom buddies with Abaddon. The missing hyperlinks were definitely intentional. Well, bad news, boys. Belial wasn't about to return to Hell a failure, the laughingstock of all the fiends who had envied him his starring role as Satan's right-hand demon. Especially not if it meant being replaced by that perv Asmo. It would effectively end his chance for promotion.

"We don't know that she made me. And anyway, if she had the skills and knowledge to identify me, she'll be able to identify him."

"Maybe," Satan said. "Maybe not. We'll review the game tapes and figure out what clued her in. Then Bad can tweak Asmo's identity so this doesn't happen again."

Belial refused to return to Hell in disgrace, the butt of jokes, with other demons sniggering as he walked by. He wasn't about stand in the vestibule, playing bogeyman to new arrivals. Bile rose in his throat at the image.

"Asmo has a strong field record, especially with women." At the other end of the phone, Satan was thinking aloud. "Bad can fix the problem with the identity and..."

A frail human vessel like Dara Strong could not be allowed to best Hell's most accomplished demon. Not even if she came of demon-fighting stock. Not even if she was the Enemy's chosen champion. Belial would rethink his approach and come at her again. And the next time, he'd succeed.

"Asmo has only one arrow in his quiver—lust," he said. "Of all the evils you created, lust is the most unreliable. Gluttony creates new hunger, and greed satisfied generates more greed, anger more anger. But lust fulfilled is subject to satiation. If the feeling is purely physical, with no emotional component, it quickly grows stale and looks for other temptations.

"Dara must come to believe that she cannot live without me, that life without me is not *worth* living. This is a woman who has been conditioned to loss since childhood. She endured bereavements that would throw most humans into an irreparable depression, but she mourned for only six months before deciding the best way to memorialize her husband was to help others. Do you truly believe that if I seduce her today and abandon her a few weeks from now, it will yield the result you're looking for?"

Satan didn't say anything. Encouraged, Belial went on. "We need a multipronged approach."

"And what is your 'multipronged approach'?" Satan's voice was a sneer, but at least he was still listening.

"The same snares I've used successfully since time immemorial—wealth, fornication and corruption of the sanctuary."

"She doesn't care about wealth."

"She's an American. Of course she cares about wealth."

"She didn't respond to your seduction technique. As near as we can tell, she hasn't had sex since her husband died."

Belial looked back at the building that housed his adversary. She might try to resist, but she would fall, as all women eventually fell. "She will."

Satan didn't bother to argue the point. "She doesn't even attend church."

Overhead, the sky opened up again. Fucking Florida. Belial ran for the car, diving into the driver's seat and slamming the door behind him as a bolt of lightning split the sky. It lit up the solid cement-block structure of the clinic like a miniature fortress. Dara Strong was a fool. Death was inescapable. Her efforts to treat disease changed nothing but the timing.

"For Dara, her clinic is her sanctuary."

There was a moment's silence. He was right, and Satan knew it.

"I still think we're better off starting fresh."

It was time to bring out the big guns. "Aren't you forgetting something? Your deal with the Enemy specified me."

"He won't care about that. We'll just slide Asmo into—"

"You're talking about the guy who invented the phrase 'letter of the law.' Do you really want to lose this bet on a technicality?"

Satan let out a string of curses that threatened to melt the phone. When he finally ran out of breath, Belial said, "We need a new way to approach her."

"Like what?"

"Something that doesn't involve the clinic. DemSec should be able to tell us where she spends her time."

"There was a pie chart in the dossier on that." Papers rustled again. "The only other places she goes are home and to visit her grandmother. Are you planning to seduce her in a nursing home?"

"Of course not. She has to buy groceries. Or I can waylay her on the way to visit the old woman. Or run into her at the gas station again. There are lots of possibilities."

"No." As he often did when Belial won an argument, Satan dug in on a small point. "You'll never get anywhere stalking her as she runs errands. It has to be the clinic. If you don't think you can get in there..." He let the sentence hang in a clear threat.

Of all the idiotic... "Fine, the clinic it is."

"And how do you propose to do that?"

Through a brightly lit window, Belial watched the volunteer doctors and nurses go about their lifesaving work. Places like the clinic needed two things: volunteers and money. If those were removed, its very survival would be threatened. Dara would be forced to accept whatever assistance was offered, no matter what the source.

"I'm afraid things are about to go badly awry in Mrs. Strong's clinic."

CHAPTER 8

Nana was in bed, reading her Bible, when Dara came in and closed the door behind her. The old lady lifted her head and sniffed. Then she sneezed.

"You smell of demon again."

Dara set her purse down on the nightstand. Any hope she was imagining things died. "I think one came into the clinic tonight."

"Lord save us." Nana clutched the ruby cross that hung around her neck with a frail hand. "What was he doing there?"

"He was disguised as a doctor. He wanted to volunteer."

"You never let him?"

"Of course not." Leaving out their initial meeting at the gas station, she described their encounter and the way Dr. Lyle's pupils had turned rectangular. "So I broke my necklace, those seed pearls Matt gave me? And I saw him counting them."

Nana's hand jerked on the cross. "He's a demon, all right. What did you do?"

"I ran his application through the shredder. He left in a huff."

Nana chuckled. "That's my girl." When was the last time her grandmother had praised her like that? Not since she'd stopped attending church.

"What kind of car was he driving?" Nana asked.

Dara blinked. "What difference does that make?"

"If he has an expensive car, then he's not just some stray demon sent to pick off whatever soft-willed soul he can find. He's been equipped. That means he's on a mission."

Dara had already figured out he had a lot of resources at his command, but her breath hitched at the thought of the Lamborghini. If what Nana said was true, what did the Lamborghini tell her?

"What kind of mission?"

"Your soul."

But it was worse than that. "He's after my clinic."

Nana shook her head. "Demons come after people, not places. He's targeting you."

The memory of the encounter at the gas station, and those perfectly sculpted lips descending toward hers, slammed into Dara's brain. She pushed it away.

"Why would he target me?" she asked.

"Because you're Lonnie Perdue's granddaughter."

"But why now? I've been Lonnie Perdue's granddaughter for thirty-five years. Why would they target me now?"

"Satan works in mysterious ways," Nana said.

"His wonders to perform?" Dara's flippancy was a defense mechanism against the danger, but it didn't go over well.

Nana drew herself upright against her pillows. Her skinny gray braid fell over her shoulder, landing amid the gathers of her high-necked nightgown. "Don't blaspheme."

"Sorry." Dara dipped her head in contrition. "So what do I do now?"

"Stay away from him." Nana clasped her bony hands in her lap. Even folded, they shook like she had Parkinson's.

Dara felt bad about upsetting her, but if the demon was on a mission, he wouldn't give up. "Everywhere I went tonight, he was right there beside me." With his melodious voice murmuring in her ear.

"That's why I can smell him on you so plain." Nana sounded satisfied, as though a mystery had been cleared up.

"It made me sneeze."

The old woman cackled. "You're allergic to demons, just like me. Those sneezes are the Lord's way of protecting you."

"Here's the bad news. It only works if I've skipped my antihistamine."

"Then stop taking it."

Dara blew her nose to demonstrate the drawback to that approach.

Nana ignored that. "Every demon has a signature scent."

"Have you smelled this one before?" When had she gone from demon agnostic to true believer? When one invaded her clinic.

Nana sniffed and then fought down a sneeze. She shook her head. "Judging from his scent, though, I'm guessing he's a fine-looking man?"

Reluctantly, Dara nodded. She preferred not to think about how fine-looking the demon doctor was.

"Did he apologize for driving Dr. Wilson away?"

"No." If anything, he'd seemed pleased to have an obstacle removed from his path.

"I didn't think so." Nana looked grim. "Demons can't ask for forgiveness. They committed an unforgiveable sin when they rebelled and left Heaven. They're doomed to live outside God's mercy for all eternity."

Dara took a deep breath and expelled it. "Okay, so we've established that he's a demon. Now what do I do?"

"Move away." The expression on Nana's face said she wasn't joking. "Get in your car tonight and drive to the other side of the country."

"And leave you here alone? Abandon the clinic?"

"If you have to."

Dara shook her head. "I'm not leaving you. Or the clinic. Anyway, if he's targeting me, he'll follow. I just have to stay one step ahead of him."

"They're faster than you think. That she-demon that come after your granddad had him out of his pants and flat on his back before he knew what hit him."

"Granddad...?" Dara goggled. It was impossible to imagine her highly principled grandfather in such a situation.

"If I hadn't come along, she would've had him, too." Nana's tone was grim.

"What did you do?"

"I whopped her up the back of the head with a broom." A smile played at the corners of her wrinkled mouth. "Then your granddad told her to be gone. He was so ashamed of hisself. That was the one time in sixty years of marriage he ever bought me jewelry." She lifted the ruby-encrusted cross and fingered it lovingly. "Rubies protect the wearer from demons. Remember his ring? I bought that ring for him the day after that she-demon come after him."

Granddad's wedding ring had included a square-cut ruby set in a bezel. Dara couldn't remember ever seeing him without it. She stared at Nana's ruby cross. Its grimy stones seemed to sparkle with a new light. "How do they work?"

"Of all things, rubies are the most painful to a demon. When nothing else will stop them, a ruby will. They can't touch one without being burned." Nana's age-spotted hands moved behind her neck to fumble with the clasp.

Dara put her hand on Nana's arm. "What are you doing?"

"Giving it to you."

She scooted back. "I can't take that. I bet you haven't taken it off since the day he gave it to you."

Nana smiled proudly. "Never once to this day." Her face clouded. "But you need it more than I do."

"You're Lonnie Perdue's widow," Dara said. "What if they come after you?"

"They won't come after an old woman who's at the end of her life." Nana's arthritic fingers worried the clasp without success. "Here, girl, help me with this."

With reluctant fingers, Dara undid the catch. "I really don't think..."

"Put it on."

Dara secured the necklace behind her neck. The cross needed a good cleaning—the rubies were a dull red instead of the glowing gems they could be—but it was still beautiful.

"Don't take it off," Nana said. "Not even to shower."

"I won't." Dara slipped the cross inside her scrubs and sat down on the bed. "I'm still worried about them coming after you, though."

Nana shook her head. "It's you they want."

"But why? Why me?" The question kept coming back.

"Because you're a good woman. Because you're Lonnie Perdue's granddaughter." Nana paused and added softly, "Because of your anger."

"I'm not angry." Dara's voice was too loud, and the look Nana gave her over the top of her reading glasses said it hadn't gone unnoticed.

"I'm not angry," Dara repeated, more quietly.

"You're angry at the Lord for taking Matt and the baby." Nana's flat tone allowed no room for argument.

"I don't think it's me the demon is after. The clinic seems to be his real focus. I mean, why else would he come here disguised as a doctor?"

Nana shook her head. "Satan wants souls."

"But he also wants to create human misery."

"Misery is just the means to an end—gathering in more lost souls."

Dara sighed. "I don't suppose it makes any difference whether he's after me or the clinic. We're kind of a package deal." She fingered the ruby cross. "This makes me feel safer."

Nana patted her arm. "It can only stop him from touching you if you don't want him to."

Dara's face heated. Given Dr. Lyle's beauty and sexual magnetism, it was a valid warning.

"I'm an old woman with prune juice in my veins instead of red blood, but that demon smells mighty good."

Dara couldn't smell it anymore, but at the gas station, his aroma had been almost irresistible. The recollection brought back her desire to run her tongue over his throat, lapping up that delicious scent. She'd tracked it down his chest, feeling the rough texture of his chest hair beneath her... She looked up to find Nana's shrewd eyes on her. Dara's face grew even hotter.

"I've got a solution for your antihistamine problem." Nana threw off her quilt and hobbled over to her dresser. From the top drawer, she extracted a small jar made of dark blue glass and handed it to Dara.

Dara stared at it in bemusement. Nana had rubbed the pungent salve on her chest when she was a child and had a cold. When she was a teenager, Nana had massaged it into her temples to cure a headache. And when they sat outside at night, Nana made everyone dab it on their necks, wrists and ankles to deter mosquitoes.

But even from a lifelong evangelist of the salve's healing properties, this was a bit much.

"If you have to be around the demon for very long, dab a little on your upper lip. It will drown out his smell."

Dara choked back a laugh at the image of herself gazing up at Dr. Lyle, reeking of menthol, her upper lip glistening with salve.

"This isn't a joke." Nana's voice was sharp, and the lines in her face seemed deeper than usual.

"Sorry." Dara fingered the cross hanging around her neck. "I thought this was supposed to protect me."

"It will. He won't be able to touch it without it searing his miserable hide. But you need help before he lays his hands on you." The shrewd look was back. "The salve will mask his scent."

Dara's face warmed again. She tucked the little jar into her purse.

She would need every defense she could muster.

CHAPTER 9

"Just the demon I was hoping to see." The heels of Lilith's stilettos made a rat-a-tat-tat on the stone floor of the hallway outside DemSec, where Bad had just re-checked Belial's pheromone mix. Although it was clearly flawed—no woman had ever sneezed at him before—the other demon had pronounced it perfect.

"I don't have time to chat, Lil," Belial said. "I'm on deadline."

"I can help you move this along."

"I don't play well with others."

Lilith caught up and fell into step beside him. She was wearing a skirt that barely covered her buttocks and a sweater that fit like paint. "Sometimes it's good to have someone who's got your back."

He snorted. "If someone has your back down here, it's because they're preparing to plunge a knife into it." He lengthened his stride.

She picked up her pace and trotted alongside him. "Not if you have a situation where you can both benefit from working together." She was panting, but she didn't give up.

He glanced at her. "You can only trust another demon as long as the advantages accruing to her outweigh the benefits coming to you."

"Don't be such a cynic. You helped me out with Zeus; I'll help you with this mission."

Belial didn't answer, just pressed his lips together and waited for her to continue.

"You don't think there's ever a situation where two parties can mutually benefit from an alliance?" she asked.

"Absolutely," he said. "Right up to the point where one member of the alliance has something to gain by betraying the other. Then the alliance ends." He increased his pace. She fell behind a step.

"It's a shame you feel that way," she called breathlessly. "Because I was thinking of going to the boss and offering to be your wingman."

He stopped so abruptly Lilith ran into him. He turned around and took her by the shoulders. She blinked at him in a show of innocence that didn't fool him for one second. "Don't you dare."

Lilith was very competent, and she'd work like...well, a demon to see the mission succeed. The problem was, she'd work even harder to ensure that she got credit for the win. And in pursuit of that goal, she'd undermine everything he did.

She cocked her head, tapping her cheek. "Did you just dare me?"

"No." He hated backing down, but the last thing he needed was for the insane wench to take this up as a challenge. He loosened his grip and patted her shoulder. "That was a figure of speech. What I meant was I've got this covered."

"You're being very selfish, keeping this opportunity for yourself." Her lower lip, as crimson as the flames that dotted the stone hallway, thrust forward in a pout.

"Let's be realistic." He touched the clingy knit covering her shoulder. "This wager is a much better opportunity for me to screw up than it is to succeed. You know how wily the Enemy is. I'll probably earn a few centuries in the maggot pit."

"Come on, Bel." She batted her eyelashes at him. "It won't cost you anything and it will improve my position. Women never get a fair shake down here."

He couldn't deny that.

"We've done some great work together in the past." She stroked his arm suggestively. "Remember Solomon?"

How could he forget? Under their partnership, Solomon had gone from being the wisest king Israel had ever seen to single-handedly destroying the United Monarchy of Israel and Judah. Belial's first snare had worked flawlessly. Solomon grew addicted to gold and horses and fine chariots. Then Lilith took over, presenting him with dozens of beautiful women from many countries. The women lured him away from the Enemy and into worship of foreign gods.

The plan was that Belial and Lilith would join together to execute the final snare—corruption of the sanctuary—to seal Solomon's fate. Instead, Lilith had returned to Hell and proclaimed victory, reaping the rewards for herself.

Before he could remind her of that little incident, she cut him off.

"You do realize that if you don't take me with you, I'm going to be here, poisoning the boss against you? Every time something goes wrong, I'll point out how badly you're screwing up. On the other hand, if you do take me, I can be a big help."

He looked down his nose. "And exactly how do you propose to help?"

"I can befriend your target, become her confidante. I can herd her into your arms."

"Since when have I ever needed help seducing a woman?"

"Never." Lilith shrugged. "But this needs to go well beyond simple seduction. She needs to fall deeply in love with you. She needs a confidante to encourage her to trust you, to push her to risk everything for you."

For a moment, he actually considered it. Lilith was right. When he abandoned Dara, it must break her heart into pieces so tiny that not one was large enough to harbor an iota of love for the Enemy.

Perhaps his next move should return to his strong suit—seduction. Bad's research indicated she'd be at the grocery tonight. Belial would run into her there, seemingly by chance, and offer to make her dinner. With no bumbling policeman to intervene, she would be helpless to resist.

"I don't need your help," he said.

He thought Lilith would get angry, but she must have expected his response. "Do you remember how we wiled the time away on that Solomon mission?"

In truth, it had been a very protracted mission. Solomon had lived to be eighty. More from boredom than attraction, they'd begun an affair. Lilith had exceptionally clever fingers. They seemed to know more about a man's pleasure centers than he knew himself. Belial had a sudden vision of Dara's scarred hands, sorting through the patient cards. Inexplicably, his sex stirred.

Lilith saw his reaction but mistook its cause. With a laugh of triumph, she sank to her knees and unfastened his belt. He put his hands over hers. "Right here in the hallway?"

She smiled up at him, her eyes sultry. "Why not?"

He stared at her for a long moment and then shrugged. "Suit yourself." Triumphantly, she freed him from his trousers. Before she could take him into the warm grotto of her very talented mouth, he added, "But you're still not going with me."

He arched his hips back just in time to prevent her from gelding him.

"You bastard." She got to her feet. Her eyes, which had appeared heavy with desire a moment before, were as angular as a goat's and hard as anthracite. "If you don't take me with you, I will undercut every mission you attempt for the next thousand years."

"As long as I succeed, nothing you say will affect the boss's opinion." He buckled his belt. "And if I fail, nothing can make it any worse."

CHAPTER 10

After five years of nagging, pleading, cajoling and threatening, Dara had finally convinced the landlord to take a look at replacing the clinic's leaky roof.

"I'm not making any promises." He looked at the water-stained ceiling tiles and the rust on the metal supply shelves. "I'm just getting estimates."

After Dr. Lyle left the night before, the skies had opened up. As if mimicking the demonic doctor's fury, the wind had blown horizontal sheets of rain against the clinic windows. The storm had reinforced Dara's decision not to bring Dr. Demon on board, but it hadn't done much for the roof. Buckets stood everywhere.

"By the way"—the landlord cleared his throat—"there was one other reason I came out."

She braced herself. "By the way" always seemed to preface bad news.

"We need to talk about your lease," he said.

She blinked. "What about it?" The lease was annual, renewed every year.

"We agreed to set the rent low when you first opened up because of all the renovations you did, but that was five years ago."

"Renovations" was an understatement. "What kind of rent were you thinking?"

He named a figure that was nearly twice what they were currently paying.

"You can't do that." Shock numbed her lips. She could barely get the words out. "We operate on grants and donations. There's no way we can come up with that much."

He shrugged. "I got a call this morning from someone looking for medical office space. This place would be perfect for him. He's willing to pay that much."

I plan to set up my own practice here in Alexandria, the demon doctor had said last night.

"When I first approached you," she said, "this building was on the verge of being condemned. If I hadn't renovated it, it would have been demolished." She hated manipulating him with guilt, but a rent increase like that would wreck the budget.

"The thing is"—he ducked his head—"I need the money."

"People depend on this place," she said. "People with diabetes and high blood pressure, who could die without care."

"My daughter's hooked on opioids." He looked at her pleadingly. "She has a chance to get into a good treatment facility, but she doesn't have insurance."

Dara swallowed. "I understand."

With a last guilty look, he was gone.

She leaned her elbows on the Pit counter. Shock made her so lightheaded she could barely feel her fingertips. How would they ever come up with that much money?

Gabby spoke behind her. "Dr. Fakhoury is here."

She straightened. Dr. Fakhoury was one of their most dependable volunteers, but it was unheard of for him to come in off-shift. Gabby pressed the door release and Dr. Fakhoury came into the Pit.

"Mrs. Strong." He dipped his head in a tiny bow. "I felt I must tell you this news in person. I have received an offer of employment as head of internal medicine at Denver Methodist in Colorado. I will no longer be able to volunteer in your clinic."

Dara gazed at him in surprise. “I didn’t know you were thinking of moving.”

“I wasn’t.” His eyes were wide with wonder. “The call came out of the blue, as you say.”

“That’s fantastic.” It was impossible to be anything but pleased for him. “I’ve heard Colorado is a great place to live. Are Mrs. Fakhoury and the children excited?”

His shoulders relaxed and a smile creased his cheeks.

“They are very pleased. My wife’s sister lives in Denver. Once we are settled, I will find a similar clinic and volunteer there. Do you perhaps know of one?”

“I don’t, but I can research it and email you with a name, if you like.”

He thanked her and left. That was twice this morning that people’s circumstances had changed unexpectedly.

She was no sooner back in her office than Kelsey appeared in the doorway. Her posture was even more ramrod straight than usual. There was a glint in her eyes that could be anger or even tears. Dara stifled a sigh. She had been expecting this, but that didn’t mean she was looking forward to it.

“Javier told me you refused to let Dr. Lyle volunteer,” Kelsey said.

Dara nodded. “After careful consideration, I decided he wasn’t a fit for the clinic.”

“He’s family practice and endocrinology. How could he not be a fit?”

“I wasn’t referring to his skills. I was talking about his personality. His rudeness caused Dr. Wilson to quit.”

The color in Kelsey’s cheeks deepened. “The way I heard it, you were the one who hurt Dr. Wilson’s feelings.”

That was true, and the memory still flooded Dara with shame. She took a deep breath, waiting until she could speak in an even tone. “Let’s call the problem a function of how Dr. Lyle and I interact.”

“Then why can’t you change the way you interact with him? I mean, we’re really short on doctors around here. It’s crazy to turn someone away just because you don’t like them.”

Dara caught a glimpse of shirt sleeve behind Kelsey at the edge of the doorway. Javier was waiting to hear her decision too. It would be much simpler it she could tell them that Dr. Lyle was a demon, but they wouldn't believe her, and their disbelief would undercut her credibility in other areas. This was a battle she would have to fight alone.

"You'll have to trust my judgment on this," she said.

Kelsey stomped from the room. It was clear that wouldn't happen.

Later that afternoon, as Dara was checking the exam rooms to be sure they each had a supply of "I Had a *Muy Bien* Exam!" stickers for the evening's pediatric clinic, Gabby came to find her. "Dr. Henderson is on the phone."

Dara fought down a feeling of dread. Surely nothing else could go wrong today.

"My reserve unit is being deployed." He sounded shell-shocked.

"Oh, no." The words felt inadequate. Dr. Henderson's husband was also serving overseas. "What about your children?"

"My parents will keep them until Chris's rotation ends."

Dara bit her lip. "If there's anything we can do to help, let us know."

After promising to keep in touch, Dr. Henderson hung up.

If you counted Dr. Wilson, that made three lost volunteers in less than twenty-four hours. She broke the bad news to Javier. "Where does that leave us with the schedule?"

He checked his calendar. "They both worked the second Thursday of the month. With them gone, that only leaves Dr. Sanders." He stroked the soul patch below his lower lip, a sure sign he was nervous.

"What?" she asked.

He pulled a card from his desk drawer. The left-hand side of the card featured a picture of Dr. Ben Lyle, smiling his arrogant smile. Script letters printed on the other three-quarters of the card provided contact information.

"If you called him and apologized," Javier said, "Dr. Lyle might be willing to come in. He seemed pretty keen to join us."

A demon with a business card. She'd have to tell Nana about that one. She shook her head. "Even if I were willing to have him in here, we haven't verified his credentials and malpractice insurance."

Javier looked at his shoes. "He's good." Before she could speak, he added, "He worked for Doctors Without Borders for the past two years. And he has tons of five-star reviews from the practice he was at before that."

The demon had gone to elaborate lengths to set up a background. That suggested substantial resources. With effort, she kept her voice level. "You checked his credentials, knowing how I felt about him?"

Javier didn't meet her eyes. "I figured, once you were over being upset about Dr. Wilson, you'd change your mind."

"You figured wrong." She took the card from his hand and tore it into pieces. "No Dr. Lyle." She started to drop the pieces into Javier's trash can but thought better of it. She would take them home and burn them with a little rosemary and sage. It would be safer. She blinked as the old knowledge surfaced. Maybe she hadn't forgotten everything after all.

The amount of damage the demonic doctor could do if he ever got into the clinic was staggering. She touched Javier's wrist. "I need you to have my back on this."

"But why?" he asked.

It was a reasonable question. It was too bad she didn't have a reasonable answer. "Something about Dr. Lyle doesn't feel right."

A couple of years earlier, an OB/GYN had offered to set up a weekly gynecology clinic. Alexandria desperately needed such a service—there were women there who hadn't had a pap smear or a breast exam in years—but something about the man felt off. Six months after she refused his offer, he was indicted for molesting his patients.

"Okay." Javier lifted his hands. "I'll see if any of the current docs have friends who would be willing to volunteer."

"Thank you, Javier." She poured every watt she possessed into her smile. "I really appreciate it."

Dara spent the next two hours combing through her donor database, looking for people who might help make up the financial shortfall. The problem was, Alexandria was a small town and she'd asked everyone on the list for donations before, some of them multiple times.

She was girding her loins to make her first call when the phone rang. It was Ed Norris from the county commission. Hope rose like bubbles in a scrub sink. She hadn't expected to hear from him for at least another week.

"I don't know how to tell you this." Ed sounded so miserable that her soap bubbles burst, one by one. "After reviewing all the numbers, we have to decrease your funding."

On top of everything else that day, it was like a punch in the stomach.

"How bad?" she asked, screwing up her face in anticipation. Even a ten percent cut would be almost impossible to make up on top of the rent increase.

"It looks like we'll have to cut your budget by fifty percent."

She gasped. "What?"

"I'm sorry, Dara." The wretchedness in his tone told her how sincere he was. "The firefighters haven't had a raise in two years. Their union contacted us to say if they don't get one, they'll strike." After another apology, he hung up.

She stared at the phone in her hand, trying to understand what had happened. Her fingers felt numb. In the space of twenty-four hours, they'd lost three volunteers, their rent had doubled, and their biggest source of funding had been cut in half. The clinic's financial status, always precarious, had tipped into outright disaster. Her stomach heaved, and for a moment she thought she might vomit. The clinic's run of trouble was more than mere mischance. Their misfortune had the demon's handprint all over it.

CHAPTER 11

Belial found Dara at the supermarket. Dressed in flamingo-pink scrubs, she stacked small, rectangular tins with pictures of over-bred felines on the lids in the bottom of her otherwise empty cart. Under the bright overhead lights, her upper lip gleamed with some shiny substance.

The fact that she was buying cat food indicated that a low-level operative was stationed in her household. He tucked the information away for future reference. You never knew when such an operative might come in handy.

After loading perhaps two dozen cans, she picked up a box of cat treats from the shelf. She hefted it in her hand as though she were weighing whether the recipient truly deserved such a reward. Probably not, but people were often very fond of operatives from the Feline Division. According to Dara's dossier, this particular cat had been brought into their home by her husband and was assigned strictly to surveillance duty.

"If I were to check your cupboards," he said, "would I find any people food at all?"

The box of treats slipped from her fingers and bounced into the cart, knocking over the stack of cans with a crash of metal on metal.

She wrapped her fingers around a ruby cross that had replaced the string of pearls she'd broken at the clinic. A faint odor of camphor reached him. She not only knew who he was, but she'd taken steps to counter his influence.

"I'm imagining your kitchen." He closed his eyes and pressed his fingertips to his temples. "I see expired canned goods on the shelves and a refrigerator bare except for a wedge of moldy cheese."

He hoped to elicit a smile, but her cold expression didn't waver.

"Why aren't you shopping out at the beach?" she asked.

She knew he lived at the beach. She must have read the application he'd faxed over to Javier this morning.

"Prices are better here. They charge a fortune out at the beach." He kept his tone bland. "Just because I'm a doctor doesn't mean I have money to throw away." Accounting would certainly agree with that.

He waited for her to confront him, to say, "You're not a doctor, you're a demon." Instead, she inched her cart forward.

He looked into her basket, frowning his disapproval. "Name three items of fresh food I'd find in your kitchen."

"I don't cook much." Was it courtesy or a lingering doubt about his identity that forced her to respond?

"You won't be much use at the clinic if you neglect your health," he said. "It's possible to create quick, nutritious meals, you know."

She hunched a shoulder, dismissing his input.

"Trust me," he said. "I'm a doctor."

Her face betrayed nothing but frustration that he was blocking her escape. She knew what he was, but for some reason, she wasn't prepared to confront him. To test that supposition, he pushed a little harder.

"Let me be your personal shopper." He lowered his voice on the word "personal," investing it with a hint of eroticism that made her cheeks flame.

Before she could call him to account, he added, in the most everyday of tones, "I could help you find quick, healthy food that's low calorie."

She caught her breath at the subtle jibe. He found her figure alluring, but every woman in America thought they were fat. She'd been about to jerk her cart out of his way and stalk off, but now she peered into his basket.

"Are you asking me to believe that you're a health-food addict?" she asked.

He smothered a smile. Women never could resist the push-pull of alternating praise and criticism. She scrutinized the contents of his cart—a pair of tuna steaks, some arugula, a cucumber and an avocado. Nourishing, delicious, and it would all fit easily into the saddlebags of his Ducati.

"I am," he said. One of the greatest pleasures of Aboveworld missions was fresh produce. "Come home with me—I'll make you a healthy dinner."

Color flooded her cheeks. "No, thank you."

He smiled. "We can cook at your place, if that would make you more comfortable."

"What would make me comfortable is for you to leave me alone," she said, but she didn't move on. The fact that she lingered told him her feelings toward him weren't as black-and-white as she wanted him to believe.

"The situation with Dr. Wilson was very unfortunate." He deepened his voice, making it sound sincere. "Surely you realize that wasn't my intention."

"I have no idea what your intentions are." Her grasp on her cart tightened, but still she stayed near him, where she could smell his scent and verbally spar with him.

"I can see how badly you need volunteers," he said. "Can't we put our first meeting behind us and let me bring my skills on board to help in your clinic? The work you're doing is worthwhile. I'd like to be part of it."

She shook her head without meeting his eyes.

"Why not?" he asked. He hoped for a glimpse into her thought processes, but all he could read on her face was stubbornness.

"You're not a good fit for the clinic."

"Why not?" he asked again. "I'm exactly what you need. How many diabetics do you see in a week? A dozen?"

"More." Her tone was short, but she didn't refuse to answer.

"Then why not bring me on?" He pitched his voice low and persuasive, willing her to breathe his scent deep into her lungs. "I have all the skills you need."

"Except *people* skills."

"Viola liked me," he said. "So did Kelsey. And Javier. And Gabby."

Her eyes flashed up to his. She looked startled.

"Remembering names," he said. "It's a people skill."

Her jaw muscles tightened. "Not badgering people is another. Why is this so important to you? There are dozens of other places that would welcome you with open arms."

He smiled. "I can never resist a challenge."

"Try," she said.

Satan must see that this dogged pursuit of a position at the clinic was only irritating her.

"Is it your decision?" he asked. "Unilaterally?"

"Yes."

"There's no one to whom I can appeal your verdict? A board of trustees, perhaps?"

"I have final say over all matters pertaining to day-to-day operation." Her eyes swept over him, dismissing him as a threat. "Now, please stop bothering me." And before he could frame another sentence, she walked away.

He stared after her, his eyes narrowed. She was wrong about his potential as a threat.

Very wrong.

CHAPTER 12

Dara stared at the nameplate beside the door to the office of the Bermuda County General Hospital community liaison in surprise.

"Lilith Rojas," it read. Where was Ruth?

Dara had planned to use this monthly meeting to ask for help with the rent. Without an infusion of cash, the clinic was in trouble. Her shoulder muscles tightened. Based on her encounter with Dr. Demon at the grocery, even with an infusion of cash, they were probably in trouble.

And now her go-to person at the hospital had disappeared. She tapped on the doorframe.

Inside the office, a woman with jet-black hair and eyebrows as sleek as a swallow's wings looked up from her computer. At the sight of Dara, her scarlet lips widened into a broad smile and she rose to her feet.

"You must be Dara Strong." She beamed as though meeting Dara was a privilege. "You were on Ruth's calendar." She crossed the room in a few strides on long legs, made even longer by a pair of stiletto heels that would give a mountain goat a nosebleed. Dara's feet, in their sensible flats, ached in sympathy.

Lilith had the figure of a Barbie doll, with the same tiny waist and high, pointed breasts. The hand she extended had long fingernails, painted blood-red. "Craig Jenner can't say enough good things about you."

"That's very kind of him." Craig was the CEO of the hospital and Matt's old tennis partner. Dara shook her hand. "What happened to Ruth?"

"She relocated to Seattle to care for her mother."

Dara couldn't remember Ruth ever mentioning her mother being ill, or even that she'd had a mother. "I wish I'd known. I would have come to say goodbye."

"It was very sudden, I understand."

"It's fortunate they were able to hire you so quickly." Dara had dealt with the hospital, first as a nurse and more recently as executive director of the clinic, for over ten years. She'd never seen them move so rapidly on a hire before.

"Craig and I met at a symposium last year. He knew I was interested and contacted me when Ruth turned in her resignation." Despite Lilith's friendly smile, there was something piercing, almost clinical, in her gaze.

To break away from that penetrating stare, Dara looked around the room. Her eyes widened. "Goodness."

The office had changed beyond recognition since the previous community liaison occupied it. Ruth's furniture had consisted of sleek pieces of canvas and chrome, her only vegetation a snake plant shoved into one corner. Now the room overflowed with leafy green plants, including a fig tree that filled one entire corner of the room. Even the smell of the room was different. Instead of toner and coffee, it smelled like sugar donuts and black licorice.

How had all this happened in such a short time?

Lilith shrugged. "I made redoing it part of my employment negotiation."

The community liaison had a lot of influence over the clinic—they sat on the board of trustees—but it had never been a position of power within the hospital. If Lilith had convinced them to invest in redecorating her office, she must have a lot of sway.

Lilith strolled over to some overstuffed chairs grouped around a low, round table. She dropped into one of the chairs and her skirt rode up, displaying smooth, tanned thighs. She waved toward the opposing chair. "Come. Sit."

Dara sat and folded her hands in her lap.

The table held a coffee carafe and a tray of braided pastries shaped like figure eights. Lilith broke a piece off one and popped it into her mouth. Her eyes closed and her shoulders moved sinuously as she chewed. "Mmmm." Her tongue—small, pink and surprisingly pointed—flicked out to lick a bit of glaze from her lips, and her humming increased in volume.

Dara shifted in her chair and wondered if she should leave and come back later.

As if she'd read Dara's thoughts, Lilith gave a throaty chuckle and her eyes popped open. "*Rosquitas*—they're a Peruvian pastry, made with anise and sesame. My one addiction."

That accounted for the donut-and-black-licorice odor.

"I used to work at the California Hospital Network." Lilith offered another smile. "I was public relations manager."

No wonder Craig was so pleased to acquire her. Dara accepted a cup of coffee and one of the little pastries. Where to begin? She didn't want to start with a request for money.

"So tell me all about your clinic." Lilith's friendly request made it easier.

Dara described her patients' demographics—the one trait they all shared was their poverty—and the community health profile. Lilith asked the occasional question, but Dara sensed the information she was providing wasn't what the other woman wanted to hear.

Lilith picked up a manila folder from the table. "I was looking over your budget numbers. I'm trying to get a sense of where the money goes, but there's no detail here."

Dara blinked. Ruth had never asked for detail. "I can email you our profit and loss statement as soon as I get back to the office."

"That would be great." Lilith was beaming again. "I want to help however I can."

Her interest and support were almost too good to be true, especially after the week Dara had had. She decided to go for it.

"There is one area where I could use some assistance." She described the rent increase that the landlord was demanding. "And I don't know how we'll come up with the money."

For an instant, Lilith's eyes seemed to glitter. Then her charcoal-tinted eyelids swept down. When she reopened her eyes, the gleam was gone.

"That's outrageous." She sounded as indignant as if the money were coming out of her own pocket. She entered a note on her tablet. "How bad a position does that put you in?"

She looked so concerned that Dara shared her next bit of bad news.

"We've also lost funding from the Bermuda County Commission. Next year's grant is being reduced by fifty percent."

Lilith's fingers twisted in the heavy gold chain she wore around her neck. "That's terrible. Don't they realize what a community asset you are?" Despite her indignant tone, the flicker was back in her eyes. It gave Dara pause. "Sounds like you're in a crisis, then?"

Without knowing why, Dara backed it down a notch. "Not yet, but if something doesn't change, we could be."

"Your clinic is too great an asset to be allowed to fail," Lilith said. The gleam Dara thought she'd seen was gone. Lilith appeared to be genuinely worried. "The hospital has an interest here. I'll talk to Craig and see if he's got any pull to make your landlord or the county commission reconsider."

Dara gave herself a shake. Demonic influence wasn't the explanation for every bad thing that happened in life. She had a sudden image of Sarah convulsing in the aisle of the church, her eyes rolling back in her head as her body went limp. Although Nana wouldn't agree, most often, the forces at play were not supernatural.

"Any other issues?" Lilith asked. "How about volunteers? Any problems in that area?"

The demon doctor sprang to mind, but Dara could hardly tell Lilith about him.

"Only the usual." Dara forced a smile. "Never enough of them."

Lilith peeped at Dara from beneath her lashes. "Not according to rumor. The hospital is abuzz with gossip about a certain handsome doctor who got his hat handed to him at the Strong Clinic Tuesday night."

"Gossip?" Dara stared at her in dismay.

Lilith waved away her concern. "Don't worry about it. In a town this size, there's not much to talk about." She picked up another *rosquita* and nibbled at it. "I don't suppose you want to give me the skinny on what happened with Ben Lyle?"

Dara started to say he wasn't a fit for the clinic but stopped herself. His credentials, however he'd assembled them, documented a perfect match. "Our personal styles are at odds."

"And you'd turn down a volunteer for that?" Lilith's swallow's-wing eyebrows lifted.

Dara winced. It did sound capricious.

"I'm sorry," she said. "I'm really not comfortable discussing this."

"Well, we certainly have to respect your instincts." Lilith glanced at her watch. "Oops, I'm afraid I'm late for another meeting."

She got to her feet and walked to the door. Dara followed her. As Dara neared the door, the smell of *rosquitas* became so strong it was almost sickening. Why would that be? The pastries were on the other side of the room.

Every demon has a signature scent.

It hadn't made her sneeze, but she'd taken her allergy meds that morning, so that didn't mean anything. And there was that strange glint in Lilith's eye. Was yet another demon invading Dara's life? She felt for Matt's pearl necklace, but it was currently nothing more than a baggie filled with individual pearls, waiting to go to the jeweler to be restrung.

Instead of Matt's seed pearls, her hand encountered Nana's ruby cross. Maybe she should press the ruby against Lilith's arm and see if it left a mark. The chain was too short to permit that without being obvious. If Lilith wasn't a demon, such an action would be impossible to explain.

How else could she out her? The only way Dara could think of was the rectangular pupils that manifested when a demon got angry. That had the same drawback as the ruby. If Lilith wasn't a demon—and she probably wasn't—Dara needed to maintain a good working relationship with her.

"Perhaps I can some visit the clinic sometime?" Lilith smiled her wide smile.

At the clinic, it would be easy to engineer spilling some grains.

"Of course," Dara said. "You're on the board. You're welcome anytime."

Lilith smiled even more broadly. "Excellent. I'm looking forward to knowing more about you."

Dara smiled right back. "I'm looking forward to the same thing."

CHAPTER 13

Belial had just finished designing his next snare—one so perfectly geared to Dara's needs it guaranteed him entry to the clinic—when his cell phone buzzed. He read the text message: *C ME ASAP @9R.* It ended with an emoji of a glaring devil. Well, bliss. Exactly how he didn't want to spend his evening.

He'd planned to reward himself with a dinner of fresh vegetables and seafood. Now he'd have to spend it calming Satan instead. If last night's encounter at the grocery had been a disappointment to Belial, the boss would be having a golden cow.

He drove to I-95 and pressed on the accelerator of the Lamborghini, building up speed until he exceeded 120 miles per hour. He was about to run up the tailpipe of a tanker truck when the portal finally opened and he was in Hell. Under his tires, the road grew rough and the air became foul with the stink of sulfur and rotting flesh.

Home, sweet home.

He tried to speed down the spiral, but blowing debris in Ring Two covered his windshield and forced him to brake or risk going in the ditch. As soon as the car slowed, a she-wolf's dripping muzzle appeared at his driver's-side window, her dark eyes leering.

This was what happened in Hell when word got around that you were in danger of failing. One misstep and you became prey rather than predator. Well, news of his failure was premature. He flipped on the wipers and stomped on the gas. The car shot forward.

The further down he drove, the hazier the air grew and the stronger the smell of brimstone. By Ring Eight, his eyes watered and his nose burned. Every breath he drew scorched his lungs. He usually had immunity to the more noxious qualities of Hell. Were these symptoms a not-so-subtle warning that the boss was not pleased with his performance, or were they just a side effect of the human DNA Bad had spliced into Belial's genes?

Satan's office was a cavern hewn into the rock wall of Ring Nine. Belial parked the car and went inside. In the reception area, Andras, Satan's secretary, pecked away at a computer. Belial drummed his fingers on her desk to get her attention. "Where's the boss?"

Without turning her body away from the computer screen, the big owl rotated her head to look at him. She blinked her huge eyes.

"Lake of Fire," she squawked.

Well, bliss. The Lake of Fire was the scene of the only deaths that had ever occurred in Hell. A few millennia after Satan opened his establishment, three young demons conspired to break away and set up a rival business. Satan, less trusting than his old employer, uncovered their treason. He'd sentenced them to death, but destroying an immortal proved a difficult task.

It took Hell's scientists nearly a thousand years to formulate a substance that could permanently destroy demon flesh. For days, the traitors' screams had echoed all the way to Ring One as the acid slowly consumed them. Sometimes Belial thought he could still smell traces of their burning flesh in the fetid air, even all these centuries later.

He made his way, on foot, to the bottom of Ring Nine. As he drew closer, the stink grew stronger. The lake belched sulfurous yellow clouds that were responsible for most of the stench in Hell. At the lakeside, Satan was ensconced in an Adirondack chair, a picnic lunch on a small table beside him. He filled a single glass with red wine and took a sip, motioning for Belial to sit at his feet.

So that was how it was to be. Belial sank, cross-legged, to the ground.

"She recognized you as a demon," Satan said.

"We don't know that." Belial's policy was never to admit anything voluntarily. "And even if she did, who's to say she wouldn't recognize another demon if you sent one in? She comes of demon-fighting stock."

Satan grunted. "Finally got around to reading the dossier, did you?"

Belial had finally gotten Bad to send him an updated version with working links. The tech demon "couldn't imagine" how the oversight had happened.

"She didn't recognize Lilith," Satan said.

Belial tensed. "Where did she meet Lilith?"

"Oh, didn't I tell you?" Satan sorted through the picnic basket until he found a morsel of raw lamb and tossed it in his mouth. "Lilith is the new community liaison at Bermuda General Hospital."

She'd managed to worm her way into his assignment. Damn the bitch. The last thing Belial needed was the kind of complications Lilith would introduce into this already fraught mission.

"What was she able to discover?" He kept his tone mild. Satan mustn't know how annoyed he was.

"The clinic has financial woes."

"Stop the presses." The fact that Belial had caused those financial woes didn't seem to have won him any points.

The boss regarded him through narrowed eyes. "At least Lilith was able to make a positive connection."

Time for some damage control.

"I realize this first leg is taking longer than we expected." Belial chose the pronoun "we" deliberately, drawing the boss into the fray. "Dara Strong is more resistant to demon wiles than the average human. That is no doubt due to her heritage, which is probably why the Enemy chose her."

The truth was that she'd cut him off before he could use his wiles. What a strange, prickly woman she was. To look at, she was rounded and feminine—any man's dream of a gentle, nurturing soul. In reality, she was more like a wasp, with a sting for any man foolish enough to get too close to her tail. The excuse worked, though. Satan didn't respond, but his talons relaxed a tiny bit on the stem of his wineglass.

"These first forays are intended to let me get her measure," Belial said. "To determine the most effective way to seduce her to our side."

"And have you figured that out?"

"Of course. She may be a Perdue, but she's still a woman. She's a lot more attracted to me than you realize. Go back and look at the game films. Watch her respiration, the way her pupils dilate, the flare of her nostrils."

"Her nostrils did more than flare—she sneezed all over you," Satan said.

"She didn't sneeze at the gas station. Nor at the grocery last night. Allergies or no allergies, my scent did its job on her. Once I'm able to spend more time with her, she will no more be able to resist than any mortal in the past. I'll have her on her back, ready to do anything for me, long before the wager expires."

"Since she won't allow you in the clinic, how do you propose to spend more time with her?"

"I'll leverage the operative you have stationed at her house."

Satan grunted. "It's about time one of those beasts earned its keep. When?"

Belial would have liked to allow a little more time to elapse since his last meeting with Dara before he approached her again. It was clear, though, from the puff of smoke issuing from Satan's left horn and the ominous presence of the lake, that he didn't have that luxury.

"Tonight," he said.

CHAPTER 14

"Milton," Dara shout-whispered from the front doorway of her condo. It was after eleven o'clock and she didn't want to wake the neighbors. Where was that stupid cat, anyway? Matt had brought him home as a bedraggled tortoiseshell kitten when they were first married. She'd kept him more out of respect for Matt's memory than any real bond.

Off in the distance, a motorcycle roared. The sound brought back her brush with the demon at the gas station, before she'd had any idea who or what he was. She shivered.

"Milton," she called again, more urgently. She'd lock him out for the night, but the one time she did that, he returned the next morning with his ear torn. It felt like she'd betrayed Matt's trust.

She looked down at the t-shirt and running shorts she wore as pajamas. The last thing she wanted to do was go outdoors braless and barefoot to search for the cat.

"Milton!" she called again.

As though she'd summoned it, the black Ducati rounded the corner and glided to a stop in front of her door. Dr. Demon pulled his helmet off. She gritted her teeth, painfully conscious of her bare legs and lack of bra.

"Did you lose something?" he asked.

She considered stepping inside and slamming the door, but that felt like cowardice. At any rate, what did she have to fear? With Nana's ruby pendant hung around her neck, she was safe. "My cat."

She bellowed Milton's name.

Dr. Demon swung his leg over the saddle. Pendant or no pendant, her mouth went dry. He was dressed in black again. His jeans were so tight he could have modeled for an anatomy class.

"Perhaps I can help you find him," he said.

"I don't need your help." She caught a whiff of petrichor and vanilla and wished she'd put on her salve.

"Here kitty, kitty, kitty." The way he crooned the words made her imagine his melodious voice in her ear as they made love. She pressed her hand against her shirt, feeling the shape of Nana's pendant underneath. The image backed off, but she suspected that was less the ruby than the image of Nana's face, pinched in disapproval at her thoughts.

There was a rustle in the bushes beside the front door, and Milton appeared. The cat looked from her to Dr. Demon. He jumped lightly into the demon's arms.

She fought down a stab of annoyance. "He always did prefer men."

"You have very poor taste," the demon told the cat, rubbing its lumpy head. Milton emitted a rumbling purr. "Here you are, graced with the loveliest owner a cat could wish for, but you cuddle up to a brawny, hairy man instead."

That actually didn't seem like such poor judgment. As Kelsey had pointed out just that afternoon, Dr. Lyle was a very fine specimen of a brawny, hairy man. Or he would be, if he actually were a man.

"Do you want me to set him inside for you?" he asked.

"No." She didn't want him invading her home the way he seemed to have invaded her life.

"I'm afraid if I set him down, he'll take off again. He seems to be ready to make a break for it, for some reason."

Dara locked eyes with the cat. "Put him down. If he wants to run, he can just run to a new home."

The demon bent and set the cat on the ground with the same grace he always displayed. Milton stalked into the house.

Dr. Demon looked amused. "I see you have him well trained."

"If he were well trained, I wouldn't be on the doorstep in the middle of the night, calling for him."

"Perhaps your expectations are too high." His eyes seemed to glow in the semidarkness. They did a slow survey of her body, leaving a trail of heat everywhere they passed. Her traitorous nipples pebbled inside her t-shirt. Fantasies filled her mind of what it would be like to have his hands touch everywhere his eyes had.

"My expectations are well within reason," she said, but her voice sounded a little breathless.

"Are you sure you wouldn't like to invite me in for a drink?" he asked. "I did retrieve your cat, after all."

"I don't drink." She heard the prim note in her voice with irritation. Did she have to be everything he already thought she was? She might as well paint a target on her back.

He pulled a flask from a leather compartment on his handlebars and held it out to her. "Are you sure?"

For a moment, she felt a tendril of temptation. Then she shook her head. "No, thank you."

He took a step nearer, and the fragrance of petrichor wound itself around her. She backed away and bumped into the closed door. How had it gotten closed?

"Have you ever even tasted alcohol?" he asked.

"Of course."

"Then you know one drink won't corrupt you." He advanced closer. Her eyes focused on his lips. A drink wouldn't corrupt her, but another kiss might.

"No, thank you," she whispered again. Why wasn't she feeling for the doorknob? Why wasn't she backing her way to safety? Because she couldn't seem to drag her eyes away from his lips, which moved toward hers as inexorably as a grass fire. He stopped a scant few inches away. She could feel the heat coming off his body.

"Shall I kiss you?" he asked.

For a moment, she was confused. Was he asking for consent? Or was he asking himself if kissing her would yield a reward worth the effort? His scent and his heat and those perfectly sculpted lips enticed her toward him. *Say no,* she ordered herself. *This man is a danger. He's out to harm you, to destroy your clinic, to steal your soul.*

"Yes," she said.

His lips touched hers and the world seemed to whirl around them. His hands cupped her jaw and his mouth massaged hers, encouraging her to open to him. Tantalizing touches on her lips from his tongue seconded the invitation. Although it felt as though every organ in her torso had liquefied, some shred of common sense kept her lips stubbornly closed. He kissed along her cheekbone, his mouth seeming to melt flesh from bone.

His hand moved behind her head, trapping it in place.

"Kiss me," he murmured against her ear. His warm, damp breath brought out gooseflesh all the way to her ankles. "Forget about your clinic for a moment and kiss me the way a woman kisses a man."

But he wasn't a man. He was a demon. With that, the spell was broken. She pushed him away and pointed at the Ducati. "Go."

He tried to draw her into his arms again. "That's not what you want."

He was right, but she wouldn't give him the satisfaction of admitting it. She pulled her cell phone from the pocket of her shorts. "Go or I call nine-one-one."

He raised his hands as though she were being unreasonable, and backed away.

"If you approach me again," she said, "I will file for a restraining order."

He threw his leg across the saddle. "You have no grounds. Every caress I've given, you've responded in kind. You asked for my kiss."

Her face and neck flamed, but she kept her gaze steady. "I have friends at the courthouse. I can make it happen."

He was too far away for her to see his pupils in the darkness, but she was sure they turned rectangular.

As soon as the Ducati roared off into the darkness, she headed straight for the shower. She scrubbed every inch of her body under a spray of cold water, shivering at her close call. Even with Nana's pendant, she'd put up practically no resistance. If he hadn't reminded her that he was a demon, not a man, she wasn't sure what would have happened.

Was Nana right? Was the demon after her? Or was seducing her merely a route into the clinic, where he could create all sorts of havoc? There was no way to know.

She got out of the shower, but she didn't even need to towel off. The cold water had already evaporated from her skin.

On the dark stretch of road that lay between Alexandria and beach, Belial crouched over the Ducati, taking it through its gears until it roared to maximum speed. The wind slipped inside the back of his t-shirt, and for a dizzying moment, it felt as though he were flying.

There was no question in his mind that he'd touched something in Dara's core, something that had been in abeyance since the death of her husband. At the thought of her beneath him, his loins burned. Sex with her would be a moment of rapture in an eternity of damnation.

Her rounded body was on his mind far more than it should be. He needed to bed her, so that he could slot her back into the category where she belonged—prey.

He pushed on the clutch, taking the bike down through its gears as he slowed to a more reasonable speed. He was doing a mere five miles over the limit when red and blue lights strobed from the darkness. As though for emphasis, a siren yelped.

Well, bliss. He hit the clutch again, halting the bike along the roadside. A white cruiser pulled up in front of him and the fat policeman from the service station got out. He swaggered up to the bike, his gut lapping over his belt.

"License and registration." It was an order.

"Certainly, officer." Belial extracted the documents from his wallet and handed them over. "May I ask why you stopped me?"

"Step off the bike."

Behind his face shield, Belial glared at him. This mortal had no idea with whom he was dealing. He put down the kickstand and slung his leg over the saddle, making it a point to land close enough to the cop to emphasize his superior height. He removed his helmet.

"What's the problem?" He stared down his nose. The cop didn't say anything, but Belial could tell he didn't like having Belial tower over him. After a moment of studying the documents, he grunted. He looked Belial in the eyes for a long moment.

"I've known Dara Strong for a long, long time." He hooked his right thumb into his belt, so that his hand hovered just above his gun. "Went to high school with her."

"Did you?" Belial toyed with the idea of making the fool shoot him, but quickly abandoned the notion. Demons weren't to draw attention to their otherness while on mission.

"Folks around here think the world of her."

"Indeed. Why wouldn't they?"

The cop squinted at him. "I think you should steer clear of her."

"Did she ask you to deliver that message?" Demons couldn't read minds, but they could get a pretty clear reading on emotions. Belial probed, looking for jealousy or resentment, but all he found was protectiveness.

"You were doing twenty over the speed limit." The officer's face dared him to argue. After scribbling for a moment, he tore a page off his pad and handed it to Belial. It was a ticket for a two-hundred-dollar fine. Mammon would be livid. In ages past, Belial would have made the man's cow go dry in retribution.

Sometimes he really missed the old days.

"Think about what I said." The cop handed him back his license and registration, the threat implicit. He trudged back to the cruiser and got in.

Belial mounted the bike, flicking his fingers toward the car in a subtle movement, invisible in the dark. Inside the shadowy patrol car, the officer put on his seatbelt and turned the key in the ignition. Nothing happened.

Of course, there was a lot to be said for the present, too.

CHAPTER 15

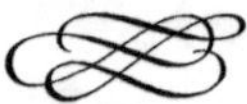

By five o'clock Friday, Dara had made thirty phone calls and hadn't received a pledge of a single dollar. That could be because this part of Florida was still recovering from the last hurricane, but it felt more like demonic interference.

She rubbed her temples. Thank God it was Friday. Over the weekend, she would come in and write out payables checks for the month and see where that left them.

Even worse than the rebuffs in her canvassing calls were the disturbing sensations she felt every time she recalled her encounter with Dr. Demon the night before. Each time the memory assaulted her, she shoved it away, but at every unwary moment, it was back, taunting her, luring her.

She was shutting down her computer when the phone rang. She eyed it hopefully. Maybe someone had changed their mind. She picked up.

"Hey, *chica*, this is Lilith Rojas. It's been a long first week. Care to join me for a drink to celebrate surviving?"

Dara hesitated. Lilith's exotic beauty, coupled with her unusual scent, made her a prime candidate for demon-hood.

"I hear that Slyders has great fries," Lilith said.

There would be salt shakers on every table, enabling an on-the-spot demon test.

"Slyders sounds great," Dara said.

A half-hour later, Dara walked through the bar, where kitschy fishing nets studded with sand dollars and dried starfish festooned the ceiling. Out on the patio, Mother Nature did the decorating. A salty breeze ruffled tufts of sea oats that dotted the expanse of white sand lying between the patio and the restless ocean.

Lilith was already there, along with two glasses of wine. "I hope you like red."

The glass at Dara's seat stood right beside a salt shaker that was nearly full. It couldn't have worked out any better if she'd planned it herself. She reached for the wineglass and knocked over the shaker. Grains of salt scattered across the table top.

"That was clumsy." Lilith barely glanced at the spilled salt. She looked amused, her tone light, displaying none of Dr. Demon's compulsion to count the spilled grains.

Here in the sea breeze, the smell of *rosquitas* wasn't perceptible. Dara felt a little ridiculous, but just to be certain, she dropped the shaker as she attempted to right it, making sure salt grains landed directly in front of Lilith. This time, Lilith didn't even look at the salt.

She wasn't a demon after all, just a woman that had recently moved to the area and was in search of friends. Dara tilted her head to one side and then the other, loosening muscles that felt like they'd been rigid for days.

Lilith watched her with a smile. "To never having another week like this one." She raised her wineglass.

Dara clinked hers against it. *Have you ever had a drink?* And then his lips on hers, teasing, taunting, drawing her closer. She squashed the memory.

"What happened?" she asked. "You seemed to have it all together when I was there yesterday."

Lilith crimped her mouth into a crimson rosebud and rolled her eyes. "I put up a good front."

"So, what happened?"

"Nothing. It's always tough, starting a new gig. High expectations and all that." Lilith was wearing a red lace camisole and a tiny black skirt that showed off her amazing legs. The matching jacket hung on the back of her chair. Her red-and-black heels were even higher than the ones she'd had on the day before, if that was possible. She attracted a lot of glances to the table.

Dara looked down at her own outfit. Next to Lilith's upscale elegance, she felt like a frump. At least she wasn't in scrubs.

"I never pictured Craig as a tough boss." She relaxed back in her chair and took a sip of her wine.

"He probably isn't." Lilith's smile was wry. "You may have picked up on the fact that I'm a wee bit of an overachiever." Her jaw went square. "I want to *destroy* this assignment."

Dara blinked at the sudden passion in Lilith's voice. "I'm sure you will."

Lilith lifted her glass and drank. Her mouth left a scarlet imprint on the glass, but her lipstick didn't smudge.

"You were having a pretty bad week, too," Lilith said. "Did things get any better?"

Dara thought about Dr. Demon's late-night visit. Unless having your immortal soul placed in jeopardy counted as a step up from losing your clinic funding, her trajectory hadn't improved. She shook her head.

A pretty waitress appeared. "Can I interest you ladies in an appetizer? They're half-price until seven p.m."

Lilith lifted her eyebrows. Dara shook her head.

"No appetizers," Lilith said, "but we'd like a round of martinis."

"Not for me," Dara said.

"Oh, live a little," Lilith said. "If you haven't earned one after the week you've had, I don't know who has."

It was tempting. Dara had never been drunk in her life. Her grandparents were teetotalers. After she moved to Jacksonville for college, she'd been too busy trying to keep up her grades and earn enough to cover expenses to party. She wavered and landed on a compromise.

"No martinis," she said, "but I will take another glass of wine."

Two hours later, Lilith had polished off four martinis and Dara was sipping at her third glass of wine. She was feeling decidedly mellow. For the first time in her adult life, she'd be taking a cab home.

Excusing herself, she went to the ladies' room. As she washed her hands, she checked herself out in the mirror. Even allowing for the fact that her unstructured jacket wasn't the most flattering cut in the world, her body looked dumpy compared to Lilith's voluptuous curves. For the first time in years, she looked at herself, really looked at herself. She didn't like what she saw.

Behind her, the bathroom door opened and, speak of the devil, it was Lilith. Although, if they were talking about the devil, strictly speaking, it should have been Dr. Lyle. For some reason, that struck Dara as hilarious. She giggled. Without asking why, Lilith joined in. Soon they were both bent double, tears rolling down their faces.

That lasted until a pair of young women who didn't look old enough to legally be in the bar came through the door. They were dressed in micro-shorts that displayed long, tanned legs that rivaled Lilith's, and crop tops that showed off taut bellies. They took one look at Dara and Lilith and exchanged eye-rolls. That made Dara laugh even harder. Lilith drew herself up, giving them a look that should have flayed the skin from their lithe young bodies.

Suddenly, Dara didn't feel like laughing anymore. She took Lilith's elbow. "Let's go back to the table."

Lilith shook her head. Her charcoal-shaded eyelids were half-closed, hiding her thoughts as well as her eyes. "I need to use the toilet first."

For a bizarre moment, Dara wondered if it was safe to leave Lilith alone with those girls. But that was ridiculous. She'd already determined Lilith wasn't a demon. The woman hadn't achieved the position of public relations manager for the California Health Network by getting into bar brawls with young girls.

Back at the table, Dara switched to water, keeping an eye on the bathroom door. She didn't see the girls come out, but Lilith rejoined her a few minutes later.

"So tell me about Dr. Lyle, and why you really kicked him out," she said.

Kiss me the way a woman kisses a man. "He's just so arrogant." The words popped out of Dara's mouth without intention.

"You refused to let a doctor volunteer because he's arrogant?"

Dara thought about shutting down the conversation, but she needed to talk to someone and she couldn't discuss this with Nana. Maybe she could share how she felt without actually saying why she felt that way.

"Doctors have big egos," she said. "They have to, to handle all the pressure they're under. And good-looking men usually know that about themselves—I realize that."

"So you think Dr. Lyle is good-looking." Lilith's lips quirked up.

"Not as good-looking as he does, but yes, he's handsome."

"Go on." Lilith was openly grinning now.

Dara felt a stir of irrational anger. This wasn't a joke. This was her clinic they were talking about. She'd poured every ounce of energy she had, along with every dollar she possessed, into making it work.

"Dr. Lyle is so egotistical that he's soulless." That was true, although his lack of soul was a separate issue from his ego. "He doesn't care for anyone but himself. He gears every move he makes toward his own betterment. At some point, what's good for him and what's good for my patients would conflict, and my patients would get hurt. And I won't allow that."

She had the impression Lilith was pleased, but she had no idea why. She opened her mouth to ask, but a voice said, "Dara?" in a tone of pure astonishment.

Jeremy Stevens, Nana's doctor and one of Dara's favorite volunteers, stood beside their table. He was accompanied by three other men. They were all dressed in golf shirts and chinos. The others weren't volunteers, but something about them said "doctor" all the same.

Jeremy introduced her to his companions, recommending they look into volunteering at the clinic. They answered politely, but it was clear they couldn't be less interested in adding another three or four hours onto their already long days, even if it was only once a month.

From the other side of the table, Lilith cleared her throat. Flushing, Dara introduced her.

More hand-shaking. The men eyed Lilith appreciatively and Dara felt like a frump again. Lilith's gaze traveled from her to Jeremy and back. As soon as they left, Lilith pounced. "Are you two an item?"

"Not at all," Dara said. "Jeremy's a volunteer."

She expected something like "why not?" but Lilith said, "Oh, good. Then you won't mind if I go after him."

Go after? The phrase had a predatory ring that made Dara blink. She looked at Lilith, with her blood-red lips, her strong white teeth, her dagger-like fingernails. This was not a woman who would wait, hands folded, until a man approached her. She would go after what she wanted. Even so, Dr. Stevens didn't seem like her type. "You and Jeremy?"

Lilith smiled. "Why not?"

Dara couldn't imagine two people who were less alike, unless it was her and Ben Lyle, and he wasn't actually a person. "No reason I can think of."

She drank some more water and decided to call it an evening. Her head was starting to ache. She wasn't cut out for this partying life.

"I was wondering…" Lilith's voice trailed off. Uncertainty seemed so out of character for her that Dara reached across the table to touch her elbow. "I was wondering if perhaps you'd like to go shopping sometime," Lilith finished in a rush.

There was something touching about her shyness, a vulnerability Dara wouldn't have expected. She thought about the admiring glances men had given Lilith all evening. It might be nice to have some clothes other than scrubs and business suits. "I'd love that."

"Tomorrow?" Lilith asked.

The stack of unpaid bills at the clinic had to be dealt with first. "Sunday might be better."

They set a time and walked out to the parking lot. Outside the front door, a pair of ambulances pulled away.

"What happened?" Dara asked a barmaid.

The barmaid shook her head. "A couple of young girls. Looked like alcohol poisoning."

Belial was sitting on one of the black leather couches facing the massive fireplace when Lilith walked in the door of the beach house. The house had an open floor plan, with white tile floors and black marble counters separating the kitchen from the great room. The triangular back wall of the house was made up of windows from floor to roof.

Mammon had refused to pay for separate housing for Lilith, so she was staying in the maid's quarters. It was hard to say who was less happy with the arrangement.

Belial turned off the big-screen TV when she came in, but not before she recognized the patio at Slyders.

"How did an old-school demon like you ever figure out how to tap into the surveillance system?" she asked.

She didn't have to sound quite so surprised.

"Bad helped me," he said.

She slipped off her heels and curled up on the other couch. "Play it again. I want to see how brilliant I am."

He considered hurling the remote at her, but curiosity won over annoyance. He punched the on button and watched as Dara spilled salt not once, but twice. Even watching the replay, he couldn't resist counting the grains. Lilith retrieved her lipstick from her purse and touched up her lips without so much as glancing in that direction.

He glared at her. "How are you doing that?"

She dug into her purse again and held up a pill bottle with a childproof lid.

"I got a prescription for Prozac." She dimpled. "It really is as effective at controlling compulsive behaviors as the literature promises."

Why hadn't he thought of that?

"Admit it," she said. "I'm smarter than you."

He considered throwing the remote again, but then relaxed back onto the sofa instead.

"You're brilliant," he said.

Her gaze became wary.

"In fact, rumor has it you were clever enough to make off with a trove of Solomon's jewels."

Wariness escalated into outright panic. "You can't believe everything you hear."

"I don't." He got to his feet. Reaching into his pocket, he retrieved an emerald the size of a hen's egg. "Unless I see proof."

She lunged at him, but he held the jewel out of her reach. After a moment or two of fruitless jumping on her part, he tossed the jewel to her.

"You might want to stay on my good side."

CHAPTER 16

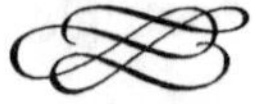

Belial strolled into the Accounting Department and tapped the little bell. A clerk with ten bandaged fingers dragged herself up to the counter.

"Can I help you, Lord Belial?" She turned her head and let out a long, gagging cough. "Sorry," she said. "Paper dust."

"I need some cash," he said.

She tapped a few keys on her computer, wincing as each bandaged finger pressed a key. Blood seeped from beneath the wrappings. In life, she'd probably been an embezzler. Most of the clients assigned to Mammon were. She read what was on the screen and swallowed.

"It says here you've exhausted the budget for this mission." Her voice trembled.

Mammon had been eying the CED slot for years. This was part and parcel of his efforts to ensure Belial didn't win the promotion.

Belial had never been a demon for taking things out on the clients. Besides, he'd come prepared. In his pocket, he had a prospectus for a tech startup he'd strong-armed from Bad. Mammon loved getting in on moneymaking ventures.

"Let me talk to your boss," Belial told the clerk.

A few minutes later, she returned, carrying a large pitcher, a cutting board and a dozen lemons. "He says I'm to make you lemonade while you wait."

"I don't want any lemonade."

She cut into a lemon anyway, yelping as the juice seeped into her paper cuts. It was only after she filled the pitcher with a pale yellow liquid laced with red swirls that Mammon appeared.

The Accounting manager was huge. He wore a gold crown and a cream-colored silk cape shot with gold threads. Sharkskin boots covered his massive feet. To Belial's irritation, Lilith was with him.

Mammon glared at him. "What do you want?"

"My multipronged approach to this assignment requires bribery." Bribery. The last refuge of the second-rate demon. Just saying the words left a foul taste in his mouth.

"Bribery's good." Mammon swept his arm around the huge cavern. Everyone at the thousands of desks sported the same little bandages as the clerk who had waited on him. "That's how I recruited most of my staff."

"I'll need about half a million dollars."

"A half-million dollars?" The flesh where Mammon's eyebrows should have been rose almost to his hairline. He rubbed his hands on his cape, leaving greasy streaks on the fabric. "That's a lot of money, demon. Exactly what do you propose to do with it?" He said the words like they caused him physical pain.

"I plan to award it as a grant."

Mammon picked up his pen, but Lilith asked, "What kind of grant?"

Belial clenched his jaw. He could lie and say the grant was to increase the use of tobacco products or the availability of heroin, but not with Lilith standing there. She'd take too much pleasure in outing him.

"It's funding for a free clinic."

"Are you insane?" Mammon's fat jowls trembled. "The operations of free clinics are diametrically opposed to everything we stand for."

"I don't need a lecture on the mission of Hell," Belial said. "I need money for the boss's top priority."

Mammon lifted a sheet of paper from a wire in-basket. It said MEMO across the top in glowing red letters. Dated the day before, it was from Satan, instructing Mammon to contain expenses, no matter how important the demon requesting extra funding claimed his mission to be.

Belial pulled out his cell phone and dialed 666. The boss didn't pick up.

"He never answers when Jerry Springer is on," Lilith said. "It's his favorite."

Oh, for Hell's sake.

Lilith turned to Mammon. "How about this? How about if he returns the Lamborghini? You can sell it and return the money to his budget."

Belial didn't want to give up the Lamborghini, but with Dara as his target, the car was probably counterproductive. She was not a woman who would understand spending hundreds of thousands of dollars on a beautiful piece of machinery when you could waste it helping the poor.

"Who will want a second-hand Aventador?" Mammon said.

"I know a B-list celebrity." Lilith's answer came out so pat Belial knew she'd been waiting for this opportunity. "A minor prince. He's been wanting one of that model. I'm pretty sure he'll take it off our hands."

Mammon pinched his thick lower lip for a moment before he spoke. "It won't bring anywhere near what we paid for it. There's a huge penalty for just driving one of those things off the lot."

Lilith shrugged. "It should fetch at least a quarter of a million."

"A quarter of a million?" Belial was outraged. "How am I supposed to complete my mission with that pittance?"

Mammon, who been known to crawl into a sewer to retrieve a penny that had fallen through the grate, drew himself up. "You need to learn the value of a dollar, demon. Take it or leave it."

"What will I drive for the remainder of the mission?" Belial was probably back to that pathetic Porsche.

"Whatever's left in the garage," said Mammon. He snapped his fingers, and one of the clerks hurried over with a tablet computer. The small screen displayed closed-circuit footage of the motor pool. All but one of the stalls were empty. The lone remaining vehicle was a beat-up Hyundai Accent.

Belial eyed it with repulsion. "You don't expect me to drive that?"

"Take it or leave it," Mammon said again.

Belial took it.

Lilith followed him out the door of Accounting.

Now that he had money, he could execute his planned snare. He didn't need her help for that.

"If you want a thank-you," he said, "I'll drop you a card. Why don't you stay here and wait for it?"

"Satan's blood, but you're an ungrateful prick," Lilith said.

That was her constant craving for recognition talking.

"This is why everyone down here hates you," she added.

He frowned. "That's ridiculous. They don't hate me."

"They do." Her tone was matter-of-fact. "You've been voted Least Popular Demon for the last thousand years running. Unanimously."

"That's not true."

"I can show you the trophy room, if you like. Your name is on a whole lot of trophies."

"You must be mistaken. I'm known as Hell's Politician."

"And you just proved my point. Politicians are only popular when they're doing favors for someone. And you only do favors for yourself and Satan."

He decided to take her word for it. The way his current mission was going, the last thing his ego needed was a room full of evidence showing how unlikeable he was. "Why do they dislike me so much?"

"They don't dislike you. They hate you."

"Fine. Why do they hate me so much?"

"Because you don't care about anyone but yourself."

"This is Hell! No one here cares about anyone else."

"Not true. Have you ever heard of the term 'a cadre of demons'?"

"Of course."

"What cadre do you belong to?"

He opened his mouth to say only a weakling relies on others, but that would make her case. "I'm not a joiner."

"Exactly. Everyone else down here is in a cadre. We know that our friends will eventually betray us—that's the nature of Hell—but for the short term, we have other demons to pal around with."

He glared at her, offended to his core. What she was saying was ridiculous. He had, if not friends, at least close acquaintances in Hell. Other demons he could play handball with, or cribbage. He tried to remember the last time he'd played handball.

"Even you don't like you," she said.

He wanted to roar a denial, but she was enjoying this conversation far too much already, so he kept his tone mild. "Why do you say that?"

"You've never gotten over falling. You hate being in Hell."

"Don't be ridiculous. If I hate it so much, why am I so successful?"

"You're successful because you're a workaholic."

He shrugged. He was all right with that.

"And you're a workaholic because you're a narcissist."

He was a narcissist? She forced clients to wear sunglasses so she could see herself in the lenses.

"And that's why everyone hates you," Lilith finished.

"So why did you help me out?"

"Because I want this mission to succeed," she said. Her eyes were wide.

He stared at her until she finally said, "Okay. At first, I wanted your mission to succeed in a way I could take credit for. I figured if we made a go of it, the boss might award me some little token of appreciation. It's not much, but it's all a woman is likely to ever get in this place."

That, at least, sounded like the truth. "If you're so hot to see me succeed, why did you just sabotage my effort to increase my budget?"

"If I hadn't been there, Mammon wouldn't have given you that much."

That was probably true, but he refused to give her the satisfaction of agreeing.

"If you're so big on seeing me triumph, loan me some money."

"I'm not that invested, but I did manage to get an extra ten thousand for the car."

That was surprising. He would have expected the opposite. "Why are you helping me? You said you were originally hoping to get a little spotlight from this. Did something change?"

Her mouth twisted in an expression of revulsion. "I met that smarmy little do-gooder, Dara Strong. Those whack-job grandparents of hers shoved a giant stick so far up her ass when she was a kid that it's never coming back out."

She clasped her hands in front of her in an imitation of the heroine in a cheap melodrama. "'Even though God has taken my husband and my baby, I'm still his loving child.'" She raised her eyes toward Heaven. "'And no matter how much abuse he heaps on my head, I won't think a word against him.'"

He blinked at the depth of the loathing in Lilith's voice. Her depiction of Dara didn't strike him as accurate. Dara had unplumbed depths of anger that made her a more likely convert than Lilith recognized. That had to be the case.

Because if it weren't, he was well and truly screwed.

CHAPTER 17

By the time Dara finished paying bills on Saturday, the clinic's cash reserves had dwindled to almost nothing. Maybe it was time to take out a loan. They had a line of credit with the local bank they'd used in the past when cash flow got tight. The problem was that any money they borrowed, they would have to pay back. Between the rent increase and their impending funding cut, she didn't see where the principal for the loan repayment would come from, never mind the interest.

When she left the clinic, she stopped in to see Nana. Even though Dara didn't mention the demon doctor's house call, the old woman was beside herself.

"You need to close down that clinic and move away." Nana's arthritic hands squeezed into shaky fists. Immediately, she insisted. Leaving no forwarding address.

She was deaf to counterarguments that taking such a dramatic step would do nothing to rid Dara of the demon pursuing her. If they had the technology to find her in the first place, they would find her wherever she went.

"Well, you have to do something," Nana said. Worry had sent her blood pressure skyrocketing. That felt like a much greater threat than any the demon posed.

On Sunday, Dara went shopping with Lilith. She hadn't planned to spend any money, but she'd gotten paid Friday and she was sick of looking dowdy next to Lilith's chic elegance. She bought a new outfit and a pair of strappy black patent-leather sandals with four-inch heels. She initially resisted buying the shoes. They looked great, but she couldn't imagine wearing them in the clinic. She spent far too many hours on her feet.

"Don't be such a prude," Lilith said. "Every woman needs at least one pair of slutty shoes. What if you meet a hot guy who's into feet?"

An image of Dr. Demon rubbing her feet sprang to Dara's mind. She pushed it away but, cheeks flaming, took the shoes to the cash register and paid for them. Lilith didn't say anything, but her grin said she knew exactly what Dara was thinking.

After shopping, they hung out on the patio at Slyders until after eleven, drinking wine and swapping stories, though Dara refused to allow herself to get drunk. To her relief, Lilith didn't even mention Dr. Lyle. Whatever curiosity Lilith felt about Dara's reaction to the supernaturally handsome doctor, she must have put it behind her. They talked and laughed until the sky was black as ink. It was the latest Dara had been out in years.

Now it was Monday morning and she felt exhausted and overwhelmed. No more going out on school nights.

She stared at her computer. Maybe changing to a larger font would magnify potential donor names to the point where they'd become visible to the naked eye. If not, she had no idea where the money would come from. She was about to give up and go for another cup of coffee when Kelsey appeared in the doorway, bouncing on the balls of her feet. In her hand was a sheaf of papers. It was the first time she'd smiled at Dara since the incident with Dr. Lyle. Dara hoped this wasn't another attempt to change her mind.

"You'll never believe what I found." The words bubbled from Kelsey like soda pop from a shaken bottle. "An operational grant for two hundred and fifty thousand dollars."

"An operational grant?" It was relatively easy to find grants to fund new programs, but grants to pay operational expenses were practically nonexistent.

"It's a healthcare grant, specifically for a small clinic in the southeastern United States." Kelsey bounced a little faster. "It says that at least fifty percent of the labor must be volunteers." She held out the stack of papers. "It's like it was designed specifically for us."

Dara skimmed through the document. It looked like a dream come true. Preference would be given to a clinic serving a demographically diverse population living below the federal poverty line, with special emphasis on clinics carrying a large number of chronic patients. That was them. There were no restrictions on how the money could be spent—rent, utilities, payroll, anything. The deadline for applying was in two days and the money would be awarded within a week after that. Her breathing sped up. It was the answer to her prayers.

Except, of course, that she hadn't done any praying. Not for years. Not that God—or the randomness of the universe—wasn't capable of sending some good luck without being asked but, given their current state of siege, she had to consider the alternative.

"That's amazing." She injected enthusiasm into her voice. On the off chance that the grant was the answer to a prayer she hadn't even prayed, she didn't want to spoil Kelsey's triumph. "How did you find out about this?"

"I got an email this morning." Kelsey's pretty face was flushed with pride.

"Really?" It was pleasant not to have Kelsey sulking at her. "Who from?"

"Grantfinders.org."

The name was unfamiliar. "Are we registered with them?"

"Not yet." The pace of Kelsey's bounce increased. "To tell you the truth, I'd never heard of them before today. I registered our name, though, so we'll get future notifications."

With every word Kelsey spoke, Dara's suspicions rose a little higher and her spirits sank a little lower.

"Great work." She gave Kelsey a broad smile and gathered up the sheaf of papers. "Would you mind leaving these with me so I can look them over?"

"Sure," Kelsey said. "I'll start working on the proposal. We've only got two days." And she hustled away, happier than she'd been in the past week.

Dara's first read-through revealed nothing out of the ordinary. Other than the fact that her search engine couldn't find anything about Grantfinders.org, everything seemed to be in order. They weren't requesting a processing fee or asking for the clinic's checking account information. It wasn't until her second read-through that she found the poison pill. It was tucked away in a huge paragraph so long and boring she'd skimmed it the first time and nearly did so again.

All volunteer recruitment for the recipient organization shall be subject to final decision by the organization's board of trustees.

Is there no one to whom I can appeal your decision? Dr. Demon had asked in the grocery store. *No,* she had told him, the buck stopped with her.

He must be behind the grant.

She tried to imagine telling Kelsey that they were walking away from the opportunity to win a grant they desperately needed. Given the clinic's current circumstances, Kelsey would think she was insane.

Dara groaned. Nana had warned her that once the demon had her in his sights, he wouldn't give up. Once again, Nana was right. Dara mentally reviewed each member of the board of trustees. She had cordial business relationships with all of them, but none were what she would call a friend.

Except for one. Recent, but a friend all the same. Having one person to back her up might not ensure she could keep Dr. Demon out of her clinic, but at least she would have someone in her corner. She made the call. Lilith answered on the first ring.

"Hey, girlfriend. Are you wearing those kicking shoes we picked out?"

"Not today."

"Why not?"

"I'm saving them for Friday," Dara said. "We are going out Friday, aren't we?" She hadn't planned on it, but it seemed tactical to throw out the offer.

"Sure. Was that why you called?"

Dara explained about the grant Kelsey had found. "Right now, I have final say on all volunteers. If a proposed volunteer approached the board but I recommended against him, could I count on you to side with me?"

Lilith didn't beat around the bush. "This is about Dr. Lyle, isn't it?"

Dara sighed. "Yes. He might cause trouble if he gets wind of the grant."

There was silence at the other end of the line.

"Lilith?" she said.

"I hate to do this to you," Lilith said, "but there's no way I can back you on this. Not when you've never provided an adequate reason why you're so opposed to having him volunteer. The man has impeccable credentials. He's exactly what you need at the clinic."

Listening to Lilith praise Dr. Lyle made Dara want to vomit. How neatly he'd snared her. He had blocked every exit, cutting off every possible escape, before springing his trap. If she couldn't count on Lilith, who knew her personally, to take her word about Dr. Lyle, how could she expect anyone else to?

It had come down to two choices: either she allowed the demon access to her clinic, where he would create who knew what sort of mayhem, or she closed the doors forever, abandoning her patients and walking away from the clinic she had worked so hard to build.

"Thank you for your honesty," she managed to say through numb lips.

"Are you okay? You sound upset. If you hate him that much, why don't you let another nurse work with him? Give yourself a night off when he's there so you won't have to be around him."

There was no way on earth she would allow that spawn of Satan to roam her clinic unsupervised.

It was time for a new strategy.

CHAPTER 18

"I don't have any choice, Nana. Either I take his money or I shut down the clinic." Dara perched on Nana's bed. Nana sat in her usual chair.

"Then shut down the clinic." Nana thumped her fist on the Bible in her lap. If she didn't calm down, she would fret herself into a stroke.

Dara tried to be patient. "The clinic employs six people. It would put them all out of work."

"When people came to your granddaddy for counseling when they'd lost their jobs, he used to tell them, 'If you found one job, you can find another.'"

Empathy was never Granddad's strong suit.

"If I close the doors, lots of people in town won't have any way to see a doctor—people with diabetes and hypertension and asthma. People who could die without treatment."

"They can go to the ER at the hospital."

"The hospital is only obligated to deal with acute situations. They don't have the staff or facilities to deal with chronic disease."

Nana crossed her arms. "Your patients are better off losing their lives than their souls."

"They're not going to lose either one." Dara stuck out her jaw, as mulish as Nana. "Because I'm not closing down my clinic. The sooner you accept that, the sooner you can help me figure out how to protect against him instead of fighting me."

They glared at each other.

"You are as stubborn as your granddaddy." Nana leaned forward. "And I don't mean that as a compliment."

Dara folded her arms, waiting.

"You're going to do what you're going to do." Nana flicked her bony fingers, as though brushing away any responsibility for the inevitable bad outcome. "Bring him here to me."

"What? No!" Dara's instinctive reaction made her realize how dangerous she considered Dr. Lyle to be. She didn't want him anywhere near Nana. "I'm not putting you at risk by bringing him in here."

"But you're willing to put your patients at risk by letting him be around them."

She looked at her grandmother. Sitting there in her chair, all wrapped up in her afghan, her silver hair gleaming under the harsh overhead lights, she looked so frail.

"That's why I need your help. I need you to tell me what he's likely to do and how to stop him."

"Then bring him here. I need to see him to know how you can best defend yourself."

"How would I even get him to come here?" *Hey, Dr. Demon—would you like to meet my grandma?*

"You never told him you know he's a demon, did you?"

"Of course not, but that doesn't mean he hasn't figured it out."

"Tell him you're reconsidering letting him volunteer. Say that your grandmother is a good judge of character, and if she says he's okay, you'll take him on."

Right, because professional women hauled prospective employees in front of their grandmothers all the time.

"He already knows if I take his grant I'll have to let him into the clinic," Dara said. "What does he have to gain by coming here?"

"Because his purpose in volunteering isn't to mess with your clinic, it's to come after you. He'll want to smooth things over now he's gotten his way."

Dara looked at Nana's ankles, camouflaged by the afghan. If she could get Dr. Lyle to examine Nana, Nana could assess how much of a threat he posed to the clinic. He'd displayed no interest in her. Whatever his target was, it wasn't her. The risk to Nana from seeing the demon doctor was very small. The risk to her patients if she closed down the clinic was huge.

"Fine. I'll give him a call and see if he can come out this afternoon."

"I'm very flattered you've asked me to examine your grandmother." Belial smiled down at Dara in the lobby of Mercy Care. Her boat-necked cotton sweater provided a tantalizing glimpse of her collarbones. His groin stirred. He made himself think of the larvae pit until it subsided.

She led him down a gleaming hallway lined with doors. DemSec had warned him to stay away from the old lady, but he didn't see how he could refuse Dara's olive branch. He might have found a means to force his way into the clinic, but that was only because the boss had insisted. His tactics had done a huge amount of damage. He had a lot of ground to make up.

The old woman was ninety-four. How dangerous could she be?

"I've been told I'm very good with older people," he said.

Dara glanced at him over her shoulder. The ghost of what might have been a smile tugged at the corners of her lips. "Thank you for giving up your evening. I appreciate it."

Her composed expression gave no indication she remembered their little tête-à-tête by the gas pumps or the kiss they'd shared in her doorway. Beneath the overhead lights, though, her upper lip gleamed with shiny salve. She had come prepared.

The hallway they walked through was dotted with blonde oak doors every ten feet. Some were closed, but most were open, revealing wizened old people sitting in chairs or lying on beds. This was where humans warehoused their elderly these days. The boss loved these places.

They passed a room containing an old man with huge ears and a confused expression. He sat in front of a tiny television showing a black-and-white western. His rounded shoulders listed hard to the left. The corner of his mouth drooped, and his left hand curled uselessly in his lap. Dara stopped.

"Give me a moment, please." She entered the room and straightened the old man in his chair, tucking a pillow in beside him to keep him upright. "Is that loud enough for you to hear, Mr. Tobias?" She turned the volume on the set up a notch.

The old man patted her arm. "You're a good girl, Susan."

She covered his hand with her own and smiled. "Thanks, Dad."

Was it her compassion that had made her the Enemy's choice? Belial didn't think so. Compassion was not really an asset in battle.

At the end of the hall, she knocked on a door exactly like all the ones they'd passed. A brass slot beside the door held a plastic name plate: Esther Perdue. Other demons might quail at the sight of that name, but Belial just smiled. He hadn't gotten this far by being afraid of a puny old woman who should have gone on to her reward years ago.

He was painfully aware of the cell phone in his pants pocket. DemSec had installed a highly sensitive microphone that would relay every syllable of his coming confrontation back to Ring Nine. He considered muffling it with his handkerchief, or even leaving it out in the hall, but such tactics would gain him nothing. Balked of the chance to listen in, Satan would assume the worst. Belial couldn't afford to inflame him any further.

Dara opened the door and stepped inside. He tried to follow but was brought up short at the threshold. When he swung his foot across the doorsill, a thousand stinging bees seemed to swarm his leg. He leapt backward.

"Is something wrong?" From inside the room, Dara raised her eyebrows. The little smile he'd noticed earlier widened.

"Ague-weed and five-finger grass," a very old voice wheezed from farther inside. "They call it demonweed."

Dara reached above the doorframe and pulled down a small cloth bag. She reached across the threshold and brushed his arm with it. From elbow to wrist, his skin erupted in needlelike stabs of pain. He yelped and backed away.

"It works really well, doesn't it?" Dara retreated, looking surprised.

"Stops them every time," the old voice said.

"I've heard you talk about it," Dara said, "but I've never seen it in action."

The stinging sensation in Belial's arm subsided but didn't go away.

"Come on in, demon," the old voice called.

Belial stayed where he was. It was one thing to suspect Dara knew his identity. It was another to have her confront him. Dara's smile broadened.

"My grandmother is an excellent judge of character," she said.

The cell phone in his pocket buzzed. He decided to ignore it. He would not return to Hell a failure. He would not cede the field to Lilith, allowing her to reign in triumph while he was reduced to terrorizing new clients as they entered Hell. If these mortal women thought they could vanquish him with a handful of weeds, they were mistaken.

"Are you coming or not?" Dara asked.

"Of course." He threw back his shoulders and strode into the room, ignoring the pain that attacked like a swarm of stinging insects. He'd suffered far worse in Hell.

Enthroned on a blue corduroy recliner, surrounded by a circle of herbs, sat a tiny old woman. Beneath a silvery bun, her face was a wrinkled roadmap of her life. In her lap she cradled a worn Bible. Dara stood in front her chair, inside the circle of herbs. While she was thus protected, neither his scent nor his snares would affect her.

"Get behind me, girl," the old woman said.

Dara didn't move. "It's too dangerous."

"It's more dangerous if I can't see what I'm doing."

Reluctantly, Dara moved behind the chair. It was clear her every sense was on the alert for any threat to her grandmother. He wished he could reassure her that he meant the old woman no harm.

The tray table beside the chair held a glass salt shaker and a cut-glass perfume bottle with a squeeze bulb. He'd pilfered one of Lilith's Prozac capsules, so he would pass the salt test. He'd just have to stay out of range of the holy water.

"Come closer, demon," Esther said.

He didn't move. His mind raced. How much did they know, and how much was guessing?

"Who are you?" Dara asked. "And why are you here?"

"I'm a doctor." He assumed a look of exaggerated patience. "I came to examine your grandmother."

"You're a spawn of Satan is what you are, and you've come after my granddaughter."

He wasn't a spawn of Satan. The boss would never trust one of those tadpoles with a mission of this importance. He was a fallen angel, no less than Satan himself. He set his bag on the floor and pulled a stethoscope from it.

"How long has she been exhibiting signs of dementia?" he asked Dara.

"You mean demon-spotting? I'd say her whole life. Right, Nana?"

Esther nodded. "Saw my first one when I was five. No one believed me until I met your granddaddy, though. That's how I knew him for my soul mate."

Belial stepped inside the line of the herbs. Flaming arrows seemed to pierce his foot and leg, but with effort, he kept his face smooth. "I'll listen to your heart, if that's all right, Mrs. Perdue." He put the tips of the stethoscope in his ears, ignoring the fiery sensations shooting up his calf. This pain was nothing to what the boss would inflict if he let these women best him.

"Your granddaughter is concerned that you may have fluid building up around your heart." He listened for a moment, careful not to come in contact with the Bible, and nodded. "She sounds pretty congested." He offered the stethoscope to Dara.

As he'd hoped, Dara's face drew into worried lines. She came around the chair to listen. "I'll talk to her regular doctor about increasing her diuretic."

"The edema might account for the dementia we're seeing." He twitched aside the afghan to expose the old woman's swollen feet. "When the body retains this much fluid, it becomes difficult for the lungs to clear out the carbon dioxide. The oxygen-starved brain begins to manufacture hallucinations."

Dara looked bewildered. "You really do know something about medicine."

Logic, ever the demon's friend, was prevailing. "Of course I do. I'm a doctor."

Esther's face colored. She picked up the salt shaker and shook it over the tray table. His eyes swept over the loose grains. Forty-seven. There were forty-seven spilled grains.

"He's a counter, all right," Esther said. "No demon can resist counting."

Why hadn't Lilith's drug worked?

"None?" Dara asked.

"None that I ever saw."

Dara kissed the top of the old woman's head. "She may be old and ill, but she's not demented."

Recovering, Belial shook his head. "Perhaps I should check *you* for water retention, too."

Dara picked up a scrapbook from the bed and opened it to a middle page marked with a Post-it note. Staring up from the page was a woodblock print of an angel with shattered wings, tumbling from Heaven. The angel was Belial.

He staggered back and his heel came into contact with circle of herbs. Burning arrows jabbed his foot in a dozen places. He lost his balance and lurched toward Dara.

The old witch brandished the little perfume bottle. "Get away from her."

"I'm not touching her." But his foot skidded on the herbs and he grabbed Dara's elbow to steady himself. Esther aimed the bottle at his hand and squeezed the bulb. As soon as the spray touched his skin, his flesh blistered with a burn that went all the way to the bone. He leapt backward, howling.

"What is your mission?" No glimmer of the compassion Dara had shown the old man down the hall was evident on her face. "Why are you here?"

In that instant, she bore an uncanny resemblance to Joan of Arc. He had badly underestimated her.

He tried to back out of range, but she blocked his way. The old woman sprayed him again, this time in the face. It felt as though his flesh was melting from his skull.

"Gaaah," he shouted, trying to sound as pathetic as possible.

Esther cackled, baring a mouthful of dentures, but Dara frowned. "Are you sure that's just holy water?"

Esther spritzed some onto the back of her own hand. It beaded up harmlessly.

He groaned. "It may not hurt you, but it hurts me."

Dara caught her lower lip between her teeth, but Esther said, "He's a demon. He'll heal."

His skin was already regenerating, although it seemed a touch slower than he remembered in the past. Dara watched as though he were a specimen under a microscope. She reached her hand out but snatched it away before she made contact with his face. "That's fascinating."

"That's Satan." The old woman set the perfume bottle down on the tray. Dara circled back behind the chair again and put her hands on her grandmother's shoulders. Esther patted a scarred hand. "Why are you targeting my granddaughter?"

"I'm not," he said. What would the old woman have thought if she'd known that her beloved Lord had thrown her granddaughter under the chariot wheels? No doubt she would have managed one of those mental contortions that allowed humans to maintain their belief in a kind and loving God. "My focus isn't Dara—it's the clinic."

"That's it, then." Dara's shoulders sagged. "I'll have to close it."

If he couldn't convince her to keep the clinic open and allow him in, his mission was as good as done. It had taken him ten thousand years to claw his way up the ladder, and that had been from a neutral starting point. This time, he'd have to overcome Satan's bitterness over the loss of the wager.

"This is a research assignment," he said. "I have instructions not to take any action."

Dara rolled her eyes. "And I can believe that because you're a demon and demons never lie, right?"

"Don't be ridiculous. Demons lie all the time. But at least you know I'm a demon. You may not recognize my replacement." He was thinking faster than he'd ever thought in his entire existence. He needed a cover story, one she'd believe, but that wouldn't cause her to close down the clinic and go into hiding. DemSec would find her, of course, but the timeline of the wager didn't have that kind of play. His head pounded with visions of scrubbing the black lava floors of Ring Nine on his knees while other demons jeered.

"Replacement?" She was wary, but she was listening. Good.

"Of course. This mission isn't about me. The boss wants to use healthcare as a template for some other efforts he's contemplating. We've spent the last ten years training demons as doctors. They're now embedded in clinics and hospitals all over America, trying to get a handle on how they create so much misery when they're ostensibly trying to do good."

Beneath his expert touch, the lie took shape and grew like a clay pot on a wheel. "I'm under strict instructions to act like a normal human doctor. The boss believes that if he understands how the model works, he can employ it." For a story concocted on the fly, it wasn't half bad.

"You can lock me out of the clinic," he said. "You can even shut it down, but you won't stop this project. And in the meantime, with your clinic closed, the patients who depend on you will go without medical care." He laughed without mirth and then made the first true statement he'd spoken all day, "It doesn't matter what you choose. The boss wins either way."

The old woman lifted the leather-bound Bible from her lap. "Put your hand on this and swear you don't plan to harm my granddaughter or her clinic."

He eyed the book. There were tales of demons who burst into flame when lying while touching Bibles. "Was that your husband's?"

Esther nodded. "He studied this Bible from the time he learned to read until the day he died."

According to legend, the more time a human had spent reading and praying over a Bible, the stronger its power. He tried to sidestep the issue. "Humans perjure themselves under oath all the time. Do you think demons can do any less?"

She pushed it toward him. "Then you won't mind swearing on it."

He was aware of Dara's eyes, watching to see what he'd do. It was make-or-break time. Swallowing, he put his hand on the book. Sparks lit along his nerve endings like a warning. In his pocket, his cell phone heated like a griddle. "I swear I am not here to harm the Matthew A. Strong Memorial Clinic or Dara Strong." Was that smoke he smelled? Trying to look like he was in no hurry, he removed his hand.

"Don't listen to him." The old lady gripped Dara's hand. "His tongue can only speak deceit." But she sounded less sure of herself.

Dara eyed him across the old woman's silver topknot. "Could you give us a moment?"

"Of course." He picked up his leather bag and left the room. Once the door closed behind him, he raced to the men's room with demon speed. He plucked the phone from his pocket and tossed it into the sink, then stuck his head under the tap and turned the cold water on, full force. Steam billowed from his head. When the steam finally thinned, he turned off the tap. He rubbed a paper towel over his hair, put his warm-but-no-longer-scorching phone back in his pocket, and zoomed back to Esther's room.

A few moments later, Dara opened the door and motioned him back inside. He stepped across the threshold, ignoring the effect of the demonweed.

"What kind of time frame does this mission have?" Dara asked.

That was easy. There were only forty days left in the wager. "Six weeks."

Her shoulders relaxed, and he knew he'd won.

"I'll take you on as a volunteer." Her voice was harsh. She wasn't happy with her decision.

"Dara Perdue Strong, mark my words, you will live to rue this day." Behind her, the old woman's gaze was pure venom. Belial stayed by the door, out of range.

"That's probably true, but I need his grant. My only other choice is to close the clinic, and I'm not willing to do that. Too many people would suffer." Dara looked at him with the same dislike she'd shown the first day he came into the clinic. He might have succeeded at volunteering, but he'd made negative progress on his real mission, to convince Dara to curse the Enemy.

He eyed Esther. The old hag was furious. He might make progress with her granddaughter—he *had* to make progress with her granddaughter—but Esther would be his bitter enemy until the end. Her knowledge of demons was problematic. His arm still stung from the demonweed sachet, the skin on his face and arm burned like they had been drenched with acid, and his scalp felt like it might reignite at any moment.

"Thank you." He tried to sound humble and reassuring. "You won't regret it."

Esther snorted. "If you do anything to harm my granddaughter, I'll teach you a whole new meaning of the word *regret.*"

He inclined his head to show that he understood, but inside, he knew that wouldn't happen.

He already knew all there was to know about regret.

CHAPTER 19

Belial arrived at the clinic at three p.m. the next day. Through the reception window, he gave Gabby a dazzling smile. She smiled back as though she couldn't help herself, but there was a crease between her brows. She made no move to buzz him in.

"Dara said to let her know when you arrived." She picked up her phone and punched a button. "Dr. Lyle is here."

According to her DemSec dossier, Gabriella Munoz lost her nursing license after medicating a patient without doctor's order. The doctor in question, a candidate high on Hell's prospect list, had already cursed her out once that night, telling her to use her brain instead of interrupting his sleep. When the patient's pain escalated, she bumped up his dosage, assuming the doctor would back her up. Instead, he'd filed a complaint. Dara was the sole employer in Alexandria who would hire her. Despite Gabby's dazed smile, it was unlikely she could be swayed against the woman who had stood behind her.

Belial turned to check out the waiting room. Although an adult clinic was scheduled, the movie *Pinocchio* played on a small television. A couple of children sat cross-legged in front of the screen. Nearby, a curly-haired toddler pulled a battered toy from a basket on the floor. She tasted it and squealed. Her mother yanked the toy from her mouth. *"No te lo metas a la boca."* Don't put that in your mouth.

Then, to Belial's horror, the infant lurched over to him and clutched his pant leg. He flinched. Even through the barrier of fabric, the touch of one so innocent made his flesh burn. He looked down. At his knee, a round baby face stared up at him. He forced himself to smile at her, but as soon as her big eyes met his, she screwed up her face and wailed. She released his pant leg and sat down with a thump, shrieking as tears rolled down her face. Her mother scooped her up with a quick apology.

Behind him, Dara cleared her throat. "You don't like children?" Her tone said she'd expected as much.

"Of course," he said. Strictly speaking, it wasn't a lie. He had no opinion one way or the other about children. He'd never had any as mission targets, so he'd never spent any time with them.

He followed Dara past the high counters of the Pit. It was surrounded by the painted white walls of the clinic. He breathed in the stinging smell of rubbing alcohol and disinfectant. These people had no idea what a *real* pit was.

Inside her office, Dara closed the door and picked up a plastic spray bottle and a baggie of crushed vegetation from her desk. His skin prickled.

"Here are the rules for working in my clinic," she said. "First, you work with me as your nurse at all times. If I discover you alone with a patient, I will douse you with holy water, sprinkle on demonweed for good measure and close this place down.

"Second, you will use AMA-approved best practices for diagnosis and treatment. Another doctor will review every test and treatment you order. If you deviate from those practices by so much as a tonsil check, I will douse you with holy water, sprinkle you with demonweed and close this place down.

"Third, you are not to try to win anyone over to your master's way of thinking. If I see you attempting that, I will douse you with holy water and I will close this place down."

"You forgot the demonweed," he said. Her hand moved toward the spray bottle. He held up both hands in surrender. "Just joking."

"Not funny." She didn't smile. "Fourth, you may not bring any other demons into this building."

He held one palm toward her. "I am not here to harm your clinic." If you discounted the collateral damage that would occur when he succeeded in destroying her, it was a true statement. "I'm only here to observe."

"Fifth," she went on as though he hadn't spoken, "you may not be in contact with any other demons, including Satan, while you're working."

That actually sounded pretty good. Since he'd been on this mission, the boss had been driving him crazy. Like a needy girlfriend, he called or texted twenty times a day.

"I don't know that I can control his texting me," he said. "He is my boss, after all." And Satan.

"Figure it out." Dara stuck out her chin. "It's bad enough I have to deal with one demon. I am not taking on a whole army of them."

He nodded.

"Sixth," she said, "do not flirt with any of the workers."

He glanced at the sheen on her upper lip, proof that she wasn't immune to his charms. "Are you feeling possessive?"

"No, I'm trying not to feel *possessed*." Her tone was tart, but color rose in her cheeks. She hadn't forgotten their little rendezvous. "Seventh, do not form relationships with any of the workers or volunteers."

"Including you?"

"That won't be an issue." As though to make up for blushing a moment before, her tone was icy.

"I won't fraternize with the troops. I'm here on a mission, and the boss doesn't like it if it looks like we're having a good time."

"Finally," she said, "I had Javier create a special login for you. It will give you access to the records of the patients you're scheduled to see and will leave an audit trail of every screen you access in our system and every piece of information you add or change."

She was locking the door to a barn he had no plans to enter, but he nodded.

"If I see you taking any photographs, or making any recordings, I'll—"

He held up his hand. "I know the drill."

"Be sure that you do." She looked at him, unsmiling. "Follow my rules and you can stay for the next six weeks."

The wager expired in thirty-nine days. Six weeks would be more than enough time.

Lilith lifted a small plastic box from the console of the Miata and opened the car door. Swinging her legs out, she set her Jimmy Choos on the cracked asphalt of the Strong clinic parking lot and exited the car in one fluid motion. Across the lot, a young man in a white lab jacket with the UFL Medical School logo on the breast pocket smoked an electronic cigarette. He looked at her legs. She put a little extra swivel in her hips for his benefit as she crossed the lot.

At the front desk, she introduced herself. "Lilith Rojas. I'm on the board of trustees. Is Dara available?" To her delight, the receptionist said Dara was currently occupied.

"Is it all right if I look around?" She glanced at the woman's nametag and added, "Gabriella. What a pretty name."

Gabriella's smile wavered. The lobby was packed, and it was almost time for evening clinic hours to begin. She clearly wanted to say no but knew that wasn't an appropriate answer to a member of the board.

"How about if I have Javier, our volunteer coordinator..." Gabriella began a counterproposal as the medical student from the parking lot came into the lobby. She buzzed him through the locked door to the clinic area.

Lilith followed on his heels and headed for the closest examining room.

Once inside, she pulled the little plastic box from her pocket and dumped the contents on the paper sheet covering the examining table. Three dozen lice scattered in all directions. It was a minor action, but one she hoped Dara would associate with Belial's first night in the clinic. She slipped the box back into her pocket just before Javier came into the room and introduced himself.

"Gabby said you wanted to see the clinic?"

For the next fifteen minutes, she followed him on a screamingly dull tour. Why in the world Javier thought anyone would be interested in the huge windowless file room or the cramped little staff kitchen, she couldn't imagine. He insisted on showing her every office, explaining in detail what each boring occupant did. They returned to the clinic area as Dara and Belial exited Dara's office.

Both of them caught sight of her at the same moment. Their reactions were so comical it was almost enough to make up for the boredom she'd endured. Dara's cheeks flamed as though she'd been caught in *flagrante* with the handsome doctor. Belial looked pissed.

Dara recovered first. "Lilith. What are you doing here?"

Lilith gave Dara a saucy smile. "I came to offer moral support."

Dara's face grew even redder. Lilith eyed Belial the way she might eye a handsome doctor she'd never met. Dara introduced them.

"Oh, Dr. Lyle," Lilith cooed, offering him her hand. "I've heard so much about you."

"All good, I hope?" He gave her hand the briefest of shakes before dropping it.

She slid her gaze sideways to Dara and smiled. "Good doesn't even begin to cover it."

Dara's face looked like it might catch fire. When the receptionist called her to the front desk, she excused herself and escaped.

"What are you doing here?" Belial asked as soon as Dara was out of earshot.

"Being supportive," Lilith said. "She didn't want you here, and I want her to know that if anything goes wrong, I'm here for her. It's what friends do."

He glared at her. "Why are you really here?"

"The boss thought it would be good to have one demon around she hasn't recognized."

His fists clenched and his pupils squared off. Lilith trilled a laugh. He was so easy to provoke. At the reception desk, Dara turned to stare at them. Lilith waggled her fingers in a cheeky wave. Dara blushed again and turned her back.

"Why didn't the Prozac work for me?" His gaze should have scorched her to a cinder. It was all she could do not to hug herself.

"You mean the pill you stole from my purse?"

He rolled his eyes. "Whatever."

"That wasn't Prozac," she said. "That was for menstrual cramps." She sashayed away. Behind her, Belial cursed under his breath.

The clinic was growing more crowded. Nurses, student nurses and medical students stood in clumps around the large, rectangular counter, making it difficult to traverse the room. The waiting room was filled to capacity with patients. Then, like a conductor leading an orchestra, Dara directed patients and workers into various examination rooms. In a matter of minutes, every exam room was full and the lobby and the area Javier called the Pit had breathing space again. Belial remained in the open area.

"What made you stop by?" Dara asked Lilith when things had finally settled down.

"I knew tonight was Dr. Lyle's first volunteer shift. I thought you might want some backup."

Dara's mouth twisted. "Helping me keep him out of here in the first place would have been more useful."

Lilith patted Dara's arm. "Even if I'd backed you, we would have been overruled. You know that as well as I do. And, to be honest, I still can't see what your problem is with him." She waited for Dara to answer that, but she didn't respond. "He's kind of hot."

Dara's face turned pink again, but before she had to answer, one of the student nurses came running from exam room one.

"Ms. Strong," she said, "I think we have lice."

Dara hurried away. Lilith wandered back to where Belial stood. He was reading a medical article on a computer screen. Her lips pinched. To see him, you'd think he was a real doctor.

A moment later the triage team and the patient came out of room one, relocating to one of the back offices. Dara fastened yellow caution tape across the door of room one and directed the receptionist to call the cleaning service.

"What did you do?" Belial glared at Lilith. Her only reply was a taunting smile. When Dara returned, Lilith asked what happened.

"We have lice," she said.

"You don't seem very concerned."

Dara shrugged. "It's pretty common. Kids bring them home from school and pass them to the parents, who bring them in here. The cleaning service will take care of the exam room." She turned to Belial. "It does mean we're down a room for the evening, so it looks like you and I will be restricted to working in room five. As soon as the nurses finish triage, I'll have them put a patient in there."

A few minutes later, they disappeared into room five. Lilith frowned at the closed door. They were far too cozy. They were already beginning to form a team. Dara's lack of response to the lice was also disappointing, but Lilith wasn't worried.

She had a lot more tricks up her sleeve.

CHAPTER 20

The demon's first evening in the clinic went better than Dara expected. He'd said Hell had spent years training demons for this mission. Maybe that was true. She had paired with a lot of doctors in the dozen years she'd been a nurse. His skills and knowledge were on par with the best she'd ever seen.

More unnerving—although she guessed it shouldn't have been—was how gifted he was at dealing with patients. The only downside to the evening, as far as she could see, was being cooped up in the tiny exam room with him for three straight hours.

His nearness made it difficult to ignore his allure. Her body tingled with awareness of him. The smear of salve on her lip only partially cloaked his scent. Maybe she'd be better off not taking any antihistamines—when her head was clogged, she couldn't smell him at all. Unfortunately, she also couldn't breathe through her nose.

Inappropriate questions pestered her like gnats as they worked. Would his dark hair feel crisp beneath her fingers, or smooth? Was his well-muscled chest bare or covered in the same fine black hair as his arms? He bent forward, and the smattering of hair that showed at the neck of his polo shirt answered that question, but from there it was far too easy to follow the trail of hair southward.

Whenever it got too bad, she wrapped her fingers around the ruby cross. That made the images scatter, but he caught her at it and slowly smiled a knowing smile that made her want to smack him—or do something else with him. Well, if he thought she'd act on her fantasies, he was mistaken. Only a self-destructive idiot would fall for a demon.

When he checked out the computer in the exam room, he'd touched the black tape she'd used to cover the camera.

"Don't remove that," she told him sharply. "It's there to ensure patient privacy."

"I wouldn't dream of it," he'd said. "The computers in the exam rooms don't have speakers?"

"Or microphones," she said. "There's no need."

She had the sense he was pleased, but she didn't know why.

All in all, though, it was worth it. Viola Finch lit up like a Christmas tree as soon as he walked into the exam room. She insisted on giving him full details of her battle with nighttime heartburn. He listened with an attentiveness that surprised Dara, asking questions about Viola's diet, exercise and sleep habits. Her answers were more straightforward than Dara had ever heard her give before. When she finished, he turned to Dara.

"She needs to see a gastroenterologist." He dropped her chart onto the counter with a thud. They hadn't had time to enter Viola's extensive history into their system, so it was still on paper. "The doctors here have been treating her for nearly three years with no real progress."

Warmth rose into Dara's cheeks at the accusation beneath his words.

"Unfortunately, the clinic doesn't have a relationship with a digestive specialist." She fought to keep the defensiveness out of her tone. Over the years, she'd cultivated affiliations with the specialists in town. Many had agreed to see a limited number of clinic patients pro bono. Alexandria was a small town, though, and there were only a couple of gastroenterologists. She hadn't been able to enlist their support. "That's why we've been treating her here."

"Give me a name," he said. "I'll persuade them to see her."

That riled her. "Why would they do it for you when they refused me?"

"Call it professional courtesy."

Viola cackled. "You know any woman doctor will say yes."

That was probably true.

"I'd like to see one of those specialists, doc, if you can arrange it," Viola said.

He turned his smile on the old lady. "I'm sure we can."

Viola beamed back at him, her former cantankerousness completely gone.

He finished up his exam. Viola slid off the table. "You've finally got a good doctor in here. You hang on to him, you hear?"

At the end of the evening, Jeremy invited everyone to go out for drinks to celebrate the new recruit's successful first night.

Dara was surprised to see Lilith still there. Despite her career in healthcare, spending time watching a free clinic operate didn't seem like her kind of evening. Then Dara remembered Lilith was interested in Jeremy, who also didn't seem like her type. Dr. Demon, at least on the surface, seemed a better fit for her—they were both exceptionally good-looking, and in the same dramatic way. And they were both quick thinkers, able to respond to complex questions in an instant.

This was why Dara had originally thought Lilith might be a demon. Dara's eyes narrowed. She was suddenly wary again. She'd had a lot of fun with Lilith over the weekend, but that didn't mean anything. It was the nature of demons that they were fun to be around. Lilith had passed the salt test, though, which Ben Lyle had flunked—twice. And Nana said the test was foolproof. *Relax,* she ordered herself. *Not everyone is a demon out to get you.*

Lilith and Kelsey both said, "I'd love to."

And that was another thing. Kelsey seldom stayed past five unless a potential donor was coming in. Dara was pretty sure she knew why the grant-writer was still there, and it worried her. She could hardly discourage her from working late, though.

"You're coming, aren't you, Dara?" asked Lilith. "And you, Ben?"

When had he become Ben?

"I don't think Dr. Lyle can make it." Dara felt like the world's biggest wet blanket. "He mentioned that he had an early day tomorrow."

"Come on, Ben," Jeremy said. "Just one drink."

Dr. Lyle looked at her with the beseeching eyes of a teenage boy grounded from the party every other kid in his class was attending. She pretended not to notice.

"I should probably go home and turn in." His shoulders drooped so low she had to stifle a snort.

"You're not coming?" If he was disappointed, Kelsey was devastated.

Dara was glad she'd stood firm. He was a demon, a minion from Hell, here to cause mischief. The last thing she wanted was for Kelsey to spend time in his dangerous company, even if other people were around.

"Not this time." He straightened his shoulders and his tone was impersonal. The rebuff was gentle, but it was clear he wasn't interested in her.

He'd paid absolutely no attention to Lilith or to Kelsey all evening, and they were both younger and more attractive than Dara. When he wasn't focused on his patients, all of his attention had been on her. A tiny part of her, ruled by ego, found satisfaction in that. But the bigger part, the part that answered to her logical brain, said there was a reason.

Nana thought she was his target. If so, he would be very disappointed. She had no intention of succumbing to his wiles.

The lights in the lobby went dark and the pharmacy's overhead door rattled closed. A few moments later, Gabby, Javier and Chris, the clinic's pharmacist, joined the group. As soon as they learned a group outing was planned, they were all in.

"Really, Dr. Lyle," Lilith said, "you should join us. All work and no play make Ben a dull boy."

It felt like there was a barb in her words, though Dara couldn't imagine why. He must have heard it, too, because his jaw tightened.

Lilith turned to her. "Tell Ben that he should reconsider. After all, this shindig was organized in his honor."

Dara was about to shrug that off when his earlier words, about Satan not liking it when he got too chummy on a mission, came back to her. Maybe she could get rid of him that way. She looked around the group, weighing the pros and cons. She didn't like the idea of exposing Kelsey to his influence, but he'd displayed absolutely no interest in her. Lilith seemed intent on bringing him along, although Dara got the sense her new friend didn't like him all that much. She finally decided it was better if she knew what the demon was doing than if she didn't.

"She's right, Dr. Lyle. You should join us."

He eyed the pocket where she kept her pouch of demonweed. "Are you sure?"

She spread her hands to show him she was holding no weapons. "Completely."

Belial looked out at the sand court next to Slyders' patio, where a life-and-death game of volleyball was being played out. As soon as they ordered the first round, Lilith had shucked off her stilettos, declaring herself a captain. Chris captained the other team. Lilith selected Jeremy and Kelsey for her side, while Chris drew Javier and Gabby. Lilith and Chris pursued the game like lives were at stake, though the other players lacked their killer instincts.

"You don't play?" he asked Dara.

"Not really an athlete." Dara sipped from her glass of wine. "What about you?"

As he reached for his beer, he brushed his hand against hers. She gasped, a sound she quickly smothered, and a bolt of pleasure seared its way straight to his groin. He wanted to stroke the back of her hand, to feel the smoothness of her scars beneath his fingertips.

"I was instructed to stay away from your staff," he said.

"You can take instruction. Who knew?" Her tone was even more acerbic than normal.

He grinned and let silence fall between them. Dara was a smart woman, a strong woman, but she was no match for ten thousand years of training in deceit. Once she capitulated to him sexually, she would be as enslaved to him as he was to Satan. It had been that way with every woman he'd ever seduced. Once that happened, it would take little to convince her to curse her maker.

He took a sip of beer and stared out at the ocean. The tide was low, and the waves were almost sluggish beneath the silvery moon. Beyond the shoreline, stars winked against the blackness. He could make out the Big Dipper, Orion and Cassiopeia. They'd changed little in the past ten thousand years. They would change equally little over the next ten thousand.

This bet, on the other hand, had the capacity to change his life. Once he had the CED job, he would be above every demon except Satan himself. When Satan was away, scouting for new populations to corrupt, Belial would become the de facto boss. And all he had to do to make it happen was seduce the woman sitting beside him in the darkness into damning the Enemy.

He gave himself pretty good odds of success. Over the salt-and-seaweed smell of the ocean, he could detect a hint of camphor. She could smear on smelly salves, douse him with holy water and pepper him with demonweed, but she would still fall. He could already read it in the way her pulse accelerated when he came near. He admired her spirit, but she was fighting insurmountable odds.

The holy water and the herbs gave her a false sense of security. Their effects were uncomfortable, but they were pinpricks compared to the torments awaiting him if he failed. Beside him, her eyes were on the others. Laughter and taunts streamed from the beach, along with the intermittent thud of a fist striking the ball. The quality of the play had gone downhill as the night grew darker and the blood alcohol levels rose, but it didn't seem to inhibit their enjoyment.

"Lilith is certainly an aggressive player." Dara sounded surprised. She didn't know the half of it.

Sometime soon, he would need to figure out what Lilith was up to. Why had she come to the clinic tonight? She was pretending to be enamored of Jeremy. She had chosen him first for her tiny team, despite the clear indicators that he was no more an athlete than Dara. Jeremy was now playing the best volleyball game of his life, thanks, no doubt, to snares Lilith threw to spur him on. Out on the sand, he launched his rotund body at the ball like a pudgy javelin. If she didn't let up soon, he'd have a massive heart attack and they'd forfeit the wager.

"I have a couple of possible gastroenterologists for Viola." Dara's words pulled his thoughts away from the children playing in the sand. "I assume you'd prefer to approach a female?"

It annoyed him that she thought his skills were limited to his sexual magnetism.

"If you have a male doctor on your list, let's go with him," he said.

"You think you can get anyone to do anything you like."

"Not at all. I present options and make those options look attractive. Ultimately, people have free will to make their own choices."

"So he could say no."

"He could," Belial said. *But he won't.* Less than one out of a thousand people refused demonically provided opportunities. It was the nature of snares that the prospect being presented looked beguiling, while any downside disappeared from people's minds.

"I only allowed you into the clinic because the only other choice was to close down."

In the darkness, he smiled at the defensive note in her voice. "You have an unusual ability to resist enticement." There was even some truth to that.

"And that's why you had to spend so much money on the grant."

"Very perceptive."

She rolled her eyes. "Save your enticements for people who buy them."

He chuckled and they both fell silent again, watching the volleyball game.

"They must seem like children to you," she said after a moment.

"You all seem like children to me." The truth slipped from his lips without conscious intention. He thought she might take umbrage at that, but she nodded.

"What has changed the most about people over time?" she asked.

He was surprised to hear her echo his earlier thought. "There is nothing new under the sun."

"What about under the earth?"

He wasn't sure what she meant.

"What is your life like, in Hell?" she asked.

He stared across the flickering flame of the citronella candle at her face. In ten thousand years, no one had ever asked him such a question. The handful of individuals who had discovered his identity had either avoided his company or done their best to pretend it wasn't true.

"You seem to like being a doctor. Is that what you do down there?"

He did like being a doctor. Even treating that cranky old bat Viola was satisfying.

"We don't need doctors," he said. "Demons are immortal. The only pain we ever suffer is when we're punished for some failure, and Satan wouldn't permit anyone to intervene, even if they wanted to, which they wouldn't."

"What about the—what do you call them?—inmates?"

"Clients," he said. "Everyone has their own terminology, but I call them clients."

"I imagine that feels better than inmates." Her tone was wry. "What about the clients?"

He stared at her, perplexed. "What about them?"

"How do you interact with them? Do you poke them with your pitchfork?"

"Don't be absurd." He wanted to tell her that such acts were much more in character for her new best friend, but outing another demon was forbidden. Not to mention counterproductive. If she thought there was an entire team targeting her, he'd never get any closer.

"Then what do you do? Do you even have a pitchfork?"

"Of course not." He did, in a closet somewhere, left over from when the boss had first set up Hell, and they were trying to figure out what worked. Tridents definitely had not worked. Even the earliest clients of Hell, Neanderthals with their jutting brows and terrible breath, hadn't taken them seriously. "I try to minimize my interactions with them."

The whole conversation had taken a bizarre turn. He was all too aware of the legions back in Hell, listening and laughing their tails off. It must amuse them no end to hear Hell's soon-to-be second-in-command interrogated about his demonic duties by this woman who should have succumbed to his charms nine days ago.

"Why is that?" she asked.

"Why is what?"

"Why do you avoid interacting with the clients?"

"My role is more managerial."

"You're a supervisor?"

He wasn't sure what irked him more—her surprise, or the fact that she chose the lowest-level managerial job.

"Yes, I'm a *manager*. Why wouldn't I be?"

"Exactly what is your role?"

He hesitated, but the need to impress her was too strong to resist. "I'm the equivalent of the chief executive officer in a human corporation." It was a tiny lie. Once he was successful here, he would be.

"You're the CEO?"

"Something like that."

"Then what are you doing here? Isn't field work pretty far beneath you?"

Dammit. He had allowed himself to grow too comfortable talking to her.

"The boss thinks it's important to stay hands-on," he said.

"You said you don't interact with the clients." She turned to look him in the face.

Just his luck to get a target that actually listened.

"The in-house stuff is one facet of what we do. Activities that occur Aboveworld are a lot more interesting."

She pounced on that. "'Aboveworld'? Is that what you all call

Earth? Or is that one of your terms again?"

How had he let the conversation get so far out of control? "No, we all call it that."

"We all call what what?" Lilith flung herself into a chair, panting. The others trailed her to the patio.

"Nothing," Belial and Dara said simultaneously.

Lilith looked from one to the other and smiled. "Sounds like something."

"Who won?" Dara said, trying to distract her.

Good luck with that. Once Lilith had something between her teeth, Satan himself couldn't shake it loose.

"We did." Lilith grabbed a mug from the table and held it aloft. "To us."

Kelsey and Jeremy, who had followed her up from the beach, picked up mugs and clinked them against Lilith's glass.

"To us." Jeremy sounded exhausted.

"We'll take you next time," Chris said. Sweat plastered his spiky hair to his head.

"Not a chance," Lilith said. They made plans for a rematch.

Belial was content to let them talk. He'd had enough conversation for one evening. Dara's questions, her curiosity about his life, had been surprisingly enjoyable. She was a good listener, with a genuine interest in other people's circumstances. Even his. How very odd.

He thought about her at the beginning of tonight's clinic, organizing patients, nurses and doctors like an impresario conducting a finely tuned orchestra. Her little clinic thrived because she shared the music of her compassion with each person who walked through her door. When she was gone, it would close.

The thought left him strangely disturbed, so he turned his focus to his own concern: the wager. That was a better topic to ruminate on. Success was within his reach. Despite her best intentions, she was succumbing to his allure. Her interest in his life proved it.

It was the best of all possible outcomes. Not only would he win his coveted promotion, but her lush body, which had haunted more than a few of his dreams, would be his. It wouldn't be much longer now.

CHAPTER 21

When Dara arrived at Mercy Care the next morning, she leaned over to kiss Nana on the cheek. Nana wrinkled her nose.

"Is that demon I smell?"

Dara didn't see how. She'd showered and put on fresh scrubs that morning.

"He worked in the clinic last night," she said. "We all went out afterwards."

"To a tavern?" Nana's expression said Dara was headed straight for Hell.

"To Slyders." Before Nana became so frail, they used to go there for the buckets of peel-and-eat shrimp. "We had some snacks and played volleyball." Dara left out her glass of wine.

"Hmmph." Nana looked her over and evidently decided she wouldn't burst into flames anytime soon.

"I found out some things about him. He says he's some kind of bigwig down there, second-in-command."

"They all say that," Nana said.

Dara nodded, though she thought he was more than a foot soldier.

He carried himself like someone who was used to being in charge. "He told me Satan doesn't like it when he gets too friendly with mortals."

"Anything he tells you is as like to be a lie as the truth. He's here to spin a web. And that web is meant to trap you. Why are you so fascinated by him, when you know he's a danger to you and everything you stand for?"

"Beneath all the arrogance and the false charm, he feels broken," Dara said.

"He is broken," said Nana. "He's as broken as he can be. But you can't heal him the way you healed Matt. He's broken through his own choice. He had everything—the Lord's love, a celestial home, holy work—and he threw it all aside."

The drugs Matt took to get through his grueling residency had nearly cost him everything, too, but prayer had gotten him through that. The exact kind of prayer Dara couldn't seem to pray anymore.

"Why?" she asked. "Why would he do that?" He seemed too smart for that.

"Ambition, arrogance, anger—take your pick."

The next time Dara got a chance to talk with him, she would ask.

"Dara Perdue Strong," Nana said, "I see that look on your face. You listen to me. Ben Lyle is a demon. You can't heal him. Do you understand that?"

"Of course," Dara said. "But to fight my enemy, I need to know my enemy."

"Your granddaddy said the same." Nana plucked at the afghan covering her legs. "He'd get one in the church and he'd stay up all night long debating with him. He called it 'getting an alternative view of the scripture.' I told him there's plenty of folks from right here on this Earth will give you the other side of the scripture if you let them, but he said demons' ways of looking at things was interesting."

Dara frowned. That didn't sound like the upright grandfather she remembered.

"That was back at the big church," Nana said. "Do you remember the church in Atlanta?"

Dara shook her head. She had no memory of ever living anywhere but Alexandria.

"I didn't think you would," Nana said. "You were just a little thing when we left."

"Was that before or after my parents died?"

"Right about the same time. You stayed with us while they went on that mission trip."

While they were in Africa, the little four-seater plane her parents used to get around in the bush went down. Dara was only four. She could barely remember them.

"Our congregation had nigh onto three thousand people," Nana continued. "That was when those *60 Minutes* people came to interview your granddaddy." She tapped an arthritic finger against her chin and seemed to come to a decision. She nodded toward the bureau. "Get in the bottom drawer and get out my green scrapbook."

Dara didn't recall a green scrapbook, but she opened the bottom drawer that held Nana's sweaters. Beneath a stack of cardigans, she found a moss-colored photo album. It was a little smaller than the other scrapbook. She carried it back to the bed. Nana opened the cheap cover to reveal yellowed newspaper clippings. One included a photograph of a young Granddad, still with all his hair, standing behind a wooden pulpit, his arms lifted in supplication.

"There was a time when your granddaddy traveled all over these United States, casting out demons and teaching others how to do the same. I wasn't supposed to keep the pictures." Nana's cheeks turned pink, but her jaw took on a mulish set. "But I wasn't the one that was given the lesson—he was. I never let on to Lonnie that I still had them."

She turned the pages so fast it didn't give Dara time to do more than skim the headlines. The early articles were about Granddad's triumphs—all the places he'd been invited to speak, all the demons he'd cast out. There was one particularly startling snapshot of a young girl, seated at the end of a pew, vomiting into the aisle.

"He did a lot of good, your granddad." Nana tapped the picture.

"But after that movie come out, that news program come to interview him. It went to his head."

Nana turned the thick pages to reveal bigger articles, with larger headlines and even more dramatic pictures of Granddad. Perhaps because of Nana's reference to his escalating pride, Dara could see a change in him. The poses became less natural, more staged. In one, he pointed at a man writhing on the ground. He held a Bible over his head. Behind him, a backlit cross seemed to beam energy to the leather-bound Bible and channel it through Granddad to the man on the floor. The man looked like he might be suffering an epileptic seizure.

"What happened?"

Nana turned the page over. This clipping showed Granddad preaching inside a coliseum. Thousands of people listened, rapt, as he spoke. On the facing page was a picture of him talking to Mike Wallace. "That's how he come to be on *60 Minutes*."

Dara had always wondered how the pastor of a little backwoods church had drawn so much attention. Now she understood.

"He stopped focusing on the Word," Nana said, "and got focused on hisself as a vehicle of the Word. The more demons he drove from the face of the Earth, the cockier he got. That's when he started debating the scripture with demons. And they egged him on, telling him how smart he was, until he started taunting Satan." Nana flipped over another page. The headline proclaimed, "SATAN, I AM YOUR WORST NIGHTMARE."

Dara stared at it, shocked. The blustering man in the photo was unrecognizable as her gentle grandfather.

"What did you mean when you said he was given a lesson?"

Nana tapped the picture. "By this time, he was out on the road on his own a lot, staying in fancy hotels with saloons in their lobbies. He was traveling to a different town every night, and he had trouble sleeping. He took to stopping off for a nightcap before he went to bed. Then it became two, and then three."

Maybe this was why they never had alcohol in their house.

"And then liquor wasn't enough, and someone in a bar offered him some pills. The next night, he ordered a demon out of a man, and the demon laughed and told him, 'You have no authority over me.' Your granddad tried to beat the demon out with his Bible. Three men had to pull him off. They took the man with the demon to the hospital and your granddad to jail."

Dara stared at her, sick with horror.

"The police found the pills on him. He was convicted of possession of a narcotic and assault. He did sixty days, but it wasn't the jail time that hurt him—it was knowing that demon was right, that he'd lost the authority to cast out Satan. That humbled him. He come back to his home church and vowed never to leave again."

She put her hand over Dara's. Her flesh was so thin you could see the network of tendons and veins beneath.

"So don't you let that demon talk you into believing you can stand against him," she said, "because you can't."

CHAPTER 22

Ben was already at the clinic when Dara got there at ten the next morning. She stifled a groan. She wasn't ready to deal with a demon before she'd even had a cup of coffee.

"What are you doing here so early?" she asked.

"No rest for the wicked."

Nor for someone who was trying very hard not to be wicked. She headed for the kitchen. The coffeemaker was dark and cold, with only the dregs of yesterday's last pot in the carafe. Was she the only person in this clinic who knew how to operate a coffeemaker?

He followed her, standing far too close for comfort. She'd taken her antihistamine that morning, but hadn't remembered to put salve on her lip. His scent slammed into her like a pile driver, literally making her mouth water. It was going to be that kind of day. Great. She looked at the clock. Ten a.m. Only ten hours to go.

"Here, let me make that." With one hip, he butted her out of the way. "Go put your purse away or whatever you have to do."

The warmth of his flesh penetrated through the thin fabric of her scrubs all the way to her bones. Low in her belly, it was like wax had melted, leaving a puddle of heat. If he was going to be in the clinic for the next several weeks, she would have to start bringing a change of underwear. Maybe more than one.

The worst part was that he knew what she was feeling. The vibrating tension of his flesh told her so. He was like a panther, waiting for his prey to make a move or give off some kind of signal, however slight, so he could pounce.

If he kissed her again, she'd be lost. Deep inside, she knew this to be true. Which meant all she had to do was never betray, with the smallest sign, how much she craved his touch.

She stepped back and let him take over the coffee pot, but she didn't leave the kitchen. "Why are you here? You're only scheduled to work the evening clinics."

"I thought you could probably use help with the daytime clinics, too."

That was impossible to argue with. "We don't start seeing patients till eleven."

"Dr. Edwards has agreed to see Viola. I wanted to get the referral filled out before patients arrive."

"How did you manage that?" Exasperation flared, and Dara fanned that tiny flame. Better to feel exasperation than lust. She had approached Dr. Edwards when she first opened the clinic. She had begged him to see one or two patients. She'd gotten nowhere.

"I visited him this morning," he said.

"I didn't even give you his name."

"Of the two gastroenterologists in Alexandria, one is named Emily," he said. "It was reasonably simple to figure out the identity of the other one."

"And he agreed to see Viola just like that?"

"He agreed to accept five referrals a month."

Dara gawked at him. "Five? None of the other specialists will take that many." She narrowed her eyes. "Is he another demon?"

"No, of course not."

"There's no 'of course' about it. How did you convince him?"

He shrugged. "It's what I do." His eyebrows lifted. "Do you want me to visit others?"

It was tempting. There were so many patients who needed to see specialists. Dara shook herself. Of course it was tempting. It was what he did.

"No, thanks." She headed out the door, but his voice stopped her.

"By the way, I arranged to cater in lunch today from Oakley's." He'd named the most expensive place in Alexandria. "The staff works hard. They deserve a treat."

She stared at him. "Is this going to be a regular thing?"

He smiled blandly. "As regular as I can afford."

"So, every day."

"Something like that."

She went to her office, where she smeared a thick layer of salve on her upper lip before putting away her purse. She had to keep him at arm's length. It was the only way she'd survive without giving in to the cravings he aroused.

She pulled a red marker from her center desk drawer and looked at her wall calendar. He wouldn't be here on weekends, of course, and she'd convinced Javier not to schedule him for the tiny pediatric clinic on Mondays. She scrawled an X across the previous day.

Only thirty-eight to go.

"Did Viola Finch come in tonight?" Belial asked Gabby. Dara stood two feet away—close enough to observe him, but not close enough to be drawn in.

He'd been in the clinic for two weeks now, but beyond that, he'd made very little progress. Dara was professional to the point of being chilly, and he never saw her without the gleam of salve on her upper lip. She was also very skittish. If he brushed her arm as they worked, she jerked away like she'd been burned.

And he badly wanted to make some progress. The wager's end date loomed, now just three and a half weeks away, Satan was breathing down his neck, fretting about the amount of time that had passed without a completed seduction, and Lilith had begun making snide little comments about demons that were past their prime.

Even more disturbing was the way Dara's lush body filled his dreams. Fantasies of touching her scarred clavicles as he buried himself inside her haunted his nights.

Days weren't much better. He'd taken to sporting an erection at the most inopportune times. He blamed the human DNA Bad had inserted into his genome—after ten thousand years, his demon body had long since stopped reacting except on command. Now he was like a lusty schoolboy.

The receptionist pointed to Viola through the big sliding-glass window to a corner of the lobby. Belial spotted the Day-Glo orange beret. "Give me five minutes to talk to Mrs. Strong about her case and then call her in, please."

"Okay," said Gabby. "Oh, and Dara—Lilith dropped by."

Dara's eyes swept the clinic. "She didn't stay?"

Gabby shook her head. "She brought coffee. She said she noticed we were almost out the last time she was here, so she donated some."

There was as much chance Lilith had come by to donate coffee as there was that he was there to heal the sick. When Belial got home tonight, they would have a little black-heart-to-black-heart talk. He'd discover what she was up to.

In the exam room, he pulled up Viola's record on the computer. Gabby had entered her long history into the system before sending his referral on to Dr. Edwards. The results of her visit to the specialist were there.

"What did he say?" Dara sounded worried.

"Why do you care?" he asked. "She's hardly your favorite patient."

"No." Dara was honest, as usual. "But she is a patient. She's also a lonely old lady, and a human being."

He'd seen Dara tell lies of commission to avoid hurting people's feelings and lies of omission to evade confrontations, but she didn't lie simply to make life easier for herself. That meant she lied far less often than most of the humans he'd observed over the centuries. Other than her demon resistance, it was the sole trait she'd displayed so far that offered any hint why the Enemy had chosen her as his champion.

"And that's all it takes for you to care what becomes of her?" He didn't bother to hide his skepticism.

Dara's shrug said she didn't care what he thought. "Pretty much."

He examined the record. "The specialist put her on a new drug. He thinks there's a good chance it will completely relieve her symptoms."

Dara let out a long breath. She hadn't been exaggerating. She did care what became of the old woman, whether she liked her or not. He frowned. Was this the Enemy's reason for selecting her? It seemed unlikely.

Someone tapped on the door, and a student nurse ushered Viola into the room. Viola thumped her way to the exam table. Using her cane for leverage, she climbed up onto the table.

"How are you feeling tonight?" Belial asked.

"Fit as a fiddle," she answered. "Last night was the best night's sleep I've had in years."

"No problems with your new medication?"

"I miss my grapefruit juice."

He smiled. She was following directions.

"Are you seeing any other side effects?" Dara asked.

And there lay the crux of the problem. The drug in question had been all but removed from the American market because of the impact it had on heart rhythms. They should do an echocardiogram on Viola every time she came in, but if he told Dara that, she might decide the digestive specialist was demon-influenced. He wasn't, as far as Belial knew, but he didn't know the details of every mission currently underway. What he did know was that the boss was intent on staying within the terms of the wager. That meant nothing their side did would put the old woman at risk. He tossed a snare in Viola's direction, just a small redirection of her thoughts.

"Not a thing," she said.

They had just finished with their last patient and Belial was entering his notes into the computer while Dara pulled clean paper over the exam table. He kept his back to her, hiding the erection that had manifested itself as soon as the patient left the room. Just a glimpse of Dara's scarred collarbones, or a brush of her hand, was enough to bring him to painful rigidity.

He thanked the stars for the black tape that covered the computer's camera. If the crew below realized his near-constant state of arousal whenever he was near Dara, he would never hear the end of it.

"What did you prescribe for him?" she asked.

In the two weeks he'd been there, she had never stopped double-checking, even second-guessing, his work. "A beta blocker."

"Are you sure he wouldn't have been better off with an ACE inhibitor?"

"Who's the doctor here?" he asked.

"Who's the demon here?" she responded.

"If you don't trust my judgment, have Jeremy double-check my work," he said over his shoulder.

"Oh, believe me, I will," she said. "But you've been seeing so many patients he's falling behind."

"Am I supposed to apologize for being competent at my job?"

"That depends. Which job are we talking about?"

Before he could respond to that, screams sounded from the back hallway. Dara turned pale. She dropped the wad of discarded paper and ran out the door. Belial followed close on her heels.

They reached the kitchen as a pair of student nurses erupted through the doorway, squealing like piglets. The last one out slammed the door shut behind her.

"What's wrong?" Dara grabbed the closest one by the shoulders.

"Bugs." The girl was almost hysterical. "Giant bugs."

He expected Dara to smile in relief, but she flinched. "What kind of bugs?"

"Huge ones," said one girl.

"Noisy ones," said another.

"With wings," said the third.

Dara shuddered.

Belial stifled a laugh. The chaos had allowed his erection to wane. "Don't tell me you're afraid of bugs."

She shivered again. "Ugh."

"Just two weeks ago you dealt with lice without batting an eye."

"I've gotten used to them. I've had to, working here. But I draw the line at big, noisy, *winged* bugs."

He laughed. This woman who faced down demons without faltering was afraid of bugs.

Now that the girls had stopped shrieking, he recognized the racket coming from the kitchen: locusts. It had been like pushing a boulder up the side of a pyramid to keep Neferhotep from caving in to Moses's demands when the little beasts had darkened the skies above Thebes. But why would locusts invade the Strong clinic?

As soon as the question formed, he knew the answer: Lilith. That was why she had dropped by tonight. She was making mischief, trying to sow discord so that Dara wouldn't trust him. When he got home that night, he would do everyone a favor and strangle Lilith.

"Would you like me to take care of them?" he asked.

"Could you?" Dara's voice was tremulous. For the first time since he'd come to work in the clinic, her defenses were down. It would have been the perfect time to draw her closer if it weren't for the bevy of students underfoot.

"How in the world did you survive growing up in Florida?" he asked.

She shuddered.

Laughing, he opened the kitchen door a crack and slipped through the opening. From the other side of the window, Dara watched, the students peeking over her shoulders. How best to capture the creatures? He could chase them around as a human would, looking clumsy and foolish in the process. He could summon them to him, but Dara might recognize the demonic method and eject him from the clinic, and her life.

Then he spied a stack of Styrofoam cups beside the coffeemaker. He picked up the entire stack and then threw a tiny snare, bidding the insects to remain where they were. He scooped the nearest bug into the top cup and sealed it in by taking the bottom cup and fitting it inside the top one. He repeated the process eleven more times. Lilith certainly hadn't stinted on her effort.

The insects reacted to their captivity by ratcheting up their whirring calls until the noise was deafening. Once he had them all confined, he carried the stack of cups outdoors. Dara followed him. He set the cups on the ground and lifted his foot to crush them, but Dara put her hand on his elbow.

"Don't kill them."

Her scarred hand on his arm made his flesh tingle. He thought about snaring her to his will. He could sow the idea that she wanted to be in his arms, and in her current state of mind, there she would be. Finally, he would get to experience the pleasures of her body. With regret, he let go of the idea. There was too much at stake to lose the wager over a minor infraction.

"I thought you wanted them gone," he said.

"I did. I do." She released his arm. Without her warm hand, his arm felt cold. "But trespassing isn't a capital offense."

He knelt on the pavement and unstacked the cups, one by one. The cicadas flew away.

She cleared her throat. "Thank you." Then, as though she might as well get it over with, she added, "I talked to the doctors that have seen Viola in the past. They agreed with your approach. They said, with all the other things we've tried, and with the state of Viola's esophagus, there was nothing else left to do."

Belial got to his feet. "I'm not here to harm your clinic."

"Then why are you here?" Her voice was tense. "Thirty miles south of us, in Jacksonville, there's a world-class hospital where you'd get a much better cross-section of American medicine."

"Another demon was assigned there."

"You told me you're second-in-command," she said. "Why would you send someone else there and come to a little country clinic? That doesn't make any sense."

Once again, the comfort that he felt in her presence caused him to share too much.

"I didn't make the assignments," he said.

"The question still stands."

He looked down at his loafers. "I may have made a misstep on my last mission."

"And you're here as a punishment?" She sounded like she was torn between disbelief and insult.

"A demon with half my rank landed the Mayo, while I"—he gestured toward the cement-block building with its faded paint—"got sent here." He pulled a handkerchief from his pocket and wiped a rivulet of sweat from his temple.

"You don't much like Florida, do you?"

"It's like a more humid version of Hell," he said.

"With bugs."

He thought about the giant wasps in the vestibule of Hell. She knew nothing of insects.

"With bugs," he agreed. "How did you come to be so afraid of them?"

She tilted her head. "I think I've always just been..." Her eyes widened. "No, wait," she said. "I wasn't always. I remember Nana saying when I was small—three or four—I'd drive her crazy, bringing them in the house all the time. One time, I threw a fit. She asked what was wrong, and I said someone took the spider I had put under my pillow the night before. She turned my room inside out, worried it was a black widow."

"What happened?" he asked. "What made you go from 'future entomologist' to 'woman who screams and runs from the room'?"

"I'm trying to remember." Her brows knitted together with the effort.

She was so beautiful when she was like this, defenses down, talking to him without her usual wariness.

"I got stung," she said suddenly. "I was playing in the yard barefoot and I stepped on a bee. I ran into the house, crying. I remember feeling totally betrayed. I told Nana, 'We were supposed to be friends.'"

"So you did a one-eighty from friends to bitter enemies," he said.

Dara shrugged. "They started it."

Belial walked through the door of the beach house to find Lilith seated on the black leather sofa in front of the big-screen TV that hung over the huge marble fireplace. She was painting her toenails crimson. As he closed the door, she arched her foot and pointed her freshly lacquered toes toward him.

"What do you think of this color? Is it me?"

"Is it called Troublemaker?"

She widened her eyes. "Troublemaker? *Moi?* Why would you say that?"

"Because of the locusts you released in the clinic tonight."

She set her foot on the floor and splayed her toes. She picked up a magazine from the glass-topped end table and fanned them.

"Don't be ridiculous," she said. "Why would I do something like that?"

"To screw up my mission and make me fail."

"Belial," she said, "I know you have trouble understanding this, but this mission is bigger than you. It involves all of us. If you fail, all of Hell fails."

"Not if someone else succeeds in my stead."

"How would that be possible? What other demon can compete with your skills, your beauty, your incisive understanding of the human condition?" She stared at her toes admiringly.

Someday, he thought, he would ring the calculating harpy's neck. "I know you released those cicadas into the clinic. I've seen you pull the same trick a dozen times in the past. It's your signature. Every time the target is female, you plague her with insects." Realization struck. "The lice last week—you planted those, too, didn't you?"

Lilith set the bottle of acetate down on the table and picked up the nail polish.

"I don't know what you're whining about." She nodded toward the TV. "I was watching the feed from the camera in the parking lot. She said 'thank you.' Twice. That's the nicest she's been since you met her. You should let me help you strategize. Working as a team, we could really move this thing along."

"I don't need your help." Letting Lilith get closer to the mission would only grant her more opportunities to sabotage him. But it was more than that. When Dara came to him, as she inevitably would, he wanted it to be because of his own actions, not the manipulations of her so-called friend.

"As the ranking demon on this mission, I command you not to release any more insects into the clinic. Do you understand?"

Lilith bent over once more, her hair falling forward to cover her face.

"Fine," she said. "No more bugs."

CHAPTER 23

Dara massaged lemon verbena lotion into Nana's feet. It was the only way she ever got a chance to look at her grandmother's ankles. The old woman's skin was so taut with fluid it had no wrinkles.

"You're retaining water again," Dara said. She circled Nana's ankle with her thumb and forefinger to demonstrate that they wouldn't touch. "I'll give Dr. Stevens a call."

"Get that demon back in here to look at me."

"No way." She slid Nana's slipper back onto her swollen foot. "I don't want him around you."

"I don't want him around you, either," Nana said, "but he's there every day."

Dara pulled a wipe from her purse and wiped her hands. "Not every day."

Close enough, though. He'd been working in the clinic just over two weeks and, since she wasn't willing to leave him unsupervised, she'd worked side by side with him every day but Monday, when they held the pediatric clinic.

"He's going to lead you to your destruction," Nana said.

They had this argument every time Dara came to visit.

"No, he won't." Dara refused to be that stupid. "To be honest, he's done a lot of good."

Nana snorted.

"No, he really has. He diagnosed several things other doctors missed. I can think of at least three patients he convinced to quit smoking and lose weight, and they're actually doing it."

He'd also been no further away than her elbow on any given day, smiling down like she was the only woman in the world. She went home every night with sore muscles from clenching her jaw and her thighs, trying to resist his allure.

"He's lying low, trying to lull your suspicions."

Dara thought so too, but she didn't want Nana to worry any more than she already was.

"Last week he even chased some bugs out of the clinic." Dara shuddered. "You know how I feel about bugs."

"They're God's creatures, same as you and me."

"Maybe. Or maybe cicadas come from the other place." She spread the afghan back across Nana's legs. "Maybe that's why he was so good at getting rid of them."

Nana grabbed her wrist. "What kind of bugs did you say they were?"

"Cicadas." She patted Nana's hand.

"Locusts." The old woman nodded like she'd suspected as much. "How many?"

"A dozen, maybe." Dara shivered at the memory.

"Have you ever had an infestation of locusts before?"

"Never." Where was Nana going with this?

"And it happened on a night when the demon was in the clinic?"

Dara nodded.

"Have you had any other infestations or visitations since he started? Flies? Frogs? Wild animals?"

"Nothing like that." Dara knew where this was coming from, and she wasn't going there. It was ridiculous.

"Lice?"

That pulled her up short. They'd found lice the first night he was at the clinic. And he'd seemed surprised she was unfazed by them.

"His first night, we had an infestation of lice. The cleaning supervisor told me he'd never seen anything like it."

"There's your answer, then." Nana settled back in her chair, nodding grimly. "Your demon is visiting the plagues of Egypt on you."

"That doesn't make sense. The plagues were sent by God, not by Satan."

"That demon of yours—"

"He's not my demon."

"—is a smart aleck. He probably thinks he's being cute."

Maybe it wasn't so ridiculous. Dara had grown complacent, thinking her only danger was in his potent attraction. "What other plagues are there?"

"Frogs, blood, wild animals, boils, hail, darkness, pestilence and death of the firstborn."

Dara's heart picked up speed as she listened to the litany. Anything on that list had the power to damage the clinic's reputation, though most posed no real threat to her patients. But the last item was different.

Every eldest child who came into the pediatric clinic would be in danger. No, the threat was broader than that. Even the adults had been children once. Everyone fell somewhere in their family's birth order. Panic choked her at the thought of all the patients who were the oldest child in their family.

Her pulse thumped so hard she could hear it in her ears, till an image pierced the fog of fear—an image of Sarah, motionless, her eyes rolled back in her head while Granddad prayed over her without results. Dara's panic receded. Not all troubles were demonic in origin.

"He didn't bring in the lice or the locusts," she said, though she didn't really know that for a fact. She'd been at his side most of the time, but not every minute.

Nana folded her arms across her chest. "Get rid of him."

"How?" Dara asked. "What do I tell my board? 'I want to fire this volunteer because he's bringing the plagues of Egypt to my clinic'? They'll think I'm crazy."

"He said his mission will only last another three weeks, right?"

"Three and a half," Dara said reluctantly.

"Then close for four weeks. Take a vacation and go somewhere."

Dara opened her mouth to point out that she had patients scheduled throughout the next four weeks, hypertensives and diabetics that needed continual monitoring to keep their meds balanced. And what would the staff say when suddenly presented with four weeks of vacation? How would she justify paying them for a month when the clinic was closed? Then she looked at Nana's flushed face. Her wrinkled nostrils flared with each quick breath.

"Okay," Dara said.

Nana's mouth fell open. "What?"

"Okay," Dara said. "I refuse to risk losing you. We'll shut down for a month. You're going to worry yourself into a stroke if I don't."

Fury filled her. What right did the demon have to inflict himself on them and upset Nana like this?

In between patients, he'd enticed Dara to share anecdotes from her childhood, from nursing school, even from her relationship with Matt. She'd tried to keep a wall of professionalism between them, but it was impossible with him always there, enthralled by every detail of her life. It made her feel fascinating, but it seemed to go deeper than that for him. It was as though she held the answer to some existential riddle.

She had thought she'd kept up her guard, but the betrayal she felt now said she'd begun to trust him. As he'd said, it was what he did.

Nana uncrossed her arms. "Oh, no you don't."

"What?" Dara recalled herself from her reverie with effort.

Nana banged her fist on the arm of her chair. "You're not closing down your clinic because of me." A vein beat in her temple.

Dara stared at her, stupefied. "You've been driving me crazy for the past two weeks to close the doors, and now that I've finally agreed to do that, you say don't?"

"Not over me." Nana lifted her head, bringing back memories of when she'd fought alongside Granddad as an equal partner. "A Perdue never gives in to demonic forces."

Dara tried to regroup. "So, you want me to keep the clinic open?"

Nana nodded firmly.

Thus far, the demon had won every round. He had aligned Dara's board on his side. Her patients loved him. Thanks to the daily lunches, her staff worshipped him. He had maneuvered her into a corner where she had no choice but to let him do as he chose.

Well, those days were over. It was time to stop letting him have everything his own way.

"I need to restrict his time in the clinic," she said, thinking out loud, "to the bare minimum."

For the first time since Dara had walked in the door, Nana's shoulders relaxed.

"I need to put him someplace where I can watch him every second," Dara continued, "and minimize the number of patients he sees."

"You shouldn't let him in there at all."

"Agreed," Dara said. "Since that's not an option, my next best choice is to put him where he can do the least damage."

Reluctantly, Nana nodded.

Dara picked up her purse and got to her feet. She leaned over to drop a kiss on Nana's white hair.

"Pray for me," she said.

"I always do," Nana said.

Lord knew someone needed to.

CHAPTER 24

On the way back to the clinic, Dara all but talked herself out of her plan to alter Dr. Demon's schedule. It was just Nana's background that made her insist that a couple of perfectly ordinary swarms of insects were a re-enactment of the Plagues of Egypt. After all, it wasn't like Dara was Pharaoh, refusing to bend to God's will.

Unless her non-existent prayer life fell into that category. She pushed the thought away. If God came after everyone who didn't pray, the world would be a mess of broken lives.

When she approached the back door, though, she heard screaming. A second later, the door slammed open and Gabby, Kelsey and Javier ran out. Her heart jumped into her throat.

"What's wrong?"

"Raccoon," Javier said, his eyes wide. "It just ran in the door when Kelsey came in this morning. It hisses if you try to get near it."

What are the other plagues? she had asked Nana.

Frogs, blood, wild animals, boils, hail, darkness, pestilence and death of the firstborn.

Dara sent the staff to the local coffee shop and called Animal Control. When the specialist left a couple of hours later with the raccoon in a cage, he confirmed that the animal was likely rabid.

As soon as her staff returned, she went to the doorway of the office Javier shared with Kelsey.

"Could you come to my office," Dara asked Javier, "and bring the October schedule?"

"Sure." He picked up his laptop and followed her.

She looked over the schedule while she waited for her own computer to boot up. Just as she thought. Ben was scheduled for every clinic for the entire month, with the exception of the Monday pediatric clinics.

"Please remove Dr. Lyle from the schedule," she said. That would limit his opportunities for mischief, and it would have the added benefit of removing him from her immediate proximity.

Javier stared at her, open-mouthed. "But he volunteered for all those shifts. He wants to work."

"Please schedule him into the peds clinics." It was counter-intuitive, but while she'd waited for the animal control expert to remove the plague of wild animals from her clinic, she'd decided the pediatric clinic was the safest place to put Dr. Demon. Most local children had coverage, so the pediatric clinic had very few patients. Some nights there were none, and even on the busiest nights she would be able to stay right by his side.

Javier's expression changed from aghast to confused. "He specifically asked me not to put him on for peds."

"Did he say why?"

"He's not that comfortable working with kids."

"Then this will be an opportunity for him to hone his skills." The board had final say over who she brought on as a volunteer. They had no say over how she chose to use those volunteers.

Javier eyed her, looking baffled. "Are you sure about this? I mean, he's—"

"I'm sure." She cut him off before he could tell her how great Ben was.

"I thought the two of you were getting along better. What happened?"

She considered telling him she'd discovered his wonderful Ben had planted lice and cicadas in the clinic, but there was too much chance he or Kelsey would follow up, and Dara didn't want the demon forewarned.

"I know this seems capricious, but I need your support. Please?"

Javier nodded, but she could tell his heart wasn't in it. This was probably the last time he would back her solely on her say-so.

"What about tonight?" he asked.

Much as she would have loved to boot the demon immediately, she had her patients to think about.

"You can leave him on for tonight."

"Are you going to tell him?"

She nodded. "I'm sorry about all the extra work this creates," she said. "Leave the schedule out and I'll rework it before I go home."

He shook his head. "You already do too much around here."

After he left, Dara pulled up the template for the patient medical history form on her computer. Because of the plagues, it was now painfully clear who his intended targets were. To protect her patients, she would need to identify the ones most at risk.

She hesitated. Was Nana right? Should she close down the clinic, at least for the next couple of weeks? Her eyes fell on a sticky note, reminding her that Dr. Salujah, a lung specialist from Jacksonville, was coming in Tuesday. Dara had four patients with COPD, including one she thought might have idiopathic pulmonary fibrosis. He had been waiting months to see a specialist.

To the questions about family history, she added one more: *Are you the oldest child in your family?*

Around four p.m., Gabby appeared in Dara's doorway.

"Ben is on the phone." Gabby looked wary. Dara's cancellation of his future volunteer shifts had already made its way through the office grapevine. "He's at the Hyundai dealership in Jacksonville. He had to leave his car for service and he was wondering if someone could come pick him up."

The Hyundai dealership? Why would he be at a Hyundai dealership?

"I'll go get him." Kelsey's voice floated down the hall. Did she listen to everything that came from Dara's office, or were her antennae attuned to mention of Ben's name?

"Couldn't he get a loaner car?" Dara asked. "Or an Uber?"

"I didn't ask," Gabby said.

"I'll go get him." Kelsey appeared behind Gabby. She already had her purse on her shoulder.

Over my dead body. "How's the Robert Wood Johnson grant proposal coming?"

"It's almost done." Kelsey's eyes didn't meet hers.

"Isn't it due tomorrow?"

Kelsey's pretty face turned an un-pretty shade of red. "I'll finish it when I get back. I was planning to work late anyway."

Dara opened her desk drawer and pulled out her purse. "I'll go get him. I have some things I need to talk to him about."

Kelsey flounced back to her office. Dara pretended not to hear the grant writer's desk drawer slam as she put her purse away.

Belial was inside the dealership, chatting with one of the saleswomen, when Dara's rusty old Toyota pulled onto the lot. Excellent. Maybe, given his heroic rescue of her from the cicadas the previous night, she would let him make her dinner.

The prospect of a long, uninterrupted evening made him smile. Without a patient there, playing chaperone, he'd finally have the perfect opportunity to kiss her again. At the thought of her soft body pressed against him, her mouth opening beneath his lips, his groin awoke.

"There's my ride," he told the blond saleswoman.

She gave him a long, melting look. "Are you sure I can't buy you a drink?"

He chuckled and shook his head. While it felt good to have a woman respond readily to his charm, it was Dara's challenging company he craved. "I have to go to work."

He expected Dara to wait for him in the parking lot, but she'd gotten out of the car and was almost to the door by the time he reached it. He smiled at her quizzically. She marched straight past him without speaking.

"Are you finally thinking about replacing that old rust bucket?" he asked. Maybe he could help her negotiate a deal on a replacement. He hovered behind her, envisioning her gratitude.

Dara yanked the door open, hard. He was following so close behind that it slammed into his face. He leapt back, grabbing his nose. "Ow!"

She turned. Her eyes widened at the damage to his face, but her lips were pinched with anger. She had done it intentionally. What the devil?

He checked his face in the showroom window. His nose was crooked and his eyes were already swelling.

"You broke my nose. Why did you break my nose?"

She put out her hand as though to touch his cheek, but immediately withdrew it. Her jaw tightened.

"Maybe if you had a little more respect for personal space, it wouldn't have happened."

He goggled at her. "What is your problem?"

She stared at him fiercely, with none of the compassion he'd come to expect from her toward anyone in pain. "What happened to your Lamborghini?"

He tried to read her body language to understand what had set her off, but he was reduced to peering through two swollen slits for eyes. Bad had injected too much human DNA, leaving him far too fragile.

"I was forced to downgrade," he said.

"Why?"

There was no point in lying. She'd already figured it out.

"I needed the money for something else."

She shot him a glance that should have singed the hair off his head. "To fund that grant."

"The money went to a variety of—"

"To buy your way into my clinic."

He watched her, thinking fast. Had she decided his story of being assigned to the Strong Clinic for a past failure was a lie? Her face was stone-like, giving nothing away. He decided truth would serve him best.

"Yes," he said.

She muttered something beneath her breath that sounded suspiciously like "asshole," and walked into the dealership. She flagged down the saleswoman he'd been speaking with.

"Did you wait on this gentleman?" Dara jerked her thumb toward him.

The saleswoman gaped at his battered face. "What happened to you?"

"He ran into a door," Dara said. "He'll be fine." When the woman didn't look convinced, Dara added, "I'm a nurse. I know about these things."

"Are you sure—"

"I'm okay," Belial said thickly.

"He didn't talk you into anything, did he?" asked Dara. "Or out of anything? Like a new car in trade for his old piece of junk?"

"No, no." The woman swallowed. She clearly thought she'd stepped into the middle of domestic violence. "He said he came in for service. We just chatted while he waited for his ride."

"Thank you." Dara turned and stomped out the door. Belial had no choice but to follow her.

"What's got your panties in a twist?" he asked, once they were back in the car. His face hurt like hell.

She turned a fulminating gaze on him. "Like you don't know."

Through puffy eyes, he stared at her in astonishment. She was the most extraordinary woman, prickly as a camel thorn tree. "My knowledge of what goes on in this world, while extensive, is not absolute. I have no idea what's got your hackles up."

It was fortunate she could only look metaphorical daggers.

Otherwise, he'd be a ringer for Julius Caesar by now. She backed the car out of the parking space.

"I told my grandmother about the locusts in the clinic last night," she said. Ah, so that was it. His gut tightened. "She pointed out that locusts and lice were two of the ten plagues of Egypt. This morning, a wild animal invaded us."

He frowned. Lilith had gone too far. "What kind of wild animal?"

"Like you don't know," she said. "Would you like to explain what you're hoping to achieve? Or is this part of your 'observation of the American health system'?"

Well, bliss. Once again, Belial was aware of the confining presence of the cell phone that relayed his every word back to Hell. He considered tossing it out the window, but that would only send Satan's suspicions into overdrive. Belial needed a way to handle this that didn't undercut his greater objective—his promotion.

"I don't know what you're talking about," he lied. "Nor why you would accuse me. I was the one who got rid of the locusts—humanely—if you remember."

"Is that what this was? Setting up a situation where you could play hero?"

"No." Though that wouldn't have been a bad idea, had it worked. "I have no idea how the cicadas got into the clinic." He didn't mind lying, but it was annoying to have to expend so much creativity covering Lilith's actions. "And you said yourself that you see lice all the time."

Her conviction didn't waver.

"The plagues didn't come from my side," he pointed out. "They were a punishment on the Egyptians from G—" He couldn't get the word out. "The other side."

She nodded like he'd just proved her point. "My guess is you thought it would be funny—this very ironic, hip way to spread your evil."

Actually, she was probably right. That was likely exactly what Lilith had been thinking. He preferred his own evil a little more straightforward.

"If that was your plan," she said, "it backfired. I've asked Javier to remove you from the October schedule."

He went rigid on the poorly sprung seat. "You're firing me as a volunteer?" Without the opportunity to spend time in her presence, his chances of success dropped to almost zero.

Her hands tightened on the steering wheel. "We both know that's not an option. You'd go straight to the board and they'd want to know why, and I wouldn't be able to give them a reason that didn't sound insane."

That was exactly what he would do. Such an action was not conducive to seducing her, but neither was never setting eyes on her again. He'd been making steady progress in the clinic, wearing down her ability to resist. Despite her wariness, even despite her current anger, she was attracted to him. He could see it in the way her nostrils flared when he was near, and in the way her color fluctuated when their hands brushed while working with a patient.

"I had Javier schedule you for the pediatrics clinic," she said.

He stiffened. Those clinics occurred only once a week. "I'm not comfortable working around children."

"If the shift doesn't appeal to you, drop out."

She had him on this. If she fired him for no reason, the board would intervene. But she had run the clinic with great success for the past five years. They were unlikely to interfere with the day-to-day operations.

His cell phone rang.

"Bad's got an upgrade for your identity," Satan said. "Get down here and let him install it."

"I just dropped my car off at the shop." A headache stirred behind Belial's eyes. "I'm not sure how soon I can get there." He didn't know if it was the bump on the head, the complaints from the boss or his backward progress with Dara that lay behind the pounding in his skull.

"Then ride the Ducati."

"I'll have the Hyundai back tomorrow. The Ducati's too unprotected for that environment."

Dara's head whipped around. "Are you talking to Satan?"

It was clear she already knew the answer. He covered the receiver with his hand. "Yes."

"In my car?"

He nodded.

She plucked the phone from his hand and tossed it out her window.

He stared at her in astonishment. "Are you insane?"

She veered to the curb. "Get out."

"What do you mean?"

She pulled an atomizer of holy water he hadn't noticed from the cup holder in her door. "Get out."

"You broke my nose. And did you see the size of this knot?" He touched his forehead. "I think I may have a concussion."

She wavered for a moment before her face hardened again. "I've seen how fast you heal. A half hour from now, you'll be good as new. Get out."

"How am I supposed to get home?"

"Take the bus." She nodded through the windshield at a Plexiglas bus shelter a few yards away.

He stared at her, aghast. "Demons don't take buses."

"Then walk. I don't care how you get home. You know the rules."

"He called me."

"Not my problem."

"The rule was that I couldn't talk to him in the clinic. You didn't say anything about your car."

"Allow me to clarify. You are not to talk to Satan in my presence. Or in the presence of anyone else who works at clinic. Or around anyone who visits the clinic. Or anyone who walks past the clinic."

"I must be thirty miles from home." And he had a hellish headache.

"More like forty. I'll tell Javier you won't be in tonight. Out." Her hand tightened on the trigger of the spray bottle. He crawled from the car.

His head was pounding like Thor's anvil. He'd barely closed the car door when she peeled away with a squeal of tires.

CHAPTER 25

It took Belial over four hours to get home. Without the phone, he couldn't call anyone for a ride. He tried hailing a taxi, but the driver took one look at his bruised face and sped away.

With no remaining options, he made his way to the bus shelter. There was a map on the wall, but between the pounding in his head and his swollen eyes, he couldn't make out the appropriate route. A heavyset woman pulling a wire shopping cart filled with groceries took pity on him.

"Where do you live?" She surveyed his bruised face curiously but didn't ask any questions.

"In Alexandria, out by the beach."

She looked him up and down, taking in his designer clothes and handmade shoes. She pursed her lips. He could almost hear her thinking "drug dealer."

"You're a long way from home." She traced her finger from the red dot marked "You Are Here" and showed him the route. It required three transfers just to get him within two miles of the beach house. She peered at his face. "Are you sure you shouldn't go to a hospital instead?"

"No, thanks." His identity wasn't displaying the quick-healing properties Dara had alluded to, but human doctors wouldn't know what to do with his hybrid body. Once he got to Hell, Bad would be able to fix it. At which time he'd damned well better fix its frailty, too.

The woman reached into her grocery sack. She brought out a pack of frozen peas. "Here," she said. "Press this against your face."

The ice pack felt like balm on his bruises. "Thank you."

With his free hand, he dug out his wallet, but she patted his wrist. "You don't owe me anything."

By the time the No. 6 came along, his face felt like it had been pounded to hamburger. He should be healed by now. Why wasn't the identity repairing itself?

On the bus, the other passengers peered at his battered face, but no one offered any comments. It was, after all, Florida. At the bus terminal, he purchased a ticket for Alexandria, only to learn the bus wouldn't leave for an hour and a half. He eyed the grubby station with disfavor. Demons should not have to spend time in such a place. Not unless they were targeting someone there.

The boss would be livid about this latest development. His contact with Dara was now limited to a few hours once a week. And because of Lilith's damned plagues, even then Dara would be on alert the entire time. The possibility that he would fail at this mission loomed large, but he refused to accept that. There had to be a way back into her good graces.

What else could he give her? She had enough money for the clinic, at least for the present, and even if she didn't, Mammon wouldn't release any more funds. Buying everyone lunch every day had eaten up what was left from the sale of the Lamborghini. He tried to think what else she had in her life: her grandmother, the cat, who was useful for some tasks, but not really helpful in this situation—and now her friend, Lilith. He smiled grimly. Lilith had created this mess, and she would damned well help him out of it.

The bus arrived in a cloud of diesel fumes. He took a seat by the window. According to the timetable posted on the wall of the bus station, the forty-mile journey to Alexandria would consume two hours. It stopped in every little seaside village along the way.

Once he was back, he would have to head straight to Hell to see the boss and get this identity fixed. Then he remembered that his pathetic excuse for a car was in the shop. That meant he'd have to ride the Ducati down the rings, with insects and debris peppering him every inch of the way.

An obese man with a large shopping bag squeezed into the seat beside him. The man spread his knees and put the bag between them. His plump thigh and upper arm pressed over onto Belial's side of the divider. Belial turned to ask him to put the bag in the overhead luggage rack and found himself looking at the man's earlobe. It had a vertical crease. He checked the man's hairline. Receding. That wasn't good. Bumpy patches of cholesterol marred the flesh surrounding his eyes. Someone should advise him to get a checkup.

Belial checked the ceiling of the bus. He saw no cameras. DemSec might have tracked him here, even without his phone, but he doubted it.

"Have you had your heart checked recently?" he asked.

The man twisted in his seat to stare at him.

"I'm a physician." Belial looked over the telltale signs of heart disease again. The man was a ticking time bomb. "You should have your heart checked out."

"Right," the man said. "Because doctors ride the bus all the time. It's the new in thing to do." He didn't say it, but his gaze made it clear that Belial's injured face further undercut his credibility.

Belial leaned forward to dig his wallet from his back pocket. The seat was so cramped his elbow rubbed against the metal wall of the bus. Why was he even doing this? He didn't know this man from Adam. Well, not Adam, because Adam didn't have a navel, and the indentation in at the man's waistline made it obvious he did. But Belial didn't know him from any other currently alive mortal on this bedeviled planet.

He was doing it just because he could. With no prying eyes watching, electronic or otherwise, he was free to do as he chose. He took out the ID card that the clinic had provided him and showed it to the man.

The man's plump lips formed an O of surprise. "You really are a doctor."

"I am."

"Yeah, well, here's the bad news, doc. I don't have any insurance."

Belial rifled through his wallet until he located the business card Javier had given him the first night he'd come into the clinic. It listed the address and hours in flamingo-pink script. He handed it to the man.

"Go here. The hours are on the card." He opened his mouth to say, "Tell them I sent you," but stopped himself. The man had enough problems without Dara misidentifying him as a demon.

He studied the card. "You really think I need to do this?"

"Yes," Belial said. "I really do."

Dara drove back to the clinic, experiencing such a welter of emotions she didn't know how to process them all. She was still furious at what Dr. Demon had tried to do to her clinic. She felt guilty about injuring him, even though she knew he'd heal quickly and he'd brought it on himself by hovering over her like a stalker. She was terrified of what he might do in the future.

Still, every time she pictured his outraged face when she'd told him he could take the bus, she laughed until tears rolled down her cheeks. Her laughter had an edge of hysteria, but it was laughter nonetheless.

Back at the clinic, she stopped by Javier's office to let him know Ben wouldn't be in that night. Javier's shoulders sagged. "I'd better start making calls and see if I can get someone else to fill in."

She continued on down the hall. Behind her, Kelsey muttered, "What do you think she did to him?"

"Should we send out the cadaver-sniffing dogs?" Javier asked.

Kelsey giggled.

All at once, Dara had had it up to here with the clinic. For five years she'd given it every ounce of her attention and every penny of her money and every minute of her life, and what did she have to show for it? Nothing. For the past three and a half weeks, she'd fought an uphill battle against the forces of Satan alone. No one else in the clinic knew a battle was being waged, but that didn't excuse them. A little support wasn't too much to ask.

She walked into Tia's office, where the nurse practitioner was processing referrals.

"Can you cover tonight?"

Tia cocked her head. "Of course, sugar. Aren't you feeling well?"

If Dara said she wasn't sick, Tia would want to know why she wanted to take off. And the explanation would take more energy than she had to spare right now.

"Upset stomach and a headache," she lied.

CHAPTER 26

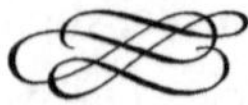

"What have you done to yourself?" Bad gawked at Belial's worse-for-wear body as he limped into DemSec.

The trip down the rings on the Ducati had been a nightmare. As he'd anticipated, insects battered him all the way down, nicking the modified flesh of his identity. In Ring Three, Cerberus chased the bike. Every time Belial managed to kick one set of teeth away from his ankle, another of the hound's three heads lunged in and chomped down. That had gone on for two solid miles. By the time he reached the entrance to Ring Four and Cerberus trotted away, slobbering in triumph, Belial's ankle was in ribbons.

"Why am I not healing?"

"What do you mean?

Belial checked himself in a floor-length mirror. His face was almost repaired. The wounds on his ankle were already closing up. He gestured toward the mirror. "This happened five hours ago. Why is it just now mending?"

Bad stroked his chin as he examined the almost-healed injuries. "Were you around people? People who didn't know you're a demon?"

Belial thought of all the individuals he'd come into contact with that afternoon, from the woman at the bus stop to his overweight seatmate, not to mention all the other riders.

"Nonstop," he said.

"That's why. The genes we spliced in were designed to help maintain your demonimity."

Belial snorted. "If that's the case, then why did the target recognize me?" If that hadn't happened, he'd be done with this mission by now and enjoying his new office.

"That's a head-scratcher." Bad rubbed the back of his head, making his fedora bob up and down. "We're still trying to figure that out. We reviewed the footage a few times, but nothing jumped out at us." He wandered back to his desk, where an oversized monitor displayed a halted image of a video game. The game appeared to revolve around guns, sleek cars and large-breasted women.

Belial tried to control his temper. "I want this identity fixed."

"There's nothing wrong with it."

"Then why does she continue to resist me?"

"Operator error?"

Belial clenched his fists. His pulse pounded in his ears. After the frustrations of the day, the other demon's casual dismissal was just too much. Not one single other demon was prepared to help with this mission. All they had to offer were jibes and sabotage.

Behind Bad's glasses, his dark eyes went wide. "Bel, your eyes have gone goat. Are you pissed about something?"

"Yes, I'm pissed," Belial snarled, glad of an excuse to vent some of the rage pounding in his veins. "I'm pissed that you gave me unproven technology and it screwed up the most important mission I've ever undertaken."

He expected Bad to shrink back from his fury, but the other demon came out from behind his desk and to peer into Belial's eyes.

"That's it." Bad punched him in the arm. Belial gave him a look that should have shriveled him where he stood, but he didn't even notice. "That's how she made you. With her grandparents, it's a given that she can spot angry demons. You got pissed, and your eyes went goat. That's how she knew you were a demon."

That first night in the clinic, when Dara had refused his offer to volunteer, he'd been furious. But why had the identity allowed so much of his true nature to come through? That had been the point of developing the hybrids—because they were much less susceptible to identification.

"It's your gene-splicing," Belial said. "You gave me a faulty identity." It didn't help the state of the mission, but at least the blame for the screw-up did not lie on his doorstep.

Bad shook his head. "It's not the identity, Bel. We've done thousands of hours of road tests and we've never seen bleed-through before. It's you. Your demontude is so strong it overwhelms the presets."

"What in Hell's name is 'demontude'?"

"It's like attitude. You know, how you carry yourself, demonically. It gets stronger the longer you live *la vida diablo*."

That was bullshit, but the boss, with his bias toward technology over agency, would probably buy it.

"Why doesn't she see through Lilith?"

"The only alterations Lilith gets are to keep her looking hot."

Belial was outraged. "Why did she get to skip all this identity crap?"

"The boss didn't put in an order for it," Bad said. "He never does for the she-demons."

Suddenly, Belial was bone-tired. All he wanted was to get the upgrade and get back to Dara. Then he could finish this damned mission and be done with it.

"Do you have a phone for me?"

"Sure." Bad pulled a phone from a drawer and tossed it at Belial. Then he drew a needle the size of a railroad spike from another drawer. "This serum will splice in a little more human genome to tone down your demontude."

More? Belial was already so human it took him five hours to heal, but maybe if he was more human Dara would distrust him less.

Bad jammed the needle into his arm like he was throwing a dart. Belial yelped.

"Stop jerking," Bad said.

"That hurts," Belial said.

"When did you turn into such a wuss?" Bad depressed the plunger and the serum burned its way into Belial's system. "You used to be the toughest demon down here."

When the vial was empty, Bad peered into his eyes. "You should probably stay below for a couple of hours, till we see how you react to the new splice."

"What am I supposed to do for the next two hours while we're waiting to see if you screwed up again?"

Bad didn't take offense. He looked at Belial with an expression that almost looked like sympathy. "Didn't you know? The boss wanted to see you as soon as you got back."

In the vestibule to Satan's office, Andras was typing the agenda for the next leadership meeting. There was some good news. At least he'd be away for that.

"The boss asked to see me," Belial said. "Is he here?"

"Lake of Fire," she squawked. With a ruffle of feathers, she returned to her screen.

Not that again.

The stone road was scorching beneath the soles of his Burberry deck shoes as he made his way to the lake. His footsteps echoed off the cavernous ceiling. He'd left the Ducati outside his personal quarters in Ring Eight.

What would Dara think if she saw him now? He smiled a humorless smile. Probably not much different than what she already thought. The image of her face, softened by compassion when she was working with a patient, furious when she accused him of visiting insects on her clinic, heavy-lidded and sensual on the rare occasions she dropped her defenses, danced before his eyes. What a beautiful woman she was.

Then he imagined a different expression on her face, one of soul-destroyed devastation after he convinced her to betray her deepest beliefs. He shook his head to banish the image from his mind. There was no point in dwelling on it; it was what it was.

He found the boss sitting at a picnic table, consuming a plate of *griot ti-malice*, a Haitian dish of pork and plantains guaranteed to burn the taste buds from your tongue. Even from two feet away, the spices made Belial's eyes burn. Satan motioned for him to sit down.

"What happened after she tossed the phone?"

Belial could see no advantage in lying. Even though the boss didn't have video evidence, Dara would probably tell Lilith what happened, and Lilith would tattle to Satan.

"She kicked me out of the car. I wound up taking the bus home."

Satan chuckled and inhaled a mouthful of peppery sauce. He choked, coughing until Belial had to pound him on his bony back. When he was able to catch his breath, Satan wiped the moisture from his eyes with the curve of his fore-talon.

"Why are you telling her so much about operations down here?" he asked.

Because it was the only topic Belial had found so far that would keep her talking to him.

"Recruiting tool," he said. "That's how you recruited me, by making this organization sound more interesting than where I was working before."

It was a startup, Sataniel, as Satan was called back then, had told him during guard duty one night. Guard duty was one of the most boring jobs in Heaven—who would attack the Almighty? Sataniel had called his new venture "a ground-floor opportunity." And, though Belial had known what a jerk Sataniel was, he had believed him. "I'm doing the same thing with her."

"What's your next step?" Satan raised his skinny eyebrows. "Do you even have a plan? Because it feels like you're winging this."

"The same plan I've used since time immemorial—wealth, fornication and corruption."

"You've said that from the beginning, but all I've seen so far is you spending my wealth and getting no fornication, much less corruption, for my money. I'm starting to wonder why I picked you for this mission. I need someone in there who can think on his feet. Lilith has made more progress than you have."

Belial managed to hold on to his temper. Without Lilith's "progress," he'd be a lot further along.

"Yes, but Lilith isn't likely to be able to deliver on the next step, is she? It's not like she can seduce Dara."

"Oh, I don't know." Satan shrugged. "You know what they say—every straight woman is just a six-pack away from being a lesbian."

Belial's mouth fell open. "You think Lilith can seduce her?"

Satan's eyelids drifted to half-mast. He was picturing the scene in his head. In detail. Belial fought to keep his disgust with the boss from showing. After a moment, with obvious reluctance, Satan let go of his fantasy. "That woman is so straight not even Sappho couldn't turn her head."

"Then pull Lilith out of there. She's getting in my way, complicating things."

Satan pursed his lips as he considered that. After a moment, he shook his head. "She's shaking things up. If it weren't for her, there wouldn't be any progress on this mission at all."

Belial thought about Dara's fury over the "plagues" being visited on the clinic.

"She's making progress, all right, but it's negative progress. You've admitted she's unlikely to corrupt the target. Get her out of my way so I can do my job."

Satan shoveled another bite into his mouth. He spoke around the food. "The old woman has made the target so paranoid she's likely to see any change in her environment as suspect. If her new best friend disappears, she'll blame you."

Although that was true, Belial couldn't resist saying, "At least she won't be blaming me for whatever mischief Lilith has planned next."

Satan slammed his fist down on the slate picnic table, making Belial jump. Cracks appeared in the tabletop, radiating out from the spot where Satan's fist made contact.

"Stop making excuses. Stop blaming everyone but yourself." His voice assumed a whiny, singsong quality. "It's Lilith's fault for interfering. It's Bad's fault for giving me a flawed identity. It's Mammon's fault for not giving me enough money." Oily smoke poured from Satan's horns.

"From the beginning, you've treated this mission like a junket. Your focus was on the car and the motorcycle and the beach house to amuse yourself, when you should have been using them as weapons in the first head-to-head conflict we've had with the Enemy in four thousand years."

Satan rose from the table and reached into the picnic basket, bringing out a red-eyed rat with a forked tail. He carried the squirming animal over to the shore of the lake and hurled it into the roiling waters. The rat squealed and tried to scramble back across the surface. The lake sucked it down, only to belch it back up a moment later with its skin gone. Its muscles and organs gleamed in the low light as it scrabbled toward the shore, still screaming.

It slipped beneath the surface a second time. What came back up was a skeleton, but the bones still writhed in agony until finally the rat's carcass disappeared for the last time.

"Full-sized demons take a lot longer, of course." Satan plucked a splinter from the shattered table and used it to pick a bit of food from his teeth. "Two or three days. With no hope of escape."

Belial was shaken, but showing fear would be a huge mistake. He assumed the ultra-patient voice Dara used when talking to Viola. "Do you feel better now?"

For a moment, he thought Satan's head would explode.

"Not everything's a joke, demon," Satan said. "I'm not willing to piss away this opportunity because you didn't take it seriously."

Belial drew himself up in unrighteous anger. "Since when have I ever failed to take my responsibilities seriously? For that matter, when have I ever failed to deliver? And don't bring up Joan of Arc again, because I've heard everything I want to on that bitch. One failure in ten thousand years, and we knew she was a long shot from the beginning."

Furious, he snapped a slab from the broken table top and hurled it into the Lake of Fire. Acid splashed back onto the shore. He jumped out of the way, but a few stray drops splattered Satan.

"Gaaah!" Satan's pupils went rectangular.

Thrall crept over Belial's limbs. It was stronger than it had been the last time. He battered against it without success. Was this the end? Was he really to die over a spat with the boss? A foolish, wasted end to a foolish, wasted existence. Sweat poured down Satan's forehead as Belial's left foot took a dragging step toward the shoreline. He fought with all his might, but his right foot followed.

Step by step, inch by inch, he trudged toward the lake, struggling to throw off the force that commanded his limbs. Finally, as Belial was about to plunge his foot into the lake, Satan's hold wavered. A tiny crack in his concentration.

That was all Belial needed. He slammed against the invisible bonds and broke free. The lake was so close his arms and face burned from the proximity. He sucked in a lungful of sulfurous air, fighting the urge to cough. His shirt was soaked with sweat. He'd won this round, but barely. Satan had been practicing, as Belial had taunted him to do at poker night.

"Dara Strong is different from Joan of Arc, in any event." Belial stepped back from the shoreline and continued as though he'd wandered down to the water under his own power. "She was disaffected before I ever came on the scene. I'm not sure what the Enemy is trying to achieve, but I can tell you this: that woman has more anger in her than I've ever seen in a woman before. Before tossing me out on the road, she physically attacked me at the car dealership.

"All she needs is a little push to topple her over to our side. And whether everyone gets out of my way and lets me work, or does everything in their power to stop me, I'm going to make that happen."

At last he allowed himself to make eye contact.

Satan glared back at him, smoke pouring from his horns. Deliberately, he looked out over the lake where the rat's body had disappeared and Belial's had almost followed.

"See that you do, demon. See that you do."

CHAPTER 27

The last two days of the week were not good days. The patient loads were heavy, made heavier by being short a doctor. Dara's staff was barely speaking to her. She made it a point to avoid the kitchen at midday, when everyone came in to retrieve the lunches they once again brought from home and sullenly heated in the microwave.

The only bright spot was the patient whose life they'd possibly saved. On Thursday night, an obese, middle-aged man appeared at the reception window and showed Gabby one of the clinic's business cards. He said someone had given it to him and suggested he come to the clinic. She fit him into the walk-in schedule. After a brief exam, Dr. Bell had sent him straight over to Bermuda General in an ambulance. He'd had a heart attack in the ER, but with lifesaving equipment instantly available, the doctors there had minimized the impact.

It felt like a vindication of her decision to keep the clinic open.

Now it was nine o'clock on Saturday night and she already had her pajamas on. A bag of popcorn perfumed the air with the aroma of movie night. Her favorite film, *Ghost,* was cued up in the DVD player. In the long, sleepless nights following Matt's death, she had watched it over and over, wondering if Matt was out there, somewhere beyond her consciousness, hovering and trying to take care of her. After a while, she'd reached the conclusion that he'd moved on to his reward and no one was interested in taking care of her. The movie was a good reminder that, save for Nana, she was on her own.

She had just settled down to watch Patrick Swayze and Demi Moore demonstrate a love that lasted beyond life itself when her phone buzzed.

"I'm at Slyders," It was Lilith. Music blared in the background, accompanied by laughter and clinking glasses. "Come join me."

Dara explained that she already had her evening planned. "You're welcome to come over, though."

"And I would totally do that," Lilith said, "if I was ninety. Come on, *chica*. Don't be such a stick in the mud. There'll be plenty of time to sit around and watch old movies when you're in a nursing home. Come party with me."

Dara looked around her cozy living room. Lilith had a point. Away from work, Dara's life wasn't all that different from Nana's.

"Come on. I'm lonely, and that always gets me into trouble. This bar is chock-full of cute young sailors."

"Where's Jeremy?" Ever since Ben's first-night celebration party, Jeremy and Lilith had been an item.

"He played golf today with the boys."

Dara looked out through the tinted sliding glass doors at the setting sun. "It's getting dark. He can't still be playing."

"He said I kept him out late last night and he was too tired to go out." Lilith sounded disappointed and pettish, but there was a ring of loneliness there, too.

"Come on," she said. "Friends don't let friends drink alone."

Dara looked at the cued-up movie and the bowl of popcorn on the coffee table. How many Saturday evenings had she spent like this over the past five years? All of them, or nearly all. Lilith was right. She was thirty-five, not ninety-five.

"Give me a half hour." That included the twenty-minute drive to the beach. She lived inland, where property values and hurricane insurance were a lot cheaper than out by the ocean.

"Put on some makeup," Lilith said, "and wear those slutty shoes we bought."

Dara walked through the crowded bar, acutely aware of the looks she was drawing from the sailors Lilith had mentioned. They didn't look any older than a lot of the teenagers she saw in the peds clinic, but that didn't stop them from staring. She wished she hadn't put on the formfitting sundress and strappy, high-heeled sandals she'd bought with Lilith. The boys' interest told her she looked good, but she was much more comfortable in the anonymity of her scrubs.

Out on the deck, Jeremy was sitting at Lilith's side. He blinked when he saw her.

"Look who decided to join me after all," Lilith said, snuggling against him.

Jeremy had volunteered at the clinic for five years. It was probably the first time Dara had ever worn a dress around him. He gave her an uncomfortable smile.

She smiled back with a confidence she didn't feel and sat down across the table from them. A tall drink was already waiting. "What's this?"

"A Long Island iced tea," Lilith said. Jeremy started to say something, but she shushed him. "I think you'll like it."

Dara took a sip. There was clearly some alcohol in it, but it tasted very smooth, a lot like iced tea.

"Is it okay?" Lilith bit her lip. "We can order you something else."

"It's fine," Dara said.

Lilith grinned and raised her glass. "Cheers."

An hour and a half and two iced teas later, Dara caught a whiff of petrichor and vanilla, and there he was. He was dressed in jeans and a white shirt that was open at the neck. His feet were encased in a pair of loafers that probably cost more than a week of her salary. His face bore no trace of the damage she'd done on Wednesday, the last time she saw him. He was back to being totally gorgeous. She took a long sip of her drink and pictured him with his nose smashed to the side. She giggled.

"May I join you?" He smiled, and his eyes crinkled at the corners. She pictured herself smoothing out those crinkles with her lips. *No crinkle-kissing,* she ordered herself. Then she frowned, trying to work out the correct response to his question. Before she could come up with an answer, he sat down beside her.

"Looks like I have some catching up to do." He ordered another round of drinks, and a beer for himself.

"I wasn't expecting to see you till Monday," she said.

He smiled. "Yet, here I am."

Dara waited for her allergies to kick in and clog up her nose so that she couldn't smell him anymore, but for some reason, maybe because of the breeze coming in off the ocean, that didn't happen. So she sat there, breathing him in and hoping she wouldn't drool on the table.

She was drunker than she'd ever been in her life. Those iced teas were much stronger than a similar-sized glass of wine. Through the fog of alcohol, it occurred to her that her grandparents' teetotaling home had not prepared her for having a friend like Lilith.

Jeremy and Ben—it felt odd to call him Ben, but she was pretty sure it would sound even odder if she called him Dr. Demon—talked a bit about a case that had come into the clinic on Tuesday night. Ben, she noticed, didn't mention his new schedule. Lilith chipped in some information about a public relations outreach the hospital was doing.

Even if her lips weren't too numb to talk, Dara didn't have anything to add. They were already aware of most of what was happening in the clinic. And what they didn't know was better kept secret. She wasn't too drunk to know that.

At some point, a band started playing inside the bar. Lilith grabbed Jeremy's hand. "Come dance with me." They headed inside.

"Would you like to dance?" Ben asked.

"I don't dance." Dara enunciated each word carefully, so he wouldn't realize how inebriated she was.

He smiled a slow smile that said he knew exactly how drunk she was. "You may be better off not trying to stand up anyway."

"I'm fine," she said. "I just don't engage in the devil's pastime." Ugh. She sounded exactly like Nana.

"He's never been that much into dancing," Ben said. "Gambling is more his thing."

She put her elbows on the table and folded her hands, making a cradle. With care, she balanced her chin on top of the cradle.

"Really?" she said. "That's fasssscinating."

His lips quirked as though he wanted to laugh, but he didn't.

"What else?" she asked.

His smile deepened. "What do you mean, 'what else'?"

Her chin rocked a little on her hands. She stilled it. "What else do you know that's fascinating?"

"Lots of things." His lips—his beautiful, smooth, shapely lips—quirked again. "What would you like to know?"

At the moment, the only thing she could think of was what it would be like to have hot demon sex with him. "Nothing."

"I see," he said. She had the feeling he knew exactly what was going through her mind.

From inside the bar, the strains of "Can't Help Falling in Love with You" flowed out the door. It was a challenging piece, but the lead singer was surprisingly good for a bar band.

"I love this song." She hummed along, swaying in time to the music.

He tilted his head. "Are you sure you don't want to dance?"

She did want to dance. At that moment, she wanted to dance more than anything in the world. She wanted to be self-confident and fun, like Lilith. But she'd never learned how. Granddaughters of ultraconservative demon-fighters did not dance. That struck her as very sad.

"I don't know how to dance." She sniffled. A tear slowly rolled down her cheek.

Ben made a choking sound that might have been a laugh. Then he stood and held out his hand. "Slow dancing requires absolutely no skill whatsoever. You just shuffle your feet and sway in time to the music."

She shook her head. "I can't."

"Come on. What do you have to lose? Lilith will make sure I don't step over any lines."

It was so tempting. "Will you steal my soul?"

"On the dance floor?" He gave the ghost of a laugh. "No."

She stood, and the deck tilted beneath her feet. She grabbed the table to regain her balance and noticed her purse. She held up a finger. "One moment." She dug through her purse until she located the jar of salve and smeared it on her upper lip. The pungent scent filled her nostrils.

He took her arm and half led, half dragged her inside. Even drunk, she was all too aware of the warmth of his palm cupping her elbow. Out on the deck, the evening had cooled off, but inside the bar, it was still hotter than Hades and reeked of liquor. It was a veritable den of iniquity. And there she was, the granddaughter of Lonnie and Esther Perdue, right in the thick of it, dancing with a demon. Without giving her a chance to change her mind, Ben pulled her into his arms and they began to sway.

To her disappointment, he held her far more loosely than she'd expected. The only places where their bodies touched was where his hands touched her shoulder and her waist. She took a half a step closer to him but, so smoothly she might have missed it if she weren't paying attention, he stepped back.

She frowned. After four weeks of stalking her, why didn't he want to hold her?

Then he ran his fingertips along her exposed collarbones. The sensation was electric, and it wasted no time traveling south. As though he sensed her desire, his hand slipped around behind her neck. As she arched her back with pleasure, Nana's ruby pendant slid down her chest, lodging between her breasts.

She grabbed it before it could drop any further, wrapping the chain around her hand. She inspected it. The link holding the clasp was twisted and pulled apart.

"You broke my necklace," she said.

He shook his head. "The clasp must be bad. You should put that in your purse, so you don't lose it."

Nana had told her the truth about the ruby. He didn't want to brush against it. That was why he held her so loosely.

Inside her brain, two women circled each other. The honorable woman who had been raised by demon-fighting grandparents had self-respect and moral certitude going for her. The human woman who hadn't been touched by a man in five years had biology on her side. They locked arms to wrestle for domination, but with three of Lilith's iced teas flowing through Dara's system, it was no contest.

She opened her little evening bag and dropped the ruby inside. As soon as she snapped the purse closed, he pulled her hard against him.

She was still a little dizzy, but that feeling was quickly overwhelmed by another. Pressed against his chest, with her face buried in his neck, she wanted to nuzzle his throat. And it wasn't his scent that was doing it, because all she could smell was eucalyptus. She rolled her head back, which made her miss a step. His arms tightened around her. She trailed her mouth up the side of his throat, then licked her lips, tasting skin and sweat and vanilla and that hint of sulfur. He tasted even better than she'd imagined.

The effect on him was immediate. She lifted her face to look at him. "Demons are easy."

He smiled down at her. "In that dress you're wearing, any male would be easy."

She pressed her pelvis against his again. What would happen if she led him out to the Toyota and climbed into the back seat? He cupped her glutes and ground himself against her, and she knew the answer. He would make her feel better than she'd ever felt in her life.

Recklessly, she lifted her head and pressed her lips against his. As though that were a signal, his arms tightened around her and his mouth crushed hers. It was the kiss she'd dreamed of since that night by the gas pumps. Beneath the persuasive pressure of his lips, she opened her mouth, as she'd wanted to the night Milton got out. Why had she resisted? All she had done was delay the inevitable. His tongue stroked hers with a copulatory cadence that awoke an answering rhythm low in her belly.

Working beside him day after day was like being an asteroid pulled into the gravitational force of the sun. It had worn down her defenses far more than she'd realized. She no longer had the strength to resist him. Desire seared through her, pooling in her belly like mercury, liquid and deadly. His erection pushed against her, thick as her wrist and hard as bone. He rubbed her back in slow circles, giving her no option to pull away, even if she'd wanted to. One hand traveled up the side of her ribcage, making her aware of how little fabric was covering her body.

He pulled his mouth away from hers to press kisses against her collarbones.

"So beautiful," he murmured.

She wanted to melt into a puddle on the floor, but even more, she wanted to pull him outside, away from the crowd, and discover what it would be like to fill herself with that demon heat.

The song ended and he straightened.

"Come," he said. "I'll take you home."

She tried to lean into him again, but he took her elbow and steered her out to the deck. Jeremy and Lilith were already there, snuggling. When the cool air hit Dara's face, some of the fog lifted.

"You can't drive." She blinked at him. "You've been drinking." The Toyota's back seat still beckoned.

"I had one beer," he said.

She looked around the table in surprise. There was a single mug sitting in front of his chair, still half-full. "You did just have one beer." A little more fog drifted away. She frowned at him. "I don't think it's safe to go home with you. You're a demon."

"Whoa, Dara." Jeremy reared back. "That's a little harsh, don't you think? I mean, Ben is a doctor."

"Not really," she said. "He's really a demon."

Lilith chuckled. "Yeah, we saw you on the dance floor."

"No," said Dara. "He's a real demon. Nana says he was sent here from Hell to destroy me."

"Okay," Ben said, shrugging at Jeremy in a way that said these were the drunken ramblings of a woman with a grandmother who disliked him. "Time to cut you off."

She leaned across the table.

"I tried to resist," she told Lilith. "You saw that, didn't you?"

"You fought the good fight." Lilith made a fist and bumped her knuckles against Dara's.

Jeremy frowned. "Maybe we should take her home."

"I want to dance some more." Lilith nestled against him. "She'll be safe with Ben."

She wouldn't, of course, but that was okay. She didn't want to be.

CHAPTER 28

Belial walked Dara out to the parking lot, one hand cupped beneath her elbow. His erection hadn't ebbed since his fingertips first grazed her scarred collarbones. He expected his condition to abate a little once her supple body was no longer pressed against him, but it didn't. He was harder than any of the stalagmites jutting up from the floor of Ring Nine.

In ten thousand years, he couldn't recall ever reacting like this to a woman. He could only hope that, once he'd possessed her lush body, his cock would stop pulling in her direction like a dowsing rod that had located life-giving water.

Beside him, Dara stumbled. He swept her up into his arms. She put her arms around his neck and rested her head against his chest. She felt so natural there he gathered her closer. For an instant, he wished the Enemy had not chosen her as the pawn in this cosmic wager.

"I'm being carried off by a demon," she said, her tone dreamy.

He set her down and opened the car door. "And that doesn't bother you?"

She attempted to place her thumb and forefinger an inch apart but couldn't manage it. "A little bit."

"But not a lot."

"Not a lot," she agreed. "It's been a while, you know."

He gave her his most seductive smile. "I promise I'll make it worth the wait."

She pressed soft fingers against his lips. "Don't do that."

"Do what?"

"That 'I'm a sexy demon' stuff. Just be real."

He had no idea how to respond to that. It felt like she'd peeled away a layer of his identity. To cover his discomfort, he helped her into the car. She made no move to fasten her seatbelt, so he leaned across her and pushed the buckle into the catch. When he straightened, she stroked her hand down the length of his shaft, squeezing when she reached the head. He was so caught off guard he almost ejaculated right then and there.

He peeled her hand away. Her lower lip protruded in a pout that made him even more rigid.

"Just a few more minutes and you can play with it all you want," he said.

Eve's daughter that she was, she smiled at him with heavy-lidded eyes and licked her lips. It was a side to her personality he hadn't expected.

Ten minutes later, he was sitting on the leather sofa in the beach house, watching her check out the great room. Would she notice the tiny cameras DemSec had installed in the upper corners of every room? She didn't. Instead, she stared out the floor-to-ceiling windows that comprised the back of the house. He turned down the lights. Beyond the glass, stars twinkled above the ocean.

"So pretty," she said.

He stretched his arms along the back of the sofa. "I like it." He did, too. There was nothing like it in Hell, just endless vistas of rock and flames. "Now come over here."

She kicked off her shoes, leaving her several inches shorter, and crossed the room to sit beside him. He moved his arm so that it rested on her shoulders. With his other hand, he lifted her chin and stared into her eyes. She stared back, unafraid. She reminded him of a doe he'd once seen, drinking from a clear pool near Gibeah. It had looked at him with that same liquid, fearless gaze. He'd killed it with a spear and eaten its heart for breakfast.

Down in Hell, the other demons would be watching, courtesy of those cameras, raising their glasses and chanting their approval. A wave of distaste caught Belial off guard. Satan would retain the videos, of course. When the wager was over and Dara became a client, they would appear onscreen everywhere she went. And that would be only one of the humiliations Satan would heap on this favorite of the Enemy. Belial shoved any guilt away. It wasn't he who had chosen her to be the pawn in this cosmic wager.

Her eyes drifted closed and her lips slightly parted, inviting him. He kissed her, at first softly, then with more insistence. She was less enthusiastic than she'd been at the bar or in the car. He took her unresisting hand and placed it on his pulsing erection, but she didn't stroke and squeeze it.

Instead, her eyes flew open and she gasped. "Oh, no." Before he could react, she bent forward at the waist and vomited all over his shoes.

Dara woke the next morning to find herself in a strange house. She lay on a black leather couch, facing a black marble fireplace set in a bare white wall. A black afghan, so finely woven it felt like silk, draped over her.

Beyond the massive windows that made up the back wall of the house, a red sun crept above the horizon. The ocean slapped steadily onto the shore, but she couldn't smell it because the air was filled with the scent of some kind of disinfectant. She turned her head a few degrees and saw an empty bucket on the floor beside her. The surrounding carpet appeared to be clean, but wet.

Fragments of the previous evening filtered back. How many drinks had she had? She turned her head a little further and saw a second couch, set at right angles to the one she was lying on. There,

Ben slept. She muffled a groan, dragged herself to a sitting position and took inventory.

She felt a lot better than she would have expected. Her head wasn't pounding, her hands weren't shaking, and her stomach was only faintly upset. On the other hand, her mouth felt like it was filled with cotton and tasted like a garbage dump. The end table beside the couch held two bottles of water. One was nearly empty. The other was full, the seal still unbroken. She opened it, tilted it up and didn't stop drinking until it was half-empty.

Ben's eyes opened. "You're awake," he said. "How do you feel?"

"Better than I have a right to." That was true. She did feel a lot better than she should, considering how drunk she'd been. She glared at him. "What did you do? Did you use some demon trickery so I wouldn't have a hangover when I woke up?"

He sat up, and the throw that had been covering him slipped to the floor. He was wearing a pair of black silk boxer shorts.

Oh, God, what did it mean that he wasn't wearing clothes? She racked her brain but couldn't remember anything that happened after they left the bar. She still wore her sundress and could feel the elastic of her panties around her hips. And they had slept on separate couches. A whisper of something that felt like disappointment surfaced, but she buried it beneath outrage.

"Cover yourself," she snapped.

He twitched the afghan back across his lap. "Sorry. Someone threw up all over my jeans last night."

Her eyes widened. "I did that?"

"Yes, you did. I'm pretty sure you ruined a five-hundred-dollar pair of Forzieri loafers, too."

Her cheeks burned. She started to apologize until she realized what it meant that she was here, instead of safely home in her own bed.

"Serves you right for taking advantage of me," she said.

"You asked to come here."

"Because I was drunk out of my mind."

"Yes, I wanted to talk to you about that. I'm not sure Lilith is a very good companion for you."

She wanted to argue, but he had a point. It was Lilith who'd supplied her drinks. As a teenager, Dara had been pretty good at resisting peer pressure. She needed to call up some of that backbone now. She wasn't about to share those thoughts with him, so she returned to her earlier question.

"Why don't I have a hangover? What did you give me?"

He got to his feet, wrapping the afghan around his waist. "Water and ibuprofen," he said. "The biggest part of hangovers is dehydration. Once you stopped vomiting, I made you drink lots of water and take an Advil to reduce the inflammation." He spread his hands. "No black magic, just common sense."

Somewhere during his mini-lecture on the care and feeding of hangovers, she stopped listening and her mind wandered to his bare chest. It looked like something out of one of those reality shows where the men hang around the tropical island with their shirts off. Above the afghan, his abdomen displayed a grid of muscles, and his deltoids were like scoops of ice cream. She licked her lips. She might be sober, but she wasn't out of the woods yet.

She looked around for her shoes. "Take me to my car."

"Okay," he said. His gorgeous body whispered, *Stay awhile longer*.

"Now." She wiggled her foot into a ridiculous shoe she should never have bought in the first place.

He raised his hands, as if in surrender. "Can I put on some pants first?"

CHAPTER 29

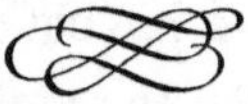

When Lilith arrived at the beach house late that afternoon, Belial was slumped on the couch, staring at the television.

"No dice, eh?" she said.

He sat up. "Where have you been?"

"At Jeremy's, making sweet, sweet love." She curled her lip. "And giving you time to do the same, or so I hoped."

"Call Dara and find out how she's feeling," he said.

She set her purse down and cocked her head to the side. "Should I ask her if she likes you likes you, or just kind of likes you as a friend?"

"How about if you're not a bitch for once and just do what I ask?"

"Tsk, tsk," Lilith said. "What if the boss hears you? What will he think?"

"The boss couldn't give a shit how demons treat each other, as long as the mission moves forward."

"Fine." Lilith pulled out her phone and called Dara. It rang once, twice, three times. She was about to give up when Dara answered, sounding sleepy and cranky.

"So," Lilith said, "how was he?"

"I'm mad at you." From her tone, Dara wasn't kidding.

"Mad at me?" Lilith pretended to be surprised. "Why are you mad at me?"

"For giving me those Long Island iced teas."

Belial could hear every word, and so could the boss. Lilith chose her response with care.

"I thought it would be good for you to loosen up a little. You've been under a lot of stress."

"And I don't appreciate you letting me go home with Ben when you know how I feel about him."

"How was I supposed to stop you? You're a grown woman."

"You could have offered to take me home yourself."

"I was as trashed as you were."

"Or suggested I call a cab."

"Dara, let's be honest here. You went home with him because you wanted to go home with him."

"You're right." Dara's anger collapsed. As Lilith anticipated, Dara's overdeveloped sense of responsibility outweighed her resentment. "It's my own fault. I could have chosen not to have that third drink. I could have chosen not to go home with him."

"You are all right, aren't you?" Lilith asked. "He didn't do anything you didn't want him to, did he?"

"I'm fine," Dara said.

"So, what exactly happened?"

"I don't want to talk about it."

Lilith suppressed a grin. Guilt and humiliation would make excellent barriers to keep Belial at arm's length. "Hey, how about if I come over and we watch that movie?"

Belial shook his head. She turned so she couldn't see him.

"I thought you didn't like sitting around watching movies," Dara said.

"I've had enough partying for one weekend."

She hung up and turned back around. Belial was glaring at her.

"It will give me a chance to talk you up," she said. Like that was going to do him any good.

"See that you do," he said. "I'll be monitoring every word."

It was unfortunate for him that most of communication was facial expression and body language.

Thirty minutes later, Lilith knocked on Dara's door, carrying a six-pack of sodas and movie-sized boxes of Goobers and Sno-Caps.

"I'm so glad you suggested this." She settled onto one end of Dara's sofa with a comfortable sigh. The movie would make it difficult for Belial and the boss to hear what was said. That didn't matter, as it turned out, because Dara nodded without saying anything. Still unforgiven, apparently.

A cat wandered in from the kitchen. He hopped up onto the couch and snuggled into Lilith's lap.

"Who is this?" Lilith rubbed him behind his crooked left ear. He rolled his head back until her hand cupped it, and purred.

"That's Milton. I can't believe he's letting you pet him. He hates everyone."

Lilith stroked her nails down his back and he moaned a little. "How can you say that? He's a sweet kitty."

Dara frowned at the cat. He shifted his head so he didn't have to see her. *I know just how you feel, buddy.*

Lilith tried again. "I've always had this thing, where I just run and run and run until I'm exhausted. Thanks for interrupting that self-destructive cycle."

Dara just nodded.

"Are you okay? From last night, I mean?" Lilith stopped petting the cat to touch Dara's scarred hand. She looked deep into her eyes, trying to convey a guilt she didn't feel. "Really okay?"

Dara sighed. Lilith sensed a thaw.

"I'm fine. Let's just watch the movie, okay?" Dara put *Ghost* in.

Ah, perfect. When the demons appeared, Lilith picked up the remote and hit the pause button. Setting Milton on the floor, she said, "Potty break." This would give Dara plenty of time to think about the demon in her own life.

When she returned from the bathroom, she sat down on the couch and leaned forward so Belial and the boss could hear her clearly.

"Okay, I have to ask you this. Why were you so upset when I called earlier? People do have sex, you know. All the time. And it's not the worst thing that ever happened to them. It's pretty clear you're attracted to him. What's the issue?"

Dara huddled into the corner of the couch, clutching a bag of microwave popcorn like a shield. "You know how I feel about him."

"I'm not sure I do." Lilith put on her puzzled face. "I know how you tell me you feel about him, but I also know what I see when I see the two of you together."

Dara went still. "What are you talking about?"

"Sparks. Fireworks. Thunder. Lightning. A woman could get singed just being in the vicinity of you two."

"Don't be ridiculous."

"I don't get how you can treat this so casually. Do you know how many people never get to experience the kind of intensity you two have? Do you know what I'd give to know a great passion? I mean, Jeremy's a nice guy and all, but he's hardly Ben Lyle. But you're determined to walk away from it." She gestured toward the frozen TV screen. "Even though you know what it's like to love someone and lose them."

Dara's face took on an expression of longing, but it was impossible to tell if she was thinking about Belial or the husband she'd lost. After a moment, the look faded, replaced by one of resolution.

"Ben Lyle isn't who you think he is," she said.

"Then who is he?"

Dara shook her head. "I don't want to get into that. But there are things... It's impossible for us to ever be together."

"With great loves, there are always things. I'm black and you're white; I'm old and you're young; I'm a Jew and you're a Muslim; we're both guys; we're both women. There's always something. But a truly heroic love can transcend that." It was a great speech. Down in the Ninth Ring, the boss would be getting a hard-on from the sheer beauty of it.

Dara's mouth twisted. "Do you read a lot of romance novels?"

Lilith shrugged. "Discount it if you want to, but there's something special between you two. Life is short. You should be grabbing that with both hands."

She could see the image of grabbing something with both hands take root in Dara's mind, but almost immediately she shook her head.

"I'm not grabbing anything. This is what's going to happen, and if you're really my friend, you'll help me: I will not spend any more time with Ben Lyle outside the clinic. If we're out and he shows up, I will leave. I don't care how rude it looks. So don't engineer any more 'chance' meetings between us."

Busted. "You're running away from your feelings."

"No." Dara pushed the button to start the movie back up. "I'm running away from Ben Lyle."

CHAPTER 30

Belial pulled into the clinic parking lot on Monday morning and blew out a long breath. He would have to play it cool. It would take only a tiny misstep on his part for Dara to banish him from the clinic altogether. With just thirteen days left in the wager, he didn't have time to regain lost ground.

Inside, he pushed the buzzer and glanced around the lobby. In the far corner, two little boys had their heads together, whispering like they were plotting something. He didn't see a parent with them. Something about them set his demon senses tingling, but before he could investigate, Gabby buzzed him in.

He went to one of the computers on the Pit counter and pulled up his patient list. He was scheduled to see three children.

Dara appeared at his elbow. Her jaw was set. He nodded at the screen. "Not many patients."

He kept his tone businesslike and saw her relax as she realized he wasn't planning to bring up the events of the weekend.

"The pediatric clinic is always light," she said. "We mostly see immigrants or recent arrivals to the area."

Belial stifled a feeling of regret. He'd grown used to seeing thirty or forty patients a day. "Makes sense," he said. "Shall we take a look at our first patient?"

The first two patients were routine—strep throat and a case of poison ivy. The third was more interesting. The little boy sitting on the table was perhaps five years old. His face was flushed, and his eyes had the dull glaze of fever. His mother stood beside him, holding his hand, her face drawn with worry.

"This is Timmy Gonzales," Dara said.

"How are his vitals?"

"Blood pressure of ninety-five over seventy, fever of a hundred and three."

"We need to get that down. I'm going to look at your throat," he told the boy. "Okay?"

The child nodded. Then he opened his mouth and coughed into Belial's face.

His mother apologized, but Belial waved her aside. "Happens all the time."

The boy's tonsils appeared normal, but his lymph nodes were swollen. Belial lifted his shirt to reveal a rash. "We'll need to take a blood test to confirm, but this looks like chickenpox." The mother's thin face sagged with relief.

Belial washed his hands and left Dara to obtain the blood sample. As he exited the exam room, the two boys he'd seen in the lobby earlier came out of the patient bathroom. He tried to cut them off, but they dodged past him, giggling as they ran for the front door. He'd gotten the closer look he needed to verify his earlier suspicion.

They were imps.

Just as demons had once been angels, imps had their beginnings as cherubs. Created tiny, they would never grow in size. Since they'd fallen, they'd never outgrown their love of pranks.

He opened his mouth to order them to halt, but Dara was in the next room. If she found demons of any kind in the clinic, she'd blame him. He'd started to follow them when a gleam caught his eye. Water seeped beneath the bathroom door, pooling on the tile floor.

The toilet was overflowing. The single bright spot was that the water was clear. Whatever they'd done was less disgusting than what they might have done. He reached behind the toilet and turned the shut-off valve. The water ceased cascading over the rim, but something prevented it from receding.

He looked for a plunger but didn't find one. Beneath the sink was a pair of elbow-length rubber gloves. He took off his lab jacket and hung it on the door. After rolling up his shirt sleeves, he donned the gloves. They were a tight fit, meant for feminine hands, but he managed to drag them on.

He crouched beside the toilet and, with a grimace of disgust, plunged his arm into the bowl. Something lay just beyond the reach of his fingers. He pushed his arm in a little further. Cold water seeped inside the glove and down his arm. Ugh. Lilith was undoubtedly behind this.

"I hate demons," he said to the toilet tank. He pushed his arm in a little deeper. More water invaded the glove, but his fingers closed around something squishy. He pulled it out. It was a dead frog. "I really, really hate demons."

"And you're not alone."

Dara stood in the doorway. A recessed light bulb in the ceiling backlit her like a halo. She held the spray bottle of holy water in one hand and the baggie of demonweed in the other, clearly prepared to smite him, hip and thigh. She glared at the frog corpse in his gloved hand. "I warned you about releasing any more plagues in my clinic."

Damn Lilith to the Ninth Ring of Hell and back. She hadn't brought in the frog herself, but he was willing to bet his promotion she'd recruited the imps who did. And no matter what he said, Dara would blame him, which meant that the boss would be pissed, not at Lilith, but at him.

He got to his feet. His pant legs stuck to his shins. Somehow he'd managed to soak his pants as well as his shirt. With toilet water. He could feel his temper slipping its leash. He'd been endlessly patient with Dara, but he was tired of being falsely accused while she continued to pal around with the real author of her problems.

"If I were planning a prank," he said, his voice vibrating with frustration, "would I choose one that involves sticking my arm in a toilet?"

She didn't respond to that. He got a tiny amount of satisfaction from the fact that he'd stumped her. He tossed the dead frog into the trash can, washed his hands like he was prepping for surgery and put on his lab coat.

"And now for the hate of all that's holy," he said, "can we just finish this clinic so I can go home and shower?"

"You can't see patients when you're soaked in toilet water," Dara said crisply. "I'll finish up with Timmy."

She looked him in the eye and there was no mistaking the triumph in her gaze.

"You're done here," she said.

CHAPTER 31

Over lunch the next day, Dara dropped by to see Nana. It was rare for her to miss a Sunday visit, but after what she'd nearly done Saturday night, she was so ashamed she skipped the next two days.

"What's wrong?" Nana asked as soon as Dara walked in the door. Well, at least she didn't say, *What have you done?*

Dara told her about the frog in the toilet.

"I told you that demon would bring your clinic no good." Nana smiled grimly. "Now you can finally throw him out."

But Dara had had time to think since Ben's exit from the clinic the previous evening. "What will I tell my board? I'm mad that he unclogged our toilet?"

Nana's mouth opened, but nothing came out. She didn't have an answer, either. Fear washed yellow into her skin and brought all her wrinkles out in sharp relief, making her look all of her ninety-four years. She twisted her hands together like she would wring a solution from them. This was the worst part—what the demon assault was doing to Nana.

"Besides," Dara said, "I'm not sure it was him. He was so frustrated. And it's like he said—he worked so hard to get into the clinic. Why would he throw it all away for a childish prank? It's almost like someone is trying to keep him from completing his mission."

Nana sat upright in her recliner. "I hope that someone is you."

"Someone besides me." Dara hated to frighten her grandmother any more than she already was, but she needed help. "Is it possible that there's a rival demon involved?"

"Lord save us." Nana groped for her ruby cross, but it was hanging around Dara's neck. "You think there are others?"

Dara described Ben's reaction to the frog.

"He truly didn't seem to be behind it," she said. "But someone is."

"You need to close that place down. Today. Don't even set foot under that roof again. If Satan has unleashed his minions there, it isn't safe for you or anyone else."

Only seventeen days remained in the demon doctor's mission to "observe healthcare." With his presence limited to the pediatric clinics, he'd see maybe a dozen patients. Less, if Dara added another doctor to the roster. In fact, using this strategy, she could stop him seeing any patients at all.

"I'm not going to do that, Nana. Tell me again what plagues are left."

"You've had lice, locusts, frogs and that raccoon. That leaves blood, boils, hail, darkness, pestilence and death of the firstborn."

That final one hung between them. Every firstborn who came into the clinic was at risk. Even before the frog, Dara had begun double-checking the new box on the medical history form, routing them to another doctor if they were the firstborn in their families. She had thought the other volunteers were safe, but if a second demon were involved, she'd need to screen every single practitioner.

She told Nana about moving Ben to the peds clinic, and about adding the birth order question to the patient history form.

"It won't keep them from targeting someone, but at least we'll know who's most at risk," she said.

Nana wasn't buying it. "Why in the world would you bring that demon into the children's clinic?"

"Children are at no more risk than adults. Old or young, a firstborn is a firstborn."

Nana squeezed the arms of her chair. "But their innocence makes them more of a target for Satan. How would you feel if someone had placed your baby in Satan's crosshairs?"

Dara sucked in a shocked breath. Nana was using her lost child against her.

But Nana was uncompromising. "Well?" she asked.

"Not good, obviously," Dara said. "But if I put the demon in an adult clinic, he's going to see a dozen patients a night, minimum. If something pulls me away, he could wind up seeing them without supervision. In the peds clinic, he'll see one or two kids, and I can be sure of being in the room the whole time. And I can add a second doctor to that clinic. That way, I can keep him from seeing any firstborn children."

After a long moment, Nana nodded.

On the way back to the clinic, Dara walked through what happened the night before, step by step. When Ben denied responsibility for putting the frog down the toilet, she'd assumed he was lying because he got caught. The more she thought about it, though, that didn't make sense. There was already a substantial amount of water on the floor when she walked up. The frog must have gone into the toilet while they were with the Gonzales boy.

Unless demons had the ability to levitate frogs into toilets from another room while simultaneously examining a patient, Ben wasn't to blame.

She exited the highway, aware that she was far more relieved than the situation warranted. For some reason, the demon she knew worried her more than the demon she didn't.

What demonic purpose did these plagues serve? Were they intended to intimidate her? That was another problem with holding Ben responsible. If he had succeeded in hiding the frog, she would never have known about it. That toilet backed up all the time because patients flushed paper towels down it. She wouldn't have thought twice about it if she hadn't seen the frog. A plague she wasn't even aware of had no intimidation value. That suggested he was telling the truth.

When she'd first come upon him, he was muttering something about hating demons. He could have known she was there and said it for her benefit, but she didn't think so. What she'd heard was his frustration that another demon was horning in on his territory, upsetting his mission.

She stopped for a red light and her heart sank a little at the thought of that mission. Why was she trying to convince herself that he didn't have it in for the clinic? He was a demon, and a demon's nature was to cause misery and heartache.

At the front desk, she stopped to talk to Gabby. "Can you give me the names of everyone who was in the clinic last night while Dr. Lyle and I were with Timmy Gonzales?"

Gabby pulled up the patient list. To Dara's disappointment, there were no names she wasn't already aware of.

"And there were those two little boys," Gabby said.

"What little boys?"

"They said their mother was out in the car, but I never did see her. They asked to use the bathroom, but when they came back out, they disappeared."

Bingo. "How old were they?"

"I don't know. We never got patient cards on them. I'd guess maybe ten. Why?"

Dara forced a smile. "I think they put a frog down the toilet."

Gabby shook her head. "What a pair of imps."

She didn't know the half of it.

At her desk, Dara tried to figure out what to do. It looked less and less like Ben was behind the frog incident. Did that mean he wasn't behind the other plagues, either? But if it wasn't him, who could it be? Was it someone she knew? Through the clinic, she met dozens of new people every week. It didn't even have to be a demon, she supposed, although the timing seemed too coincidental for it to be a human playing pranks.

She pulled up her contacts list and scrolled through it. They fell into four groups: volunteers, board members, vendors and donors. None had been in the clinic the night before. Most were people she'd known for years. With many, she knew their parents.

Except for Lilith Rojas.

She was a new person in Dara's life, and she'd come on the scene, out of the blue, at the same time Ben appeared. She frequently tried to tempt Dara into doing things that were unwise—drinking, buying sexy clothes, going off with Ben. It was easy to picture her as a demon.

The problem was that Lilith had passed the spilled-grains test, and Nana said it was reliable.

Dara gnawed her lip. What if it wasn't reliable? Lilith was smart. Maybe she'd used some kind of hypnosis on Dara so she wouldn't see her count.

There was one other way to identify a demon, but it involved some risk. If she made Lilith mad enough, she could check her pupils. She thought about the lice and the locusts and the raccoon and the frog. If she didn't put a stop to these plagues, they were only going to get worse.

She picked up the phone and dialed Lilith's number. "I need some ideas for fundraisers. How about joining me for lunch? I'll buy."

At Crab Louie's, a Cajun seafood bistro by the shore, Dara asked for a seat out on the patio. The light would be better there. Lilith was dressed in a black silk suit with an ivory shell and chunky accent pieces that looked like they might be real gold. A squirt of catsup in her direction would wreck that beautiful shell. Given Lilith's reverence for clothes, that should be enough to set her off.

"It's going to be hot out there," Lilith said.

"They have an awning. I'd really like to be outside. You can take your jacket off." She'd make an easier target that way. Dara tried not to think about what this would do to their friendship if Lilith wasn't a demon after all.

Lilith rolled her eyes. "Fine."

Once they were seated, Lilith ordered a salad, while Dara asked for a cheeseburger and fries. Lilith surveyed her in surprise. "What's that about?"

Dara shrugged. "Sometimes you get a craving." And sometimes you needed catsup to use as a weapon.

"You're in a weird mood." Lilith slipped off her jacket, revealing tiny cap sleeves with black embroidery on her silk shell.

What if Lilith wasn't a demon? What if Dara defaced Lilith's beautiful blouse for no reason? The thought made her feel a little ill. Well, she'd just have to apologize and pay for the damage.

Lilith noticed her gaze. "Do you like it? I just spent a week's pay on it."

It would take one of Dara's entire paychecks to cover for the damage, but she couldn't just let the plagues continue unabated. She cleared her throat. "About that fundraiser..."

Lilith held up her hand. "Before we get started on that, I want to talk about doing a spa day."

"A spa day?"

"You know, a day where you check into a resort and they pamper you."

"Sounds expensive." Especially if Dara had to replace an expensive blouse.

Lilith pulled a slip of paper from her purse. "I happen to have a two-for-one coupon for Exhilaration."

Exhilaration was a trendy new spa that had recently opened in a high-end shopping complex near the golf course and Slyders.

"Even with a coupon—"

"I already made us an appointment for Saturday," Lilith said. "I'm going whether you do or not, so the money is already spent. Come on —join me."

"Only if I can pay my half." *And you pass my demon test.*

"Deal," said Lilith. She picked up her phone and began typing. After a few minutes, she nodded in satisfaction. "I set us up for hot stone massages, facials and mani-pedis."

The waiter brought their food.

Dara picked up the squeeze bottle from the table and aimed it at her fries. At the last second, she jerked and squirted catsup directly at Lilith's blouse. It landed dead center, a bright red stain blooming like a gunshot wound in the middle of Lilith's chest.

Lilith reared back, grabbing for a napkin and dabbing furiously. "What the hell, Dara?"

Dara inspected her eyes. Even in the midday light of the patio, her irises were so dark that it was difficult to differentiate between iris and pupil. From what Dara could see, though, they appeared to be round.

Maybe Lilith wasn't mad enough.

"There must be something wrong with that catsup bottle." Dara picked it up and squirted again. Bullseye.

"Damn it, Dara." Lilith's face turned red. "What the fuck?"

Dara leaned across the table to get a better view. Lilith's face was scarlet with rage. Her teeth were clenched and her eyes were narrowed, but her pupils remained perfectly round. Perfectly human.

It didn't make sense. There were too many clues, too many coincidences. She had to be a demon. In for a penny, in for a pound. Dara squeezed the catsup bottle again, this time aiming at Lilith's face.

Lilith fended off the flow of tomato sauce with her napkin, causing it to splatter.

"What is wrong with you?" she screamed, but her eyes didn't change.

She wasn't a demon.

With a sick sense of horror, Dara surveyed the destruction she'd caused. Lilith's blouse, jewelry and face dripped catsup. Now that she'd passed the test, Dara felt terrible.

"I am so sorry," she said, wincing. "I don't know what came over me. I'll pay for your blouse."

Without speaking, Lilith tossed her catsup-stained napkin down on the table and stalked across the restaurant to the ladies' room.

Inside the ladies' room, Lilith removed her blouse and rinsed it under the tap. She loaded some liquid soap onto a paper towel and pressed it against the fibers.

Just wait until she got that little bitch down to Hell. No client had ever received the treatment she'd give Dara. She'd heap on the humiliation. No torment was too painful, no task too degrading. She was even willing to shepherd the vapid little twit into Belial's bed, if that was what it took.

His bedroom at the beach house had strategically placed cameras. One day soon, Dara would watch a porno reel of herself fucking a demon. Lilith could barely contain her glee.

She checked her eyes in the mirror. The contact lenses she'd gotten from DemSec had worked as intended. They obscured her rage and gave her the innocent round pupils of a mortal.

You had to love technology.

Lilith was gone a good thirty minutes, leaving Dara to realize just how badly she'd screwed up. She'd alienated the one person who seemed to be in her corner.

When Lilith got back to the table, her jaw was still taut with anger. She bent to pick up her purse without speaking.

"I am so sorry," Dara said again. "Let me make it up to you. I'll replace your blouse. Let me pay for our spa day. I don't know what came over me."

For a long moment, Lilith remained frozen in position. Then she straightened and shook her head. A grin broke over her face. "You are one crazy bitch, you know that?"

Dara ducked her head. Five weeks ago, no one would have ever described her that way. "Are we still friends?"

Lilith gave her a broad smile. "Honey, we are so much more than friends."

CHAPTER 32

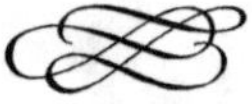

Belial arrived in Ring Nine to find Satan's office door closed.

"You can take a seat," Andras said. "It will be a few minutes."

"Why did he call me down here if he doesn't have time to see me?" Belial dropped into one of the chairs lining the wall behind Andras's desk and wiped sweat off his forehead. The heat was bothering him more than usual. Why had he allowed Bad to blend in still more human genes? He would soon be more human than demon.

"Lord Satan is a very busy demon," Andras said without looking up from the letter she was typing.

He picked up a copy of *Modern Demon* and fanned himself. Bad was on the cover. "The Face of Tomorrow," ran the blurb beneath it. That didn't improve Belial's mood any.

"He's been crazy all week," Andras said. "Because of the interviews."

He stopped fanning. "Interviews? For what?"

She turned her head one hundred and eighty degrees to look at him. "Chief executive demon."

That was his job. He wanted to voice his outrage, but he couldn't summon the energy. He'd actually been expecting this. The boss had written him off and was just waiting for the time limit for the wager to expire before executing him.

Satan's office door opened and Bad strolled out. He hitched his chin in greeting but didn't speak.

Andras jerked her feathered head back to her computer screen. Apparently it wasn't safe to be seen conversing with Belial.

"There you are." Satan appeared in the doorway, looking annoyed, like he was the one who'd been kept waiting.

Belial stood, more weary than he could remember feeling in his entire existence.

Inside the office, Satan parked his skinny butt on the corner of his ebony desk and motioned for Belial to take a seat. Even though he knew the order was intended to give Satan the height advantage, Belial was grateful. He wasn't sure how long he could stay on his feet.

Satan looked him up and down and spat on the floor. "Give me one reason why I shouldn't call it quits and tell the Enemy he's won."

Belial's head ached. Another flaw in this thrice-damned identity. These frailties had to be deliberate. No doubt they represented Bad's best shot at the CED position. "It's not over until it's over."

Satan received that cliché with the disgust it deserved. "Do you even have a plan? Even a glimmer of an idea how you're going to close this?"

Belial had had an idea, but his head was aching so badly he couldn't think of it.

Satan tapped his front tooth with a talon. "Maybe we can get Lilith to lure her out, try the alcohol route again."

"I don't think that's a good idea." Although Belial had enjoyed seeing Dara lose her inhibitions, he hadn't liked the idea of having sex with her in that condition. It had been almost a relief when she'd spewed vomit all over his shoes. "This wager is about free will. Getting her drunk deprives her of her ability to choose."

Satan snarled. "Do you have a better idea?"

"I was thinking about doing some kind of fundraiser, to show her I mean the clinic no harm."

Satan rolled his eyes. "Money again? Been there, done that. Don't you have anything new?"

"I just need to get her alone."

Satan sneered. "Been there, too."

"This time I'll make sure she's not on the edge of alcohol poisoning."

"How do you propose to do that? She told Lilith she wants nothing to do with you."

Belial frowned. He'd had a plan. What was it? His head felt like a thousand anvils being struck by a thousand hammers. "I've made arrangements to start seeing patients at Mercy Care. That will put me in her path."

"The smell of liniment and urine aren't conducive to seduction."

Before he could formulate a response, his phone buzzed. It was a text from Dara. Pleasure zinged through him.

I need to talk to you. Can you meet me?

She wanted to see him. Warmth that had nothing to do with his surroundings filled him.

"What have you got to smile about?" Satan growled.

Both his horns spouted smoke, bringing Belial's attention back to the present. *Bless you, woman, you just saved my ass.* He showed the text to the boss, who pinched his lower lip and nodded.

Belial typed back: *Sure. Slyders?*

The response was almost immediate. *Nowhere with alcohol or food.*

Hallelujah, she'd finally wised up. *Where?*

Public parking lot, Alexandria Beach, 6 p.m.

He typed, *See you then*, and hit send.

"You can go back," Satan said.

With Belial's pounding head, it took a minute for that to sink in. Before Dara's text arrived, the boss hadn't planned to let him return Aboveworld. He dragged himself to his feet and trudged toward the door.

His hand was on the doorknob when the boss's voice stopped him. "Demon?"

Belial turned around, trying to look sharp and like he was on top of things. All he could think about, though, was how much he wanted to drink a glass of ice water and crawl into bed. For a delirious moment, he imagined Dara applying a cooling cloth to his head.

"Don't fuck this up," Satan said.

It was less of a warning than a promise.

It took all the concentration Belial could muster to drive up the Rings without putting the Hyundai in a ditch. Like his front wheels, his mind kept wandering. He found himself thinking, for the first time in many centuries, about his life before the Fall.

Heaven was a place of sunlight and blue skies. Soft music from harps and wind chimes played in the background. And having wings had been amazing. He imagined he could feel them again, sprouting from his shoulder blades. If he'd had any idea that signing on with Sataniel would mean giving up his wings, he would never have done it.

He'd been a complete fool, buying the line of Sataniel. How devastated he'd been when he arrived in Hell and discovered the grand stories of the new organization were outright lies. The Enemy had staked out all the good territory. All that was left for Satan's new empire was the bad.

For the first few centuries, Belial took out his disappointment on the mortals with whom he came into contact, both above and below. Every life he touched, he made miserable. But being evil grew stale. He switched to a model of doing his work with a maximum of efficiency and a minimum of carnage. His machinelike competence impressed the boss even more. So began his ascent through Hell's hierarchy. Eventually he rose to where he was now, the level just below the boss that he shared with the demons of sloth, lust and greed. Where it now appeared he would end his days, if Satan's threats were to be believed.

He pulled onto the exit ramp to Aboveworld and thought of Dara in the little sundress she'd worn Saturday night. Her beautiful scarred collarbones were on display above, her dynamite legs below.

He remembered the day she'd brought him to meet her grandmother. She'd stopped to help the old man down the hall. Not for any personal gain, but because she was made that way. He'd doubted it at the time, but her behavior since then—her affection for her staff, her visits to her grandmother, which couldn't always be very pleasant, the sacrifices she made to keep her clinic open and available to the poor—proved she was sincere. Loving others as herself—no, loving others *more* than herself—was built into her as much as those shapely legs and elegant clavicles. She was the most amazing woman he'd ever met.

He got to the beach parking lot fifteen minutes early, so he made a side jaunt to a convenience store. There, he purchased two bottles of cold water, one to drink and the other to press against his forehead. He tried to drum up some anger at Bad for sabotaging his identity in order to steal his job, but he couldn't come up with the energy. He just hoped Dara wouldn't make him walk very far.

He had emptied the first bottle and broken the seal on the second when her rust bucket Corolla pulled in beside the Hyundai. He crawled out of the car. He had to lean against the door for a moment before drawing himself upright and giving her what he hoped was a devastating smile. She was wearing her usual flamingo-pink nursing scrubs. They offered a tantalizing glimpse of her collarbones.

When she saw him, her eyes narrowed, but she didn't say anything. With a thrust of her jaw, she indicated she wanted to walk on the beach. Without a word, she set off across the asphalt toward the boardwalk. Stifling a groan, he followed her. At the bottom of the steps, she kicked off her clogs and stepped out onto the sand.

He slipped off his deck shoes and tried to follow, but the sand was like something out of Hell. The sun was low on the horizon, but the pulverized quartz was still hot as lava. It shifted beneath his bare feet at every step, making him fight to stay vertical. On about his fifth step, he lost his balance and fell flat.

It was even hotter on his face than it had been on his feet, but he couldn't summon the energy to get back up. With effort, he rolled onto his back and stared at the sky. It was a clear cerulean blue, truly worthy to be the underside of Paradise. He was glad he'd gotten one last chance to see it before Satan executed him.

In the distance, Dara exclaimed, "Oh, for heaven's sake." Then she was there, looming over him, blocking his view of the celestial subfloor. "What are you doing?"

He didn't have an answer for that, so he didn't attempt one.

She bent to look at him more closely. Her eyes narrowed. She put her hand on his forehead.

"You're burning up."

The palm of her hand was cool and soft and smooth. For a moment, it felt like he was back in Heaven. He turned his head and coughed into his elbow.

Her jaw dropped. "Are you...sick?"

"Demons don't get sick," he mumbled.

"Then what do you call this?" She waved at his prostrate body.

He groaned. "I don't know. I've never felt like this before. Is this what being sick feels like?"

Biting her lip, she studied him. "Tell me your symptoms."

"My skin feels like I'm on fire. My head is pounding. And my muscles ache like I've been on the rack." He coughed again.

She looked him up and down, frowning. Then she tilted her head and said, "Oh. My. God."

Without asking permission, she lifted the hem of his shirt and looked at his belly. Then she laughed.

He wished Satan had just executed him and gotten it over with. "What's so funny?"

"I think you've got chickenpox."

He struggled up onto one elbow. "What?"

"You've got chickenpox. You must have contracted them from the Gonzales boy."

"Demons don't get chickenpox." He tried for his usual hauteur, but it came out sounding more like a whine.

"This one did. And fast, too. It usually takes ten days to two weeks to develop." She studied him again. "Did they equip your—what did you call it? identity?— with immunity to human diseases?"

"I don't know."

Dara helped him to a sitting position. "Let's get you to the clinic and find out how bad your fever is."

"I don't want you to get sick, too."

She stared at him, as though he'd said something odd. Then she said, "I've been vaccinated. I won't get them."

He stumbled to his feet. Leaning on her shoulder, he made his way back to the boardwalk, feeling worse every minute. By the time they reached the foot of the stairs, the four steps to the walkway looked like Mt. Ararat.

Dara bent over to retrieve their shoes. "You can do it."

Hand over hand on the rail, he dragged himself up the steps. With Dara's support, he managed to navigate the quarter-mile boardwalk to the parking lot. At the end of the wooden walkway, he collapsed onto a built-in bench.

She knelt in front of him and lifted his foot, brushing the sand off. Her hands were cool and gentle. Then she slipped his shoe back on. From where he was sitting, he could see down the neckline of her scrubs to her scarred collarbones and round breasts, but he couldn't even summon any lust.

"Why are you helping me?" he asked.

She shook her head. "I couldn't tell you. I'm still furious about Saturday night."

"Yeah, I'm sorry about that," he said.

Her hand stilled on his foot. "What did you say?"

"I said I was sorry."

She stared at him, frowning, her eyes searching his.

"What?" he asked.

She shook her head. "Let's get you someplace and take your temp."

CHAPTER 33

By the time Dara got Ben back to the car, she realized she couldn't take him to the clinic. Even without a thermometer, she could tell that the amount of heat he was putting out didn't fall within normal human ranges. However much his identity might look like a human body, it wasn't one. For the same reason, she couldn't take him to the hospital.

His beach house was less than a mile away, but she headed for her condo instead. The idea of caring for a sick demon, whose physiology she knew nothing about, was overwhelming enough without trying to work in an unfamiliar location. He sat in the passenger seat, his eyes closed and his head lolling against the headrest.

Why was she going to so much trouble? Throughout the drive, she kept asking herself that. There was no question that the world, especially her world, would be a safer, better place without him. But as she looked at him, slumped in the passenger seat, a five o'clock shadow shading his beautiful jaw, his eyelashes inscribing dark crescents against his flushed cheeks, she couldn't do it.

And then there was his apology. Nana said demons couldn't apologize, but he had. Twice. Could Nana have been wrong?

At her condo, she pulled into the garage and lowered the garage door so that none of the neighbors would see him get out of her car. Alexandria was a small town, and the last thing she needed was for the rumor mill to go crazy with stories of the Widow Strong bringing home the gorgeous doctor who gave her clinic two hundred and fifty thousand dollars.

He was so limp she had to support him as he stumbled into the house. It was like being draped with a huge, sweaty tarp. She led him to the couch, where he sat down and looked around. She would have suspected him of doing demon reconnaissance, but he didn't seem to be taking in his surroundings.

"Go ahead and lie down," she said. He toppled over sideways. She took off his shoes and lifted his feet onto the sofa. There were still grains of sand clinging to his soles.

She retrieved an oral thermometer from the bathroom medicine cabinet, poured rubbing alcohol over it and rinsed it under the tap.

When she got back to the living room, Milton had jumped up on the couch and was sniffing Ben's breath. He must have liked what he smelled, because he kneaded the couch cushion in front of Ben's head with his front paws and curled up there. Ben was so out of it that he didn't even react.

She scooped Milton out of the way and set him on the floor. He gave an offended meow and stalked out of the room, tail in the air. She stuck the thermometer in Ben's mouth. Three minutes later, when she took it out, it simply read "H." He was off the scale.

He lay very still. He hadn't even moved when Milton sniffed him. He seemed to be barely conscious. What should she do? She needed some way to measure the effects of any actions she took.

After a moment, she went into the kitchen and located her candy thermometer. She repeated the routine with the rubbing alcohol and tap water before putting the bulb under his tongue. When she pulled it back out, it read 120 degrees. His physiology was definitely one she knew nothing about.

What next? She could give him acetaminophen, but what if it poisoned him? She turned on the ceiling fan and sponged him down, but the water dried as soon as it touched his heated skin.

Then she remembered a method that worked with small children when they had high fevers: letting them play in a bathtub of lukewarm water. She went back into the bathroom and turned on the taps.

When the water got deep enough, she woke him. "Let's get you into some cool water."

He bolted to a sitting position. His eyes were wild. "Not the lake."

She laid a comforting hand on his arm. "Of course not the lake." What lake was he talking about? She tugged on his wrist.

He tried to crawl backward to get away from her.

"Just a bathtub," she said, making her voice as soothing as possible. "A bathtub filled with cool water, to bring your fever down."

He stopped trying to crabwalk away from her. "A bathtub?"

"It will help cool you." She half led, half dragged him to the bathroom. There they encountered another issue. She didn't want him to get into the water in his clothes, but she felt awkward about undressing him.

"Can you take your shirt off for me?"

He pulled his polo shirt over his head, swaying as he did so.

"That's it," she said. "Now your pants."

He unbuttoned his khakis and dropped them to the floor. He was down to a pair of burgundy silk boxers like the black ones he'd worn Saturday morning, after he tried to seduce her.

If she'd ever entertained any idea of sleeping with him, the semi-nude body in front of her was enough to put an end to that. His torso was shaped like a funnel, with the emphasis on fun. Every inch of him rippled with muscles, and his skin, the parts that weren't speckled with blisters, looked like satin. There was no way she would ever allow her own scarred body to be contrasted with this work of art. Then she realized he still had his shorts on.

"I'm a nurse," she said. "I've seen men's butts before."

Turning away from her, he shucked off his boxers, standing on the fabric with one foot while he pulled the other free, holding on to the shower curtain for support. She breathed out a tiny sigh. She'd seen men's butts before, but never one as fine as this one. Her eyes traveled upward and she sucked in her breath. Both of his scapulae bore jagged scars. It looked as though a part of him had been torn away.

"My wings," he said, bowing his head.

Her heart twisted with horror.

"Let's get you into the water." She took his elbow and helped him into the tub.

He sat down and relaxed against the slanted end of the tub. She tried to ignore his penis, bobbing in the water. She'd fantasized about seeing him naked more than once, but she'd never imagined it would be under these circumstances. She glanced up to find him watching her. Her cheeks flamed. A smile touched the corners of his lips, but he didn't say anything. Instead, he closed his eyes and rolled his head back against the lip of the tub, as though he were exhausted.

After twenty minutes in the water, he seemed a little more alert. She checked his temp,

"You're down to a hundred and six," she said. "Unfortunately, I didn't know what your normal temperature runs."

"Hand me my phone. I'll text Bad and find out."

It was good to see him more aware, but... "Bad?"

"Abaddon—the demon in charge of mission identities."

She debated refusing, but her medical training was too ingrained to let her fly blind as she attempted to treat a patient, demon though he might be.

"This is a one-time thing." She fished his phone out of his pants pocket and handed him a towel to dry his hands. "It is not a precedent."

He nodded and tapped the screen. A moment later, he said, "Normal temp is ninety-eight point six."

That made sense. An identity designed to be intimate with a human would need a human body temperature.

"He said not to worry about the fever—the identities are designed to withstand temperatures in Hell."

"Can you take acetaminophen?"

He texted again. "I can take it, but it won't do any good."

"Thank goodness the tub works, then."

But, of course, goodness had nothing to do with it.

After she got him out of the tub, she went back to straighten up the bathroom and saw his cell phone. She considered smashing it, as she had his last one, but what if she needed another medical consult? After a few minutes' careful thought, she carried the cell phone to the kitchen and sealed it in a plastic baggie. After verifying Ben was asleep, she got in the car and drove the phone to his house, where she tucked it beneath a shrub.

She straightened and looked at the house. This was the place where Ben had come so close to seducing her. The memory was a little hazy, but what she did remember made her squeeze her thighs together and bite her lip. She almost wished he'd succeeded.

By the time the next morning rolled around, they'd gone through three more rounds of tub time, each of them a little less effective than the one before. During the most recent cycle, Dara dumped all the ice cubes from her freezer into the water. Ben shivered like he had ague, but the ice was almost melted before his temperature nudged downward.

Despite the tech demon's lack of concern, Ben's fever spikes worried her. He had no immunity to human maladies. When new diseases entered the biosphere, it wasn't unusual for them to prove fatal to large numbers of humans.

He said he was immortal, but what if she, through her inept nursing, was the first person to ever kill a demon? What if she did it on purpose? Would God reward her? Or would it be a sin, like killing another human?

The thought of losing him disturbed her far more deeply than it should have. Nana would have viewed his death as a win over the demon hordes, but it didn't feel that way to Dara. Over the past few weeks, she'd felt alive in a way she hadn't in years. Despite her worries about the clinic, she'd come to look forward to their verbal jousting. His obvious desire for her had made her feel…desirable.

On Wednesday, she called into the clinic and told them she'd picked up a bug from one of the patients and wouldn't be in for the rest of the week.

When his temperature was down and he was lucid, they talked.

"What was it like, having wings?" she asked.

He hesitated, then pantomimed a listening ear.

"I took your phone to your house," she said.

He pointed at her and cocked his head.

She turned off her phone, then carried it into the bedroom and stuck it beneath her mattress. When she returned, she told him what she'd done.

He looked around the room, his face still worried.

"I don't have a computer," she said.

Then his eyes fell on her television, an old analog set she'd never bothered to replace. A tiny smile curled his lips and his shoulders relaxed.

"Wings were incredible." His face filled with longing so intense her chest ached in sympathy. "Imagine being able to soar and see the Earth drop away beneath you, to glide and feel the currents holding you up. We had this game where we'd dive into the ocean, deep, deep, deep, and then shoot straight up, spraying water everywhere. The sun would catch the droplets and make them sparkle, like a shower of diamonds."

Except for a single blister between his dark eyebrows, his face was free of the disfiguring pox. Memories of his time as an angel made it radiant. She caught her breath at the sheer beauty of his features. Why had he abandoned all that? Why hadn't he remained on the side of good?

Not that it made any difference. In one guise, he was off-limits. In the other, out of reach.

"If DemSec can make you into a doctor, why can't they fix your scars?"

"The scars are supernatural wounds, symbols of our betrayal."

"The God I was brought up on is generous with forgiveness."

"'To him whom much is given, much is required.'"

"You're saying God gave angels a lot more power than he gave humans, so he expected more of them?"

"That's always been my belief. Or maybe he just mellowed over time. Despite what the televangelists say, no one really knows what's in his mind."

Then his temperature rose again, and soon he was tossing and muttering about that lake.

The next day was more of the same. Dara snatched sleep whenever she could, wondering what she would do if the tub stopped working. How would she explain a dead body in her bathtub? Especially when an autopsy revealed that body to be other than human? She made broth for him, taking far too much pleasure in his gratitude when she spooned it into his mouth.

On Thursday, she called Mercy Care and asked for Nana.

"Where have you been, girl?" Nana's worried voice filled Dara with guilt.

"I caught a bug from one of the patients. I don't want to give it to you."

"What's going on with that demon?"

"I don't know," she lied. It was better than having Nana fret herself into a stroke.

She got off the phone with promises to take care of herself and come visit as soon as possible.

"What was it like in Heaven, before you fell?" she asked Ben the next time he was clearheaded.

He grew wistful. "It was very beautiful, very serene. God doesn't allow any bad juju in Heaven. It's also very structured. Everyone has an assigned role."

"What was your role?"

"I was a Virtue. I helped humans realize their dreams." He sounded sad.

"Why did you leave?"

"I was ambitious. I wanted to be more than I was, and I knew that would never happen there. I saw Heaven as a very unfair place, where some got rewarded while others didn't."

"But you don't think that anymore?"

"I think God knew I had it within me to betray him, long before I ever did."

"That's how Nana and Granddad saw God," Dara said, "as totally omniscient."

"You don't believe that?"

"I've always been a little skeptical. If he knows everything before it ever happens, doesn't that pretty much eliminate free will?"

"Good question," said Ben.

"And if he's omniscient, why didn't he see what Sataniel was about to do?"

"Everyone has their blind spots."

The next time, she asked, "What's it like, working for Satan?"

"About like you'd think."

"You mean awful."

He shrugged. "It has its pros and cons."

"Tell me one good thing about it."

"I'm a better poker player than he is." He looked smug, shades of the old cocky Ben.

"And you're proud of that? I guess you take what you can get."

"Not everyone has the luxury of being self-employed and not answering to anyone."

"Are you kidding? Being self-employed means answering to everyone."

He shrugged. "I guess you take what you can get."

Another time, he asked about Matthew. "Did you love him very much?"

"I did," she said. "He was a wonderful man and a wonderful doctor and a wonderful husband."

"And yet you can only spare a single adjective to describe him."

She shrugged. "What can I say? He was wonderful."

He picked up a picture of her and Matt that was sitting on the end table. They'd gone down to Epcot for a day, and another tourist had snapped their picture outside The Land exhibit. The agricultural experiments there fascinated Matt, so she had arranged for a behind-the-scenes tour.

"The car accident that killed your husband killed your child, too," he said, "and left you barren."

She snatched the picture from his hands.

His face turned a dull red. "Sorry. I didn't mean to overstep."

And there it was again. An apology, this one clearly sincere. When she'd asked about his wings, he'd been honest, without attempting to pretend or glaze over the truth. She took a deep breath.

"I was on my laptop, working on the budget for the new house we planned to build. Matt and I were arguing about the construction costs. It was raining, and he wasn't paying attention. The car skidded out of control and hit a bridge abutment. My seatbelt gave way. The laptop slammed into my abdomen. They said the baby died on impact. The damage was so extensive they had to take my uterus and both my ovaries."

"How far along were you?"

"Eight weeks. We'd only just found out."

"And your scars?"

"My airbag caught fire."

He shook his head. "How did you escape dying?"

"Some good Samaritans came along and pulled me from the car." For a moment, she was back at the scene, rain dowsing the burning nylon that clung to her hands and chest, hearing the horrified exclamations of her rescuers at the trail of blood left in the soaking grass as they dragged her from the wreckage.

"You're angry at God about losing your family."

"I don't think so." She shook her head. "I was heartbroken, but I got past the anger stage fairly quickly."

"If you weren't angry, why did you stop going to church?"

She drew another deep breath. "I wasn't angry at losing Matt or the baby. I was angry at never being able to have another."

He nodded. "Because it felt like a punishment."

"Yes." How strange that she could tell this to a demon when she couldn't admit it to her own grandmother. And that a demon would understand. "It felt like God was saying, 'You are not worthy to procreate.'" Shame bowed her head and filled her eyes.

He put his hand under her chin and lifted it, wiping away her tears with the edge of his thumb. "I think you misinterpreted the message."

"What?" And why was she listening to him?

"I think he was just telling you that ramming a laptop into your gut at sixty miles an hour is a bad idea."

CHAPTER 34

On Friday afternoon, Ben's fever finally broke. She could almost see him healing as his hybrid body figured out how to deal with the microbe that had laid him low. His skin cleared up as if by magic. She considered taking him back to his house, but he lived alone. She didn't like the idea of him being on his own if he relapsed or experienced follow-up complications.

They spent Friday afternoon on the sofa, with his feet in her lap. She hadn't sneezed since he'd been here, she realized, even though she hadn't taken any antihistamines. She shared Nana's theory of demon allergy with him.

He told her about Abaddon's experiments. "I'm too human to even make you sneeze."

They watched reruns of *Buffy the Vampire Slayer* all afternoon. Every time Buffy offed some vampire, he'd snort and say, "No real demon would fall for that move."

"Those aren't demons. They're vampires."

He snorted again. "Why do you mortals persist in making up creatures to frighten yourselves? Isn't there enough evil in the world to satisfy you?"

She realized he was healthy again when dinnertime rolled around.

"Let's order a pizza," he said.

"You can't have pizza. They're full of fat and grease. You're still convalescing."

"I'm well now. Get one with peppers and olives and onions."

"What, no pepperoni?"

He made a face. "I don't eat pork."

"Why not?"

"I never developed a taste for it."

He still followed the dietary laws laid out in the Old Testament. She stored that up to share with Nana.

"If you're well, then I can take you home and have my house back." She had enjoyed having him here, especially the long talks, but she wasn't about to let him know that.

He flopped back on the couch and moaned. "I think my fever just spiked again."

Dara placed her palm on his forehead. "Feels normal to me."

He wriggled back to a sitting position. "Why do all women believe they can convert their hands into digital thermometers simply by applying them to someone's forehead?"

"Do you want me to get a real thermometer?"

He pulled her back down beside him. "No, stay. I'm pretty sure I'm within normal ranges, at least for a demon."

She didn't want him to go when she wasn't sure he was healed, so she suggested a compromise for dinner.

"How about we order Chinese?" she asked. There was a Chinese restaurant in downtown Alexandria that delivered. The owners had moved from Brooklyn and kept a kosher kitchen.

"Excellent idea. I love duck *gan guo*." That was the spiciest dish on the menu.

"You can have egg drop soup and steamed rice."

His face fell, but he didn't argue. She ordered his food, plus kung pao chicken for herself.

While they were waiting for the food to be delivered, the phone rang.

"What's going on?" Lilith asked. "I talked to Tia and she said you haven't been in since Tuesday."

"I picked up a bug," Dara said.

"Bummer. Do you want me to bring you anything? Aspirin? Pepto?"

Dara imagined Lilith's face when she walked in and found Ben half-naked on the couch.

"No, that's okay. I'm pretty much over it, just giving myself a final day to recuperate."

"Oh, good. I'll bring over a couple of movies tonight. We'll stay in and watch them."

"Maybe another time," Dara said.

"I should at least come and check on you. It's what friends do. I'll swing by after work."

"No!" Dara cleared her throat. "That is, I appreciate it, but I mostly want to rest. Thanks."

"Well, if you're sure." Lilith sounded hurt.

"I appreciate the offer," Dara said. "I'm just a little tired. I'll be fine by tomorrow."

"All right. I'll see you at ten tomorrow, then."

"Tomorrow?"

"For our spa day."

Argh. Their spa day. And since it was her treat to make up for destroying Lilith's expensive blouse, Dara couldn't very well back out.

"Right," she said. "Tomorrow."

Dara and Ben spent the evening watching *Hellboy*, which he found hilarious. At ten o'clock, she said goodnight and went to shower.

When she came out of the bathroom, there were noises coming from the darkened kitchen. Was Ben sick again? She hurried to investigate. When she flipped on the overhead light, he was standing in front of the microwave.

"What are you doing?" she asked.

"I'm ready for some real food." He pulled the carton containing her leftover kung pao chicken from the microwave and sat down at the counter. He was dressed in the silk boxer shorts she'd laundered while he was in the tub that morning. She was wearing a thin nightgown suitable for a September night in north Florida, but her hair was loose and covered her almost to her waist. It seemed safest to ignore their lack of clothing.

"Do you want some?" he asked.

"At eleven o'clock at night?"

"I'm hungry."

She sat down next to him and he offered her a bite off his fork.

"How's the clinic doing without you?" he asked.

"Okay," said Dara. "Tia had to cover all my shifts, and I hate to think of what my inbox will look like when I go back, but okay."

"It's probably good for them to function without you," he said.

She swallowed. "I supposed that's true. When I talked to Javier, he said he had to get creative to cover Thursday night, but he figured it out. And Kelsey's pursuing a grant from the Family Foundation I never would have considered."

"She has a lot of potential," Ben said, "once she really gives up on being a dancer."

"That has to have been so difficult," Dara said. "To work and plan for something your entire life, only to have it snatched away in an instant."

In the dim light of the kitchen, his eyes were gentle. "You would know."

She started to shoot back an answer but stopped herself and nodded.

"That's why I'm so patient with her," Dara said. "Tia gets frustrated with me sometimes. She wants me to tell Kelsey to grow up or get out, but she has to deal with her loss in her own time and her own way."

It was an oddly intimate moment to be sharing with a demon. What would Nana say if she knew? Dara winced. She'd have to see her grandmother soon.

After they finished up the leftovers, she rinsed the plate and put it in the dishwasher. The detergent packets were in the cabinet overhead. She stretched to get one out.

When she turned around, Ben stood in the doorway, watching her. Over the past few days, he'd stopped seeming like a demon to her. He was a patient, and a platonic friend. Now she became aware of his body again.

The front of his boxers told her he was equally aware of her. She leaned across the counter and flipped off the revealing overhead light, but it was too late. Quicker than any human could move, he was beside her. His arms encircled her and his mouth came down on hers and everything else in the world went away.

When he lifted his head, he wrapped his fist in her hair and used it to draw her closer. His lips hovered above hers. She was so tired of trying to resist him. Then his hand moved behind her head and he crushed his lips to hers, and it was the most pleasurable pain she'd ever experienced.

His scent filled her nose. The smell of vanilla and rainwater coiled around her in all its deliciousness, with only the faintest note of sulfur. She hadn't taken an antihistamine since morning, but she didn't sneeze. She pressed her pelvis against his.

He took her jaw between his long fingers, turning her face to his so he could claim her lips again. His mouth moved on hers until her lips opened and their tongues tangled in a thrust and parry that set her senses on fire. He searched out her breast and cupped it from beneath, as though checking it for heft. Then he bent his head and sucked her nipple through the thin cotton of her gown. That felt so good her knees buckled. She clung to him for support.

Any concerns she had about whether he was healthy enough for sex were put to rest when he scooped her into his arms and carried her into the bedroom like she weighed nothing. She wanted him so badly that even the idea of revealing her scarred body to him didn't dissuade her.

He laid her on the bed and stood there for a moment, gazing at her with the moonlight streaming in through the windows. His glowing eyes reminded her that he was no mortal man, but before she could process that thought, his body covered hers and his knee nudged between her thighs to part them.

It was too soon. There was no way she was ready to accommodate what he had inside those boxers, but there was a part of her that wanted him to claim her that instant. Inarticulate with desire, all she could think was *mine, mine, mine*. She wrapped her arms around his neck and pulled him down to her.

"Gaaah!" There was a sound like fajitas sizzling, and the smell of burning flesh rose up between them. He rolled off her.

On his chest, the shape of a cross was burned into his skin. His face twisted into one giant wince. Garbled sounds came from his throat.

"Oh my gosh. I am so sorry." Dara undid the clasp and tossed Nana's ruby cross onto the nightstand. "Are you okay?"

He nodded, sliding his knee back between her thighs. He lowered himself to her body again, but the break was enough to bring her back to sanity.

"Condom." She pushed at his shoulder. "We need a condom."

He ignored her. His breath was hot and damp on her skin. His knee grew more insistent. She clenched her knees together.

"Condom," she said again.

He stopped trying to spread her legs and stroked his hand down the side of her face.

"You worry too much. You need to be more adventurous."

This was the old, arrogant Ben, the one she didn't much like.

She pushed him off.

"I was about to have sex with a demon. I think that's adventurous enough. And I won't risk getting some two-thousand-year-old disease by having sex without protection." The realization of what she'd almost done hit her like a thump from Granddad's Bible.

He struggled up onto his elbow. "You have nothing to worry about. Demons can't catch sexually transmitted diseases."

"Tell that to someone who didn't just spend three days nursing you through chickenpox."

He rolled over, shoved his face into the pillow, and yelled. The sound was muffled, but his frustration came through loud and clear. It was a frustration she shared, but that only fueled her return to reality.

"Put your clothes on," she said. "It's time for you to go home."

The ride back to his car was silent. She pulled into the adjacent parking space and he got out of the car. Then she drove off like the hounds of Hell were on her tail, without so much as a goodbye.

He drove the twenty minutes out to the beach trying to figure out what had just happened. Why had he tried to rush things? He had made love to thousands of women over the last hundred centuries, and he knew to a nicety how to bring a woman to the point where she was incapable of worrying about pregnancy or disease or anything but the imperative to mate with him. Why hadn't he brought that experience to bear with Dara tonight?

Instead, he'd climbed on top of her like some callow teenage boy at the mercy of his hormones. The thought that had been pulsing through his brain, the thought that had drowned out logic and experience and even common sense, was: *mine, mine, mine.*

At home, he found his cell phone lying on the kitchen counter. It had been so pleasant, having time alone with Dara without spying eyes or listening ears. DemSec must have tracked down the phone and had Lilith rescue it.

As he reached to pick it up, the flesh over his breastbone pulled painfully. He pulled the neck of his shirt out. The faint imprint of the ruby cross was still etched there. In addition to being susceptible to human illnesses and injuries, he appeared to be healing more slowly from supernatural ones.

On the phone, there were a pile of texts from the boss, ranging from *WHERE RU?* to *REPORT IN, ASSHOLE,* but there was nothing from today. Bad must have reported Belial's illness to Satan.

There were no lights on at the beach house. With any luck, Lilith was staying over with Jeremy. He opened the garage door, and her Miata was sitting there.

He needed time to think. He circled around the house to the deck and sat down on the bottom step. Yards away, beyond the shadowed sand, the ocean moved like mercury beneath the moonlight. It was low tide, and the encroachment of the waves on the shore was no more than a quiet whoosh.

Two thoughts vied for his attention. The first was: why had he been in such a hurry with Dara? He didn't know. He'd never felt such a need to possess a woman before. The chant of *mine, mine, mine* had been as forceful as the tide that made the waves seek the shore.

The second was that the wager was as good as won. If he'd had a condom, Dara would have had intercourse with him. That told him she was infatuated with him. She wasn't a woman who took sex lightly. She would never have let him get so far if she weren't poised on the edge of falling in love, and he knew just what to do to draw her the rest of the way.

Once they had intercourse, he would be able manipulate her however he liked. He had never, in ten thousand years, had sex with a woman and then failed to corrupt her. And though Dara lived her life well within the letter of the Enemy's rules, her disaffection from her creator ran deep. It still nagged at him why the Enemy had chosen this exact woman, with these exact issues, but that was a puzzle Belial wouldn't solve. The Enemy had his reasons, and he rarely shared them.

The important thing was that Dara was ripe for a fall. The losses Belial would heap on her, stacked atop all the other losses in her life, would tip her over the edge. He had played this game too often to have any doubt of it. So why didn't the knowledge of his ultimate victory bring him any pleasure?

She had spent the last several days caring for him—a demon she knew meant her harm. She might not know exactly what his plans were, but she understood they meant nothing good for her. Her treatment of him in the face of that reality showed her unselfishness was genuine. She was a truly compassionate woman who set self-interest—self-preservation, even—aside to put others' welfare first.

He didn't want to complete this mission. The thought of damning

Dara to an eternity in Hell was unacceptable. Some remnant of his angel nature recognized the good in her and drew a line at her destruction.

More than that, he wanted to stay beside her. He wasn't in love with her, of course—demons couldn't love—but he wanted more time with her. She would likely live another fifty years. In cosmic time, it was an instant, but it was an instant he would very much enjoy spending at her side.

There had to be some way to make that happen, some clever con he could pull to convince Satan and the Enemy to let him draw out this wager until they lost interest, distracted by other things.

He just had to figure out how to stack that deck.

CHAPTER 35

At her condo, Dara tried going back to bed, but the sheets smelled of rainwater and vanilla. She couldn't even smell the sulfur. Nana's ruby cross was on the end table where Dara had tossed it. The chain lay in the shape of a mangled heart. She gritted her teeth against the desire to call Ben back and punched a spot for her head into the pillow.

To her surprise, he hadn't spoken a word on the drive back to his car. He hadn't even looked up when they passed an all-night pharmacy that almost certainly stocked condoms. It was annoying to think that their aborted sexual encounter frustrated him less than it frustrated her.

He had mumbled, "Thank you," when he got out of the car, refusing to meet her eyes. From the way he'd acted, you'd think it was she who had tried to seduce him and not the other way around. She was so irritated she'd barely waited for him to close the car door before she sped out of the parking lot.

She was not a woman who took sex lightly. Part of her envied women like Lilith, who treated sex as a pleasure to be enjoyed without too much thought, like good chocolate or a fine glass of wine, but that was not how she was made. She and Matthew had sex before they were married, but not before she was sure he was the man she would marry.

For the first year after Matt died, she was too devastated by his loss, and the loss of their child, to be interested in meeting anyone. By the time that first anguish faded, she had filled her life with work. Her job was soothing, it was worthwhile, and it couldn't die on her.

But something had happened to her since Ben came into her life. The parts of her that had been slumbering for the past five years had awakened. She'd spent more than one night alone in this bed, her hand creeping between her thighs as she imagined what it would be like to be in his arms. She tried to tell herself she wasn't the kind of woman who would have sex with a demon, but tonight's events made it clear that she was lying to herself.

The scary part was that she didn't feel any different. She didn't feel like she had relaxed her moral code. She hadn't become an intrepid sexual explorer, like Lilith. She wasn't interested in remarrying, or even starting to date again. She just wanted the demon she knew as Ben Lyle. His scent wafted up from her pillow and her body chanted another chorus of *mine, mine, mine*.

With an exclamation, she got up and yanked the sheets from the bed. She bundled them, along with the pillowcases, into the washer and sprayed the mattress with Febreze. She put on new sheets that smelled of lavender and crawled back into bed. His scent wrapped around her, fainter, but still there. She groaned. It was as impossible to drive his odor from her bed as it was to drive his image from her mind.

Ben's behavior over the past three days was not what she would have expected. In her experience, illness did not bring out the best in people. They were ruder, more short-tempered and more difficult to please when they were sick. And the longer they went on being sick, the truer that was.

But while she'd nursed him, Ben had been the perfect patient. He was grateful for everything she did for him, saying thank you at every turn. It was hard to know what to make of that. Was that a con all demons pulled to gain pity? Or something particular to this demon? She didn't have enough experience to know which was true.

In the morning, she'd go see the expert.

Belial arrived in Hell as Satan and Bad were taste-testing atomic chicken wings prepared for tonight's poker game. The air in Ring Nine felt hot, and in comparison to Alexandria, very dry.

"What's he doing here?" Belial asked.

"Zeus can't make it. Hera's on the warpath. Bad is filling in."

Belial dove straight in. "I think we should challenge the Enemy to increase the stakes."

Satan's lips flattened into a straight line. "First things first. Did you bang her?"

"Yes." In ten thousand years of telling lies, it felt like the worst falsehood Belial had ever uttered, but it was for Dara's own good.

"Since you ditched the mic," Bad said, "we only have your word for that." He bit into another wing.

Belial drew himself up, flaunting his beauty. "Do you doubt it?"

Bad flushed. "All I'm saying is this supposed carnal action had no witnesses. The beach house has cameras in every room. If you want credit for the score, provide some documentation."

"You're just looking for a peep show. Get your jollies somewhere else." Belial turned back to Satan. "She succumbed to me. This wager is as good as won."

Satan pinched his lower lip. "What changes were you contemplating? Another soul? Because we're already ten to a bunk down here."

Belial was prepared for this question. "I was thinking, if we win, Heaven hosts the next poker game."

Satan's hands stilled. If there was anything Satan craved, it was recognition of his sovereignty. An invitation from the Enemy to play poker in Heaven would constitute an acknowledgment of the Hellish state.

Belial sweetened the pot. "Picture it. Michael brings you a beer while Gabriel lights your cigar."

A spark glinted from Satan's left horn. Belial had found the right lure.

Satan frowned. "Why would the Enemy let us change things up at this point?"

"Because he's about to lose."

"What will you offer him?"

"I was thinking—Silicon Valley." Some of Hell's best work was being played out in the tech companies of California. "No intervention for some period of time."

"You can't do that," Bad protested. "Silicon Valley is my territory, not yours."

Satan whipped around like a snake striking. "Nothing is your territory unless I say it is."

The temptation of recognition was as strong as Belial had hoped.

A few minutes later, the players arrived. The Enemy's white robe trailed the ground without picking up any of the black grit that coated the lava floors. Loki followed close behind.

The Norseman spied Belial. He tucked his hands into his armpits and flapped his arms like wings. "Bock-bock-bock."

Belial stared at him. He grew more deranged every month.

"Chickenpox," Loki crowed. "I heard you had chickenpox."

Everyone roared except Belial and the Enemy. Belial fought the urge to punch Loki in his helmeted head. What an idiot. It was no wonder the Norse gods had lost their following.

Satan passed out poker chips, then broke the seal on a fresh deck of cards and shuffled. He offered the Enemy the cut.

"Pass." The Enemy smiled. "After all, we're all friends here, are we not?"

"Of course." Satan smiled right back at him.

"Speaking of friendly wagers..." The Enemy turned to Belial. "How goes your pursuit of Dara Strong?"

He swallowed. Satan knew only what he could see and hear, or what was reported to him. It was less clear what the Enemy knew.

The path ahead was so narrow that even the tiniest misstep would send Belial crashing over the edge to the burning rocks below. "She's in love with me. She'll do anything I ask."

The Enemy looked amused. "Do you think so?"

Satan shot Belial a narrow look, forcing him to elaborate.

"In ten thousand years, no woman I've bedded has ever failed to do whatever I've asked." It was the kind of statement that had won him the title "Hell's Politician." He hadn't claimed they'd fornicated. He'd just said what it would mean if they had. He waited to see if the Enemy would call him on it.

"You've never taken on this woman before."

Belial let out a tiny sigh of relief. It was exactly the response he'd hoped for. "Since you're so confident, how about making things a little more interesting?"

The Enemy raised one elegant eyebrow. "Interesting how?"

Belial sat back. "Instead of the week that's left, you give me the remainder of her life." In the celestial scheme of things, it was a nit, only microscopically longer than the current term. "If, after all that time, you win, we'll cease operations in Silicon Valley for twenty years." Twenty years without demonic intervention would allow technology to veer to the good, although the moment the dark forces went back to work, that progress would probably be lost.

"What do you want in return?"

"You start hosting some of these poker games in Heaven."

The Enemy surveyed him. "Let me see if I have this right. We extend this wager for the duration of Dara Strong's natural life. Then, if you lose, you stop interfering in Silicon Valley for twenty years. If you win, I invite you lot into Heaven. Is that also for twenty years?"

Satan hissed, and Belial shook his head. "Twenty human years is one hundred and seventy-five thousand hours and change. You'll host us for an equivalent number of hours." At five hours per game, that was approximately thirty-five thousand poker games.

"You've got to be joking. I'll host once each year you leave Silicon Valley alone."

That felt more like a holiday arrangement with obnoxious relatives than an acknowledgment of the Hellish state.

"No deal," Satan said.

Belial had expected this. Time to execute his backup plan. He prodded his chips and took the ultimate gamble. "What I find myself wondering, what fascinates me, is what Dara's reaction will be when she learns of this wager."

The Enemy's heavy brows slammed together and thunder rumbled overhead. There was a collective hiss of indrawn breath from everyone at the table. Bad's eyes bounced from the Enemy to Belial and back, like he was watching a ping-pong game. Even Satan looked startled.

"There is," Belial said, keeping his voice even, "nothing in our agreement that forbids me from sharing that information."

The Enemy glowered at him. "And you think she'll believe you?"

"Probably. She has a pretty good instinct for the truth. With all that she's already been through, and with a little encouragement from me, that will be enough to make her curse you."

Work with me here. It had long been a question in Hell whether the Enemy could, or would, read demon minds. For the first time, Belial hoped he did. *I'm trying to save this woman you said you were pleased with.*

"Good point," the Enemy said. "Her rejection of me will need to be permanent, of course."

Belial sensed an abyss yawning before him. "What do you mean?"

The Enemy nodded. "Because of the new covenant."

The abyss took shape. The new covenant was the Boy's work. Under its terms, if Dara repented before she died, the Enemy would forgive her and Hell wouldn't be able to claim her soul. How had Belial missed that? Because the new covenant wasn't in place when Job was the pawn, or Eve before him.

"The terms of the wager—" Satan's color had deepened well past burgundy into puce. His horns puffed like a coal-fired locomotive.

"The terms of the wager are not specific," the Enemy said. "I only stipulated that you get a human soul, not *her* human soul. Play back the recording if you doubt it."

Satan looked like he was about to burst into purple flames. The Enemy was using the loophole to make it look like Satan was no match for him, and he'd made it crystal clear that he'd rather risk losing than invite Satan back into Heaven. But Belial breathed a sigh of relief. Dara was safe.

"So, are you in?" Belial asked, bringing the conversation back to his original gambit. He wanted those fifty years beside her.

The Enemy nudged his tower of white chips with one immaculate fingernail. After what felt like an eternity, he said, "I'll pass."

Belial felt as though something precious had been ripped from his hands. He wouldn't get to spend Dara's life at her side. Then he took a deep breath. He'd accomplished the most important thing. Dara would be all right. As long as she recanted before she died, she would be all right. Knowing her as he did, he pegged that as a certainty.

On the other side of the table, Satan's face was barely visible for the smoke streaming from his horns. He was furious that Loki had witnessed his humiliation. It would do no good to point out that the Enemy had repudiated Loki, too. Everyone knew it was Sataniel he wouldn't allow inside the Pearly Gates.

Satan was angry at Belial, but what else was new? The important thing was that, thanks to the new covenant, Dara was safe. Some other poor soul that might otherwise have received leniency would be on the hook instead.

Satan dealt the cards. When the play came around to Belial, he was feeling lucky, so he bet big. The play passed to the Enemy, who met his wager and raised him. Grinning, Belial shoved in a matching amount of chips and then tossed in a few more for good measure.

"You're bluffing," the Enemy said.

"It's the best hand I've had all night," Belial lied.

"I was talking about the woman." The Enemy spoke with a certainty that couldn't be gainsaid. "You haven't bedded her yet, and I don't think you will."

Belial's lie was exposed. Satan threw him a scorching look. Bad smirked.

The Enemy laid down his cards. His royal straight beat the pants off Belial's two of a kind. The Enemy raked in all the chips.

Nana looked Dara over with a worried eye. "You look tuckered out."

"I'm still a little under the weather." In truth, Dara felt fine, other than some fatigue from three days of constant nursing followed by a night of very little sleep.

"Your face is a little flushed." Nana sounded pleased. "The Lord probably sent you this illness to keep you out of the way of that demon."

If that was how things worked, the Lord must want Dara to spend a lot of time with the demon. She picked up Nana's Bible from the nightstand and set it back down again. "He apologized to me."

Nana squinted up at her. "What?"

"The demon—he said he was sorry."

Nana's jaw dropped, exposing a white row of dentures. "For what?"

Dara couldn't very well tell Nana he'd apologized for helping her get so drunk she'd vomited on his shoes. She wandered over to Nana's dresser and straightened the edge of the crocheted doily that covered it. "I don't remember, something trivial, but he said it."

When had she begun lying to her grandmother so easily? After the demon came into her life.

"You must have heard wrong."

"He said it twice." He'd also said thank you numerous times over the past few days, another phrase she'd been led to believe was outside a demon's lexicon.

"He didn't mean it."

"I thought demons were unable to voice apologies?"

Nana gnawed on her lip and thought about that. After a moment, she nodded. "That's what your granddaddy always said, and I for certain never heard one speak regret."

Dara had hoped Nana would have some idea of what it meant, but it was clear she was mystified, too. If she wanted Nana's help, Dara would have to tell her more.

"And he got sick."

"Sick?" Nana rubbed her chin. "Sick how?"

"He caught chickenpox from a little boy at the clinic."

"Chickenpox?" Nana's eyes flashed to her face. "And you nursed him back to health, didn't you? That's where you been these past three days."

Why had Dara thought she would get away with this? She never had gotten away with anything as a teenager. "What was I supposed to do? Let him die?"

"Demons are immortal," Nana said. "Even if his body died, he would have just gone back to Hell and gotten another one."

But I like this one.

"I couldn't do it, Nana. I'm a nurse. Nurses don't just let people die."

"He's not a person." Nana's open palm smacked the arm of her recliner. "He's a demon who is out to do you harm."

"I know that." Dara's shoulders drooped. Nana took the dream world she'd inhabited over the past three days and exposed it to harsh sunlight, where its falseness became all too apparent.

"I expect he made an awful patient."

"He didn't, though. That's what I wanted to ask you about. He was the best patient I've ever had—polite, grateful, did whatever I asked." She didn't mention that one of the things she'd asked him to do was strip off his clothes and soak in her bathtub. "He was"—Dara searched for a word—"angelic."

Nana frowned for a moment, pulling on her lower lip. Then she nodded. "Well, that is how he started out. Before he fell."

The image of his scarred shoulder blades flashed before Dara. Pity welled for her poor fallen angel. The last three days had shown what he could have been. If he'd been an ordinary man—what would it be like to spend her days in such a man's company, her nights in his bed?

"You need to get yourself married again," said Nana.

That pulled Dara out of her fantasy. "What?"

"Saint Paul said it. 'Tis better to marry than to burn.'"

Her cheeks flamed.

"And you're burning for that demon," Nana said. Dara tried to deny it, but Nana didn't stop. "That's why you're so flushed; that's why you're so restless; that's why you come in here and tried to lie to me like you haven't done since you was sixteen years old."

Dara's head dropped forward, her face hot with shame.

"It's all right, girl. I saw that demon when you brought him in here that day. No woman could be expected to resist that, not when he's after you and after you and won't let up."

Tears burned beneath Dara's eyelids. She sat down on the floor and leaned her head against Nana's knees. Nana stroked her hair.

Dara looked up, her vision clouded by tears. "What am I going to do?"

The old woman cradled her cheek, wiping a tear away with gentle fingers. "Pray, child. That's all you can do. Pray."

Dara nodded, but inside she was in despair. Nana had named the one thing she couldn't do.

CHAPTER 36

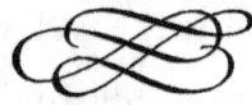

After the poker game ended and the others left, Satan parked his skinny butt on the edge of the poker table and motioned Belial to stay behind.

"So you haven't actually seduced the woman?" His voice was like acid.

Belial wasn't about to fall into the trap of defending himself for lying. Given similar circumstances, any demon would have done the same.

"Close enough," he said.

"Unless your cock was inside her, it wasn't close enough."

Belial didn't respond or look away.

After a few minutes of locked stares, Satan said, "We're not going to let him get away with this."

Belial was pretty sure the "he" Satan was talking about was the Enemy, but he had no clue what they weren't going to let him get away with.

"Of course not," he said.

"Loopholes are our gig," said Satan.

"Right," said Belial. Ah, the loophole.

"I don't want just any soul." Satan's skin darkened again. He was recalling his public humiliation.

"It's obvious he has a soft spot for the Strong woman," Satan said. "I want *her* soul. Hers. When she gets down here, we'll make her treatment the worst any human has ever experienced. Maybe we'll build a whole new ring just to torture her. We'll parade her in front of him every time he comes down. It will eat at his craw, and there'll be nothing he can do about it."

Belial listened, feeling a little ill. He'd made things so much worse for Dara. He had to get her out of this mess. He had to.

"It's not enough for her to just curse the Enemy," said Satan. "You get that, right? She'll have to kill herself afterwards, so she doesn't have a chance to repent."

Drive Dara to suicide? Horror thick as molasses rolled through Belial. Only his ten thousand years of masking his emotions allowed him to hide his feelings.

"Right," he said.

How had he let this happen? Through a combination of selfishness and arrogance. He had come below determined to have everything his own way. He would dally with Dara for the duration of her life, then return to Hell and pick up where he'd left off. He had treated her like a toy to be played with and tossed aside.

What had he been thinking? He had pitted himself against the two most powerful entities in the universe. It was no surprise he'd been bested by both. He'd boxed himself into a corner from which he could see no escape. And the one who would pay the price for his arrogance was not him, but Dara.

Satan didn't seem to notice his silence. "You'll have to be careful. It can't look like our doing. The bet stipulates no physical harm. It must be clear she chose to off herself."

Revulsion numbed Belial's lips and slowed his thinking. Dara deserved better than to be pawn in a cosmic pissing match. She deserved better than him.

"Right," he said again.

Satan drummed his fingers on the table. "So what's the plan?"

Whatever it took, Belial would save her. More than that, he would leave her in better shape than he'd found her. No matter the cost.

"The same plan still holds." Belial forced himself to focus. Satan must continue to believe he was on board. "Convince her to betray her deepest beliefs. Her suicide was always a probable outcome."

With a feeling of self-loathing, he realized that was true. The mission he'd gone above to perform had always held the risk of hurting Dara so deeply she would lose her will to live.

"I just need to take it from probable to absolute," he said.

Satan looked him up and down. "See that you do."

Deep in thought, Belial turned to leave. There were two things Dara needed for a better life: a permanent source of money for her clinic and a husband to cherish her. Over the next two weeks, he would arrange both of those things.

Before he could make it out the door, Satan's voice stopped him again. "When you fuck her, make sure it's on camera."

Belial didn't turn around, didn't respond in any way.

"That's an order," Satan said.

It was almost nine a.m. when Belial got back to the beach house. He crawled into bed, only to be disturbed by the sound of his phone buzzing. It was Jeremy.

"We're short a fourth for golf. Do you want to join us?"

He'd gotten no sleep the night before, but there was no time to waste in putting his new, two-pronged plan into action. The golf course was the perfect place for both prongs. The mate he found for Dara would likely be a doctor. That was who she'd have the most in common with and who could help her with the clinic. Also, Jeremy's friends might have ideas on the ways to fund the clinic. Belial arranged to meet them and got out of bed.

From the doorway, Lilith watched him with narrowed eyes. "Word on the rings is you just spent three days with her and you still haven't hit that."

He shrugged.

"What happened? This is your sweet spot."

"This identity Bad created betrays me at every turn." He'd made the complaint so often it would raise no eyebrows. "I spent those three days with chickenpox. It was a complete waste."

She shook her head. "Being sick made it possible for you to become close to her. Human women love that vulnerability shit. You've lost your edge."

He shrugged again. "If she was easy, the Enemy would have chosen someone else. Would you mind getting out of here? I want to get dressed."

But she didn't leave. Instead, she leaned against the doorsill with her hands behind her back. Her breasts jutted out.

"You must be frustrated," she said. "We could work some of that off before you play golf."

His eyes traveled over her curvaceous body. He could bury himself inside that and find release from the pulsing frustration that possessed him. He didn't even care if all Hell was watching, though he doubted they'd bother. They could see demons fornicate anytime.

It wouldn't help, though. He didn't want sex. He wanted Dara. He wanted to make love to her and feel her respond to him. He wanted to hear her soft sighs and watch her eyes go smoky with desire. He wanted to give her more pleasure than any woman had ever experienced.

He pushed Lilith out into the hall. "I'll take it out on the golf ball."

Lilith watched Belial pull out of the driveway. What was going on inside that demon's head? He didn't trust her, but he had always been willing to drill his frustration into whatever she-demon happened to be available.

She wandered down to the kitchen and retrieved a carton of eggs and some habanero salsa from the refrigerator. She could chip in and help him succeed, but what advantage would that bring her? He might be appreciative, but demons weren't known for acting on their gratitude. Maybe she should go to the boss and warn him that Belial was behaving suspiciously.

She shook her head. Even if she had something concrete, she doubted that would work. The boss expected demons to undercut each other. He wrote off ninety percent of what he heard as lies. He was mostly right. She pulled a saucepan from the cupboard and added a couple of inches of water.

What might be more useful was an artfully placed falsehood, something to revive Dara's distrust of Belial. The three days she'd spent nursing him would have eroded her wariness. Something to shore up her flagging sense of caution was definitely called for. But first Lilith needed to find out exactly what Dara was thinking. Today's spa day should provide ample opportunity for that.

She set the saucepan on the stove and turned the flame to maximum.

Over the course of the day, her goals might not strictly align with the boss's. As the end of the wager neared, his willingness to turn a blind eye to that type of self-interest had diminished. She couldn't risk being overheard.

She pulled her cell phone from her pocket and typed a text to Dara, double-checking on their meeting time. Just as she hit send, she bobbled the phone. It arced out of her hands and into the boiling water.

Problem solved.

Dara sat down in the lushly upholstered mani-pedi chair, submerged her bare feet in the footbath and tried to think of a place she'd less rather be. When she didn't come up with anything, she reminded herself that she owed Lilith.

"Did you get your blouse back from the dry cleaner?" she asked.

A muscle twitched in Lilith's cheek, but she covered it with a wide smile. "The catsup came right out."

Dara let out a sigh of relief. "I'll pay the cleaning bill, of course."

Lilith immersed her toes in her own footbath. "You're paying for our treatments today. That's enough."

Dara hoped so. She'd nearly had a heart attack when she saw the price list.

"I still feel bad that I didn't even come by to check on you while you were sick." Lilith peeped at Dara from the corner of her eye.

Why was Dara keeping Ben's illness a secret? It wasn't like Lilith was a demon. Dara decided to tell Lilith the truth.

Lilith laughed. "I'd have loved to have seen that—Ben Lyle with chickenpox." She gave Dara another sidelong look. "So how was it, being cooped up for three straight days with all that gorgeousness?"

"He's a lot less gorgeous covered in blisters."

"*Chica,* I'd hit that if it was covered in boils."

In spite of herself, Dara giggled.

"Come on." Lilith wiggled her toes in the aromatic water. "It's just us girls. Fess up. Did you finally let down those walls and let yourself enjoy life for once?"

Dara had enjoyed herself, though not in the sense that Lilith meant. She thought of her lingering conversations with Ben as he soaked in the tub and later, when he was feeling better, cuddling on the couch.

"I didn't have sex with him, if that's what you mean."

Lilith groaned. "That's exactly what I mean. What a waste of an opportunity. You do realize there are a lot of other women who'd be glad to slide underneath that?"

"I do." The stab of jealousy Dara felt at Lilith's words startled her.

"A guy like that is not going to wait forever." There was some tone in Lilith's voice, some note of speculation, that said when Ben got tired of waiting, she'd be happy to step in.

"He won't have to," Dara said.

Lilith turned to stare. Her mouth widened in a grin. "Did I just hear you stake a claim?"

The heat in Dara's face should have dried her masque instantly. "Maybe."

"And I should keep my hands off?"

"I'd appreciate it, but I'm surprised you even care. I had the impression you don't like him all that much."

Lilith shrugged. "You don't have to be soul mates to have fun in bed together."

When Dara didn't respond, Lilith turned to look at her again.

"Oh, please," she said. "Don't tell me you're in love with Ben Lyle."

"Of course not."

"Good," said Lilith. "Frolicking between the sheets with him is probably more fun than a Paris shopping spree, but falling for him would be a nightmare. For guys like him, it's all about collecting scalps."

Dara's joy from the past three days turned to ashes in her mouth. "What happened to this being a great passion?"

Lilith blinked. "Well, you didn't seem to think so, so I figured I was wrong."

Somehow, Lilith had taken a magical experience and turned it into something tawdry. Dara supposed she should be grateful. No matter how wonderful the past three days had been, Ben Lyle was still a demon.

CHAPTER 37

Belial spent the first nine holes doing everything in his power to ensure that the other members of his foursome had the games of their lives.

"I think I've finally got this figured out," Jeremy crowed after a particularly good drive, courtesy of a snare to the back of his head that wouldn't allow him to raise it until he completed his swing. "Maybe I'll sign up for the Gulf States Pro-Am next spring."

"Maybe we should sign up as a foursome." Ted Oakes, an internist, had shot three birdies. His freckled face curved in a beaming smile.

"Maybe we should line up more than one good game in a row before we join the tour." Tony Balsamo was a lanky OB/GYN with a practice out by the beach.

"Have any of you ever thought about setting up some kind of annual fundraiser for the clinic?" Belial asked.

The other three doctors looked at him in surprise.

"We're not on the clinic's board," Jeremy said.

"I know that, but you all volunteer there. You have an interest."

"I don't know." Jeremy was giddy with his newfound aptitude. "If the clinic goes belly up, we'll all have an extra evening to play golf." The others laughed.

Belial let him handle his own putts—four of them—to finish out the hole. "Dara works hard, but that place always seems to be on the edge of closing." He was surprised how enjoyable it was, in this group of hardworking doctors, to allow his pride and affection for Dara to come through. If the boss heard it, he would write it off as an act.

Ted punched Jeremy's arm. "Does it bug you that this guy seems to have succeeded where you spent five years failing?"

"Nope." Jeremy smirked. "Don't get me wrong. Dara's great. But who would want Dara when they can have Lilith?"

Anyone with an ounce of good taste. Not to mention self-preservation. Still, Jeremy might make a good husband for Dara, once Lilith was out of the way. If the she-demon hadn't ruined him, that was. Belial wanted a good husband who would cherish Dara, not one of Lilith's trained freaks.

"It's always been like that," Tony said.

Belial hadn't met Tony before, but he liked the self-effacing doctor. He came into the clinic once a month to do pap smears and give referrals for mammograms. He might make Dara a good husband. Belial checked out Tony's left hand. There was no ridge inside the third finger of his golf glove. What excuse could he give DemSec to get a background check on Tony?

"What kind of fundraiser were you thinking about?" Ted asked. He was married with kids, so there was no point considering him. Dara would never break up a family.

"What kind of event can we set up annually that will raise lots of money?" Belial said.

"How would I know?" Jeremy lifted his bag into the back of the golf cart. "Ask Lilith. She does that kind of thing for a living and she's on the clinic's board."

Belial wasn't about to let Lilith within a thousand yards of this event. "I mentioned it to her," he lied. "She didn't have any ideas."

"Really?" said Jeremy. "Because she never seems to be short on ideas when she's with me. Did I tell you about this thing she does with a mango and an ice cube?"

"Nobody wants to hear about your sex life," Tony said.

Shooting Tony a grateful look, Belial removed Jeremy from his list of potential husbands for Dara.

"Why don't you talk to Kelsey the next time you're at the clinic?" Ted said. "I mean, that's what she does, right?"

"You're brilliant." Belial rewarded Ted with a double eagle.

As soon as he left the golf course, Belial texted Kelsey and asked her to meet him for a drink at Slyders. He was working against a deadline and there was no time to waste. He was unsurprised when she responded right away in the affirmative.

It took her longer to arrive than he expected, so he drank a beer and did some mortal-watching. The people on the beach fell into two categories: tourists and regulars. The tourists were easily identified by their brand-new beach gear—huge umbrellas, shiny coolers, brightly colored towels—and their painful-looking sunburns. The regulars had warped beach chairs, beat-up coolers and ragged towels. Their skin was wizened to leather by the sun. They would do well in Hell.

Surprisingly, his phone didn't buzz. Had the boss decided to let him run his own mission, or was Satan occupied elsewhere? Not that it mattered. The important thing was that he had the space he needed to set up a new, better life for Dara.

An hour later, Kelsey stepped through the doorway, and he saw why it had taken her so long. Her hair, which he'd never seen out of its bun before, rippled down her back in shining waves. Her face was made up so that her doe-like eyes looked even larger. She was a pretty child. His feeling of tenderness surprised him. The softness he'd developed for Dara seemed to extend to others as well.

"Thanks for coming." He was careful to make his voice neutral, but even so, she lifted onto her toes like she was about to do a series of leaps across the deck.

"I'm happy to." She slipped into the chair opposite him, her eyes shining.

Had he made a mistake asking her here? The waitress came by and took their orders. He ordered a pizza with peppers and onions. As he expected, Kelsey asked for a salad. That was another thing he liked about Dara. She wasn't obsessed with some Hollywood ideal of what her body should look like.

"I wanted to talk to you about doing a fundraiser for the clinic," he said once the waitress was gone.

Kelsey's smile dimmed by a few hundred watts, but she quickly rallied. "That's a lovely idea. It was good of you to think of it." She tilted her head to the side in a way that showed off the graceful line of her neck. She stretched her hand across the table. Her pale pink fingernails touched his hand. "What sort of fundraiser did you have in mind?"

Trying not to be too obvious, he withdrew his hand and let it drop into his lap. "I thought maybe a golf scramble?"

She winced and shook her head.

"No good?" he said.

"There must be ten of those things here every year—leukemia, breast cancer..."

"All right, no golf scramble. How about a dinner dance?"

She wrinkled her nose. "The medical society already sponsors one of those, with a silent auction, every October. I don't think you'll get the docs to attend another one."

He tried to think of the other ways he'd seen humans raise money. "What about a poker tournament?"

Kelsey's carefully groomed eyebrows drew together. "A poker tournament? I don't think Dara would go along with that."

But the more he thought about the idea, the better he liked it. There was a certain symmetry to the idea that a poker game would start Dara's new, better life instead of ending it. For once, he would leave a target in better condition than he'd found her. "You can leave Dara to me."

The glow dimmed from Kelsey's face, as she registered the possessive note in his voice. She straightened in her chair. "Let's say Dara's willing to go along with holding a gambling event. When were you thinking about having it?"

"Next Saturday," he said.

Her jaw dropped. "That's not possible."

"Of course it is." Almost anything was possible if you had all the resources of Hell at your disposal. "Where could we hold it?"

"There's only one place in town that I can think of that's big enough—the Alexandria Ballroom. That's where everyone does their wedding receptions. It's booked every weekend for months in advance."

"I'll handle that," he said. "What's the best way to promote our event?"

"That's another reason why you need to give yourself more time. There's a lot of wealth in Alexandria—well, not in Alexandria proper, but out at the beach. Some of the older residents out there have money out the yin-yang, but they're mostly snowbirds. They don't come down here until it turns cold up north, usually not until Thanksgiving."

Thanksgiving was still a month away. Belial added the prediction of a freak snowstorm to the list of things he'd need. Leviathan, the demon who commanded the seas, could blow up the makings of a frigid nor'easter to chase the snowbirds south early.

"Let's say we can get them down here. What would make them come to the tournament?"

She considered that. "To draw them in, you'd need a celebrity with name recognition."

"Done," Belial said. Halpas, the stork who ran Vice, could deliver someone, for a price. That price would be high, but that didn't matter, because Belial wouldn't be around to pay it. Once Satan realized he had thrown the bet, Belial would be headed for a dip in the Lake of Fire.

"Then what?" he asked.

"Once you have your celebrities lined up, you book airtime on local radio and TV shows. You can also print up posters and put them in the places the people you want to attract commonly go to—groceries, pharmacies. You should mail invitations to the people you'd especially like to attend at least six weeks in advance." She held out her hands. "Can you see all this takes time?"

He didn't have time. "If I can book the ballroom and nail down a celebrity for this weekend, can you help me with emails and social media?"

She wasn't done. "And there's food. If people pay to get in, they'll expect to be fed."

"We'll hire a caterer."

"How will you pay for this?"

There was no way Mammon would release any additional funds to him. Then he realized it didn't matter.

"That's the beauty of a poker tournament," he said. "The players fund it with their buy-in fee."

"There's a lot of stuff you'll have to pay for ahead of time. You're planning this on such short notice; people here won't be willing to take a chance on you making a profit to get their money."

That stumped him, but only for a moment. Lilith could spare a few small gems. "I can cover that. Will you help me?"

She took a deep breath. "I guess so—if Dara okays it."

When Lilith stepped out onto the deck at Slyders, it was all she could do not to hug herself with glee at the sight of Belial sitting at a table with the little dancer from the clinic. They were so wrapped up in their conversation they didn't even notice her. She didn't have to harpoon him. He'd harpooned himself.

She hesitated in the doorway long enough for Dara to get an eyeful of the two of them, their heads together, looking cozy. Her stricken expression was priceless. She had suspected Dara was infatuated with Belial. The look of devastation on her face verified it.

What an idiot. A lot of women had made the same mistake over the centuries, but they at least had the excuse of not realizing what he was. Dara had fallen for him, knowing he was a demon. What a complete and utter twit.

Which would work better? To have Dara confront him or to pull her away? Better to whisk her away, Lilith decided. Belial was an arrogant ass, but he wasn't stupid, and he was all business. Whatever he was talking about with Kelsey was related to his mission. Right now, that mission was to get on Dara's good side. If she confronted him, his positive motive would become apparent, and that was not what Lilith wanted. She pushed Dara back through the door.

"I'm sure it doesn't mean anything." She guided Dara to the front entrance. Dara didn't resist. She just walked out the door like a robot. "I mean, he really seemed to be into you..." Lilith let her voice trail off, as though she were now realizing how wrong she'd been.

The shock and hurt on Dara's face congealed into anger. She pulled her arm free. "This is not okay. I told him when he came on board I wouldn't put up with him flirting with the staff. I'm going out to talk to him."

"Right now?" Lilith winced as though envisioning an unpleasant scene. "In front of Kelsey?"

"Right now," Dara said.

That couldn't happen. "Are you sure you want to do that? I mean, it seems a teensy bit controlling, saying who your employees and volunteers can get involved with."

Dara blew out a long breath. Her shoulders sagged. "Fine. I'll talk to him Monday night."

Lilith had no doubt that on Monday Belial would straighten things out, but the next thirty-six hours would give Dara plenty of time to stew about it. It would give her time to remember that he was a demon who lied as easily as he drew breath, time to realize her heart would never be safe loving him. That should amp her distrust back up to acceptable levels.

Still, Lilith might be able to wring a little bit more out of the situation. She forced blood into her cheeks and drew up her shoulders, as though warding off a blow.

"I didn't want to tell you this," she said, "but you might want to let this go. Ben told Jeremy"—she dropped her voice low, as though she didn't want to be overheard—"that your scars kind of...you know... skeeve him out."

Dara's face flamed with mortification. With anything else, her common sense might argue that Belial's reaction to her was anything but repulsed, but Dara's scars were so wrapped up with the loss of her baby and her womb that she didn't think clearly where they were concerned. It was all Lilith could do not to high-five herself. Then Dara lifted her chin.

"Dr. Lyle's reaction to my scars is irrelevant," she said. "This is about him breaking clinic rules."

Lilith arranged her features into her sad-clown face. "Of course." She took Dara's arm again. "Now where would you like to go for dinner? I'm thinking somewhere with alcohol."

"I think I'll pass." Dara withdrew her arm. "I'm going to call it a day."

CHAPTER 38

Belial spent Sunday busier than he'd been in centuries. Arranging the threat of a nor'easter to chivvy all the snowbirds back to Alexandria required some major horse-trading with Leviathan, who controlled the seas. In the end, Belial wound up giving him Abraham's *shofar,* a prize he'd lusted after for centuries. Belial handed over the ram's horn with barely a twinge.

Halpas, the stork who ran Vice, also had to be greased to gain his cooperation to bring in a celebrity. His price was the stone David used to slay Goliath. Belial had picked it up off the field the day the Philistine died. That one stung a little, but by the end of the day, a major poker star was enlisted for Saturday and a potential storm brewed off the East Coast that had the airlines overbooking every flight south.

Of course, no visit to Hell was complete without a stop at the boss's office. Satan glared across his desk. "Seriously? You're going for gratitude sex?"

"I'm cementing my position. A woman like Dara has to be in love to open her legs." Belial heard his own words with distaste, but it was imperative the boss believe he was still plotting Dara's downfall.

"How will a poker tournament make her fall in love with you?"

"Her concern about the clinic is the last barrier standing in my way. This fundraiser will convince her she doesn't need to worry about that. Once it's over, I will seduce her, give her carnal pleasures beyond her wildest imaginings. But she needs more time to think about it, dream about it, fantasize about it, until those fantasies become all-consuming. She's getting there, but she's not at that point yet." As he spun the words, he almost believed them himself.

"Lilith thinks she is."

"Lilith is a bitch who has been trying to undermine me from day one."

Satan didn't dispute that. "I still don't see where Saturday is any different from tonight."

"Saturday is different only in the emotional component, but that's the piece that sets us up for the third snare to work. That clinic is her sanctuary. Once I provide a way to fund it, year after year, her last defenses will be gone. I will have proven my sincerity. When the time comes for her to choose between me and the clinic, she will choose me. And at the same time, she will turn her back on Him. She will choose us."

Would this false promise give him the time he needed to change Dara's future?

Satan pinched his lower lip. "You realize by the time the tournament is over, we'll only have a week left."

"That works in our favor," Belial said. It worked in *his* favor, anyway. If he could string the boss along for those remaining days, promising miracles he'd never deliver, he could save Dara from an eternity in Hell. He didn't let himself think about the impact his actions would have on his own eternity. "The affair won't have time to grow stale before she's faced with a decision. Relax. I've got this."

He just hoped that was true.

On Monday morning, Belial stopped at the Alexandria Ballroom, where a middle-aged woman whose nameplate read "Betty" told him he couldn't have the ballroom on Saturday. There was a wedding reception at seven p.m.

"We'll be out of here by three," he lied, but she didn't buy it.

Behind the glass window of the small office at the front of the ballroom, Betty tapped her lower lip with one fuchsia fingernail that matched her lipstick. "Even if you were, they'll be in here on Friday, decorating. You wouldn't want their decorations—"

"I'll take what I can get."

"—and I can't risk you messing something up for them."

Why in Hell's name was it so much harder to do good than it was to do evil?

"What if I can get the bride and groom to okay it?" he asked.

Betty shook her head.

"What if they cancel?"

"They won't cancel," she said. "The bride has been planning this wedding for two years. She had her heart set on a dream wedding in the Caribbean, but this was what they could afford."

He tried snaring Betty, but she slammed the window in his face. Was he losing his touch?

Google identified the happy couple. The quickest way to break them up, of course, was for the bride to discover that the groom was sleeping with her best friend.

Even as he pulled out his phone to set that chain of events in motion, he stopped himself. It didn't feel right. If Dara ever found out what he'd done, it would destroy any joy she'd take in his gift. It was foolish, but he wanted her to remember him with fondness.

Instead, he made another unscheduled visit to Hell, where he all but begged Halpas to notify the bride she'd won a dream wedding in the Caribbean. By the time Halpas agreed, Belial was almost glad he would be dying soon. At least he wouldn't be around to see Ehud's sword in the hands of a demon that didn't have the artistry to appreciate it.

While Belial had his safe open, he removed a square velvet purse and stuck it in his pocket. He was running short on funds, and the treasure it contained would bring a substantial amount of cash at a human pawn shop. He'd considered selling the Ducati, but it was a vintage machine. For it to be worth much, he'd have to find the right kind of buyer, and that would take time.

He looked at the contents of the safe. Selling them would yield enough to set up permanent funding for the clinic. Regretfully, he set the notion aside. In the time frame available, there was no way he could dispose of that much loot without Satan getting wind of it.

Then he drove back to the ballroom, racing through the door as Betty was locking her office.

"I heard you had a cancellation," he said.

"I didn't give their deposit back." She folded her arms across her big chest. "But they won't be using the ballroom. I guess it wouldn't hurt to make a little extra profit this weekend."

He removed the last of the money he'd gotten from selling the Lamborghini from his wallet and handed it to Betty.

Dara thought Kelsey might mention seeing Dr. Lyle over the weekend, but the grant writer spent the entire day in her office. Several times during the day, Kelsey even closed her door to make phone calls in private. What did she need to keep private? Was she doing favors for Ben? Jaw tight, Dara decided to take that up with the demon doctor when he arrived.

Once, she ran into Kelsey in the kitchen, getting coffee. Kelsey filled her cup so quickly she slopped coffee on the counter. She wiped it up and scurried out of the kitchen, guilt written all over her face. Dara would definitely be talking to Ben.

At four thirty, he appeared in her office doorway. He wore a gleeful expression, like he'd put one over on her. Her hand twitched toward the bottle of holy water stashed under her desk, but she stopped herself. Instead she said, in a tone so snotty she despised herself, "Please take your cell phone and place it in your car."

"New rule?" He actually looked pleased.

Of course he did. She was helping him evade his boss's

supervision. For a moment, she considered rescinding the rule, but common sense won out.

"It is for you," she said.

He disappeared and returned a few minutes later. He turned his pockets inside out to demonstrate the phone was gone. She gave him a curt nod and turned back to her computer.

"Do you have a few minutes?" He stepped closer to her desk. "I had something to discuss with you before clinic." She dragged eyes away from her PC to find him watching her.

"Certainly, Dr. Lyle." She couldn't quite manage a smile, so she settled for keeping her features in a calm mask.

His gleeful expression returned. "I don't know if Kelsey said anything to you…"

Blood rushed to her head. How dare he waltz into her office and dangle his date with one of her staffers in front of her? *You're just jealous,* a little voice said. She ignored it. He knew how she felt about him targeting her team. And after all the time she'd spent healing him last week. After what they'd almost…

Her hand shot beneath her desk. Surging to her feet, she sprayed him squarely in the face.

"Gaaaah," he roared as his flesh turned crimson.

"Is everything okay?" Kelsey called.

Footsteps sounded in the hallway.

Dara grabbed Ben's arm and dragged him inside the office.

"We're okay. Everything's okay." She slammed the door in Javier and Kelsey's faces.

"What in Satan's name did you do that for?" Ben demanded, touching his burning face with one fingertip.

"Like you don't know," she shout-whispered. "I told you to stay away from my staffers."

"Stay away from your…? What are you talking about?"

The holy water hadn't melted his skin, as it had when Nana sprayed him, but it still looked pretty painful. He touched his face and winced. Her hand itched to squirt him again, but that would be sheer self-indulgence.

"How dare you come in here and brag about seducing that child," she said.

"Seducing…? I haven't seduced anyone," he said.

"You liar." She was yelling. She lowered her voice. "I saw you at Slyders Saturday afternoon."

Comprehension dawned on his face, but there was no accompanying guilt. Of course not. He was a demon, incapable of remorse, no matter how heinous his actions.

"You saw me with Kelsey?" he asked.

She nodded, sticking out her jaw.

Instead of looking guilty, he quirked his lips. "And that upset you enough to spray me with acid?"

"It's not acid." Even as she defended her action, she felt a little awkward. Something about his response was off, even for a demon with no conscience.

"It is to me. It burns like acid."

Now she felt guilty, which was ridiculous. She folded her arms across her chest. "I warned you to stay away from my staff."

He checked his face in the mirror over her filing cabinet. The red was already fading. He walked to the door and opened it. "Kelsey, can you come in here for a minute?"

Dara grabbed the spray bottle again, but she couldn't very well spritz him in front of a witness. Kelsey came in, carrying a folder. Her eyes bounced between the two of them. She swallowed.

"Were you able to make any progress today?" he asked.

Warily, Kelsey opened her folder. "The caterer agreed to have a buffet of finger sandwiches, cold salads and cookies set up by two p.m. The party store has a full selection of poker-related decorations that we can pick up at a reasonable price. And it looks like we'll be able to get a temporary liquor license by Saturday, though I don't know how in the world that happened. It usually takes a month."

Dara's eyes swung from Kelsey to Ben and back again. "Sandwiches? Decorations? A liquor license?"

"I'm hosting a poker tournament on Saturday, with all proceeds benefitting the Matthew A. Strong Memorial Clinic," Ben said.

"Poker…?" Nana would be horrified. Dara opened her mouth to refuse, but before she could say anything, he continued.

"We should be able to raise ten thousand dollars."

"That much?" Compared to the grant he'd provided, it was pocket change, but the right thought was definitely there. Except, where he was concerned, she wasn't sure what the right thought actually was.

"At least," he said. "Maybe more. And next year, when you have a little more time to plan, you should be able to do five times that." He turned one of his gorgeous smiles on Kelsey. "Thanks, Kelsey—you've done a great job." His tone was a dismissal, and Kelsey took it with a grace that said she'd realigned her expectations concerning him.

Dara reached out to thank him and apologize for dousing him with holy water, but at the sight of her disfigured hand, Lilith's words came back to her. *Your scars skeeve him out.* That explained why he hadn't suggested stopping to buy condoms on Saturday night, why he hadn't been in touch since then. This fundraiser was his way of paying his debt of gratitude for her nursing care.

"Thank you," she said. "That was very kind."

He looked so crestfallen guilt stirred again, but she couldn't afford to indulge her emotions. Nana was right. No matter how many nice things he did, he was a demon and a danger to her and everyone else in this clinic.

Even though she had absolved Ben of trying to seduce Kelsey, Dara tried to keep her distance. It was a difficult thing to do when they saw every patient together.

She was relieved when Gabby escorted their final patient in. Even being in the same room with him was starting to take a toll on her. Every time he glanced her way, she wanted to hide her hands, to make sure her scrub top covered her clavicles. *Grit your teeth and get through it.* She was Lonnie Perdue's granddaughter, and no demon would make her cry. Not where he could see, anyway.

The last patient's arm was wrapped in gauze. When Ben peeled the gauze away, the sight was horrific. She was accustomed to infection, but the putrid stink of the boy's wound made her stomach heave. The inside of his forearm had open lesions. Ben stared at it, intrigued.

"How did you get this?" he asked the boy.

"Wrap that back up," she said.

"It's MRSA," Ben said.

"I know what it is. We don't have the facilities to deal with it here. Our ventilation isn't good enough and the infection protocols are beyond what we can guarantee." She turned to the boy. "You need to go to Bermuda General, where they're better prepared to help you. Do you have a ride to get there?" If not, they'd send him by ambulance.

The boy nodded. "My mom can take me."

Frowning, Ben rewrapped the boy's arm.

"How did you get this?" he asked again. "Have you been in the hospital?"

The boy shook his head. "Some lady came into the restaurant where I work today. She reached for her cup as I was trying to clear her plate and she scratched my arm with her fingernail. A few hours later, it looked like this."

"Four hours?" Dara asked. MRSA took days to develop. Maybe this was some new super-infection. "What did she look like? We'll need to track her down and—"

"No time for that now," Ben said. "He needs to get to the hospital."

She spoke to the boy's mother, impressing on her the importance of taking him straight to Bermuda General. Then she called ahead to alert them to set up contagion protocols. When she returned to the exam room, Ben was still there.

Eyes narrowed, she fingered the spray bottle in her pocket. "This is another plague."

Ben didn't meet her eyes. "I don't recall Egypt having a plague of MRSA."

"No, but they had a plague of blood, and that's close enough."

He didn't argue.

"You didn't need the woman's description because you know who might have done that to him." Again, he made no denial. "Because you're in cahoots with another demon, a female."

Color rose in his face and his eyebrows crashed together. "I am not in cahoots with anyone."

"What's really going on here?" She waved her hands to encompass him and the clinic. "This clearly isn't a research mission about U.S. healthcare."

She looked into his eyes. His pupils were round and human-looking. It had been a long time since they'd turned rectangular. Even on the day she'd tossed him out of the car and made him find his own way home, they'd stayed round. But he wasn't human. He was a demon, and no matter how blameless he looked or how good he smelled, he was dangerous.

She bowed her head in defeat. "Nana's right. I should close this place—shutter the windows and lock the doors—before someone gets hurt."

She felt sick at the thought. She was so tired. She had been fighting demons nonstop for six weeks, and it had taken nearly everything she had.

Holding up his index finger, he disappeared out the door, returning a moment later with a pen and a pad of paper. Setting it down on the counter, he wrote, *The mic in my phone may be able to pick up what we say, even from the car.*

Dara frowned, trying to figure out where he was going with this.

It's going to be all right. Your clinic is safe, I promise.

She opened her mouth to argue, but he held up his index finger again and left the room. After a moment, the volume of the music playing over the PA system increased until, overhead, Lady Gaga bellowed that the boy she'd gone out with was really a monster. *I know just how you feel,* Dara thought.

Ben came back into the room and closed the door. She took a step back, but he followed, trapping her against the counter.

"I don't know how good the tech in that mic is," he murmured into her ear, "so be very careful what you say."

His breath was warm on her ear. It was impossible to think with him so close.

"I have nothing to say," she said.

He crowded even closer, till his body pressed the length of hers. "What's happened since the last time I saw you?"

"Nothing." She fought down a shiver of longing. "I've just had time to think."

"Don't think." He placed little nibbling kisses from one end of her collarbones to the other. *Your scars skeeve him out,* Lilith had said, but the erection brushing against her hipbone made that a lie. "You are the most beautiful woman I've ever seen. And these"—he nuzzled her collarbones—"drive me crazy."

It was like he'd lit a bonfire in her belly. If Gabby and Javier's voices outside the door hadn't reminded her there were people around, she would have torn off his clothes and had sex with him, right there on the exam table.

"Would you like to come back to the condo?" she asked.

"I would love to come back to your condo and make love to you until we both pass out from exhaustion." The heat in his eyes, not to mention the erect phallus bulging beneath his lab coat, said that was true. "But tonight I have a poker tournament to set up. After the tournament, I'll have time to make love to you the way you deserve."

She tried to take that with good grace. "I can't figure out how you're pulling this together in less than a week."

He kissed her again. "Don't think about it too much." He walked out the door.

On the way home, she stopped at the drugstore and bought a box of condoms.

CHAPTER 39

Dara hadn't gotten a straight answer from Ben about the she-demon bedeviling the clinic, so the next morning, she stopped to see Nana before going into work.

She explained the situation.

"So there's another one?" Nana's age-spotted hands trembled. "And you don't have any idea who it is?"

The patient's description, brief as it was, had screamed Lilith.

"I have someone in mind," Dara said. "There's a woman I met about the same time Ben appeared."

Nana raised her wispy eyebrows. "Ben?"

Dara's face warmed. "Dr. Lyle. Anyway, I gave this woman the salt test, but she passed. Have you ever heard of a demon passing the salt test?"

Nana never had.

"Things kept happening, though, and she always seemed to be somewhere in the vicinity. So I tried making her mad, but her pupils didn't change."

"She passed both tests?" Nana asked.

Dara nodded.

"But you still think she's a demon?"

Dara shrugged. "I don't know what to think. Are there any other tests that you know of?"

"Holy water and demonweed."

"Right. I know about those." Dara rubbed her face. "The problem is, I have to work with this woman. I can't figure out a subtle way to spray her or rub demonweed on her without seeming like a crazy woman."

"There's the Bible test."

"I have even less reason to ask her to swear to something on a Bible."

"Bring her by tomorrow night," Nana said.

"I can't." Dara refused to expose Nana to further danger.

"Why not?"

"I'm really busy this week."

"What are you so busy with?"

There was no point in lying. "Ben has arranged a poker tournament on Saturday with the proceeds benefitting the clinic."

Nana's jaw dropped. "And you're going to let him?"

"He thinks it will raise ten thousand dollars."

Nana looked like she might have a stroke right there on the spot. "I see what his plan is now. He's set your foot on the slippery slope. First it was drinking, now it's gambling." She didn't say, "And next will be fornicating," but the words hung in the air.

"If two hundred and fifty thousand dollars didn't corrupt me, another ten thousand won't make any difference."

The logic of this was so compelling even Nana couldn't argue. She bit her lip. "What is he up to?"

"I don't know," Dara said. He'd said the clinic would come to no harm. For some reason, she believed him, but Nana wouldn't.

"You need to stay on your guard," Nana said.

"For right now, can we focus on the she-demon?"

"Bring her here," Nana said again.

"I don't think she'd come. She's not a woman who does much she doesn't want to."

"Convince her."

"How?"

"Ask Ben." Nana's eyes swept Dara up and down. "He's good at talking women into things."

"All right. All right. I'll bring her."

"When?" Nana asked.

"Next week, after the tournament is over."

For the rest of the week, Belial worked long days, preparing for the tournament. Commandeering Kelsey, Javier and Jeremy as his team, he used the clinic kitchen as an operations base. There were poker supplies to buy—chips and cards, lammers and timers—and a thousand other details.

The ballroom supplied tables and chairs, but their plain white tablecloths didn't create the right ambiance, so Belial drove to Mobile, Alabama to buy sturdy green felt table toppers from a gambling supply house there. At least the Hyundai was good for that.

He could have gotten supplies from Hell, but by the time you factored in all the palm-greasing and bargaining, not to mention the obligatory visit to the boss, it was faster and cheaper to do everything Aboveworld. Also, it allowed less potential for meddling.

Dara kept the clinic running almost single-handedly while everyone else worked on the tournament. Whenever he caught her alone in an exam room, he pulled her into his arms and kissed her. Tuesday night brought a hot make-out session after the last patient left. He slid his hand up the front of her scrub top, but she grabbed his wrist. "Someone will hear."

The metal overhead door to the pharmacy rattled closed.

"Is anyone still here?" Chris called.

Dara opened the door a wedge. "I am."

"Everyone else is gone. I'll lock the back door as I leave."

Dara thanked him and said goodnight. When the outside door slammed, color rose in her cheeks. She was so transparent Belial chuckled. That brought even more color to her cheeks. To mask her embarrassment, she pulled fresh paper onto the exam table and tore off the used section.

He dared not make love to her and risk drawing her deeper into his web. It was no exaggeration when he claimed that no woman had ever resisted corruption after fornicating with him. He had no plans to harm her, but who knew what Satan might be planning? For her safety, Belial wanted that slim degree of separation. It felt as though he'd had a nonstop erection since the first time he saw her, but he couldn't take any chances.

She wadded up the paper and shoved it into the trash can. She looked so adorable, with her flushed face, he cornered her beside the exam table. He checked the computer camera. It was still covered with black tape.

"Are we alone in this building?" He put his hands on her shoulders. His thumbs skimmed her collarbones. His erection felt like it would split the inseam of his pants.

Dara nodded, her eyes huge. The mixture of hope and fear there undid him. There was nothing he could do about his own longings, but he could satisfy hers. On Saturday, he would do something to make her push him away again, but tonight he would gratify her in ways she'd never known before.

He crushed his mouth down on hers, reveling in her instant response. As their tongues tangled in an ancient dance, his shaft became a piece of iron. Cupping her haunches, he lifted her. She wrapped her legs around his waist. She ground herself against him and he groaned. This was the strongest temptation he'd ever resisted.

He set her on the exam table without breaking their kiss. She moaned against his mouth and locked her ankles behind him. When they finally came up for air, he pulled her scrub top over her head. Her color heightened, but she made no move to resist.

Against her breast lay the ruby cross that had burned him the other night. He eyed it warily.

She reached for the clasp. "I can take it off."

He stayed her hand. "Leave it on. It won't be in the way for what I have in mind."

He unfastened her bra and tossed it away. Reflexively, her arms crossed to cover her breasts and collarbones, but he grasped her wrists and peeled them away, kissing each palm before setting them at her sides.

"The light's a little clinical, don't you think?" she said.

"Do you want me to turn it off?" That would leave the windowless room completely black.

She hesitated. "It's up to you."

"Then we're leaving it on." He wanted her to be with him without shame or inhibition.

Before him, her breasts swayed free. Their motion made his shaft harden even more painfully. He leaned forward to suckle a breast, feeling her nipple tighten between his lips.

She arched her back, pressing her breast more deeply into his mouth. He swirled his tongue around her nipple. She grasped his shoulders. "We don't have condoms here. Unless you…?"

"We won't need them." He blessed her common sense. It was easier to be the man he wanted to be knowing she would hold him to that standard. "Tonight is all about you."

He returned his attention to her breasts, taking time between sorties to nuzzle her collarbones, even though every time he touched her scars, his shaft thrust toward her like a lance at a joust.

Reaching down, he slipped off her clogs and dragged her scrub pants off. She was wearing white cotton briefs, which should have dampened his desire, but they were so perfectly Dara they had the opposite effect. Spreading her thighs, he put his face against the cotton cloth between her legs and scraped his teeth over the fabric.

She tried to shut her knees.

"Relax." He backed off, using his hands to calm her. He stroked down her ribs, feeling the indentations between each rib and the soft skin that covered them. He smoothed her belly, his fingers drifting over the pale scar where they'd taken her womb. She had lost so much. He would not be part of her losing anything else. He kissed the scar to seal that vow.

He contented himself with kissing her until her body became soft and pliant. Then he slipped a finger inside her panties. Her portal was warm and wet and welcoming. He swallowed. There were condoms in the pharmacy. Jamie had just locked it down, but Dara would have a key. Belial pulled himself up short. Condom or no condom, uniting with her would eventually destroy her.

For a while, he contented himself with stroking lightly between her legs. When she wriggled to get closer to his questing fingers, he pulled her to the edge of the table and ground his shaft against her. She groaned and hooked her ankles around his ass, rubbing hard against him.

Her body called to him like a beacon pulling him home. It would be so easy to unzip his khakis, shove aside her panties and be inside her. For a moment, his body pulsed with a hunger so strong he could barely contain it.

Then he looked at her face. She smiled at him, her eyes drowsy with desire. Despite the harsh overhead light, she made no attempt to cover herself or mask her eagerness. She trusted him, and for the first time in ten thousand years, trust felt like something to be honored, no matter the cost.

Corralling his outsize need to join with her, he stepped back. He peeled off her underpants. Kneeling on the little step at the end of the table, he buried his face between her thighs, glorying in the heat and the taste and the scent of her. He stroked her with his tongue until her fists clenched and unclenched on the padded table.

The metal edge of the step chewed into his knees, but he would have been content to stay there, tasting the honey of her, forever. Occasionally, he would reach up to tweak her nipples, or stroke the pit of her elbow or the delicate flesh behind her knees. Every touch seemed to delight her, pushing her closer to orgasm, and that delighted him.

When certain movements of her body warned him that she was about to climax, he slid one finger inside her, then a second. Unerringly, he located the spot that magnified a woman's orgasm and pressed against it. His tongue stroked harder. With a muffled shriek, she grabbed his hair and ground herself into his face, arching off the table like a woman possessed.

Joy bubbled up inside him. Into the life of this woman who had known so much pain, he had brought pleasure. Her orgasm rolled on and on, filling him with a fierce exultation.

Only when she finally eased back against the table, releasing his hair and lying there, spent, did he remove his fingers from her body. He stood. Dara appeared to be semiconscious. He kissed her, savoring the way her body looked, more relaxed than he'd ever seen her. He probed one of her trapezius muscles with a fingertip. It was as soft as a sea sponge. She didn't move under his prodding. He couldn't help grinning.

"So that was okay?" he asked.

She opened heavy eyelids. It was clearly a struggle.

"Better than okay." She dragged herself up on one elbow, tired but game. "What can I do for you?"

That was Dara. Even exhausted, she thought about others.

"You could stay naked," he said, letting his eyes roam over her.

Unfortunately, that brought her back to herself. Blushing, she got up and dressed. She moved more slowly than normal, and that made him smile. He pulled her close and kissed her.

"Saturday," she mumbled against his shirt. "I'll pay you back on Saturday."

He kissed the top of her head.

Before Saturday, he'd have to figure something out.

CHAPTER 40

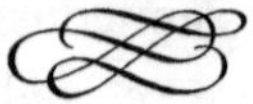

On Wednesday, they discovered they needed a special permit, a variance to the local zoning ordinances, to allow gambling at the ballroom. The zoning commission wouldn't meet until next month, so that required another trip to Hell.

This time, Belial had to blackmail Bad to get what he wanted. He threatened to tell Satan about Bad's dalliance with a certain she-demon during the same period said she-demon was also dallying with Satan. It was only after he listed dates and locations and hinted that pictures might exist that Bad agreed to have one of his minions hack into the Bermuda County computer system to file and approve the variance application.

Belial watched over the hacker's shoulder, confirming the variance had gone through.

Bad wandered up beside him. "While you're down here, the boss wants to see you." He made no effort to hide his satisfaction.

Cursing under his breath, Belial made his way to Ring Nine.

When he got to Satan's office, the boss's color was normal and no hint of smoke emanated from his horns. Belial's demon senses tingled. There was no way Satan was this calm with the wager so near its conclusion and nothing decided.

"Have you made any more progress?" Satan asked.

Belial thought about his foreplay with Dara in the exam room. "I've been busy with the tournament. That will seal the deal."

"Take her back to the beach house after the tournament," Satan said. "The boys haven't had any fresh porn in a long time."

Belial tried to cover his distaste. "I don't do my best work in front of an audience."

"Deal with it. Three-quarters of the demons down here have already lost money on the pool for how long it would take you to boink her, and they're pissed. If you're to become second-in-command, you need to start mending fences."

Belial's unease increased. Satan acted like his long-awaited promotion was a done deal rather than dependent on a mission that was behind schedule. Belial should be tap-dancing to avoid being recalled, not arguing logistics.

"She'll be a lot more comfortable in her own home," he said.

Satan's face darkened a shade. "After six weeks, she should be willing to do it in a glass elevator, if that's what you want. Fuck her in the beach house."

"Seriously? You're willing to risk the outcome of this wager to keep the troops happy?"

"You say you want to be a leader. Show me some leadership skills."

"I am showing you leadership skills. Risking an important mission to provide a circus for a bunch of louts who should be out seducing their own targets is exactly the kind of practice I want to put an end to. We could be ten times more productive if 'the boys' would get off their dead asses and get to work."

It was a speech he'd given Satan a thousand times. He'd said nothing new, but the boss's face lightened.

"You still want that promotion."

"Of course I still want that promotion," Belial said, though he could not have cared less.

"Fine. Boink her wherever works best. Then report in."

One thing that worried Belial was the attacks on the clinic. Lilith continued to deny responsibility, though he knew beyond doubt she was behind them. Worse, they appeared to be escalating.

On Wednesday, Tia called in sick because of a huge, painful boil on her perineum—the plague of boils. Dara was supposed to meet Ben and Kelsey at the ballroom to plan decorations, but Tia's illness meant she had to cover the Wednesday night clinic. That, in turn, meant he didn't get to see her. She was philosophical, but, knowing it was one of the few days they had left together, Belial was furious.

When he got home that night, he confronted Lilith. "I know you're behind these plagues. The boy you gave MRSA identified you."

Lilith widened her eyes. "I don't know what you're talking about. I'm doing everything I can to help you. Jeremy's been there every night, helping. What else do you want from me?"

"I'm glad you asked. I want you to convince every board member to participate in the tournament."

Her mouth fell open. "The buy-in for your tournament is two thousand dollars. How do you expect me to convince people I barely know to donate that kind of money on three days' notice?"

"You're a demon," he said. "Use your skills."

"Fine." Then her eyes narrowed. "How are you paying for all this?"

"You're going to help me."

"I so am not. Mammon's right—you need to learn to work within a budget."

He reached into the pocket of his jacket and retrieved the velvet purse he'd brought back from Hell. He'd considered simply stealing some of Lilith's jewels and pawning them, but again the thought of Dara finding out and thinking less of him dissuaded him. Before he even opened the flap, Lilith's eyes began to glow.

"Is that…?"

Nodding, he drew out a pair of jeweled hair combs. They had belonged to Jezebel. Before he seduced her, she'd been a nice young girl. It was a stark reminder of what could happen if he had intercourse with Dara.

Lilith's hand hovered over the combs. "May I?"

He shoved them back in the purse. “For a price.”

She glared at him. “How much?”

He knew to a penny how much he needed to finish funding the tournament. “Five thousand dollars.” Their history made them worth far more, and they both knew it.

“I’ll have the money transferred to your account.”

He shook his head. There were too many ways to interfere with electronic transactions. “Cash only.”

She pulled out her wallet and handed him fifty crisp hundreds.

“It’s a pleasure doing business with you.” He handed her the combs. “By the way—why haven’t you been hanging around Dara, helping with the tournament?”

She slipped one of the combs into her hair and pulled a mirror from her purse. “I thought it might be good to give her some breathing room.”

A flicker of hope ignited in his chest. “Did she make you?”

“Please.” Lilith stuck her nose in the air. “Unlike some demons, I know how to do my job.”

The next day brought a freak hailstorm that broke several windows at the clinic, though no other damage was recorded in Alexandria. Belial wished he’d charged Lilith twice as much.

On Friday, Dara met him at the ballroom after work.

“How did things go today?” he asked.

“Power outage,” she said. “We sat in the dark for three hours. And when the lights came back on, the computer network wouldn’t come up. The tech thinks we have a virus.”

“The plagues of darkness and pestilence,” he said.

She nodded.

Neither of them said it aloud, but that left only the death of the firstborn. He wished he could tell her not to worry about that. The terms the Enemy had set down ensured that no one would die. His cell phone was in his pocket, so he couldn’t say anything. He held her in his arms and rubbed the tight muscles in her shoulders, kissing her hair and murmuring, "Everything will be okay. I promise."

Dara spent Friday evening kissing Ben in every dark corner of the Alexandria Ballroom they could find. The interludes left her panting for more. If Kelsey and Jeremy and Javier and Gabby hadn't been there, she would have dragged down his jeans and mounted him right there in the ballroom.

On the way home, she stopped at Mercy Care to see Nana. Guilt stabbed at her. It was only the second time she'd gotten by to see her grandmother that week.

Nana was already in bed when she got there. She leaned over to kiss the weathered cheek. Nana sniffed her neck. "I smell demon musk on you."

Dara didn't deny it.

"Are you fornicating with him?"

"Not yet." She hated disappointing Nana even more than she hated worrying her, but there was no point in lying. Nana wouldn't believe her anyway.

She filled Nana in on the progress on the tournament. As expected, Nana didn't approve of funding the clinic by encouraging people to drink and gamble. "You're spending too much time with that demon."

That was probably true.

"What are you doing, girl?" Nana asked. "You know he's got ill intentions. What are you thinking?"

"He's changed since he was sick."

Nana snorted. "You're thinking with your hormones and not your head. This will come to a bad end."

Even though her heart and gut said Ben was different in some momentous way, Dara couldn't put it into words.

"Once this tournament is over, I'll bring him by and you can see for yourself."

"Demons don't change." Nana's face was flushed, a sure sign her blood pressure was up.

Dara's stomach twisted with worry and guilt. "Sunday. I'll bring him by on Sunday."

"You were supposed to bring me that she-demon, too."

Dara grimaced. "I forgot all about that. I'll see what I can do, after the tournament."

When she got up to leave, Nana pulled a thick, leather-bound book from beneath the covers and held it out. "Take this with you."

"What is it?"

"Your granddaddy's Bible."

Dara frowned. "I can't take this." She pushed it back toward her grandmother. "It's yours."

Nana tucked her hands under the covers. The flesh around her jowls sagged like the weight of the world's sins was dragging on her. "Take it home and read the Book of Revelation. That will help you see that demon for what he is."

Dara knew exactly what Revelation had to say about demons, but the demons depicted there were hard to reconcile with Ben Lyle. More and more, he seemed like an ordinary man to her, but she didn't want to upset Nana further by arguing.

"I won't be in tomorrow," she said. "By the time the tournament is over, I'll be too exhausted. But we'll see you on Sunday."

Nana looked her in the eye. "I'm praying for you."

She was praying Dara wouldn't do something she had every intention of doing.

Dara took the Bible home and set it on the dining room table. There, it served as a reproach every time she walked past.

On Saturday, Belial, clad in a tuxedo, watched the parking lot of the Alexandria Ballroom fill with Cadillacs, Lexuses, Mercedes, Porsches and Ferraris. When a Lamborghini rolled past the glass doors, he stared at the Italian car in bemusement. Why had driving one seemed so important? It was just a car, a lifeless hunk of metal and rubber.

Dara wore a short black dress with a black lace yoke that played peekaboo with her collarbones and nearly drove him crazy. She sat by his side at the registration desk and greeted the players as they came in. He took their two-thousand-dollar cashier's checks and Dara gave them their table assignments. By his calculation, even after he paid the remaining costs associated with the event, they would clear at least the ten thousand dollars he'd promised.

Whenever there was a lull, he ran his fingers up the black nylon stockings that encased her legs. They weren't pantyhose, but stockings with a garter belt. He had known it would be hard to resist making love to her later, but the dress and those stockings intensified the problem tenfold.

Scattered among the sixty-four players were the eight members of the clinic's board of trustees, looking a little bewildered. For once, Lilith had done as he asked.

When she arrived, she and Dara made a show of air-kissing cheeks, but they didn't meet one another's eyes.

"What happened between you and your BFF?" he asked after Lilith moved on.

Dara shrugged. "We discovered we don't have that much in common."

He sent up a silent hosanna.

But the highlight was when Dr. Wilson, the old practitioner who had quit during Belial's first visit to the clinic, showed up. Dara stared at him in stupefaction. By Belial's count, she had reached out to the old doctor at least a dozen times, but he'd never returned her calls.

Knowing how much the rift hurt her, Belial had dropped by the man's house and invited him to play in the tournament. When Dr. Wilson tried to shut the door in his face, he tossed a snare.

"I may be too old to treat patients," Dr. Wilson said now, "but I can still help the clinic."

Tears shimmered in Dara's eyes. Dr. Wilson reached out and patted her hand.

"Don't get yourself all upset," he said. "You were right. It was time I stepped back."

"But the med students learned so much from you."

He considered that. "What if I come back and just serve in a mentoring role?"

They made plans to reconnect the following week. As the old man walked away, Dara turned toward Belial, her face shining like Moses' when he came down from Mt. Sinai. It was the best snare Belial had ever thrown.

At twelve thirty, Halpas's celebrity arrived. He made a short speech of welcome and the games began. Belial's sense that all was right with the world suffered a setback when Dara picked up the last remaining table assignment.

"Where are you going?" he asked, trailing her into the ballroom.

"As the executive director at the clinic, I'm a member of the board. They expect me to invest as much as they do."

"Where did you hear that?"

For a moment, he thought she wouldn't answer. Finally, she said, "Lilith."

Damn Lilith and her constant interference. "You invest every day of your life into that place."

She patted his arm. "Maybe I'll have beginner's luck and I'll win."

He looked at the hard faces at the tables around the room. There was no chance of that. "Do you even know how to play poker?"

She nodded. "I read up on it online yesterday. It doesn't look that complicated."

He groaned. He had planned to roam around the room, ensuring everyone was comfortable and happy, at least till they lost all their money. Now he positioned himself behind Dara.

Tony Balsamo, the OB/GYN he'd played golf with, sat next to her. Good. She could make his acquaintance. Once Belial was gone, perhaps something would come of that. The thought was less satisfying than Belial had expected. He didn't want her with another man, even a good man.

Ed Norris, from the Bermuda County Commission, took the third spot at the table. A retired doctor who had returned early from his summer place off the coast of Massachusetts dealt the first hand.

Dara drew a pair of jacks, and an ace, deuce and trey of hearts. Belial watched with cautious optimism as she matched the opening bet of two hundred dollars. Hope turned to dismay when she traded in her jacks for what proved to be the five of spades and nine of clubs. After the hand ended, he dragged her away from the table. "Why did you get rid of those jacks?"

"The website said five in a row of the same suit is better than two of the same kind."

He took a deep breath. "Did the website also quote the statistical probability of getting five in a row?"

Dara frowned. "Maybe. I didn't have time to read the whole article."

"Think in terms of probability from now on," he said.

The next hand, she wound up with three fives. She let herself be bid up to two hundred and fifty dollars, but then folded when the old man from Nantucket doubled the stakes. Pretending there was an issue he needed to discuss with her, Belial pulled her from the table again.

"Why did you fold? You know that three of a kind is a good hand."

"He acted like his was better," she said. "And you were so upset over me losing two hundred dollars, I figured you'd freak if I lost five hundred."

He groaned.

"If you're such a great poker player," Dara said, "why aren't you playing?" He tried to walk away without answering, but she grabbed his arm. "Why?"

He flushed. "Because I spent every dime I had getting this thing set up."

She stared at him like he was still a member of the heavenly host. Then she grabbed his head between her hands and kissed him, on the mouth, in front of the entire room. Scattered applause broke out and she blushed but didn't back away.

"Are all demons like you?" she whispered.

"No," he said. "I'm not even like me." And it was true. Somewhere along the line, he'd changed into something else, though he had no idea what that something was.

Dara was out at the end of the first round. When she had good cards, she underbid or folded. When she had lousy cards, she took ridiculous chances. She knew nothing about checking, and she was careless about keeping her cards hidden. And through it all, her face displayed every thought that crossed her mind. She was, without question, the worst poker player he had ever seen.

"Well, did you at least have fun?" he asked during the break. They stood beside the buffet. Kelsey's caterer had done a great job, and even the players who lost in the first round seemed to be enjoying themselves.

"That's the fastest two thousand dollars I've ever spent without getting a case of insulin in return." She looked so shell-shocked he had to hug her.

"Hey, you two, get a room," Lilith said.

She had won her table. Jeremy, like Dara, was already out. He was at the other end of the buffet, chatting with Kelsey. After a moment, Dara excused herself to go speak to one of her volunteers. Lilith wasn't having a good day on the relationship front.

"You have two choices," Belial said as soon as Dara walked away. "You can lose sometime in the next three rounds, or you can donate your winnings to the clinic."

"Make me," Lilith said. He was surprised she didn't stick her tongue out.

He took her by the shoulders and turned her around. Taking her head between his hands, he tilted it so she was looking at one of the cameras that dotted the corners of the ceiling. "This time, I'll have proof that you tried to undercut the mission."

"Fine," she said. "I'll lose in the next round."

The final round came down to the celebrity and the old man from Nantucket. It was a hard-fought match, but in the end, the old man won the pot. In a grand gesture, he donated half of his winnings, bringing the clinic's take to over fifty thousand dollars. It was far more than he'd dared hope for. Not bad for a week's work. Dara accepted the donation with a huge smile as everyone cheered.

"I promise that we'll do a lot of good with this money," she said.

Belial was pleased. It set a great precedent for similar donations from future tournaments.

His mind was already on the next challenge, though. He walked into the men's room and stepped into one of the stalls, closing the door behind him. He pulled his cell phone from his pocket and dropped it into the toilet.

He was going to need some privacy.

CHAPTER 41

Belial pulled a table topper from the rented van and looked around the garage of Dara's condo. "What do you want me to do with these?"

She checked the rafters. "I think they can go up there, but I'll have put down plywood first. Could you please stack them inside the house for now?"

He carried the first topper into the dining room and set it on the floor. "I'll buy some plywood tomorrow so we can get these out of your dining room."

"Thank you." Dara still wore the starry-eyed look she'd had at the tournament.

A fist clamped around his heart. There was no way he could give her what she wanted—what, to his shame, he'd led her to expect. Not without putting her soul at risk.

Once the toppers were disposed of, he climbed the ladder. She handed him unopened decks of playing cards sealed in plastic. Her fingers brushed his, and it was like a flame traveled up his arm to his chest. The need for her was so great he clenched his teeth. He drew a deep breath and placed the bag on the shelf.

"Next year, you'll already have all the equipment." He was proud of how conversational he sounded. "So your expenses will be lower. And you'll have longer to plan, so you won't spend so much expediting things. I told Betty to reserve the ballroom for the first Saturday in December. She put you in her book." There. That was better. He took a step down the ladder.

Dara stroked his calf, as though she couldn't keep her hands off him. Her touch left him so lightheaded he missed a step, jolting as he caught himself.

"Careful." Her hand slid from his calf up the back of his thigh to steady him. Their eyes met, and the heat between them was like a tangible thing. The warmth of her touch penetrated the fabric of his pants, and desire rose, thick and sweet. His brain clouded as all the blood forsook it for points south.

He stepped off the ladder and she lifted her face for his kiss.

"Let's go to bed," she said.

His hands shook with the need to gather her close. He wanted to hold her and never let go. And that was the problem. If he touched her, he wouldn't be able to stop himself from making love to her. And once they had joined, she would be unable to resist doing whatever he asked.

He would have given the rest of his eternal life to be united with her just once, but he could not, would not, betray her like that. He loved her too much. The thought stunned him, but even as he rejected it as impossible—demons couldn't love—he knew it to be true.

He had always loved her, even before she was born. He would love her beyond her life's end, even after she'd gone to a place beyond his reach, where he'd never see or speak to her again.

His resolve strengthened. He would not put her soul in jeopardy. Rejecting her at this stage was cruel, but it would save her from a hellish future. The one thing he could do to make it easier for her was allow her to refuse him.

He grinned at her. "Pretty eager, aren't you?"

She blushed. "I've been looking forward to it, yes."

He was such an ass. He'd deserved to be cast out of heaven. He'd deserved every horrible thing Satan had ever done to him. He smirked. "You should be. You haven't had sex until you've had it with me."

She stopped smiling, and it was as though the sun had dimmed. "Do you think you're being funny?"

He forced a careless shrug. "No, I just think I'm the best lover you'll ever have." His tone insinuated there would be many more.

Her face froze into a glacier. "Mostly you're just a jerk." She shook her head. "Why do I keep forgetting you're a demon? Nana keeps warning me, but do I listen?" She turned on her heel and walked away. "Feel free to let yourself out."

It was what he wanted, wasn't it? He would have been fine if he hadn't caught a glint of tears in her eyes as she turned away. The sight of her tears, knowing he'd caused them, was like Ehud's sword twisting into his entrails. It hurt more than any of Satan's punishments ever had. He had approached the problem with his usual toolset—arrogance, manipulation and callous indifference to others' feelings—and hurt the woman he loved more than life itself.

"Dara, I'm sorry."

She didn't turn around. "You can't keep being a jerk and just expect that I'll forgive you."

"I know." It was no more than he deserved. "Can I explain?"

She turned, her arms folded across her chest. "You can try."

"I was afraid."

Her face didn't soften. "Humans are afraid all the time. We're not immortal. We don't have special powers. But some of us manage to get through the day without deliberately hurting other people."

He hung his head.

"What are you afraid of?" she asked. "It's not like I'm asking for a commitment here. You'll be gone in a week. Right?"

He'd forgotten she knew his timeline, even though she didn't know what lay behind it.

"I'm afraid, if I make love to you, you'll be more susceptible to corruption."

She nodded. "Uh-huh."

He blinked. "You knew that?"

"Of course. It's just common sense that being intimate with a demon increases my risk of corruption. Bad news: we've already been pretty intimate."

"No, I mean, having intercourse."

She nodded. "That's another level of intimacy."

She wasn't getting it. "No woman I've made love to has ever been able to refuse me whatever I've asked afterward." Shame filled him.

To his shock, she burst out laughing. "So, you think once you touch me with your magic wand, I'll say yes to anything you ask?"

Put that way, it sounded silly, but he knew it to be true. He growled with frustration. How to convince her? He spied the Bible sitting on the dining room table. When his hair burst into flames, she would realize he was still a danger to her. He picked up the book and waited for the warning prickle of heat, but he felt only a faint warmth.

"Where did this come from?" he asked. It looked old, but perhaps it hadn't been used much.

"It was my grandfather's. Nana gave it to me."

Six weeks ago, this same Bible had nearly ignited him in her grandmother's room. Maybe it was the lie that had sparked the fire.

"*Buffy the Vampire Slayer* is so accurate it should be a documentary," he said. Nothing happened.

"What are you doing?" asked Dara.

He set the Bible down, thoroughly confused. "My hair didn't catch fire."

"Why would it?"

"I barely made it out of your grandmother's room before it went up in flames last time."

Her eyes widened. "Really?"

"Really. That's what I'm telling you. I'm dangerous."

She considered that. "But it doesn't have the same effect anymore."

He frowned. "No, it doesn't."

She drew her ruby from inside her dress and held it out. He pressed the inside of his wrist against the jewels. His flesh didn't react.

She raised her eyebrows. "If you're done being superstitious, can we make love?"

"I'm a demon. You're a human. There's never a good outcome for your side."

She reached behind her back and unzipped the little black dress, letting it slide to the floor. Beneath it she wore a silky black bra, a matching garter belt, the black nylons he'd stroked at the registration desk and the tiniest thong he'd ever seen.

"Define 'good outcome.'"

As soon as the dress pooled at her feet and she stood before him, naked except for three scraps of black lace and her garter belt and stockings, Dara knew she'd won. Where in the world had she gotten the courage to face down his fears when her own still ran rampant? She didn't know. She just knew this was something she needed to do.

She touched the sleeve of his jacket. "I feel a little underdressed."

He untied his tie and tossed it aside, then took off his jacket, never taking his eyes off her. He removed his cummerbund. When he tried to unbutton his shirt, his fingers stumbled.

She reached for him. "Let me do that."

She made short work of the buttons and pushed his shirt off his shoulders, only to have his sleeves catch on his cufflinks. He tried to work his hands free, but she stopped him. Pressing her mouth against his, she captured his hands behind his back. Kissing him, knowing he couldn't touch her in any other way, felt exciting and forbidden. She unzipped his pants. With his arms essentially tied behind his back, she was in control. She dragged his pants down to his ankles. Kneeling in front of him, she stroked his length through the silk of his boxer shorts.

He closed his eyes and groaned. His penis was as hard as marble, but it throbbed like flesh and blood.

She wanted to pull down his boxers and engulf him in her mouth, but he stepped back. He freed his hands and his shirt dropped to the floor. Then he toed off his shoes and stepped from his trousers.

"Slow down," he said.

Dara got to her feet. "Slow down? We've been having foreplay for the past six weeks."

"You think that was foreplay? Clearly, I have a lot to teach you about foreplay." He lifted her onto the dining room table, spreading her knees so he could stand between them. He stroked along the sides of the triangle of cloth between her thighs. She writhed beneath his knowing hands.

"I want you to know that I esteem you above all women." He cupped his hand over the tiny triangle of cloth. The warmth of his palm radiated through the fabric.

She pressed herself against his hand.

"Not just the women alive on the planet today," he said, "but all women ever."

She wriggled, and her thong crept into the folds there. Her teeth clenched.

"That doesn't look comfortable." He slipped his finger underneath the fabric, taking his sweet time working it loose. Every touch made her want him inside her more.

"Condoms." She could barely form words. "We need condoms."

He unhooked one of her stockings from her garter belt and rolled it slowly down her leg, kissing his way down as he went.

"You humans. Always in such a hurry. Perhaps it's because you live such short lives. It makes you feel you must race through every experience." Then he started on the other leg, even more slowly.

"I'm ready," she said. The truth was that she'd been ready since that first night at the gas pump.

"You just think you are." He nibbled kisses up her thigh. His lips set every nerve on fire as he inched his way upward. Her hands closed spasmodically on the table.

"There's so much further to go," he said.

And she was willing to go there.

"Don't stop," she said.

He stopped. "What I feel for you goes beyond lust. I need you to understand that. I admire you. I respect you. I venerate you."

"I appreciate that," she said. "For now, can we just focus on the lust part?" Hooking her ankles around his back, she pulled him toward her. He unhooked them and stepped back.

Then he pulled her thong aside, leaving her exposed to the cool air, but only for a moment. He bent to lick what he'd just revealed. She grabbed the tablecloth, scrunching it with her hands. His mouth felt so good she thought she'd lose her mind, but it wasn't what she wanted.

"Condoms," she said.

"Where are they?" he asked. His fingers replaced his stroking tongue.

"My nightstand."

He planted another kiss on her thigh. "I'll be right back."

But he wasn't. After a few minutes, she sat up, feeling silly and more than a little irritated. Where in the world was he?

She stalked down the hallway to the bedroom. It was empty. Her nightstand drawer was open, so he must have found the condoms. She crossed the bedroom to the open bathroom door. Inside, he was patting his face dry. What in the world?

"What are you doing?" she asked. *And why isn't it me?*

"Just slowing things down a little."

"And you want to do that—why?"

He turned and smiled. He trailed his fingertips down her ribcage and over the curve of her hip. Her knees wanted to buckle. "So much loveliness."

She grabbed the hem of his boxers on both sides and yanked them down. His penis sprang out like a creature freed from a cage.

His lips quirked. "Are you trying to tell me something?"

She removed her bra, then twined her fingers in the strings holding her thong in place and dragged them down over her hips, letting the scrap of lace fall to the floor. Taking his hand, she led him to the bed. She sat down on the edge and scooted to the middle.

"I'll give you three guesses," she said, "and the first two don't count."

He crawled onto the bed and bent his mouth to the nipple closest to him. She arched with pleasure. Finally, he seemed to be getting the message.

"I want to bathe in the limpid pools that are your eyes." He slipped a finger inside her. "I want to drink from the goblet of your navel." He added a second finger, crooking it expertly against her pubic bone, but they were past the point where even expert foreplay would satisfy her. "I want to—"

"I want to fuck!" she shouted.

His head jerked back.

A wave of embarrassment rolled up Dara's chest, neck and face. Even the part in her hair felt hot. She fought the urge to hide her face in her pillow.

She glared at him. "I have never said that word in my life."

"I just wanted you to know this isn't just—"

"You've been promising me hot demon sex for six weeks." She pointed to his very erect penis. "Prove to me that's more than a prop."

Now he was grinning. "Is that a challenge?"

"Take it how you will."

"Whatever the lady wants." He shoved her back on the bed and parted her legs. With a flourish, he produced the condom and rolled it on. Then he sheathed himself inside her. It was as though half of her that had been missing all her life was finally home.

CHAPTER 42

At two a.m., exhaustion finally called a halt to their lovemaking. Dara drifted off to sleep. Belial wished he could do the same, but he had to report in. He couldn't afford to anger Satan again. He crawled out of bed and put on his pants.

"Not a sleepover kind of guy, I take it?" Dara sounded disappointed, though she tried to keep her voice light.

He finished dressing and knelt beside the bed. She reached for him, but he threaded his fingers through hers so she couldn't embrace him.

"If I had my choice"—he brushed his lips across her knuckles—"I would stay in this bed beside you forever, holding you and feeling your body respond to mine. You are the most exquisite, fascinating, irresistible woman I've ever known."

She smiled. He couldn't recall ever seeing her so happy.

"But I have to report in to he-who-shall-not-be-named."

Her face dimmed. "What happens if you don't go?"

He glanced at the clock and grimaced. "So far, nothing. But I don't think he'll wait much longer." He bit his lip. "I have a confession to make."

She sat up, clutching the sheet to her chest. He covered her hand with his and dragged the sheet even higher, until it covered her scarred collarbones.

"Stop distracting me," he said. "I need to tell you something, and I don't have much time."

She nodded.

"You've already figured out I'm not here to observe American healthcare," he said.

She grew very still. "Are you here to destroy my clinic?"

"No." Honestly compelled him to add, "Not per se."

She clutched the sheet tighter. "What does that mean? Why did you come here?"

He set his jaw. Once he made his confession, she would probably order him from her life and refuse to ever set eyes on him again. If that were the case, then so be it. She would be safe, and that was all he could ask for.

"I came here to destroy you," he said.

Her eyes went wide. "To destroy me?"

He nodded.

"Why?"

He shook his head. He would not tell her the Enemy was behind this. Someday, not too long from now, her grandmother would pass on and Dara would need the comfort of her God. He wouldn't take that from her.

"It's what we do," he said.

"Why are you telling me this?"

"Because I love you. I don't want to harm you, but I may not have a choice. You need to be on your guard. Especially at the clinic, because that's where you're most vulnerable."

"Should I ban you from the clinic?"

He considered that but shook his head. "The boss is really committed to this. If I'm not working this mission, he'll send someone else, a demon you may not recognize. Fortunately, the mission has a hard end date."

"The end of next week. Why?"

"I can't tell you that." He took her hand and held it against his heart. "But I pledge this to you: I won't hurt you or your clinic."

As he crossed through the portal, Belial realized he hadn't warned Dara about Lilith. He considered doing a U-turn and going back, but that would never fly. The boss's surveillance system would have already told him that Belial was back in Hell. He made his way down to the boss's office, his palms damp.

If the boss had even the tiniest suspicion that Belial planned to undermine the wager, he'd toss him into the Lake of Fire and let another demon finish the mission. It was impossible to predict whether the Enemy would allow such a substitution. You could never predict where the Enemy would land on anything.

In Ring Nine, Andras looked at Belial with her huge, unblinking eyes. "He's expecting you."

His gut tightened another crank. He walked into Satan's office.

"Were you able to finally complete the second snare?" To his relief, Satan was calm—relaxed, even.

Belial nodded.

"Do you have things lined up for the final act?"

"Yes," Belial said, hoping like heaven he was right.

"What's your next step?"

He paused. This next bit was critical. "The final snare is corruption of the sanctuary. We went into this wager assuming that the Enemy's champion would find refuge in his word or his church, but that doesn't seem to be the case."

He gained confidence as he spoke. Dara hadn't set foot in a church since the wager began. It would be hard for anyone to argue this point. "The target's life revolves around her clinic. It's how she spends her time, her money and her energy. It's what gives her life meaning. It's her sanctuary."

Satan smirked. "I hope you've given her something else that fits those criteria."

Belial forced a semblance of his old cocky grin. "I rocked her world."

Satan's smirk grew wider. "How do you plan to make her betray the clinic?"

Belial drew a deep breath. He had to get Satan's buy-in to letting him play this by ear. That would allow him to fritter away the last few days of the wager without delivering. "I need to wait and see what opportunity arises."

Tiny puffs of smoke erupted from Satan's horns. His face darkened to a deep maroon. Belial tensed.

"We've got less than seven fucking days left and you want to wing it?" Satan asked.

Don't say any more than you have to. Forewarned was forearmed. The less Satan knew, the better. Belial would have to provide a little bit more detail, though.

"I'll be on the lookout for a patient I can misdiagnose. Dara put me back on the schedule every night, so I'll have plenty of opportunities. I need to wait for a case that she'll believe was a simple mistake and back me. Then we can spring the trap."

With any luck, he could leverage that excuse all the way through Friday. After that, it would be too late for the boss to intervene.

Satan pinched his skinny lower lip, staring at Belial with eyes like slits. Belial met Satan's gaze, his face bland.

After a moment, Satan nodded. "Make sure you don't kill anyone. I don't want to lose this bet on a technicality."

"I won't," Belial said, and meant it.

He turned to leave, but Satan's voice stopped him. "Before you go back, stop by DemSec."

"Why? This mission is all but over."

"Whenever something's going on, you never seem to have your cell phone. I want you miked."

So much for his hopes of privacy.

In DemSec, they kept him waiting for hours, making up flimsy excuses every time he complained about the delay. Finally, Bad showed up, yawning, and motioned Belial to one of the operating chairs. He sat down, and Bad produced a tiny device.

"Where are you putting that thing?" Belial asked.

"In your ear."

"She'll see it and make me get rid of it."

"Not where I'm putting it." Bad jammed the device deep into his ear canal, and Belial screamed. "Don't be such a wuss," Bad said. The other techies snickered.

It felt like his eardrum had just ruptured. A rivulet of blood trickled from his ear.

"Hmm," said Bad. "Maybe you weren't such a wuss."

"Can I go now?" Belial rose from the chair, a little dizzy from pain.

Bad shook his head. "We have an upgrade to install."

Belial tried the same argument he'd used on Satan: "Why bother? This mission is almost over."

"There's a glitch in your current release."

Bad wandered off, leaving a pair of techs to insert long needles into every joint in Belial's body. Each one burned like the fires of Hades, and the burning pain lingered long after they withdrew the needles.

If he protested, they'd just drag it out longer. He longed to get back to Dara, to spend these last few hours by her side, so he clenched his teeth and got through it. After what felt like days of torture, he stumbled from the chair and headed back above.

CHAPTER 43

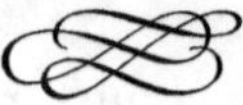

When Ben got back to Dara's condo on Sunday evening, he looked so exhausted she hated to run him through another gauntlet, but she'd promised Nana.

He pointed to his ear and pantomimed listening.

Listening device? she mouthed. He nodded.

Then he took her in his arms and kissed her like he was parched and she was his oasis. When he released her, she slipped on her sandals.

He perked up. "Am I taking you out to dinner?"

"Even better," she said. "We're going to visit my grandmother."

He groaned. "Will she torture me again?"

"I don't know what she has in mind." Dara slipped her arm through his. "Do you want to take my car or yours?"

"We'd better take yours," he said, "in case I'm too incapacitated to drive afterwards."

She threaded her fingers through his. "I'll protect you."

He followed her out to the garage. "So this is what I've come down to. Henpecked by a mere mortal."

She raised up on her toes to kiss him. "It's what all smart men come down to."

Nana was sitting in her recliner when they arrived. Her tray table held her perfume atomizer and a sachet of what Dara assumed to be demonweed. Ben hung back a little at the door, but she pushed him into the room. Once inside, he dug in like a sick toddler, refusing to take another step.

Nana's eyes raked over him. "You're right," she said to Dara. "He's different."

Dara took advantage of Ben's surprise to shove him a few steps closer.

"Give me your hand." Nana picked up the sachet of demonweed.

Wincing, he held out his hand. "What is it about you Perdue women that makes you determined to torture me?"

She scrubbed it up and down the inside of his forearm.

He stared at his arm in surprise. It had turned a little red, but there was no sign of the welts the herbs had raised last time.

"Even the demonweed don't work on him like it did." Nana picked up the atomizer, but he backed out of range.

"I can testify that still works," Dara said.

Nana's thin lips twitched.

"Though not as much," Dara said. "And he seems to heal slower than he did. What does that mean?"

"He's becoming less of a demon," Nana said.

Joy blossomed in her heart, but it wilted when Nana didn't smile. Neither did Ben.

"You've seen this before?" he asked.

"Once," Nana said. "After Lonnie prayed over a demon."

"What happened?" Dara asked.

Ben's face was impassive.

"His master called him home," Nana said. "I don't know what became of him after that."

"He was put through a reorientation program," Ben said. A world of horror lay behind those words. "I heard about it at the time, but I didn't realize it was your husband who performed the exorcism."

"Wasn't no exorcism." Nana's jaw jutted out. "It was just a praying."

The old Ben might have split hairs with her or claimed to know more than she did on the subject. The new Ben just nodded.

"I can see that you'd like to be more than you are." Nana's voice was almost gentle. "But it's not to be. Demons aren't God's children, who can repent of their sins and be forgiven."

Even though she was talking to Belial, her words were aimed at Dara.

"Demons are supernatural creatures that must live out eternity expiating their betrayal of the Lord. No matter how well you mean, you're still a danger to my granddaughter, and everything she works for."

Ben bowed his head. Dara saw something that looked like sympathy flit across Nana's face, but it was quickly gone.

"If you care for her," Nana said, "you'll return to Hell, from whence you came."

When they got back to the condo, they spent the rest of the evening cuddled up on the sofa, eating popcorn and watching *America's Funniest Home Videos,* laughing at the pratfalls. Dara offered to put *Breaking Bad* in the DVD player, but Ben had already seen it. The series was a favorite in Hell.

"Things go so well. Right up to the end, anyway."

She punched him in the ribs and he said, "*Oof,*" and they wrestled a little on the couch, but he didn't let things get out of hand. During the commercials, they talked, careful to stick with topics that posed no danger.

Soon after that, they turned off the TV and headed for bed. In the bedroom, Dara switched on a small stack stereo. The strains of Monteverdi's "Pur ti miro" filled the room. Ben smiled, and she smiled back at him. Then she turned up the volume and pressed the repeat button. They spent the next couple of hours amid a symphony of sound, exploring each other's bodies.

The next evening was the pediatric clinic again. Belial arrived early because he wanted a chance to review the charts ahead of time. There were five patients scheduled, an atypically heavy caseload for a peds clinic. The list included a ten-year-old girl with complications from Type 1 diabetes and asthma. Should he have Dara call in another doctor? No, better not. He didn't want to alert Satan.

Dara always triaged the sickest patients first, but he put the girl last to downplay the severity of her illnesses. After working his way through two rashes, a tennis elbow and case of RSV, he had Dara bring the girl in. Her HgA1c reading said she was ready for a reduction in her insulin dosage.

When he tried to input the new dosage into the computer, his fingers typed an increase instead of a decrease—one large enough to put her into a coma, depending on when she took it. He tried to correct the entry, but it was as though steel spider webs entangled his hands. The cords crept up his arms. *Thrall.*

He fought it until, finally, stabbing at the keys with one finger, he forced the correct entry. Satan's rage was like a hot breath on the back of his neck, but he ignored it.

"She's doing a great job," he told her mother. "Make sure she keeps it up."

Dara escorted them to the lobby while he finished up the computer work. When she came back, she was frowning.

"Is there a problem?"

He didn't want to frighten her, and he had things under control. "No. I'm good."

"Because you seem to be having problems with your hands."

"I'm fine."

"Are you sure? Maybe I should take you off the schedule for the rest of the week."

Inside, he was panicking. Something felt different, as though his body were less under his control than it had been before DemSec worked on him over the weekend. What had that "upgrade" consisted of?

If she kicked him out of the clinic, Satan would find another way in. She was safest with him here. He turned back to the computer and completed the log entries without issue. DemSec's technology was no match for his knowledge and experience.

CHAPTER 44

Dara wasn't sure what was going on with Ben, but the panic that flared in his eyes as he stumbled over the little girl's insulin dosage made her triple-check his work. She reviewed every chart before she left that night but could find no flaws. To be safe, she would call Jeremy in the morning and ask him to do a chart review.

That evening, Ben seemed twitchy. Over dinner, he snapped at her. Finally, Dara said, "Would you rather go home tonight instead of coming back to the condo?"

"No, I want to stay with you." It would have been touching if it hadn't felt so out of character.

That night, his lovemaking had a touch of desperation to it.

The clinic had Spanish translators on hand for Tuesday, so they were full to overflowing. Wednesday was the same thing. To make things even more chaotic, two volunteer nurses called in sick, leaving Dara short-handed.

When she put Ben back on the schedule for the adult clinics, she planned to supervise his work, but on Wednesday, between acting as charge nurse and trying to ensure that all the docs had someone to draw blood or give treatments, she was spread too thin. When Lilith blew through, Dara stifled a groan. She still needed to coax Lilith over to see Nana, but tonight wasn't the night to attempt that.

"I'm sorry," she said. "I really don't have time to talk."

Lilith waved her off. "I can see you're busy. I just brought some snacks."

Andrew Walz, who'd always worked with Dr. Wilson, arrived before the rest of the doctors. Dara drew a sigh of relief. She assigned him to shadow Ben.

"I've seen some things that look like demonic activity recently," she said in a low voice. "If you see anything that seems odd, no matter what the source, come and find me immediately."

Andrew followed her gaze to Dr. Lyle, who stood on the far side of the Pit, talking to another doctor. He looked as angelically beautiful and supremely confident as he had the first night he'd come in. Some qualities were intrinsic.

Andrew swallowed, clearly intimidated. "I can do that if you want me to."

He didn't sound too sure.

"I want you to," Dara said firmly.

Then she got caught up in triage and trying to figure out how they would see forty sick people, including her old buddy, Viola, in three hours with only three doctors. A half hour later, Andrew stopped her as she was coming out of an exam room.

"I don't know if this is the kind of thing you were thinking about." His face was almost as red as his hair. "But Dr. Lyle smells like he's been drinking."

She caught her breath. "Does he act drunk?"

"No."

"Did you ask him if he'd been drinking?"

Andrew's ears turned scarlet. "Of course not."

"Where is he?"

"In room five, waiting for his first patient."

She touched his arm. "You did the right thing."

Ben smiled when she entered the room.

"Have you been drinking?"

His smile drained away. "Of course not."

But she could smell what Andrew was talking about. "Your breath smells like alcohol."

He curved his palm in front of his face and blew into it, squinting at the blow-back. "Whoa. I haven't been drinking." His eyes begged her to trust him. "I haven't put anything in my mouth since lunchtime except for water and one of those pastries in the breakroom."

"I believe you," she said, "but patient safety has to come first. Why don't you go back to the house and wait for me? I'll even let you make me something healthy for dinner."

He stood there for a moment, shoulders tense. His shoulders sagged and he nodded. On his way out the door, Viola spied him.

"You ain't leaving, are you?" Her voice sounded like sandpaper. "I come to see you."

Ben looked at Dara. For whatever reason, he liked Viola, and the other two docs who were on that night didn't. Jeremy had dropped by over lunch and reviewed Ben's charts from the night before and found no problems. And Andrew would be right there, watching.

"All right," she said. "Go ahead."

Twenty minutes later, Dara was drawing blood in room two when someone yelled, "Call nine-one-one!"

It was Ben's voice. Her stomach clenched. She asked the student nurse to finish the draw and hurried out into the main area. On the far side of the Pit, the door to room five was open. Inside, Ben leaned over Viola, giving her CPR. Andrew stood beside them. She raced around the Pit.

"What happened?" She grabbed Ben's arm.

"She has a respiratory infection." Ben pressed and released Viola's chest like clockwork, while Andrew held the diaphragm of his stethoscope to her jugular. "It had a pretty good head start, so I ordered a dose of erythromycin."

Dara looked at Viola's pale, still form, trying to understand what Ben was telling her. "What's wrong with that?"

"I didn't take into account the other drug she was on. It's been known to interfere with the QT interval. Erythromycin can aggravate that. She had an infarction." Ben looked at Andrew. Andrew shook his head. Ben renewed his efforts.

Dara tried to take in what he meant. The QT interval was a measure of the heart's electrical system. Apparently, the combination of two drugs that could affect that cycle had caused Viola's heart to stop.

On the table, Viola dragged in a noisy breath and her eyes blinked open. Relief washed through Dara like a warm tide. Breathing a prayer of gratitude, she looked at Ben. Horror filled her. His expression was not relief, but disappointment.

Outside the clinic, sirens wailed. Moments later, EMTs loaded Viola onto a stretcher. She was conscious, but in bad shape.

Ben left after that. Dara finished the evening clinic with her nerves sparking like a stripped wire. He had dinner waiting for her when she got home, but she didn't sit down.

"Why were you disappointed when Viola's heart started again?" she asked.

He gave her an odd, slanting look, and she remembered the listening device.

"I wasn't," he said. "You know how much I like Viola."

She did know that. But she had checked Viola's medical history and found a fat black checkmark in the "yes" box beside the question: Are you the oldest child in your family?

She grabbed a piece of paper and a pen and wrote the question out. She shoved the paper at him. He tried to ignore her, but she stabbed at it with her finger, not willing to let it go. Finally, he took the pen from her hand and scrawled a response.

"It was just a mistake. That's the downside of being more human."

Was that possible? Well, of course it was possible, but was it the real reason?

She looked at him, biting her lip. His eyes pleaded with her to believe in him. Hoping she wasn't making the biggest mistake of her life, she nodded.

That night, when Ben made love to her, she couldn't relax. She kept seeing Viola's face, waxy pale and not breathing. Her muted response seemed to call forth a need in Ben to elicit an orgasm from her.

It felt less like lovemaking than like a power struggle. A memory of the first night she'd seen him, at the gas station, flooded her head. The image of him, dark and threatening in black leather, brought on her climax. As her spasms crested, he thrust into her like he was burying his own painful thoughts beneath an avalanche of desire.

When he rolled off her, she curled against him. His arms squeezed her as though he feared she'd slip away in the darkness. She fell into an exhausted slumber.

Dara had barely drifted off when a voice inside Belial's head said, "Olly olly oxen free! Time to come home."

"Not yet," he said, keeping his voice low so he wouldn't wake Dara. "I'm not finished."

Before he even got the words out, his body rose to its feet and donned its clothes. He fought for control, but Satan's power had grown exponentially since the last time. Thrall wouldn't even let him kiss Dara goodbye, wouldn't allow him even one last look over his shoulder. He walked out the door like a robot, got into the Hyundai and drove straight to Hell. There, he got out of the car and marched into DemSec.

Inside the office, a young demon with massive grommets in his earlobes was sitting at Abaddon's desk, playing a video game. The grommets transformed his lobes into pendulous bags that made Belial think of testicles. His thrall melted away.

"Where's Bad?" Belial looked around but didn't see DemSec's director. He'd probably been promoted to a corner office, next to the boss.

Scrotum-Ears tugged at one of his grommets. "Bad's in the maggot pit, man. The boss is not happy with that demon."

"Why?"

Scrotum-Ears shook his head. His earlobes swung like bell clappers. "He gave some dude an upgrade that was supposed to let the boss run him like a drone, but it didn't work like it was supposed to. The boss was *pissed*."

Belial felt a tiny stir of triumph. At least he'd put up some resistance.

Scrotum-Ears scratched his tattooed neck. "Is that all you wanted, man?"

Belial shook his head. "I was ordered here. I guess you want your hardware back."

Scrotum-Ears looked confused. "We usually just leave it in between gigs." He checked his computer screen and his eyebrows rose. "Wow, I guess they want it back."

Because Belial wouldn't be going on any future missions.

He took his seat in the operating chair and endured the agony as Scrotum-Ears dug out the microphone. Once he was done, the floppy-eared demon wiped off his instruments with a grimy cloth. Belial cringed. Aboveworld medicine, flawed as it was, emphasized infection prevention and pain relief. Hell had no such goals. His ears rang like the bells of Notre Dame.

Scrotum-Ears checked his computer screen again. "It says here I'm supposed to collect your cell phone, too."

The phone was Belial's last tiny filament of contact with Dara. He handed it over, feeling like a door was slamming shut. It didn't matter. In another twenty-four hours, he would take a swim that would free him from the life he'd lived since he joined the ranks of the damned. If all went well, the wager would end and the boss would lose.

Dara had succumbed to his wiles, taking the money, coming to his bed and corrupting her sanctuary with a demon. She had not cursed the Almighty, though, and she wouldn't commit suicide. She might bend a little under pressure, but she would not break. The Almighty had chosen his vessel wisely. She was safe.

If all went well.

CHAPTER 45

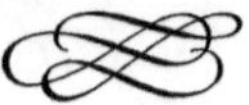

When Dara awoke the next morning, Ben's side of the bed was empty. He had been so upset the night before that he probably needed time alone to process what had happened with Viola.

She bit her lip. How was the old woman doing? Ben had promised her no one would die. She clung to that thought as she washed her face and got dressed.

He hadn't harmed Viola intentionally. Dara was as certain of that as she was of the tide coming in. She'd seen it in his eyes. This was part of the "incidental damage" to the clinic Ben had warned her might occur as part of Hell's mission to corrupt her. Well, neither one of those things was going to happen. As soon as he got back, they'd put their heads together and figure out how to end these attacks once and for all.

Her first stop was the hospital, to check on Viola. An older gentleman in a teal lab jacket embroidered with Bermuda General's logo manned the visitor's desk. She asked for Viola's room number.

He frowned. "Are you a reporter? They told me to send all the reporters who asked about Ms. Finch to the auditorium to wait for Ms. Rojas."

Dara stared at him in confusion. Her brain felt like she'd walked into a fog bank. What was he saying? "I'm sorry—reporters?"

He leaned across the desk. "Ms. Finch went to that free clinic on the other side of town, and they let a doctor who was drunk work on her. Said he almost killed her."

Dara's chest seemed to freeze. Was that what people were saying? How had that rumor gotten out? She ran through the list of people who were present in the clinic the night before. They were all staff or longtime volunteers that were committed to the clinic. Except one.

"What does Ms. Rojas have to do with this?" Dara asked.

"The hospital funds that clinic. Ms. Rojas serves on their board. She's giving a press conference."

Dara thanked him and walked away. Instead of going to Viola's room, she went to the auditorium, where she found a dozen reporters milling around. Alexandria had only a weekly paper. Even if you threw in reporters from the Jacksonville *Post-Dispatch,* that didn't begin to account for all the people in the room.

A few minutes later, Lilith arrived, accompanied by a man in a dark suit. Lilith explained that he was from the Florida Medical Board. He was investigating allegations that the Matthew A. Strong Memorial Clinic had allowed an alcohol-impaired doctor to treat a patient. Dara listened in growing horror.

"Is it true that patients of the clinic are prohibited from suing because of the clinic's status?" asked one reporter.

"Under Florida law, the clinic can't be sued in civil court," Lilith said. Half of the people in the room slumped in disappointment. So that was who they were—lawyers hoping to represent Viola in a lawsuit. "However, they may be subject to criminal prosecution. The Bermuda County district attorney is looking into that."

Criminal prosecution? Was Lilith talking about Ben or Dara? Or both? As Lilith's eyes swept the audience, they found Dara and widened. A couple of the reporters turned in their seats to follow Lilith's gaze.

"What other questions do you have?" Lilith said, distracting them.

Dara's conviction that Lilith was the demon plaguing the clinic wavered. If she were really after Dara, she would have fed her to the sharks. Dara slipped out of the room.

How had things blown up literally overnight? Medical malpractice, even with alcohol involved, wasn't unusual enough to be newsworthy, not unless the patient was a celebrity, and Viola was hardly that. It didn't make any sense.

Dara sagged as reality hit. This sudden interest by the press, and by the medical board, was part and parcel with all the other attacks on the clinic. Lilith may have called off the sharks just now, but she was also responsible for convening them in the first place.

Dara called Ben, but he didn't pick up. She texted, asking him to call.

She went to Viola's room, but the old woman was asleep. She looked so frail, her hair a gray smudge against the white pillowcase. She had tubes coming out of everywhere. Dara felt sick to her stomach at the situation Ben's mistake, *her* mistake, had placed Viola in. She bit her lip. Whatever had happened the night before, Ben had not intended to harm Viola. She believed that with all her heart.

Her next stop was Mercy Care, where she told Nana what had happened.

"This is all part of the demon attack on you," Nana said.

"I know."

"What does Ben say?"

Dara frowned at her phone. It remained stubbornly silent. "I don't know. I haven't been able to get hold of him."

Nana's face said she had an opinion on that, but she didn't share it. "Did anyone besides Andrew smell the alcohol?"

"Other than me?" Dara thought back to the previous evening. "I don't think so. No one mentioned it."

"Bring Andrew to see me tonight. Testifying against you would be doing Satan's work. He'll understand that." Nana sounded so confident a tiny bubble of hope rose. Andrew had been a member of Deliverance Mission Church since he was a small child. To the best of Dara's knowledge, he still attended every Sunday. Maybe he would understand what had happened.

After she left Mercy Care, Dara drove out to the beach and knocked on Ben's door, but no one answered. The hollow sound of the door knocker echoed the hollowness in her chest. Both said her lover had returned to Hell.

She spent the afternoon trying to work and facing the realization that Ben was gone. The evidence said he'd completed his mission and abandoned her, but she didn't believe it. The man he'd become over the past six and a half weeks would not have intentionally hurt her or the clinic. She hated to think of him back in Hell, returning to his old demon ways.

Her sense of loss was a gaping wound, but she set that aside to deal with later. For now, she needed to protect her reputation, and the clinic's. She went into the computer system and pulled up Viola's chart. There, in red print, was a warning about a possible drug interaction and the initials "BL." The computer had warned him what might happen, and he'd overridden it.

After leaving DemSec, Belial took the elevator down to Ring Nine. Andras wasn't at her desk, but light gleaming beneath the boss's door said he was in. For a moment, Belial considered walking to the end of the ring and simply throwing himself in the Lake of Fire, denying Satan the opportunity to execute him. The need to know that Dara was okay was too strong, though. He let himself into Satan's office.

"You're working late." He dropped into one of the chairs that faced Satan's desk, pretending a calm he didn't feel. This was the only way he had of keeping in touch with what was going on.

Satan didn't smile. "I had some work to finish up."

"Why did you pull me back? I wasn't finished up there."

Satan looked him up and down, and a chill ran down Belial's spine. "Lilith can take it from here."

"You'd trust a she-demon with a mission this important?"

Without warning, black smoke belched from Satan's horns. "I'd trust any demon down here before I'd trust you." His face turned burgundy with rage as he leaned across the desk.

"What's the problem?" Belial assumed his most clueless expression.

"You don't think I bought that pathetic performance, did you? I knew when you were here the last time you were scheming to betray me." Satan seemed to grow in size, but Belial refused to cringe.

"You fell in love with her." Satan's words were a howl of rage. Love, in any form, was forbidden in Hell.

Belial didn't try to deny it. "So what happens next?" He didn't much care, but he did want to stick around long enough to know Dara would be all right.

"It depends on how this wager turns out," Satan said. "If I win, you'll start over at the bottom. And by 'start over,' I mean you'll lick dung off the asses of dirt demons for the rest of eternity. If I lose, I'll rebuild morale by letting all of Hell watch your execution."

Belial rolled his eyes in pretended terror, but on the inside, he drew a breath of relief. It was everything he'd hoped for.

Satan pushed a button on his desk, and two hulking demons came through the door. "Put him in the spider hole."

When Gabby buzzed to say Lilith was at the front desk, Dara was ready. She needed to determine once and for all whether Lilith was a demon. In the top drawer of her desk was a baggie of demonweed, a spray bottle of holy water and Granddad's Bible. She also had her ruby cross. Surely one of them would expose Lilith's demon side.

She laced her fingers and hoped Gabby would remember what she was supposed to do next.

The tip-tap of stilettos sounded in the hall. Lilith appeared in the doorway.

"Are you all right?" Her voice oozed concern.

Whether Lilith was a demon or not, Dara really didn't want to open up to her. "Thank you for managing the press this morning."

"That's my job." Lilith shrugged the shoulders of her silk suit. "It's also what friends are for. And despite whatever's been going on between us lately, I still consider you a friend."

"And I appreciate that." Dara gave her a smile that wasn't quite a smile, putting the ball back in Lilith's court.

Lilith drove it straight back at her. "You're angry at me for lying about Ben."

"Yes."

"I'm sorry about that," Lilith said. "I handled things badly. You were so infatuated I didn't think you'd listen to my real concerns about him."

"And what were your real concerns about him?"

"That's the problem. I was never able to formulate them into anything that made any sense. Something about him felt off."

"Where was all this women's intuition when I was trying to get you to back me in keeping him out of the clinic?" Dara injected just a touch of bitterness into her voice, amazed at her own talent for guile.

Lilith spread her hands. "You're right. You tried to tell me. But it wasn't until that night that he got you so drunk and tried to take advantage of you that I saw him for who he was."

Dara stopped just short of snorting. "You were the one who set those drinks in front of me."

Lilith's cheeks flushed. "After that first drink, I ordered virgin iced teas for you. Ben must have bribed the bartender to spike them."

That night was a bit of a blur, but Dara was pretty sure she'd been drunk long before Ben arrived. She pasted on the foolish smile of a woman who will accept any behavior from her boyfriend. "He probably did."

"Whatever happened that night?" Lilith hovered in the doorway, too far away for tossed demonweed or sprayed holy water to reach her.

"I threw up all over his shoes." Dara let a gleam of amusement pierce her somber expression, hoping she wasn't overplaying it.

Lilith laughed out loud. "Good on you."

"He really was a jerk back then," Dara said.

"Back then?" Lilith looked outraged. "What about now? Almost killing that old lady and leaving you to face the consequences. That's pretty bad."

"How do you know he's gone?" *Because you're a demon, that's how.*

"It's all over the hospital that he isn't responding to phone calls or texts." Lilith held out her hands in spurious sympathy. "Oh, Dara—I'm so sorry. After the poker tournament this weekend, I thought you two might make a go of it. He seemed different when he was around you."

"He was different." Dara shrugged. "Just not different enough."

"What will you do? They're saying one of the medical students said Ben was drunk last night."

They had reached a critical juncture. Dara's hand closed on the drawer handle. "He hadn't been drinking. Ben has a condition that causes undigested food in his intestinal tract to make alcohol."

She told the falsehood as coolly as if she lied all the time. Anger flashed from Lilith's eyes, quickly replaced by sympathy.

"Did he tell you that? Because of the hospital's exposure, I did a background check on him. He's had two DUIs over the past four years."

Dara let go of the drawer handle. She didn't need demonweed or holy water or a Bible to tell her Lilith was a demon. Her instinct told her that.

"I guess it will all come down to what Andrew has to say," she said. "Fortunately, he's a member of my grandparents' church. He visits Nana all the time." She tapped her lip, as though suddenly remembering something. "In fact, I think he's scheduled to go there this evening after the clinic."

"Well, that's good." Lilith looked relieved, but that was just another lie. "Sounds like you've got everything covered."

Dara smiled. "I think I do."

When Lilith arrived at the nursing home, Dara would be there with Nana, waiting. Together they would take this she-demon down.

As soon as Lilith walked out the door, Tia came into Dara's office.

"What in the world happened last night?" she asked.

Dara looked at the clock. Lilith's safest bet for catching Nana alone was after dinner, when the staff were occupied settling the residents into their rooms for the night, but Dara didn't want to take any chances.

She gave the nurse practitioner a brief summary of events and picked up her purse.

"This will all blow over," she said. And it would, assuming Nana was successful in convincing Andrew of the demonic attack. "Can you start triage for me?" she asked. "I need to run over to Mercy Care and check on my grandmother."

Tia left to start triage. Dara drew a sigh of relief, but she only made it as far as her office door before she encountered another obstacle.

The president of her board of trustees blocked her way. He talked for five minutes without drawing a breath.

"Why did you let him see patients when you knew he'd been drinking?" he finished.

"He wasn't drinking." Dara checked her watch. "I don't know how that rumor got started."

"Several people have come forward to say they heard Andrew tell you Ben Lyle was drunk."

The demons were way ahead of her. Dara gritted her teeth. She'd figure that out later. Right now, her top priority was getting to Nana's before Lilith did.

She edged her way around the man.

"I just got a call from my grandmother's nursing home," she said. "I have to go."

He looked annoyed but moved out of her way.

She hurried out the door, only to find a dozen reporters milling around outside.

"That's her!" one yelled, and they swarmed her.

Her increasingly frantic "no comments" probably made her look guilty, but she couldn't think about that right now.

She had to get to Nana.

CHAPTER 46

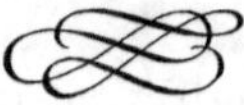

Lilith considered waiting until dinner at the nursing home was over and the residents settled back in their rooms before making her move, but she decided she couldn't afford to chance Dara showing up. She waited until a couple of aides who had come out to smoke went back in, leaving the back door ajar. She slipped silently through the gleaming hallways until she arrived at Esther's door.

There she paused. This task required delicacy. She needed to trigger a stroke in the old bitch, one severe enough to keep her from talking to Andrew, but not bad enough to kill her. At least not for another week. The Enemy had been crystal clear on that when he laid out the rules: their side was not permitted to kill anyone close to Dara within the time frame of the wager.

Like a wraith, she opened the door to Esther's room and stepped inside.

"I wondered when you'd get here." Esther sat in a recliner ringed with crumbled herbs. Her Bible was open in her lap.

Lilith viewed the demonweed almost with pleasure. She'd waited years for her revenge. The memory still rankled—Esther's broom striking her head and back until she ran from the room, naked. The herbs would sting, but the pain would make her eventual victory that much sweeter.

A bigger problem was the bottle of what she presumed to be holy water Esther held in her hands. Holy water burned like the fires of Hell. It was impossible to stay on task if you got it in your eyes.

A second problem was the nurse call button draped over Esther's chair arm. It was one thing to attack a helpless old lady. It was another to be charged with that crime. In the interests of maintaining demonimity, Satan had a strict policy of non-interference. If human law enforcement caught a minion in a crime, they were on their own. And American prisons were worse than at least the top three rings of Hell.

"The years haven't treated you well, Esther." Lilith took a step closer. "You look like a plucked chicken."

"The years have treated me the way God intended." Esther didn't rise to the bait. Instead, she wrinkled her nose and sneezed. "And you still smell like a two-dollar whore."

Rage sizzled through Lilith's veins.

"I could smell your stink clean out in the hall," Esther added, taking aim with the bottle of holy water.

Lilith feinted to the right. "You don't like my perfume? Lonnie loved it. I've had a lot of fun the past ten years, torturing Lonnie. I think the worst part for him has been seeing how he wasted his time up here."

"Lonnie's in Heaven, enjoying his reward." There was not a shade of doubt in Esther's voice. Pious old bitch.

Nearby, a cane leaned against the wall. Lilith picked it up and tossed it from one hand to the other, checking it for heft. She couldn't use it to bash Esther's skull in, the way she'd like to, but it might serve another purpose. She raised it over her head threateningly.

When Esther lifted her arms to shield her face, Lilith caught the cord to the nurse call button with the head of the cane and dragged it off the chair arm. She kicked it under the bed before darting back out of range.

"That's better. We wouldn't want to be interrupted."

Esther grabbed a handful of herbs off her table tray and tossed them, but they fell harmlessly short. She took a deep breath.

"Demon, I command you to return to Hell from whence you came. Lord, I call upon you to send your presence to banish this evil spirit." She launched into a long, chanting prayer that was like ten thousand fingernails on ten thousand blackboards.

Lilith gritted her teeth. She would not be vanquished. Only one of them could win this confrontation, and it would be her. A win here, tonight, would show the boss she had what it took to succeed where Belial had failed.

"Your slut of a granddaughter has grown quite cozy with her demon boyfriend," she said.

A tiny flicker of Esther's eyelids was the only sign that she'd heard. Her prayers grew more intense. She slipped into the hypnotic state that was the hallmark of an open conduit to the Enemy. Lilith felt herself being pressed back, back. Without knowing quite how it happened, she found herself pinned against the wall, barely able to move.

"He bought her, bedded her and corrupted her." She pitched her voice to be heard over Esther's prayers, but the old woman didn't shut up. Lilith needed to get closer, to make skin-to-skin contact, so that she could fire a stream of images of Dara having sex with Belial into Esther's brain. The crude pictures would do the trick.

Esther's voice strengthened as she said, "Lord, smite this she-demon. Smite her, hip and thigh."

What felt like an axe handle slammed into Lilith's hip joint. Her leg crumpled beneath her. Esther grunted with satisfaction. A typhoon of fury gusted through Lilith. She would not let this old hag best her again. Not with so much at stake. With the help of the cane, she dragged herself back to her feet.

She needed to get closer. "Dara will spend eternity roasting in Hell for opening her legs to a demon," she taunted Esther.

Esther's lip curled. "If every woman who ever slept with a bad boy was sent to burn in Hell, Satan would have run out of fuel long ago."

"This isn't just any bad boy. This is Belial, Satan's right-hand man, the chief executive demon of Hell."

"He's changed since he's been with Dara."

Lilith rolled her eyes. "Oh, please. Spare me the fairy tale of the scoundrel redeemed by a good woman's love. Every woman who ever fell for that did wind up in Hell, and it's cost us a fortune."

Esther returned to her prayers. "Heavenly Father, please care for my granddaughter and make her an implement of your will." As she chanted, her eyes closed.

That was all Lilith needed. She lunged forward with the cane and sent the bottle of holy water flying. Esther's eyes flew open at the sound of the bottle hitting the floor.

Ignoring the peppery sting of the herbs, Lilith broke the circle with her shoe. She wrapped her fingers around Esther's frail wrist. Before the old woman could pull free, Lilith fired a stream of images straight into her cerebral cortex—images of Dara having sex with Belial in the most wanton ways possible.

Esther gasped. She touched her throat, as though searching for something. Whatever it was, she didn't find it.

Beneath Lilith's fingers, the old woman's pulse jumped and raced. Lilith willed the blood thundering through Esther's veins to find an age-weakened vessel in her brain and burst through. Instead, Esther tore her wrist free from Lilith's grasp, rubbing it as though to wipe away the demon's touch. She was frightened, but defiant.

Lilith needed something more, some *coup de grace* that would send Esther over the edge.

"Do you know why Belial is here?" she asked. "Why he targeted Dara specifically?"

Beneath the fear on Esther's face, curiosity flickered. She'd evidently been giving this question a lot of thought.

"He's here on a bet, between your lord and mine, to see if he can destroy Dara," Lilith said.

Esther folded her arms. "The Lord would never do that to his child."

"He did it to Job," Lilith said.

Esther laced her fingers. "Lord, please protect Dara from the forces of evil." She tried to reopen the conduit, but fear wouldn't let her focus. Lilith's plan was working.

"He can't protect her. That would be against the rules." Lilith smiled as she delivered the final blow. "Your beloved Lord chose Dara as a pawn in a wager with Satan."

She hovered, waiting for Esther to crumple, but Esther straightened her spine like she was being drawn by an invisible force.

"God chose my Dara?"

"That he did."

Joy suffused Esther's face. "Just like he chose Job; just like he chose Mary. He chose my Dara because he knew she was his faithful handmaiden."

Lilith was so frustrated she wanted to scream. What would it take to break the old bat? She lifted the cane and brought it down in a slashing arc. She planned to whip it sideways at the last minute, missing Esther entirely, but Esther surged from her chair and met the stroke head-on. Under the momentum of the slashing cane, her fragile skull shattered. Blood flew everywhere.

Horrified, Lilith checked her swing, but it was too late. Esther slumped to the floor. A quick check revealed no pulse.

Shit.

Shit. Shit. Shit. Shit. Shit.

This wasn't supposed to happen. Satan would be furious. Lilith would be lucky if she escaped with a century in the maggot pit. Word on the rings was that he was threatening to execute Belial if he screwed up this mission. And he *liked* Belial.

In the circle of pooling blood, Esther's Bible lay, face up, open to Psalms. All demons were familiar with the contents of the Bible—to subvert the law, you had to know the law. Relief washed through her as she spied her way out. She wiped down the cane, placed it in Esther's stiffening hand and slipped back out the way she'd come.

Dara drove to Mercy Care like a madwoman. When she didn't see Lilith's Miata in the parking lot, her shoulders sagged in relief. She inhaled the first full breath she'd taken since Lilith left her office.

What would be the best way to approach Andrew when he arrived? Nana was convinced that, since his family attended Deliverance Mission Church, he would be on their side, but Dara wasn't sure it would be so easy.

Her heart leapt into her throat when she saw nurses and aides hurrying toward Nana's room. She ran down the long hallway. An aide tried to hold her back, but she pushed her way past. Inside, Nana lay face down on the floor in a pool of blood. Dara's heart seemed to stop in her chest.

"Nana!" she screamed. Gathering the old woman's shoulders in her arms, she tried to roll Nana over so she could see her face. A pair of aides grabbed her by the arms and dragged her away.

"She must have fallen and hit her face on her cane." The nurse touched Dara's wrist gently.

The nurse was at a loss to explain why Nana's call button was under the bed. She was at an even greater loss to explain why a mixture of dried herbs ringed Nana's chair and why a bottle of what appeared to be tap water lay on the floor. In one spot, the water had soaked the herbs, leaving a faint scent of anise in the room. The staff couldn't explain these things, but Dara knew exactly what they meant.

The demons had won.

CHAPTER 47

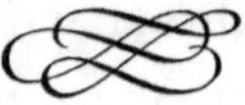

Belial could have been in the spider-hole for a day or a week when the demon guards returned to drag him out. After the blackness of the hole, even the flickering torches of the corridor made him squint. He'd been so cramped he couldn't straighten his arms or legs. He crumpled when he tried to walk. The guards lifted him by his armpits and dragged him down the corridor.

As his eyes adjusted to the light, he saw his arms and torso were in ribbons from scratching at spider bites. Away from the pit and the constant bites, his skin began to heal, but it still itched as though the eight-legged beasts crawled over him.

His guards delivered him to Satan's office, where the boss was waiting for him with smoking horns. This was it. His long life had finally come to an end, and he couldn't find it in himself to be sorry. He had only one question: was Dara safe?

"I didn't think it was possible..." Satan trembled with rage. "But I've found a demon who's a bigger fuckup than you are."

With effort, Belial shifted gears. "Lilith?" She was the sole demon he could think of who was doing something important enough to warrant this kind of fury. Hope burgeoned. He stood a little straighter.

Satan tapped his nose. "And if she's screwed up as bad as I think she has, the two of you will be performing a *pas de deux* in the Lake of Fire."

Belial heard this threat with something approaching joy. For Satan to be this angry, Lilith must have bungled things beyond redemption.

"You sit there." With a flick of his fingers, Satan tossed Belial across the room, slamming him into a chair. "And keep your mouth shut." Belial's lips sealed into a tight line.

A few minutes later, Lilith strode through the door, a broad smile on her face.

Satan's horns streamed oily black smoke. "You stupid slut, you just lost us the bet."

But Lilith tilted her head and put a fingertip to her chin. "Now why would you say that?"

The smoke coming from Satan's horns thickened. He practically danced with rage. "You know the terms of the bet. If we kill anyone before their time, we forfeit."

Lilith had killed someone? Belial hoped it wasn't Viola. Beyond the fact that he liked the old biddy, her death would implicate Dara and the clinic.

"But we haven't," Lilith said. "That's the beauty of it." Obnoxious as she was, Lilith was seldom off-base when she thought she'd excelled. Belial's hopes wavered.

"What are you talking about?" Satan didn't share his appreciation of Lilith's instincts.

"How old do you suppose Esther was?" she asked.

Esther? Lilith had killed Dara's grandmother? Bile rose in Belial's throat. Dara would be devastated.

"She was ninety-five if she was a day," Satan said. "The old bitch should have been dead years ago."

"Exactly."

Realization broke over Satan's face like dawn breaking over the Alexandria Beach. At the same moment, Belial saw the wicked genius of what Lilith had done.

"The days of man's years are threescore and ten," Satan said. "Seventy years."

"Psalms 90, verse 10," Lilith said. "His rules, not ours."

"You're brilliant." Satan offered her a high five. "Do you know that?"

Lilith preened. "I've been waiting for you to notice. The death of her grandmother will be all it takes to push that vapid little slut past the tipping point."

Satan slid his hands over Lilith's high, tight ass. Lilith rubbed herself against him. Belial thought he might throw up.

"If you can pull this off," Satan said, "you'll have your place at the poker table."

"Then save me a spot," Lilith said. "Because I'm going to deliver that sad, sad bitch like a pepperoni pizza."

Frozen in his chair, Belial racked his brain. What could he do to stop them?

Dara didn't sleep that night, sick with grief and guilt. She'd involved her grandmother in a war with demonic forces and then left her, unprotected, for the demons to murder. The next morning, she got word from the board of trustees they'd voted to suspend her from her executive director post.

It was no more than she deserved.

Lilith delivered the news via phone. "I'm hoping this will blow over, but the DA feels like he needs to come down hard. I'm already getting pushback from the hospital about continuing our support. If we leave you in place during the investigation, it could destroy your donor base for years to come."

"I'll remove my belongings from the office tomorrow, after the funeral." Dara's chest felt hollow. Matt's death, and the baby's, had left her with two things in her life—her grandmother and the clinic. Now they were both gone. She refused to let herself think about Ben.

That night was Nana's visitation. Dara spoke to people in a haze.

She'd done this for Granddad, and later for Matt. The good news was that she'd never do it again. She had no one left.

By the time she pulled into her garage afterward, depression had settled over her like a wet, gray blanket. She felt more alone than she'd ever felt in her life, even after Matthew's death.

Despite her best efforts, thoughts of Ben seeped into her mind. She missed his laughter and his quick wit and his interest in the patients at the clinic. She missed his snarky comments on humankind, but most of all, she missed his arms around her. It had taken her body no time at all to become accustomed to the weight of his arm thrown across her in sleep. The loss of that was like having part of herself ripped away.

She could sense Nana and Granddad looking down from Heaven, willing her to call on God for relief, but she couldn't do it. God had allowed her to get into this mess. What was the point in asking him for help? She cried herself to sleep.

Nana's funeral was at Deliverance Mission Church, as she would have wished. Everyone from the clinic was there, both staff and volunteers. The exception was Dara's board. None of them were in attendance. They'd evidently decided they couldn't afford to be associated with a woman who allowed her drunken boyfriend to nearly kill a patient.

Kelsey was there with Jeremy. *Ben will be so pleased.* Then Dara remembered he'd never know.

Beyond offering condolences, everyone kept their distance. It was as though they didn't want to risk infection with the misfortune that had come her way. She wasn't surprised. She'd seen the same behavior after Matthew's death. Pastor Bodine gave Nana's eulogy, reminding everyone of the years she and Lonnie Perdue had spent fighting demons and saving souls.

"Who can find a virtuous woman?" he asked. "For her price is above rubies."

Dara touched the cross that hung around her neck, letting her tears fall like Florida rain while a CD played Ricky Skaggs singing Nana's favorite song, "The Soul of Man Never Dies." The pallbearers carried her casket out to the churchyard, where the spot beside Granddad waited. Pastor Bodine said another prayer, and Dara dropped a single white rose into Nana's grave. The clods of earth made hollow thuds as they landed on her coffin.

In the recreation hall behind the church, white paper tablecloths covered the youth ping-pong tables. Folding chairs lined the sides. The ladies of the congregation had brought enough casseroles and sheet cakes to feed an army of mourners. When everyone finished eating—everyone but Dara, she couldn't stomach the thought of food—Pastor Bodine told her she needn't help clean up. The church sisters would take care of it.

"When you're ready to come back," he said, "you know that we're here for you."

She did know that. But her latest losses were one more example of God's callousness toward his children. She wanted nothing to do with him.

Dara left the church feeling drained, but she'd promised to retrieve her belongings that afternoon, so she girded her loins and drove to the clinic. Gabby got there before her. She buzzed Dara in, telling her once again how sorry she was about everything. Dara nodded. She tried to summon gratitude but felt only emptiness.

When she reached her office, her determination to get through this trial with her dignity intact suffered a setback. Lilith sat in her chair, browsing through her computer like she owned the place.

"We felt like it was important to get some new leadership in here right away," she said. "The clinic can't afford to have any more bad publicity."

Dara pressed her lips together. Her things were already loaded into a cardboard box. Beside it, another carton contained an assortment of stiletto heels Lilith evidently hadn't found a place for. Dara picked up the first box.

"I can have someone help you carry those out to your car." Lilith reached for the phone as though Dara's staff were hers to command.

A red mist rose in front of Dara's eyes. The odor she'd smelled at Mercy Care after Nana died, that cloying scent of sugar donuts and black licorice, was in this room.

Ben had said, "I'm not sure Lilith is a very good companion for you." And he'd put a lot of energy into separating Jeremy from Lilith's clutches. Dara didn't know how Lilith had subverted the grain-counting test and the eye test, but somehow she had.

"It was you," Dara said.

Lilith looked at her like she had no idea what Dara was talking about.

"You were the other demon. The one who visited the plagues on the clinic. The one who killed my grandmother."

For a moment, Dara thought Lilith would deny it, but then she laughed, a trilling sound that made Dara's hands shake with the desire to choke her.

"Guilty," she said on two notes, making it into a little song of triumph. She rested her chin on her fist as though she were posing for an executive portrait. "What are you going to do about it?"

There was, of course, nothing Dara could do about it. As Nana had pointed out, over and over, demons were supernatural immortal beings, while she was just a puny human. Rage rose in her, thick as gumbo. She grabbed one of Lilith's stilettos from the nearby box and snapped off the heel.

Lilith's gasp of horror felt so good that Dara chose a couple more at random and broke off their heels, too. It was childish, and probably actionable in a court of law, but it felt great.

"Are you insane?" Lilith said. "Those are Manolo Blahniks." Her pupils squared and Dara's last, lingering doubt disappeared.

She shrugged. "What are you going to do about it?"

Lilith's fingers curved into claws like she would attack. Dara readied herself. *Bring it on.*

Lilith dragged a long breath in through her nose and her pupils became circular again. Her hands relaxed and she smiled. "You know, you really want to stay on my good side."

Dara picked out another shoe and snapped off the heel, making sure it wasn't a mate to any of the ones she'd already damaged. Lilith twitched, but the smile didn't leave her lips.

"Truly," she said. "Because I've got something you want."

"My clinic? We both know that's never coming back to me. My grandmother? You don't have her and never will."

"I was thinking more in terms of...Ben."

It felt like Lilith had punched one of those heels through Dara's sternum.

Crossing her legs, Lilith laced her fingers together and cupped her knee. "I am empowered to offer you a one-time deal. If you will come to Hell and make your case, my boss is prepared to allow Ben to return to Earth and live out your life beside you."

Dara caught her breath. It was a trap, but a trap so alluring it was impossible not to picture it: a lifetime with Ben at her side, working with her, making her laugh, making love to her. Common sense reasserted itself.

"And afterwards I'm damned to Hell for all eternity?"

Lilith looked at the box of broken shoes. Her lips twisted. "Sister, that's gonna happen anyway."

Dara tossed and turned all through that night, imagining a life with Ben. She might be damning herself to Hell, but to Lilith's point, her estrangement from God already put her at risk. The idea of spending as many as fifty years with Ben at her side was so tempting it was all she could do not to put on her thickest-soled shoes and head straight to Hell.

She woke the next morning, bleary-eyed, and forced down some breakfast. Milton chose that day, of all days, to become needy, following her from room to room, watching every move she made with his yellow eyes. When she went to the bathroom, he meowed through the door.

In the plain light of day, the flip side of last night's internal debate was much clearer. Only an idiot would sign up for an eternity of torture in exchange for a brief lifetime of joy. In spite of that, she spent the day bouncing back and forth. She wouldn't go. She would. She wouldn't.

Late that afternoon, the mail arrived, including a notice that she was late on her association dues. She'd emptied her bank account to make the buy-in for the poker tournament, figuring she would catch up when she got paid. Now she had no paycheck coming. As dusk neared, she settled in a good place. It was time to stop grieving over what she didn't have and cherish what she did.

She would treat herself to dinner at Slyders. In the garage, she hit the button to raise the overhead door. Milton streaked past her and into the street. A speeding black sedan caught him under its front tire. There was a horrifying yowl. The car kept right on going.

She ran into the street, but Milton was dead. Sobbing, she found a piece of cardboard in the garage and used it to scoop up his poor broken body. She shrouded him in a pillowcase and dug a grave off the edge of the patio.

All the time she was preparing his limp body for burial, she kept thinking about the car. She hadn't recognized it, but she had no doubt an emissary of Satan was behind the wheel. No matter what she did, her life would not get any better. No hospital would hire a nurse with a history of making bad judgments—Gabby's experience told her that.

With no income, she would lose her home and wind up living on the streets. Anyone, anything, she got close to would become a target. She would not be able to have a friend or keep even a menial job. And God could not or would not protect her.

You haven't asked, Nana pointed out in her head.

I shouldn't have to ask. Some things, some basic human rights, like life, liberty and having a pet, you shouldn't have to beg for.

You haven't asked. The voice was inexorable.

With that, something broke within Dara. She dropped to her knees next to Milton's tiny grave and lifted her weeping face to the heavens.

"Why?" she asked. "Why have you forsaken me? Why have you given me over to my enemies?" And then she listened, and for the first time in her life, she got an answer. An answer that made absolutely no sense.

Rescue him.

Rescue who?

Rescue Ben.

That was insane. There was no way God wanted her to go to Hell and try to rescue a demon. Clearly, this was her own subconscious forcing its desires into her conscious mind. She tidied up Milton's grave, sweeping the sandy soil off the patio, and washed her hands. The voice didn't let up: *Rescue him.*

She was lightheaded from not eating, but no longer felt like going out to dinner. She opened a can of soup and heated it. As she spooned the tasteless mess of vegetables into her mouth, the voice chanted in rhythm with her chewing: *Rescue him. Rescue him.*

Outside, it grew dark and the stars came out in the night sky beyond the patio door. *Rescue him.* She tried to watch television, but she couldn't concentrate. *Rescue him.*

After a lifetime of waiting to hear God's voice, she wished he would shut up, but the voice continued to chant, *Rescue him.*

At nine o'clock, she walked out to the garage and picked up her car keys from the cement floor, where she'd dropped them when Milton ran out. She got in her car. She'd never been to Lilith's house, but she knew right where to find the she-demon.

A moment after Dara rang the bell at Ben's beach house, Lilith came to the door. Behind her, on the black granite countertop that separated the kitchen from the living area, was a row of shoes and a tube of Super Glue.

Lilith followed her gaze. "Happy?"

Dara shrugged. "It was one of my better moments from the past few days."

Lilith almost smiled but caught herself. "What do you want?"

"About the offer you made me earlier…"

Lilith's gaze sharpened. "Yes?"

Dara's heart pounded like she was standing at the edge of a cliff, ready to jump off. *Rescue him.*

"Is it still open?"

"Yes." Lilith's prompt answer should have sent Dara running back to the comparative safety of her condo. Instead, five minutes later, they were in Lilith's Miata, speeding down I-95. The car topped 120 miles per hour. Dara clung to the door handle. She'd assumed Lilith could take her to Hell in her current form, but maybe she needed to be dead first. Lilith seemed unconcerned, driving with one hand while she texted with the other.

Just before they rammed into the back end of a semi, a black hole opened in front of them. They drove into it and the blue sky and palm trees disappeared, replaced by a landscape of jutting rocks, backlit by flames. The road through Hell, it turned out, was paved with hardened lava.

Lilith slowed the car, but even so, the ride was so rough that Dara bounced around like a pinball, her teeth slamming together. Lilith smiled, a self-satisfied, feline smile. Dara's heart sank. She had taken a terrible, terrible risk, and only the goading voice in her head kept her from begging Lilith to turn around.

They'd driven perhaps a quarter mile when, outside her window, a group of nude runners dashed by, pursued by a swarm of hornets. Lilith sped up and they left the runners behind, descending a spiral over terrain so rough Dara expected the tires to blow any minute. The scenery got worse the further they went.

They saw people beset by a whirlwind. A huge wolf, her teats dripping milk, chased another group, snapping at their heels as they ran. Further on, they encountered a storm that coated the windshield with brownish-green goo. Lilith turned on the wipers and sprayed washer fluid. The windshield cleared, but the stench was horrific.

Despite her horror, Dara relaxed a little. It had nothing on the Hell Granddad had painted in his sermons.

After a half hour or so, the pavement smoothed out a little. Lilith glanced at the clock on the dashboard. She muttered, "Shit," and shoved her foot down on the accelerator. After that, Dara had no time to look at the scenery. She was too busy hanging on. The road spiraled down. With every ring, the sense of hopelessness grew stronger.

At the bottom, they came to a suite of offices hewn from rock. Lilith squealed into a parking spot and jammed on the brakes. Only Dara's shoulder harness kept her from slamming into the dashboard. Lilith got out of the car and swept out one hand to encompass the scenery. "Welcome to the funhouse."

CHAPTER 48

It was poker night, and Belial was once again at the table.

An hour before, a phalanx of demons had pulled him from the spider-hole again and cleaned him up. He assumed Satan wanted him looking his best for his execution, to show how far he'd fallen. And that was good. As much as he feared the pain, Dara was safe and that was what mattered.

But after he showered, instead of taking him to the Lake of Fire, they dragged him to the rec room. When he tried to resist, thrall swept over his limbs and forced him to the table. There, he found the usual suspects assembled. Without volition, he said, "Good evening, everyone."

Fear skittered up his spine and his mouth went dry.

He checked the clock and reassured himself. In just over an hour, the wager would expire and Dara would be safe. Satan had no power to change that. She would live out her life on Earth and then rejoin her loved ones in Heaven.

Satan would exact his revenge and the Lake of Fire would consume Belial's bones, but he cared nothing for that. All that mattered was that Dara was safe. *Stay strong, my love. You can do this. You've been through worse.*

Across the table, Loki gathered the cards from the last hand and shuffled. He loosed one of his cackling laughs as he threw cards around the table.

"Isn't the time limit for the big wager about due?" Zeus stirred a tumbler of ouzo with his pinky.

"At midnight." Satan's lips formed the V that was his version of smiling. His horns sparked with excitement.

Belial's dread deepened.

The Greek licked ouzo from his finger. "Who won?"

"It's still up for grabs." Satan cocked his head and tapped one black talon against a front tooth. "One hour left. Now what can I do, in just one hour, to destroy the woman once and for all?" He looked at the blackened ceiling as though it might hold an idea.

Nothing. There's nothing you can do.

"Hark." Satan cupped a hand to his ear. "Do I hear visitors?"

Belial's heart thumped. At the far end of the hall, the doors swung open and Lilith sauntered through the door on her mountain-goat stilettos.

"Here she is, boss," she said. "Signed, sealed and delivered."

Belial's dread took form and acquired a name. It couldn't be. He wanted to howl to the heavens, but his body sat silent and unmoving. In the doorway stood Dara.

"Mrs. Strong." Satan got to his feet, every inch the suave host—if you ignored the crimson skin, ram's horns and cloven hooves. Flames of delight danced in his eyes. "How lovely of you to visit us."

Dara seemed to shrink into herself. Belial tried to shout to her to turn and run, but his larynx made no sound. She looked around the table, her eyes widening as they fell on Zeus and Loki. They brushed past the Enemy as though he weren't even there. Mortals, even holiest of them, could never see him. Their brains were too limited.

Then her gaze landed on Belial and her face lit up like a thousand votive candles. Seeing her was at once Heaven and Hell. Heaven to gaze upon her beautiful face when he hadn't expected to ever do so again, Hell to know that her being here put her in mortal, and immortal, danger.

He was here as bait. He cursed himself for not jumping into the Lake of Fire when he'd had a chance. He tried again to force a warning from his throat, but he was no more than a marionette, able to speak only at the command of his puppeteer.

Without will, his lips widened into smile of welcome and he rose and circled the table. He pulled Dara into his arms, dipping her backward in a kiss that made Loki howl like a coyote while Zeus beat a tattoo on the table. When he set her back on her feet, her face was scarlet with embarrassment. She yanked herself away, glaring at him. He had never told her about thrall. Why had he not warned her?

Because it would have been too humiliating to admit to such weakness.

Nearby, Satan's horns sparked like Roman candles. "What brings you to my humble lair, Mrs. Strong?"

Dara lifted her chin. "I'm here for Ben."

"You mean the demon Belial?" Satan pretended to be surprised. "Belial is one of my most valuable demons. What makes you think I'd be willing to release him? "

If Belial had been able to roll his eyes, he would have.

"Lilith said you were willing to make a trade."

Satan gave Lilith a look that promised rewards beyond what any she-demon had ever received.

"A trade?" He stroked his goatee. "What are you proposing?"

"That you let Ben return to Earth with me. That you allow us to live together for the duration of my life."

It was the same gambit Belial had tried, only to fail. He wanted to shake her for her naivety. No human could bargain with Satan and win.

"And what do I get in return?" Satan asked.

Don't do it. Belial directed the thought toward her with little hope that she would heed him. *Don't do it.*

Dara swallowed. She glanced toward the spot at the table where the Enemy sat, her brows knitted. She seemed to be holding some kind of internal dialogue. After a moment, her face cleared.

"My soul once my life is over," she said.

Satan snapped his fingers at a nearby demon. A triangular grin twisted his face. "Go get the paperwork."

The demon scurried out the door.

Why was Satan doing this? It wasn't what he wanted, what he needed to win the wager. *Run, Dara,* Belial willed. *Run away.* She didn't move. He cursed his thrall-held body.

"You are aware," Satan said, "that at the end of your life, both you and Belial will be returning here for the remainder of eternity?"

"Yes." Her voice was calm. Didn't she understand the hellish bargain she was making?

"And that there's no guarantee of how long your life will be?" Satan said.

A second wave of dread washed over Belial. Satan was talking her out of the deal she'd so foolishly accepted, luring her into the one he wanted her to take.

"Are you planning to kill me?" Dara didn't seem concerned by the notion.

"Of course not," Satan said.

Don't believe him. He is the Father of Lies.

She shrugged. "With any luck, I'll live another forty or fifty years."

A fat gray cat with a crooked ear jumped into Satan's lap. Milton. Why was he here?

Satan stroked his head. "Based on your history, you don't strike me as lucky."

Dara looked at the cat. Her face tightened. "I think my luck may finally have changed."

"What if I sweeten the pot?" Satan said. "What if I offer you a guarantee of fifty years together—fifty years of perfect health, not subject to accident or disease, along with great wealth and influence over mortal events?"

Belial could tell by her face that Dara was tempted, not by the money or power, but by the promise of time together. *Don't do it.*

"What do I have to do in return?" she asked.

Satan looked at his fingernails. "One tiny thing."

"And that is?"

"Curse God and die now, tonight, before the clock strikes twelve."

The color drained from her face. "You mean, go back as a zombie?"

"Of course not. I'd allow you to continue as though you were still alive. You could still have your little clinic. You could even have a child."

Looking repulsed, Dara shook her head, but before Belial could breathe a sigh of relief, she looked at the spot where the Enemy sat, and at the cards lying on the table. She said, "How about if I play you for him?"

Was she insane? He loved her to the ends of the Earth and back, but she would have been out of her league playing poker with kindergartners, never mind this crew.

"If you win," she said, "I will curse God and die tonight. If I win, Ben comes with me as an ordinary human being and we're free to live our lives without your interference."

"But when they're over, you belong to me," Satan said.

"No." She shook her head, and the negotiation skills she'd developed running a free clinic surfaced. "We go into this with an equal stake. If I win, I get what I want. If you win, you get what you want."

Satan's face turned burgundy. "No."

Dara shrugged. "Okay by me. Can someone take me back to the surface, please?"

Satan looked like he'd caught his tail in a spring trap. If he'd had any control over his body, Belial would have laughed.

"All right." Satan held up a hand to stop her. The demon he'd sent for paperwork reappeared with a scroll and a quill pen.

Dara read through the scroll from top to bottom. She shook her head.

"This still feels like the odds are in your favor."

Satan's eyes flashed fire. Then he looked at his watch and swallowed. "How about if I play both of you? If you win, you're both free."

"Both of us?" Dara pretended not to understand, but Belial was sure, from her sharpened gaze, that this was exactly what she'd intended.

"We'll all play. If I'm out while either of you still has chips left, you win."

For an instant, Belial's hopes rose. He'd spent centuries watching Satan play cards. He knew his habits, his weaknesses, his tells. With the other gods there to prevent Satan from cheating, Belial had at least an even chance of winning. Just as quickly, his hope dissolved. In his current state of thrall, he'd be out in no time.

"That sounds pretty good," said Dara.

The scribe updated the scroll and Satan's eyes burned with unholy glee once more. Her pen hovered over the scroll. *No!*

"There's one more thing." Dara gestured toward where Belial sat. "I don't know who this is, but it isn't Ben Lyle."

"Of course it is," said Satan. "Look at his body, his beautiful face. This is the man you fell in love with."

"This may be his shell," she said, "but it isn't Ben. And I'm not risking my eternal soul for a blow-up doll."

Belial sent up a silent cheer as black smoke shot from Satan's horns and his face turned the color of dried blood. "What if I refuse to give you a ride back to the surface?"

Dara smiled at Zeus and Loki. "Then I'm sure one of these gentlemen will oblige."

"I will give you a ride in my chariot," Zeus said. He stubbed out his cigar.

Not great, but anything was better than Dara's current circumstance. Smoke roiled from Satan's horns, but Dara just stood there, her arms crossed, not yielding an inch. Satan checked his watch again and his hold on Belial's limbs loosened.

Belial stretched like he'd just awakened from a nap and smiled at Dara.

"There you are," she said.

"Here I am." He took the pen from her hand. "Now go home."

"I don't think so."

"You can't save me."

"I can try." She reached for the pen.

He held it out of range. "No. You need to go back—"

Before he could complete his sentence, she turned to Satan and held out her scarred hand. Satan took it in his leathery claw and they shook. Belial groaned. For good measure, Dara took the quill from his nerveless fingers. A splinter on the barrel of the pen pricked her finger, releasing a single drop of blood. She nodded like she'd expected that, but signed her name at the bottom of the scroll for good measure.

At the table, Satan allotted each of them the same stake everyone else had brought into the game. Whoever still had chips when the other two were out would be declared the winner. Statistically, the two of them should have had a better chance of winning, but Dara was such a lousy player, she was worse than useless.

As Belial expected, she was out before she even got a chance to deal, but Belial was unconcerned. Her contribution had been freeing him to play.

The game continued. The Enemy folded, and then Loki dropped out. It was just Belial, Satan and Zeus remaining. It was ten minutes until midnight and the stacks of chips sitting in front of Belial and Satan were identical.

Belial considered slowing the play until midnight struck, but he didn't know the contents of the contract Dara had signed. It would be like Satan to insert a clause declaring the house the winner if time ran out. Perspiration beaded his forehead. Dara handed him a napkin. Satan grinned, but Belial shrugged and blotted his face. His human genes made him vulnerable, but they'd also allowed him to love Dara.

He held his breath as the Greek dealt. When Belial fanned out his cards, he held the ace, two and three of spades, plus a pair of jacks. It wasn't bad, but across the table Satan fiddled with his goatee, a sure sign he'd drawn a strong hand. Belial's heart sank, but he gritted his teeth. It wasn't over until it was over.

He sat on Zeus's left, so he anted up a dozen red chips. Satan doubled the bet and Zeus matched him. Knowing anything less than running the table was a loss, Belial stayed in. He started to take two cards, but three of a kind wouldn't do it. He needed a straight flush. Holding his breath, he slid the two jacks, face down, toward Zeus. Zeus gave him the next two cards off the top of the deck. Satan rapped his knuckles on the table, content to stay with what he had. Zeus took three cards.

Belial looked at his cards and shoved his remaining chips to the center of the table.

"All in, demon?" Satan asked.

Belial took Dara's hand in his. "With everything I have."

Satan swept all his chips to the center.

"Too rich for my blood." The Greek laid his cards face down on the table.

"Show us what you've got," Satan said.

Belial fanned out his cards on the table: ace, two, three, four, five of spades. He didn't even have to ask Satan what he held. As soon as the old sinner saw Belial's cards, his face turned the color of cranberries and smoke gushed from his horns.

"You cheated," he screamed.

"How could I cheat?" Belial asked. "I didn't even deal."

Behind him, the clock struck midnight. The wager was over, and Satan had lost.

Satan rounded on Lilith. "This was your fault. I had matters well in hand until you interfered."

"You told me to bring her here." Lilith backed away. "I didn't tell you to play cards with her."

Satan signaled two husky demons. They grabbed Lilith by the arms. "Take her to the maggot pit. A little larva time may improve her memory."

Dara's face was a study in horror. She reached out, as though to catch Lilith's hand, but the guards dragged Lilith away, kicking and cursing.

Satan turned back to Belial. "You're not going anywhere. I refuse to be bound by the results of a bet you won by chicanery."

"Keep your word," the Enemy said, "or I'll ban you from the poker table. Forever."

Dara didn't react to that, reminding Belial she couldn't hear or see the Enemy, but Satan looked like the horns would explode right off his head. After a moment's struggle, he forced a sickly smile.

"Congratulations, Mrs. Strong," he said.

"Thank you," said Dara. "May we go now?"

They'd won. Against all odds, they'd pulled it off. Belial gave Satan a cocky grin. "Can we borrow a golf cart? Just as far as the surface?" If not, they'd walk, but either way, they'd make it to the entrance to begin their new life together.

Satan smiled again, a false smile. Worry awoke and niggled its way through Belial's gut.

"Take the Lamborghini," Satan said. "The keys are in it."

Worry morphed into fear. Belial's old boss was being too accommodating. There wasn't anything Satan could do to them, he reassured himself. Not with the Enemy watching.

"Thanks." He led Dara toward the exit.

"In fact"—Satan followed them to the door, the very picture of a gracious host—"to show I'm a good sport, keep it. Consider it a wedding present."

Fear blossomed into outright panic as thrall swept over his body. Dara smiled up at him, unaware of the change. He struggled to regain control of his limbs, but they would not obey him. He stopped walking and Dara stopped, too, her brows drawing together.

He took her face between his hands. She lifted her mouth for his kiss. His lips formed a smile and then he wrenched her head sideways, snapping her neck. His thrall melted away.

"Noooo." His howl caught the attention of everyone still at the table. They turned as Dara collapsed to the ground, her head canted at an unnatural angle. He dropped to his knees and pulled her lifeless body into his arms, swaying back and forth, as though by rocking he could pump life back into her.

"Demon." Satan affected a look of horror. "What have you done?" He turned to the Enemy. "That's the problem of pairing demons with humans. They play too rough and someone gets dead."

"You did this," Belial shouted. "Not me. You."

"All right." Satan bobbed his head playfully. "I might have had something to do with it." He put a hand to his ear. "What's that commotion I hear up in the vestibule? It sounds like they're welcoming a new client—a celebrity, by the sounds of it."

Belial stared at Satan, sick with horror. Not Dara. Not in Hell. He turned to the Enemy. "She didn't really wind up here?"

The Enemy's face, impassive as always, gave nothing away.

"She chose to come here," Satan said. "She was in Hell, by her own choice, when she died. Where did you think she'd wind up?" He tapped his cheek. "Ordinarily, she'd be assigned to Ring Two, with the other mortals who love unwisely, but I think she deserves something special, don't you?"

Belial lunged for Satan's throat. Satan's jaw dropped at the unprecedented attack, but he recovered. With a flick of his fingers, he sent Belial flying backward across the ring and impaled him on a stalagmite.

Belial stared at the cavernous ceiling, a spit of limestone protruding from his chest. The pain was excruciating, but he made no attempt to free himself. There was but one being in the universe who could save Dara. Belial laced his fingers and bowed his head to his chest.

"Father," he prayed, "please, bring her back."

The demons in the room yelped.

"How dare you pray to the Enemy inside my walls?" Satan kicked Belial in the ribs. He sank deeper onto the stalagmite and the pain increased tenfold.

"Father of light, father of love, father of mercy, hear my prayer."

"Stop," Satan shouted. "I command you to stop."

Pain from Satan's snare meshed with the pain of the stalagmite, washing over Belial in hellish waves, but he refused to be distracted. "Father who delights in his children, who delights in giving his children wonderful gifts, give your daughter the gift of life."

Throughout the ring, demons squealed like pigs being slaughtered.

"No more, demon," Satan screamed.

Thrall invaded Belial's fingers, his toes, but he pressed it back.

"Father, forgive my sins." Tears streamed from his closed eyes and choked his voice, but he kept praying. "Forgive me for my arrogance and my ambition, which led me out of your light. Forgive me for the souls I've harmed since I came below. Punish me however you will—leave me speared on this spike for all eternity; throw me in the Lake of Fire—but give Dara back her life and make her whole again." He would pray without ceasing, forever if necessary.

"Father, save your daughter. Please. Please." He had killed her. Belial had done this. Him. Not Satan, but him. He sobbed, broken. If he could, he would have crawled across the floor on his belly and thrown himself at the Father's feet. A soft hand touched his elbow.

"You know, for someone who boasts about his demon grace, you're kind of clumsy."

His eyes flew open. Dara stood beside him. She took his hands in hers and, bracing her foot against the stalagmite, tugged until he pulled free. She winced when she saw the gaping wound in his chest, but already the edges knitted and the healing began.

He dropped to his knees, pulling her down beside him. "Thank you, Lord, for your providence. Please watch over us as we make our way to the surface and protect us from the forces of evil."

"I thought you were the forces of evil," she said.

"I've changed sides."

Her eyebrows lifted almost to her hairline. "When did that happen?"

He bowed his head in shame. "While you were dead."

She put her hand under his chin and lifted it till he had no choice but to look her in the eye. "If we're going to have a relationship, you'll have to give up poker with the boys. They're a bad influence."

The broadest smile he'd ever worn split his face. "Yes, ma'am."

Behind him, God said, "You know, I like how this turned out. Let's do it again."

Satan made a sound like he was choking on his tongue.

"Let's get out of here." Belial fought laughter, though his cheeks were still wet with tears. They headed for the door.

"One more thing," said Satan.

Belial turned, prepared to turn prayer warrior again if necessary.

"The agreement was you'd return to Earth as an ordinary human." Satan flicked his fingers.

Pain wrenched through Belial's body as though half of him was being torn away. He staggered and then blinked against the burning in his eyes from the sulfurous air. Zeus and Loki looked larger than he remembered. Satan, with whom he'd worked for ten thousand years, was an unfamiliar and terrifying figure. Then his eyes settled on the chair where God had been sitting. It was empty.

He supposed that was the way it ever was. The creatures most beloved by God knew him the least.

"Do you think he planned this?" Dara asked as she climbed into the Lamborghini.

Belial knew what she was asking: had God foreseen this outcome from the beginning? Had all the hell they'd been through been part of a larger plan to free his demon soul? He thought about his final poker hand. The odds against drawing a straight flush in the last round were phenomenal. Phenomenal, but not impossible.

"I don't know." He closed her door. "No one ever knows."

He circled the car, sulfurous air burning his throat and eyes. How had he survived here all these centuries? Because he was a demon, a supernatural being with an endless life. Now he was merely human, subject to all the weaknesses that flesh was heir to. In another forty or fifty years, he would wither and die. He got in the car and took her hand.

"Everything up there is still a mess," he said. "You're still suspended from the clinic, the DA still wants our asses, and we're both broke."

"On the other hand, we'll be able to make love with no one listening in."

A feeling of contentment like he'd never experienced, as angel or demon, filled him. He leaned across the console to kiss her.

"Sounds like a fair trade," he said.

THANKS TO READERS

Dear Reader,

Thank you for reading *The Demon Always Wins.*

I know that your spare time is limited, and I'm honored that you chose to spend it with Dara and Belial.

I'd love it if you would leave a review on Amazon, Goodreads, Tumblr, Twitter, Facebook, or your blog or website. Word of mouth is also good—please tell your family, friends and fellow readers!

Book 2 of my *Touched by a Demon* series. *The Demon's in the Details* has some familiar faces, and some new ones, too!

For word of upcoming releases, author interviews, blog tours and giveaways, please sign up for my monthly-ish newsletter at www.jeanneestridge.com.

To follow me on Facebook: www.facebook.com/JeanneEstridgeFanPage

To join my Facebook. group, go here.

To read my weekly blog posts: www.EightLadiesWriting.com

To follow me on Twitter: www.twitter.com/JeanneEstridge

To follow me on Instagram: www.instagram.com/JeanneEstridge

Again, thanks for reading!

Jeanne Oates Estridge

ACKNOWLEDGMENTS

I've been writing for a very long time, so this is going to be a very long list. My thanks to:

Joe Downing and Mark Thaman, who have been at my side since we formed our writer's group in 2002. And to Teri Piatt, who joined us soon after.

Nicole Amsler, whose brilliant example and delicate criticisms led me to ask more of myself, to take more chances and to write better prose, and to the rest of the Cool Kids I met at the Midwest Writers' Workshop— Casey Alexander, April Gerard, Mary Mascari, Katie Spina and Julie Lawson Timmer.

Jenny Crusie and the Romance Writing Program at McDaniel College. The knowledge I gained from their program was life-changing, as was the writing group I formed with my classmates, the fabulous Eight Ladies Writing: Michille Caples, Justine Covington, Elizabeth Eldridge , Nancy Yeager, Kat Kaiser, Kay Keppler, Micki Haller Yamada and Jilly Wood.

Alexa Rowan, who came up with the title.

Karen Dale Harris, whose brilliant editing turned this story from a hodgepodge of dangling plot threads and inconsistent world-building into a real book.

Mary Buckham, whose writing craft books and plotting weekends were both instructional and inspirational.

Pauline Pruden Persing, who listened to me plot and replot this book every Saturday morning for several years as we hiked in the woods and identified wildflowers.

And, last but by no means least, my sister, Lelane Oates, who read at least three different versions of this story (and three really awful books that came before the McDaniel program) and never once said, "Maybe you should think about a different hobby."

EXCERPT FROM THE DEMON'S IN THE DETAILS

Chapter 1

"Not just no, but hell no." Georgia O'Keeffe Blackmon glared at her father and stepmother. "I'm not selling *John*."

The view from the floor-to-ceiling windows at the north end of her father's family room—the red sandstone cliffs and cloudless blue skies of Sedona, Arizona—was gorgeous, but Keeffe's gaze flashed right past it, to the opposite end of the room and a wooden pedestal topped by a Plexiglas case.

Inside the case, an eighteen-inch alabaster statue of an eagle soared upward, wings spread, its gaze fixed on the sky. The translucence of the stone gave the sculpture a transcendent quality. The sheer beauty filled Keeffe with bliss, and her anger moderated a little. Mom had been an incredible artist.

"I've been waiting since I was eighteen to take him home," she said. "After seven years, I'm down to my last thirty days. Why would I sell him?"

Dad responded to her question by burying his nose in his whisky glass, but Lilith, aka the stepmother-from-Hell, spread her hands.

"We're not asking you to sell it," she said. "We're just asking you to meet—"

"—someone who wants to buy him." Keeffe finished her sentence for her.

Lilith's lips tightened. Stepmom wore a black leather miniskirt that showed yards of what Keeffe had to admit were shapely and perfectly tanned legs. On her feet were strappy black sandals with five-inch heels. Her red silk top matched her toenails. Chunky red and black jewelry pulled it all together. Keeffe was aware of the contrast to her own outfit—a flannel shirt, faded jeans and down-at-the-heel Doc Martens.

Lilith didn't appear to have aged a day since she married Daniel Blackmon ten years ago. Probably because she was sucking the life force out of her husband.

"Be reasonable, Keeffe," she said. "I'm an art agent. Given your financial situation, I would be remiss if I didn't help you find—"

"My financial situation is fine." Keeffe cut her off with what was, mostly, a true statement. Lilith's face turned pink with annoyance, but before she could respond, the doorbell rang.

"That must be Seth." Lilith shot Dad a glance that looked like a warning. She left the room, her stiletto heels rat-a-tat-tatting on the hardwood floor like a machine gun firing.

The hair on the back of Keeffe's neck prickled. She wasn't much when it came to book-smarts, but she was good at reading people. This felt like more than just one of Lilith's intermittent attempts to convince her to sell her sculpture.

She turned to Dad. "Who is Seth?"

"Seth McCall, some Internet billionaire Lilith is helping select art for his new house." Above Dad's russet beard and mustache, his nose was a patchwork of broken veins. His drinking had taken a drastic uptick after he remarried.

"You don't really want me to sell *John*, do you?" Keeffe asked.

Dad's eyes flashed to the doorway where Lilith had disappeared, like he wasn't sure he was authorized to have his own opinion. *Come on, Dad. Grow a pair.*

He held up a hand. "That's between you and Lilith."

Nope. Not today, anyway.

A moment later, Lilith returned, accompanied by a blond guy who looked to be in his late twenties. He was tall, probably a foot taller than Keeffe's five-three. Above torn jeans hanging low on his hips, his T-shirt hugged six-pack abs. He must spend some serious gym-time to get abs like that. Sleeves of tattoos ran up both muscular arms and a tiny silver ring graced his left nostril.

He seemed oddly familiar. It took Keeffe a moment to realize why. He reminded her of the statue of Leonidas at Thermopylae that stood at Sparta. The statue was modern, but it had made Leonidas her personal choice for hottest historical figure of the ancient world.

Lilith introduced them and Keeffe's heart thumped a little until her gaze reached his eyes. They were a silvery-gray, with no hint of humanity, like a statue's sightless, soulless eyes. Instinctively, her fingers sought the little silver crucifix Mom had given her for her first communion. She instantly felt better. Safer.

Then McCall smiled, the killer smile Leonidas might have had if there had been modern dentistry in ancient Sparta. The sense of a soul gone missing disappeared.

"Hello, Keeffe." He extended his hand, his voice as smooth as acrylic flowing from a tube.

The handshake brought them close enough that she could smell his aftershave, an expensive mix of sandalwood and leather. She steeled herself to look at his eyes again, but they were now ordinary gray eyes.

Still, she had to resist the urge to take a step back. "What brings you to Sedona?"

McCall's gaze shifted to Lilith, focusing on her melon-like breasts. *Ew*. Lilith looked great, but she had to be twenty years older than Seth, minimum. After a long moment, he dragged his attention back to Keeffe.

"I heard it's great here in the winter. I can hike and mountain bike, even though it's January. I just built a house at the south end of town.

Lil is helping me decorate." He looked across the room to the eagle, soaring inside its Plexiglas case.

"My sculpture isn't for sale," Keeffe said.

"Everything's for sale," he said easily. "It's just a matter of settling on a price. What would you take for it?"

"Nothing."

"Well, that's affordable." His smile was like a warm caress, but it left Keeffe cold. He headed toward the sculpture.

"No amount of money could convince me to sell," she told his back.

"I saw one of your mother's crucifixes at a church in Sicily." He threw the words over his shoulder. "And another in Majorca. Her work is magnificent. I want to own one of her pieces."

Keeffe followed him across the room, "Perhaps one of the churches would be interested in selling."

She stroked the Plexiglas case. A bronze plaque on the base read, *John*.

"Why is it named *John*?" McCall stood beside her, his thumbs hooked into the pockets of his jeans, unconsciously framing his genitals.

At least, she hoped it was unconscious.

"He's an allegorical representation of John from the Bible," Keeffe said. "My sister and brothers own the other three."

"Three what?"

"Evangelists."

"Huh?" His gorgeous face was completely blank. Clearly, he had never attended catechism class.

"Evangelists. You know—Matthew, Mark, Luke, and John. They wrote the gospels."

"Okay, sure," he said.

Why did he even want her statue? He clearly wasn't religious. She looked at *John* again, studying the clean lines of the wings, the sleek head, and fierce gaze. The eagle's soaring form was magnificent in its own right, but its meaning was the source of its real beauty.

"My mother was working on this piece when she died," Keeffe said.

Inside the case, the bird's left talon wasn't quite freed from the stone. "She sculpted him specifically for me. You can't put a price on that."

"I'll give you a hundred and fifty thousand dollars for it."

Keeffe's jaw tensed. Even if she'd been interested, that was far less than *John* was worth. It was exactly what she would have expected, though. Just as she was finally about to win permanent possession of him, Lilith had brought in someone to rip her off.

"No, thanks," she said.

"Two hundred."

Keeffe glared at McCall. "He's not for sale."

McCall glanced at Lilith. She gave a tiny, almost imperceptible nod. Every follicle on the back of Keeffe's neck snapped to attention.

"Two fifty," he said.

Whatever the eagle was worth to him, he was worth more to her. When Lilith had moved in, barely a year after Mom's death, she had cleaned house, getting rid of not only Mom's clothes and personal items, but also her artist's tools. This statue and a small notebook were the only things Keeffe had left of Mom.

"Not just no, but hell no."

McCall glanced at Lilith's chest again and licked his lips. Gross. Then he turned to Keeffe and smiled his sexy, caressing smile. At least, it would have been sexy if he weren't such an asshat. He could barely take his eyes off Lilith's breasts, and right in front of Dad, too.

"Let me take you to dinner and we'll talk it over," he said.

Have dinner with someone she had no interest in, so that he could pressure her to sell something she had no wish to sell?

"No, thanks."

His mouth actually fell open. Evidently hot guys who also happened to be jillionaires didn't get turned down very often.

His eyes narrowed. "You're better off selling it to me than just losing it."

Keeffe stilled. "Why do you think I'm going to lose him?"

Lilith grasped McCall's upper arm. "Seth, perhaps we should—"

"Lil told me about your agreement," he said. "If you're not

supporting yourself as an artist by the time you turn twenty-five, the statue becomes her property."

Keeffe's fists clenched at her sides.

"There are two problems with that statement." She spoke to McCall, but her words were aimed at Lilith. "One, the statue doesn't become Lilith's, it becomes my dad's. And two, I *am* supporting myself. I make as much as a secretary does."

"Administrative assistant," Lilith said.

"Whatever you want to call it." Keeffe glared at her. When she was eighteen, she had been determined to get an art degree from Mom's alma mater in Pasadena. Lilith was equally determined Keeffe should take business classes at Coconino Community College in nearby Flagstaff. The resulting argument made Armageddon look like a tiff over which way the toilet paper roll goes.

After three weeks of shouting and slammed doors, Dad brokered a compromise: Cost wasn't the issue; it was about being practical. They'd pay for art school on the condition Keeffe signed a contract to repay them if, by her twenty-fifth birthday, she wasn't making as much from art as she would have from following Lilith's advice.

That would have seemed silly—how could an artist who wasn't even pulling in as much as a secretary ever hope to repay tens of thousands of dollars of tuition?—except they had *John* as security.

It was a gamble, but it had turned out okay. Over the past year, between Keeffe's canvases and the caricatures she drew outside Tlaquepaque Village during tourist season, she had made at least the average salary rate for an administrative assistant in this part of Arizona.

Another glance passed between McCall and Lilith. He had no real interest in her sculpture. Keeffe was willing to bet on it. No, Lilith had put him up to this. Her stepmom had wanted to take *John* away from her from day one. The only thing Lilith understood about art was its monetary value. Over at the bar, Dad poured himself another drink, shutting out the tension in the room. No help to be had there.

"I think it's time I took my sculpture home with me."

Lilith jerked. "I thought you decided it wouldn't be safe in your trailer." Her voice was sharp.

"Looks like it's not safe here either."

Lilith flushed, but it wasn't clear if that was from guilt or anger.

"Daniel, tell Keeffe how unwise it would be to try to keep the statue at her trailer." Her tone made *trailer* sound like *shack*.

Dad held up a hand. "Leave me out of this. I'm Switzerland. I'm neutral."

Lilith shot him a look that said he'd pay for that later. She turned back to Keeffe.

"If you're not concerned about it being stolen, think about the statue itself. We keep this house at a consistent seventy degrees and fifty percent humidity, summer and winter. Can you provide the same optimal conditions?"

Keeffe started to say, *It's made out of rock. It can handle a little dry air.* If you antagonized Lilith enough, you could sometimes make her pupils go rectangular, like a goat's.

Keeffe's brothers and sister claimed not to see that transformation, and in her anatomy-for-figure-drawing course in college, her professor had told her, flat out, that rectangular pupils didn't occur in humans. That trait was limited to goats, octopuses, and toads.

But Keeffe knew better. As a teenager, she had excelled at badgering her stepmother until her pupils reshaped into rectangles.

She'd spent a lot of her teenage years grounded.

She glanced at *John* again. His eyes were fixed on the heavens, away from trivial earthly concerns. She could almost hear her mother's voice saying, *Be the bigger person, Keeffe.*

She drew a breath. "I'm planning to loan *John* to museums."

She expected Lilith to relax once she learned the sculpture wasn't bound for the trailer park. Instead, to Keeffe's amazement, the circles of black at the center of Lilith's eyes lengthened and the corners squared off. Stepmom didn't like the idea of her predecessor's artwork going on tour. At all.

"I've talked to the Chicago Art Institute and the DIA in Detroit." Keeffe gave in to her baser instincts and pressed the barb deeper.

"They both have churches nearby with Mom's crucifixes on display. They're very interested."

If she'd wanted to infuriate Lilith, she'd succeeded. Her stepmother's goat-like eyes blazed. If looks could kill, one of Lilith's stiletto heels would have hammered straight through Keeffe's skull right about now.

Then Lilith's charcoal-shaded eyelids swept down, hiding her weird pupils.

"Have you ever bothered to read that contract you signed?"

Keeffe caught her breath. Her cheeks burned as her eyes flashed over to McCall to gauge his reaction. Keeffe's dyslexia made reading a challenge, and Lilith knew it. Keeffe had tried to read the contract several times, but she'd never gotten all the way through it. Fortunately, McCall had wandered away to look at another statue, a she-demon with long black hair, horns, and an arrow-tipped tail.

Keeffe lifted her chin. "Clue me in."

"It really isn't in anyone's best interests for that statue to get stolen or damaged," Lilith said. "The contract specifies that it will remain here, in Daniel's custody, until you turn twenty-five and the terms of the contract have been fulfilled."

Keeffe waited for Dad to chime in, to confirm that of course he trusted her to take care of her mother's sculpture, and even to relinquish it, if necessary. Instead, he practiced his neutrality by adding another ice cube to his drink.

Keeffe's chest tightened until it felt like it might buckle. That statue was hers. She'd spent hours watching its delicate feathers revealed at the tip of her mother's chisels. She might not be able to breeze through a contract, but she could describe every hammer-stroke that went into that statue, and the other three as well.

Her sister and brothers had taken possession of theirs long ago. *John* was the only one still within Lilith's grasp. For the first time, it struck Keeffe that she might actually lose him.

Her palms grew sweaty. What other little tidbits were tucked inside that contract? She needed to read the thing, front to back, and make sure she understood every word, no matter how long it took her or how head-splittingly difficult it was. Lilith wasn't getting *John*.

Over by the bar, Dad watched them warily, while Seth tried to take the she-demon from her case.

Probably to feel her up.

Keeffe kissed her fingertips and pressed them against the Plexiglas protecting *John* before turning to face her stepmother.

"In thirty days, I'll be back to pick him up."

Lilith's pupils returned to a normal human shape. A tiny smile tugged at the corners of her lips. The hair on the back of Keeffe's neck stood up like porcupine quills. Evil stepmom was planning something, but what?

"When I do, he'd better be here." Keeffe took a shot in the dark. "If not, I'll be back with cops, lawyers, judges—whatever it takes."

Lilith smirked, as though to say Keeffe had no money to pay a lawyer. Hollowly, Keeffe realized she was right. She took a step forward until the rounded toes of her boots bumped up against the pointed tips of Lilith's stilettos.

"Understand one thing," she said, staring straight into Lilith's dark eyes. "It will be a cold day in Hell before I let you take my sculpture."

www.ingramcontent.com/pod-product-compliance
Lightning Source LLC
Chambersburg PA
CBHW051006180726
48291CB00006B/1995
* 9 7 8 1 9 4 9 4 5 1 0 2 3 *